A MOTHER'S SECRETS

A MOTHER'S SECRETS

SECRETS OF SAEMAR
BOOK ONE

TUPPENCE VAN DE VAARST

Charlotte, NC

FALSTAFF
BOOKS
WWW.FALSTAFFBOOKS.COM

To the Council of Saemar:
Rose, Neil, Nathan, Megan, and Jonathan

And to our Mad God:
Josh

AN INVITATION, THE LADY, AND THE BOOK

T he decaying heads stared sightlessly from their posts above the city gates. Scavenger birds had pecked out their eyes, and flesh hung loosely from the skulls. Vinet shivered at the gruesome vision, grateful when her carriage moved out of view. The last Council of Saemar had paid for their treachery.

When the clattering of the carriage horses' hooves on the pavement ceased, Vinet took a deep breath and examined the imposing building from the window of the carriage.

The carved granite steps to the palace climbed before her. Some people suspected magicians of shaping them from a single stone. The palace rivaled the steps in their majesty. Rising into the sky, it towered over the rest of the buildings of the capital. The front door loomed thirty ells into the air, and murals of mythical beings decorated the walls. Giant eyes guarded the palace from their position painted on the two towers to either side of the main building, a reminder that someone was always watching. It acted as a security measure, Vinet knew, but that didn't make them any less ominous.

She looked at the person in the carriage seat opposite her. Bright green eyes stared back at her. Gwyn smiled reassuringly, her green and gold armor a proud statement of Ninaeva. Her bodyguard believed in her, at least.

Vinet considered the palace again. *How in Mazda's name did I get myself into this?* she wondered.

The invitation had been wholly unexpected. When the messenger had arrived at Ilhelm Castle, bearing a missive with the distinctive golden seal of King Andreas IV, she had had no idea of his purpose. She certainly had not expected this.

She glanced down at her dress to check that everything was in order. She wore a green gown trimmed with gold—her house colors. The cut, however, was in the Venian style. Instead of being proper and modest, like most Saemarian gowns, it cut low toward her chest, and the sleeves ended barely past her shoulder. She had chosen the cut as a statement as much as the color. Anyone who wore Venian clothing rather than Saemarian made an effort to see beyond Saemarian borders.

And these people will know what to look for, she reminded herself. She straightened her shoulders.

Gwyn nodded approvingly, causing a lock of her blonde hair to fall past her ears. She absent-mindedly brushed it back.

Vinet couldn't hesitate anymore. If she didn't enter, she would be late. "I'm ready," she said.

Gwyn straightened and opened the door to the carriage, exiting quickly and inspecting the area before returning to Vinet and gesturing. Her chain mail glinted in the light, the sword and dagger on her hips especially prominent. Another statement based on appearances. If anyone watched, they would know that Vinet was well protected.

Vinet took one last moment to confirm the plaits of her red-brown braids were securely fastened before following Gwyn out of the carriage. She had also chosen her hairstyle as a statement; a style favored by the nobles of Hillsdale, the city-state closest to her holdings of Ninaeva. The fact that the braids dipped to cover her ears was intentional. Not that her ears were different to the casual eye. Someone on the Council might be keen-eyed enough to see the slight points, however, and no one could learn of her half-elven blood.

Gwyn fell into place a half-step behind her as Vinet began ascending the steps. She kept her eyes fixed in front of her. Here in the capital, the situation was different than in Ninaeva. Here she had to appear to stand on her own.

Two guards came into view as she approached the entrance to the palace. Both stood at attention, so still she could barely tell they were human and not statues. Only Vinet's sharp eyes allowed her to see the way their eyes followed her as she ascended the steps.

Someone had noted her arrival, because a servant approached her as soon as she reached the entrance. "Lady Vinet Rochelle of Ninaeva?"

Vinet nodded, and without being asked, produced the invitation.

The servant took it, glanced at it, and then bowed deeply. "If you'll follow me, my lady."

No one asked for Gwyn to disarm, an acknowledgment of Vinet's rank. Vinet followed the servant into the palace, Gwyn still a half-step behind her.

The inside of the palace was just as impressive as the outside. A long, grand, entrance hall led straight to the large, intricately carved double doors of the throne room, where King Andreas IV held audiences. Or used to, as the doors stood intimidatingly shut, with two of the King's Guard, in their dark black armor and closed helmets, standing with their halberds crossed before them. Vinet breathed a small sigh of relief as the servant took her down a side passage to the left of the throne room and stopped before a smaller, but no less elaborately carved door.

Vinet was struck by the decorations of the palace. So many colorful murals embellished the walls, with complex abstract symbols and depictions of famous Saemarians down through its history. In Ninaeva, tapestries fulfilled the same purpose. Then again, Ninaeva grew cold. The tapestries were a necessity transformed into a luxury.

Vinet glanced back at Gwyn and gave her a slight nod. Gwyn took a station at the door, and Vinet took a deep breath before she turned the handle and pushed.

A large table, lined with chairs on each side, took up almost the entire room. At the head of the table stood a larger chair, only slightly more extravagantly embroidered than the others. The Lord of the Council would claim that seat, but until a year passed and the councilors elected one of their own to that position of power, it would remain vacant.

Only one other person currently occupied the room. A man in his thirties, wearing the thick wool and furs associated with the far north. He leaned back in one of the chairs, his boots resting casually on the table.

Only one man matched that description from the briefing she'd been given: Lord Conn MacTir, lord of Dunbarrow, self-styled Lord of the Gray Mountains.

He smiled as she entered the chamber. "Ah, another councilor!" he exclaimed. His eyes swept up and down, taking in every aspect of her appearance. Vinet felt a moment of gratitude she had taken as much care as she had.

"Lady Vinet Rochelle?" he hazarded.

Vinet gave a nod of acknowledgment. "And you must be Lord Conn MacTir," she said. "A pleasure to meet you."

Conn nodded back. "Likewise. It's good to have another northerner on the Council."

Vinet concealed a smile. Although Ninaeva sat in the far northwest of the kingdom of Saemar, and perhaps had once shared a culture with the clans which formed the basis of Dunbarrow, it now held more similarities to the free city-states along the coast.

"Do you take your position so lightly that you rest your sullied boots on the council table?" The sharp voice made both Vinet and Conn glance up as another man entered the room, appearing from the shadows by the door. He was strange, tall, with dark black hair, and eyes of two different colors, one blue and one a bright citron. A red scar over the citron eye made it stand out even more.

"Ah, Lord Dannan," Conn's voice sounded smooth, but Vinet thought she detected sarcasm. "I did not see you skulking there. I trust the prince is well?"

The knowledge from her dossier clicked into Vinet's mind. Lord Dannan Duatha, tutor to the young prince. Rumors surrounded him, varying from him being cursed to being possessed by a demon, and after taking one look at him, Vinet could understand why.

"Well enough," Dannan answered harshly.

Conn nodded amiably. "How could he not with such an exceptional tutor? And I trust Ninaeva fares well under your enlightened rule, Lady Vinet?" Slowly, he removed his boots from the table.

Vinet kept her expression solemn as she sat down at the table across from Conn. "Ninaeva fares quite well, thank you," she said. "And Dunbarrow?"

"We had some trouble with bandits recently, but we've driven them off. We believe they were attracted by our new trade routes." Conn smiled grimly.

His comment obviously poked at Vinet. Anyone who knew her public reputation knew she had been outspoken in favor of trade for her entire reign as Lady of Ninaeva.

The entrance of two other councilors saved her from the necessity of an answer, one dressed in robes embroidered with the golden sun conquering the darkness, marking him as a priest of Mazda. Ellil, the high priest of the temple of Mazda, the sun-god who kept his dark brother Manyu from conquering the world. The woman next to him, dressed in an elegant high-collared velvet black dress in the southern Saemarian style, was just as easy to identify. Only one other lady featured in the dossier Vinet had been given, and the mourning gown just made it obvious. Lady Pellalindra Duskryn, widow of the late Lord of Duskryn. Her husband had been a member of the last council and had died under mysterious circumstances before his head could grace the front gates.

"Good morning, councilors," Lady Pellalindra said, her voice smooth and melodious. "My apologies if we're late."

"Not at all," Vinet gave her a small smile. "We were just getting to know each other."

Conn gave Pellalindra a nod. "My condolences to you, Lady Pellalindra. I am sorry I could not attend the funeral, but we had a bandit problem that needed dealing with."

Vinet glanced at Conn sharply. Given the rumors surrounding Pellalindra's late husband, and that those rumors linked him with the treason of the previous council, she would not have brought him up at all.

Pellalindra's smile tightened. "Of course, domestic concerns precede others. I would prefer to invite you to my lands during a time of mirth, anyway." She surveyed the others around the table. "Shall we get started?"

Vinet frowned, recalling who else featured in the dossier. They were missing someone. "Has anyone heard from Lord Kamian?" she ventured.

"If he is late for the discussions, he has only himself to blame," Dannan growled. "Let's get this over with."

Vinet held her peace. She, just as much as anyone here, had to be careful not to make too many enemies. They all had things to lose. And with the grisly example of the last council's heads hanging prominently above the city gate, the price of losing could be far higher than any of them wanted. *And if any of them discover who my father actually was, then I will be thrown to the wolves faster than I can scream.*

Five of them. Five of them to decide where to funnel the kingdom's resources, to decide how to shape the future of Saemar. King Andreas IV wouldn't do it. That was why he had set up a council to begin with. *Three of us landed nobles, one priest, and the prince's tutor, whom some call cursed. Mazda's light.*

Or perhaps there were six of them, indeed. Vinet glanced up as the door opened again, and a young man dressed flamboyantly in the brightest colors possible stepped into the room. *Four landed nobles, then.*

"Excuse me for being late, lords and ladies," he said, bowing extravagantly. "I was delayed by a personal matter. The most charming..."

"You're here now," Dannan cut him off. "Let's get down to business, shall we?"

Lord Kamian Silas of Hinswold didn't look at all dismayed by Dannan's tone. He took a seat next to Vinet, giving her a broad smile. "A pleasure to find such a charming lady as a fellow councilor."

Vinet raised a brief eyebrow, refusing to allow herself to be flattered. She knew Kamian's reputation. His skill as a duelist was only matched by his skill in flirtation.

Pellalindra sniffed disdainfully. "Lord Dannan is right. We should focus on the reason we're here."

Vinet cast an amused glance at her. Surely, she wasn't put out that Kamian had deigned to flirt with Vinet instead of her?

"And ignore the fact that the crimson blood of our predecessors still flows down the gate?" Kamian arched his eyebrows. "I find that shortsighted, especially of you, Lady Pellalindra."

Pellalindra paled slightly, and Vinet hastily intervened. "I believe we are all aware of what happened to the previous council," she said. "And doing our job, and taking care of the kingdom, is our way of acknowledging what happened to them. As well as avoiding their fate." She looked around. "We are none of us traitors, or the king would not have sent us invitations. It is up to us to prove that his faith in us is justified."

Pellalindra cast Vinet a gaze which spoke volumes. She could read gratitude there, but uncertainty as well. Vinet didn't blame her. Pellalindra's situation could hardly be less precarious than her own. *Pellalindra's husband may not have been executed, but the rumors still circulate.*

"Exactly," Dannan said brusquely. "So, to business? I assume everyone actually read the briefings?" He narrowed his eyes, his tone making it abundantly clear he didn't believe his statement at all.

Conn's face flushed red and his eyes narrowed. Before he could say anything, Vinet hastily spoke up.

"I would recommend focusing on the Jyrian's request for soldiers to guard the trade route," she said. "A kingdom's lifeblood is built on trade, however insular they may try to be. As a small city-state, Jyria does not have the manpower to guard the trade routes, and we do." Her chest tightened as she spoke her first words as a councilor. The issues to be discussed today were simple enough, but Vinet had no doubt the king had chosen them as a test.

Kamian gave her a look of approval, but Conn and Dannan both shook their heads at the same time.

"No," said Conn. "The trade route can take care of itself. The smallfolk need the soldiers returned to them to help with the harvest."

Vinet glanced out of the window. The bright sun was indication enough that Mazda's Time still lingered, but it would only be a month or so before the leaves started changing colors.

"They've never had a problem bringing in the harvest before," Pellalindra objected. "Why should they now? Our resources could be better used elsewhere."

"The recent conscription," Dannan snapped. "The size of the Regulars has been increased dramatically, causing a labor shortage."

"A conscription which was meant to deal with Tigri," Pellalindra put in. "Should they not be sent down to guard the border, as was originally intended?"

"We just won the war," Conn snorted. "What could Tigri be doing to threaten us now?"

Vinet felt a pang of misgiving. Their neighbor, the Duchy of Tigri, had been at war with Saemar on and off for generations, ever since Tigri had successfully seceded during the reign of Andreas II. The last conflict had ended with Saemar nominally victorious, but that hardly meant Tigri wouldn't still pose a threat.

"Since we have the upper hand over Tigri, now is the time to deal in diplomacy, not swords," Vinet said. "And Jyria is a valuable trade partner. There have been bandits reported along the route. Surely you would not object to sending the Regulars to deal with them, Lord Conn?"

Conn shrugged with indifference. "That is in Jyria's land," he said. "Let them supply the warriors to deal with them. Or the merchants can empty their pockets to hire guards themselves. Saemar has its own priorities."

"Trade is a Saemarian issue," Vinet pointed out.

Ellil spoke for the first time. He spoke quietly, yet his voice carried a weight that made everyone listen. "I would be remiss in my office as high priest if I did not urge charity for the smallfolk," he said. "If they are under pressure because of our actions, that is, the conscription, then we must do our best to relieve that pressure."

Conn glanced triumphantly around the table.

Pellalindra frowned. "Surely, we would not have conscripted farmers we could not spare from the fields?"

Vinet narrowed her eyes in thought. Had they? It hadn't been the last council who'd ordered the conscription, but the Regulars. Surely the Regulars knew if they didn't have enough food for the troops, it wouldn't matter how many people they conscripted. "If we open new trade routes, then perhaps we can trade for food if there's a weak harvest," she said. "But on the basis of one plea, I cannot see that releasing the soldiers from their duties would do us any good in the long-term. Perhaps more research into the smallfolks' requirements is needed."

Pellalindra leaned back in her chair. "So, we agree, Lady Vinet. Though I believe securing the border should be of the utmost priority before opening trade routes. After all, part of diplomacy is ensuring one has the strength to threaten if words fail."

Vinet managed a tight smile. She had known this wasn't going to be easy.

The sunlight on Vinet's face gave blessed relief after the stuffy air of the council chamber. The argument, for she could not call it a discussion, had dragged on for hours. It had ended with a vote to send some of the Regulars to the fields to help with the harvest without discharging them from their duties, a decision Vinet had mixed feelings about.

"Mazda's light," she whispered.

Gwyn grimaced in sympathy. "Rough time in there?"

Vinet could only shake her head. "I don't think the king could have picked six people more inclined to butt heads with each other."

Gwyn shrugged. "At least you all have different perspectives to share, which is probably what he wants, right?"

Vinet felt like grumbling, but Gwyn was right. She nodded in acknowledgment.

Time to change the subject. The Council wasn't the only reason she'd come to the capital. The palace library had been the other draw. Old tales, maps, travelogues, histories...even old journals and treaties were of interest to her. And magical texts. One text, one day, would have to explain her abilities.

"We're taking a walk," she announced. "I inquired of the palace librarian, and he pointed me in the direction of a private collection. I want to introduce myself to the owner."

Gwyn raised an eyebrow. "Does he know why you've inquired?"

"He thinks it's curiosity, nothing more," Vinet said, smiling a reassurance. Gwyn worried for her. One didn't admit to just anyone that the Lady of Ninaeva had magical talents, after all. They might want to know why. And that would lead to inquiries about her heritage, inquiries best avoided.

Gwyn's smile this time was more genuine. "Of course, my lady," she said. "I'll be right behind you."

Vinet sighed. It was easier in Ninaeva, where Gwyn could walk side by side with her. Everyone there had seen them together for the past twenty years. Everyone there knew their relationship.

But they had to maintain the appearance of propriety while in the capital. Vinet knew that, but she didn't have to like it. Gwyn swore she didn't mind, but Vinet couldn't help but feel she betrayed her friend somehow by acting like her superior.

To maintain the appearance of propriety, she also should have called for her carriage, but she wanted to take the opportunity to see a bit more of the capital than she had previously. She'd been here before, of course. Her first presentation at court, nearly ten years ago, had been her first time in the city, and she'd been here irregularly since. She didn't enjoy the parties as much as her father had, so she had never felt a need to spend the dark cold months of Manyu's Time here.

Well, to the rest of the world he had been her father. He had even believed it himself. No one had ever found out her mother had had an affair with an elf.

Her path to the private collection took her through the main marketplace, where vendors hawked their wares, musicians played their instruments on corners, and children ran underfoot. Bright red and gold tarps covered most of the booths, designed to catch the eye. Swords, jewelry, food, and clothing begged for Vinet's attention, but as she glanced around, she noticed two Jyrian merchants in the process of packing up their wares, down to the tables and booths.

Gwyn noticed at the same time she did. "Think the trouble on the trade route is driving them home?" she muttered.

Vinet could only shrug, though she couldn't help feeling disconcerted. The Jyrian city-state brought the luxury items that the nobles loved. They would notice if the Jyrians suddenly up and left, and perhaps they would blame the Council.

She hesitated, wondering if she should approach one of the merchants and inquire as to their reasons for leaving, and perhaps ask them to stay. The sight of an old, lonely, rickety-looking bookstand on the other side of the square, however, distracted her.

She couldn't say what drew her to it. The Jyrian merchants were certainly more important, and the volume of their voices increased as they started arguing with each other, but she walked toward the book stand instead. The wood of the stand was rotting and on the verge of falling apart, but the books were in pristine condition. They were scattered about the stand half-haphazardly, and some of them appeared very old, but they were books Vinet would not be ashamed to have in her own library.

As she drew closer, she realized the book stand was not as abandoned as it first seemed. An old woman stood behind the counter, nearly concealed by shadows and books. She hunched over, her gray hair falling forward to conceal her face.

Vinet smiled. "How's business, friend?"

The old woman glanced up at her, revealing a toothless smile. "Business, mother's daughter? Business is most awful, what with those two moving and shifting and cursing and spitting. Most foul creatures, not nearly the handsome man who visited me of late. He was a gem. But you came not to hear the complaints of this one. What is it you desire? Do the books please you?"

Vinet nodded and started perusing the stacks of books. She had her interests, and this looked like the type of place she could find books to suit her tastes. There might even be magical tomes in here.

Several titles caught her eye: *Rinon's Historia, The Legend of Danyan the Great, How to Light a Candle...* "Indeed, yes," she said. Something the old woman said earlier stuck in her mind, and she couldn't contain her curiosity. "Who was the handsome man who came by earlier? Is he still around?" She reached forward to touch a book, one bound with black leather and no visible title.

"Oh, mother's daughter. Be careful what volumes you touch. Not all are...friendly." The crone reached out a hand, and Vinet nearly flinched; the hand was missing several fingers, and those that remained were old and crooked. The old woman hissed. "Oh, the man, the handsome one, the darling of the sun. Yes, nowhere near, gone, gone. Sorrow, but promises to return, though the gorgeous are deceptive."

Vinet looked at the book as the crone drew it away from her. Something had caught her attention about it, but she couldn't tell what. "He's gone? Like where those two merchants are going?" Maybe the crone had heard some of their arguments.

"Nah, no, nothing so banal, but it is not those cattle yonder that truly interests you." The crone leaned forward, whispering. "Elfsdaughter. The Book, the book, she loves it, yes. We can give it to you, it can be what you want, but…" The crone turned away, cradling the tome like a farm maiden with her first bastard child.

Vinet jerked back, all thoughts about the Jyrian merchants flying from her mind. "How do you know that?" she whispered. Only Gwyn knew that secret, and she would never have breathed a word!

Behind her, she heard Gwyn's gasp. Not daring to look around, Vinet locked eyes with the crone.

The crone's face shifted. Old, dripping skin on one side, covered in scars, but the other half seemed almost young. Vinet blinked, trying to focus her vision.

The crone grinned. "Hush, hush. We hear the buzz inside. The acidic, rancid Fear. Secrets, by Brother-Eyes, are…worry not, mother's daughter, we will not revel in these things nor reveal them."

Unbidden, a story rose to Vinet's mind. A legend, the washer-woman at the ford. The crone who knew secrets, and who kept them, and those who answered her falsely met their deaths.

The crone leaned forward, her mangled hand brushing Vinet's. "Well, are you willing? Gifts for the giver?"

She was talking about the book. Vinet took a deep breath. Sense told her to turn around and leave immediately. But this woman knew her secrets. Vinet needed to know who she was.

"What would be appropriate?" Vinet asked. "I…" she paused. "It hardly seems you're asking for gold." She paused again. "Who are you, mother?"

The scars on the crone's face seemed like they were moving. "Which comes first, mother's daughter? Knowledge or wealth? Who or what are we all? Do you look for a name or the truth? The blood, raw, truth?" she laughed, her voice sounding like pain in Vinet's ears.

A test. Vinet took another deep breath. There were two parts to the question. "Knowledge is required for wealth," she said. "And truth is better than any name."

"Yes, yesss. No. No," she coughed. "A wealth of knowledge, knowledge of wealth, like all things intertwined. Meaning. A curious..." She released Vinet's hand and stepped back into the shadows of the book stand. For a moment, her face looked entirely young, a maiden, not a crone.

Then she stepped forward into the sun again, crone again. "We are what you are and what all become. Hmmmm. Truth for truth and the book is yours, what do you want? This is so, yes, mother's daughter, Elfs-daughter." She gazed intently into Vinet's eyes. "Speak your most harbored truth, and the book is yours. Then you must leave before brother-eyes discovers you."

"Vinet," Gwyn stepped forward, interrupting for the first time.

Vinet didn't look at her, just raised a hand. She kept her eyes locked with the crone. She hesitated, thinking frantically. The crone already knew one secret of hers. There existed only one other she could be talking about. She whispered, keeping her voice as low as possible, "I have a daughter."

"Don't we all," the crone's voice was quiet. She nodded. "The Book of Truths is yours, Elfsdaughter. Take it and begone, please." She glanced around, seeming almost frightened. Her gaze lingered on Gwyn.

Vinet took the book from her, her confusion growing by the moment. She wanted to ask more questions, but the crone's fear forbade any attempt.

"Come on, Vinet," Gwyn took her arm and guided her away from the book stand, toward the market.

Gwyn didn't say anything as they walked away. Vinet remained silent, waiting for the outburst. She didn't have to wait long.

"What were you thinking?" Gwyn demanded in a hissed whisper.

Vinet took a deep breath. "I used my judgment," she said.

"Your judgment?" Gwyn exclaimed. "You told her—"

"I told her nothing she didn't already know," Vinet cut her off. "You heard her. If I had lied, something far worse would have happened."

Gwyn frowned. "How do you know that?"

Vinet shrugged. "I don't know. There're some legends she reminded me of. If AeresThonEsia wants something, she will get it."

Gwyn stared at Vinet. Vinet blinked, realizing what she had just said.

"What did you say?" Gwyn asked, her voice low.

"AeresThonEsia..." Vinet suppressed a shudder. "I have never read that name before in my life."

"And she didn't say it," Gwyn continued to stare at Vinet. "Vinet..."

Vinet glanced down at the book in her hands. "She called this the Book of Truths," she said slowly.

"Truth can be dangerous," Gwyn said. "If truths about you were known, you could be ruined."

Vinet winced. Gwyn was far more right than she wanted her to be.

Gwyn sighed. "Just be careful, Vinet," she said. "You've just become a lady of the Council. You can't afford to get mixed up in something unsavory."

"Of course, I'll be careful." Vinet nearly reached out to embrace her friend but restrained herself. They were still in public. She smiled instead. "I have you to keep me in line."

Gwyn groaned. "And that's a full-time job, I swear."

Vinet laughed. "And that's why it's *your* full-time job!" she exclaimed. She started walking again. "Come on, let's visit that private collection. There's still plenty of daylight for research."

Gwyn shook her head hopelessly as she fell into step behind Vinet. Vinet's lips twitched in amusement. She made a mental note to research anything which had anything to do with the name AeresThonEsia.

Vinet had a vision that evening, the first she'd had in weeks.

They happened like that, occurring randomly. They never lasted for long, and she often could conceal when they happened, but they always unsettled her.

This one unsettled her more than most. At first, everything was simply dark. Then a sound. A hand. A scream, a groan, the dying audible truth of ultimate loss. All around blackened timber, smoldering. Two skulls, judgmental stares. A whispering voice in the soul. The hand, surrounded by near-visual weeping, dipping a twig into a dripping substance nearby. Another hand reached down out of the shifting light and dark. Quick receding footsteps. Then nothing.

Vinet blinked and grabbed a nearby chair for balance. That had been... unpleasant.

"Vinet? You alright?"

Vinet forced herself to nod. "I'm fine, Gwyn."

Gwyn wasn't fooled. "You had another vision, didn't you."

Vinet tried to shrug it off. "It's not like it hasn't happened before."

"Yes, but…" Gwyn seemed to struggle for words. "You can't control them, Vinet."

It was just as well they were in her own private quarters. It would cause a scandal if anyone had heard Gwyn talking to her without using her title.

"I've never been able to," Vinet said bitterly. "Why should it change now? That's why I need to research, Gwyn."

Gwyn sighed. Vinet could hardly blame her. She had been researching for years and had come up with nothing.

She let her gaze wander. A tall, four-poster bed sat at one end of the room. At the other, a fire crackled in the hearth, regardless of the warmth outside. She would want it tonight. A small table rested next to the chairs around the fire. The black book sat on it.

Absently, Vinet reached for the book. She hadn't had a chance to peruse it closely yet. The private collection had been extensive, and the owner, none other than the palace archivist, had been more than willing to show it to her right then. She had even found a fragment of a map that appeared to show land directly across a channel from Hillsdale. But none of that compared to this book.

"Vinet…" the warning in Gwyn's tone was evident.

Vinet ignored her friend. She sat the book on her lap and began flipping through the pages.

For a moment, she almost thought she recognized the script. It seemed like an ancient version of Saemarian. Then it shifted, the lines blurring before her eyes. To her astonishment, they changed completely, morphing into symbols which meant nothing to her. Then the page went blank.

Vinet stared at the book in astonishment. After all that…

She closed the book with a snap. Gwyn blinked at her, startled.

Vinet shook her head, forestalling any questions. "I'll look at that later," she said. "We're heading home tomorrow, yes? I think it's better to examine it back in Ninaeva."

"As long as Niara doesn't get her hands on it," Gwyn said.

Vinet smiled fondly. At a bare five years of age, Niara, her only child and daughter, was a handful. Already reading as fluently as many adults, she constantly begged for stories from anyone who would listen to her for more than five seconds.

"I'll ensure she doesn't see it," Vinet said. She met Gwyn's eyes. "Believe me, that is the last thing I'd let her do."

Gwyn nodded in satisfaction.

Vinet smiled. She paid more attention to Niara's safety than she did her own. Something that was perfectly natural, she supposed. She sighed and carefully placed the book back on the table. "I hope the next council session goes better than this one," she said. "If arguments like this happen every time, I'm going to have gray hair before I'm thirty."

2

THE EXPEDITION

G wyn!"
Vinet nearly flew down the spiral stairs, shouting for her friend. In her hand she held a parchment lined with the familiar golden illumination of the Council.

She burst into the grand hall of Ilhelm Castle and looked around. Where had Gwyn gotten to?

"Aunt Vinet!"

Vinet barely had time to turn around before a small bundle of energy zoomed toward her and slammed into her leg, nearly toppling them both over. Vinet laughed and reached down, picking the small girl up and swinging her around. "Where are you going, my little goose?"

Niara grinned up at her, and Vinet felt her heart contract. Her own green eyes were set in that expression of utter innocence. How had she managed the deception about Niara's heritage? How could she continue to lie to her daughter? She knew the answer to that. Because it was necessary.

"Aunt Gwyn's been teaching me how to use a knife!" Niara announced with importance. "Want to see? Please, Aunt Vinet!"

Vinet laughed and set Niara down. "Of course, dearest. Lead the way!" Carefully, she folded the message from the council and put it in her belt pouch. It could wait.

Niara took her hand and nearly dragged Vinet out of the great hall and into the inner courtyard where a practice yard had been set up years ago. Gwyn had trained here, and she'd attempted to teach Vinet. A chill in the air warned of an early Manyu's Time, but the sun still shone brightly.

Gwyn waited for them, dressed in her usual chain mail, blonde hair bound in a tight bun on the back of her head. Vinet thought, not for the first time, that it was no wonder people occasionally mistook Gwyn for the true lady of Ninaeva.

Gwyn grinned as she saw Niara and Vinet approaching. "The little minx found you, did she?"

"I'm not a minx!"

Gwyn reached down to ruffle Niara's hair. "You're an adorable minx," she said unrepentantly. "Now, were you going to show your aunt what you just learned or not?"

Niara quickly moved to obey Gwyn. She took a small wooden dagger from the weapon rack and squared off against Gwyn.

Gwyn was going easy on Niara, Vinet knew. A five-year-old had no chance against Gwyn, who had been training for over twenty years. But she could immediately see Niara's potential. She spun and twisted, staying just out of Gwyn's reach. In the end, she darted forward, landing a blow on Gwyn's shins.

Gwyn's dramatics were all a five-year-old could wish for. She hopped around on one foot, swinging her sword wildly and threatening Niara with impossible fates. Niara could barely stay upright from giggling. Finally, Gwyn collapsed to the ground, and Niara darted forward to poke Gwyn's stomach with her wooden dagger.

"Ow," Gwyn complained.

Vinet laughed. "I think Gwyn has been well and truly vanquished, little goose. Well done!"

Gwyn sat up and glared at Niara. "Who told you it was acceptable to strike a warrior while he was down?"

A giggle escaped. "You did."

Gwyn crossed her arms and scowled at Niara. "Clever minx."

Niara burst into giggles again.

"At least she fights better than her aunt," Gwyn raised an eyebrow at Vinet.

"Hey!" Vinet's exclamation was indignant, which only made Niara giggle harder.

Vinet rolled her eyes. "I can't deny it. I never wanted to learn. Keep at your lessons, dear. Do as I say, and not as I do."

Niara nodded eagerly. Vinet stroked her hair tenderly for a moment.

"Go and claim some sweets from the kitchens as your reward, dearest. And make sure you clean up before dinner!" She had to shout the last phrase as Niara darted off at the beginning of her first sentence.

She extended a hand to help Gwyn to her feet. "She's hopeless."

"Gets more like her mother every day," Gwyn quipped.

If anyone else had said that, Vinet's heart would have stopped. Instead, she just shrugged. "I'm keeping my sister appraised of her," she said. "Just in case anyone goes to the convent and starts asking questions."

Gwyn shook her head but didn't continue the subject, for which Vinet was grateful.

"A message from the Council arrived," Vinet said, remembering. She fished the parchment out of her belt pouch. "Guess what one of the options is!"

There was an amused glint in Gwyn's eye as she took the parchment from Vinet. As she read, her eyebrows arched. "An expedition, hmm?"

"To ruins in the southern badlands! An ancient city!"

Gwyn's smile was indulgent. "You'll have to convince your fellow councilors of its worth," she pointed out. "And this," she pointed at the parchment, "they may feel is more relevant to their interest."

Unwillingly, Vinet looked at the parchment again. She had noted the option most likely to spark the other councilors' interests. She hadn't wanted to think about it.

A note had come from the southeast, ill-written, saying something about children taken, uniformed sons ruined, and a plea to the Light-Bringer to protect.

"I'm not certain there's anything of substance to it," she ventured.

Gwyn snorted. "You just want your expedition."

Vinet winced at the accuracy of Gwyn's words. "Would you believe it?" she asked.

Her friend only sighed.

She closed her eyes. "I'll make sure we investigate it first," she promised. "Find out who delivered it. If it seems like there's a legitimate threat, I'll support it."

"Good," Gwyn said. "That's all I can ask, Vinet. Think before you act. Especially when you're following your heart."

Vinet nodded reluctantly. Gwyn was right, she knew. She was a lady of the Saemarian Council, and she had a duty to her kingdom.

But she wanted that expedition.

Vinet had an obligation to fulfill before she went to the capital, however. On the same day that brought word from the Council, an invitation had arrived from Lord Conn MacTir, inviting her and her niece to Dunbarrow to meet his family. It would be most convenient for her to ride to visit him and then head directly to the council session. And since the invitation specifically included Niara, Niara would ride with her to the capital, and they would spend the two months until the next council session there for Niara's sixth name-day.

Vinet couldn't contain her suspicions about Conn making sure his invitation included Niara. Although Niara was illegitimate, right now she was the only apparent heir of Ninaeva. She would be quite the catch for one of his children to unite the north under one ruler.

Assuming I stay single and were inclined to let Niara be betrothed in the first place, Vinet thought. She shook her head. That suspicion was yet to be founded.

The ride was pleasant enough. Although Manyu's Time threatened, no snow had yet fallen, which made the journey easy. Vinet was grateful, traveling in snow was never pleasant.

As they rode up to the gates of Dunbarrow, Vinet allowed herself to be impressed. The city was built on a foundation similar to Ilhelm, her own capital, a circular layout built for defense. The smooth granite walls rose high, and the patrolling guards were prominently visible. A large, bear-like man stood at the gate, along with the regular guards, his fur cloak hanging about him like a mantle of victory. He hailed Vinet's party as they approached.

"Lady Vinet Rochelle?" he asked.

Vinet nodded. She didn't need Gwyn's glance to guarantee she kept her distance. Although the man was likely one of Conn's guards, Gwyn would verify that first.

The man smiled. "Aed Dubh, at your service. My lord Conn sent me to escort you to the castle."

"Lead the way, Aed."

Aed led them through the streets, where Vinet's initial perception of Dunbarrow being similar to Ilhelm was shown to be mistaken. Instead of wood, the houses were mostly of stone, and decorated with intricate runes Vinet wished she could understand. The noise of daily bustle was almost overwhelming, especially when they passed through the market.

"My lord told me you are of a mercantile nature," Aed shouted over the sound of commerce. "Perhaps you and Lady Maeve will find some time to come down here together."

Vinet surveyed the market. Despite the crowded atmosphere, the anticipation associated with trade and commerce tantalized and beckoned. It would be intriguing to come explore it at leisure. The kind of goods available would tell her a great deal about her northern neighbor.

Aed led them closer and closer to the large hill in the middle of the city. At the edge of it, he stopped. The steep hill resembled a cliff, but carved stairs traveled up the rock face. "I'm afraid your horses will have to stay here."

Vinet nodded and dismounted. She gestured to her guards to stay with the horses. The laws of hospitality required her to rely on Conn's protection now. And Gwyn.

Aed gestured at Niara. "Can she make the climb?"

Niara set her chin stubbornly. "I can do anything!"

Aed blinked, seemingly taken aback. Then he smiled warmly. "I'm sure you can. It's a long climb, though. Don't be afraid to ask for help if you get tired."

Vinet suppressed a smile, knowing Aed had just said the words that would almost guarantee Niara would never admit to being tired. She just hoped the child wouldn't be too exhausted by the top.

They started the climb, and Vinet gave a moment of thanks she was still in her traveling clothes. The knee-length split tunic was far more suited to these stairs than a formal dress would have been. She would wear a dress for dinner, one in the fur-loving Gray Mountain's style to appeal to Conn's sensibilities. Someone would, unfortunately, be assigned to haul her luggage up these stairs. It wasn't as long a climb as she had feared, however. Before her legs began to burn, they reached the top, where Lord Conn was waiting with a pale, dark haired woman and two children.

"Welcome to Dunbarrow, Lady Vinet!" Conn looked even more the image of a northern lord than he had at the Council. His entire outfit seemed to consist of fur and leather, and he wore only a simple silver coronet to signify his rank.

Vinet nodded in acknowledgment. "Thank you for the invitation," she said.

Conn indicated the people next to him. "Allow me to introduce my wife, Lady Maeve, and our children, Niall and Dinah," He gestured at the children in turn. Niall was the oldest, a serious-eyed boy around ten. Dinah appeared to be around Niara's age.

Vinet nodded at each of them. "And may I present my niece, Niara?"

Niara barely contained a bounce of excitement. It was for her sake Vinet had accepted this invitation. Her daughter needed some non-Ninaevan friends.

"A pleasure," Conn smiled at Niara. He gestured to his eldest. "Niall, why don't you and Dinah take Niara to the gardens to play?"

Niara cast a pleading expression at Vinet, who couldn't help but laugh. She gave a slight nod, and the children went tearing off.

Vinet watched them go, her expression mirthful. "They won't get into too much mischief, will they?" she asked.

Conn waved a hand. "There's not much mischief they can get up to. Niall will supervise them."

Maeve graced Vinet with a cool smile. "You'll want to refresh yourself before dinner. I'll have a servant show you to your chambers. Will your guard be accompanying you?"

Vinet glanced back at Gwyn. "Gwyn goes where I do," she answered.

Maeve nodded gracefully. "Very well. We'll see you for dinner."

———

Dinner was a comfortable affair. Maeve, although cool and unreadable, was an excellent hostess. Conn's house bard sat by the fireplace, playing a traditional hill song on a harp carved with geometric symbols.

"How long has your niece lived at Ilhelm with you?" Conn asked.

Vinet kept her eyes on her food as she cut into a slice of beef. "All her life," she said calmly.

"So, your sister was at Ninaeva when she was born?" Maeve inquired.

Vinet looked up to meet Maeve's eyes. "Not at Ilhelm, but in Ninaeva, yes. The convent of Mazda, near your border."

It was enough information for them to fill in the pieces of the story. A noblewoman who had a child out of wedlock was a shameful disgrace. A convent life was considered suitable repentance.

"Ah," Maeve was satisfied. "So that is why your sister is now at the convent. Why was Niara not sent there to become a pledged one?"

Vinet controlled her reactions. "Because I do not believe her choices should be limited by those of her mother," she said simply. "A life in a convent is not for one who does not have a calling."

That silenced Maeve, much to Vinet's relief. The children were having dinner in their own chambers, supervised by the MacTir nursemaids. Vinet hoped Niara was enjoying herself.

Filling the awkward silence, Conn cleared his throat before asking, "So, have you received your letter from the Council yet, Lady Vinet?"

She could sound out Conn's feelings about the expedition. "I have," she said smoothly. "I take it you have as well?"

Conn nodded. "I am quite interested in our options. It is sad the treasury will not allow us to pursue more than one line of inquiry."

"Which one are you leaning towards?" Vinet took a bite of the beef, finding it well-seasoned with northern spices, sage, and a hint of mustard.

"I must admit, I'm concerned about the south," he said slowly. "But the option which truly intrigues me is the opportunity to research the dwarven armor."

Vinet glanced up sharply. She had seen that on the list and discounted it. They would never have the funds to equip every single Regular with dwarven armor, so why should they research it?

"Why that one?" she asked as casually as she could, intrigued by his motives.

"Have you met any dwarves?" Conn asked. "There's an enclave in the capital. If we commission them to craft us armor, then they might be staunch allies."

Vinet wanted to bite her lip hard. That was not what she had wanted to hear.

"What about the expedition?" she ventured.

Conn laughed. "Lady Vinet, your reputation precedes you. An exploratory expedition was almost designed to draw your attention."

Vinet forced herself to smile. "And if it was?" she said. "That does not mean it comes without its benefits to Saemar."

"Or its risks," Conn said. "I would rather invest in ourselves, than send men to Mazda-knows-where to find potentially nothing."

"Or potentially everything," Vinet pointed out. "You speak of risk, but there is no gain without it. What if these explorers find valuable knowledge?"

Conn shook his head in amusement. "I'd save these arguments for the Council, Lady Vinet. Let's enjoy our dinner, shall we?"

Silently, Vinet acquiesced. If she was going to fund that expedition, she would have to search for allies other than Conn MacTir.

Vinet sighed with relief when they arrived at the capital. Conn was...
entertaining, certainly, but Vinet was tired from having to be constantly
on her guard. Her suspicion about his intentions toward Niara had only
grown as he exulted in how well the children had gotten along.

Niara gasped in delight as they rode through the marketplace. Her
little head swiveled left and right, trying to take everything in. Vinet let
Gwyn keep a close eye on her and directed her own attention to looking
for the bookseller.

Her heart stopped as she saw the corner across from where the Jyrian
merchants had been. It stood empty, no sign there had never been a stand
there.

"Vinet?" Gwyn's voice was low and worried.

Vinet shook her head. "Not now."

Despite her misgivings, they made their way to her townhouse
without incident. Almost as soon as they entered, the butler approached
Vinet with a bow and handed her a slip of parchment.

Vinet frowned as she opened it. A message already? Her eyebrows rose
as she read its contents.

My dear Lady Vinet Rochelle,

  It was an honor to make your acquaintance. Perhaps we could continue that
acquaintance over some tea at my townhouse when you arrive?

  Lady Pellalindra Duskryn

"Anything important?"

Vinet glanced up at Gwyn's question. "I think we're going to tea this
afternoon." She waved a hand at the servants carrying the baggage into
the house. "Get someone to lay out a gown for me, will you?"

The next two hours were a flurry of activity. Although Pellalindra had
not specified a date, Vinet's arrival in the capital had been later than she'd
planned. The council session was tomorrow.

She left Niara, chaperoned by her nursemaid, to happily explore and
set off to Pellalindra's townhouse with only Gwyn as her guard. Luckily,
the two noble townhouses were not far apart. The Duskryn house,
however, was far more ornately decorated than the Ninaevan one, with
gold filigree along the fence and geometric murals on the front walls.

"Someone got their hands on too much gold," was Gwyn's quiet opinion.

Vinet smiled and shook her head.

The door opened as the two women approached, and a servant bowed and ushered them in. The inside was just as ostentatious as the outside, with more murals and shelves with golden knick-knacks. "I'll let my lady know you've arrived."

Vinet nodded, and she and Gwyn were left alone in the hall. They stood in silence for only a few moments when footsteps echoed on the wood floor.

"Oh!"

Vinet's heart nearly stopped. The young man was slight but muscular with bright blue eyes that gazed guilelessly at the two women. A great sword was strapped to his back, and he wore the cobalt blue and black uniform of a Duskryn guard. That wasn't what caught Vinet's attention, however. His ears were long and pointed.

"I...umm...I didn't realize Lady Duskryn had visitors," he said.

Not for the first time, Vinet cursed the noble propriety that forced her to act aloof. She wanted nothing more than to pounce on the young elf and interrogate him about who he was, his lineage, and his people. Instead, she shot Gwyn an imploring look.

Gwyn's face was full of amusement, but she nodded imperceptibly. "My lady received an invitation to tea," she said.

"Oh, right!" the poor elf hunched his shoulders in confusion. "I shouldn't disturb you." He started backing away down the hallway.

Vinet's eyes widened. They couldn't let him leave without asking any questions!

More footsteps heralded the return of the servant. She shook her head at the elf and turned to Vinet. "Lady Duskryn will receive her ladyship in her study. Will your...guard be accompanying you, my lady?" the servant gave a superior sniff.

It was just as well Gwyn had had a lifetime to get used to such slights. She gave the servant an easy smile. "No, I think I'll be better suited joining the guards here. Perhaps you could show me around?" She indicated the elf.

He blinked but made no objection. Vinet glanced gratefully at Gwyn before following the superior servant.

The servant led them to a comfortable and pleasing study. Dark wood bookcases lined the walls, the same wood as the large desk situated at one side of the room. At the other side, a small table and chairs were set for tea.

Pellalindra rose from one of the chairs as Vinet entered. "Lady Vinet! I can't say how pleased I am you've accepted my invitation."

Vinet gave a slight curtsy. "Thank you for inviting me."

The two women sat down, exchanging more banal formalities. Vinet took the opportunity to examine Pellalindra more closely. The Lady Duskryn had shed her mourning gown, a trifle early for the sensibilities of some, but, considering the circumstances of her husband's death, a wise choice. A silver tiara held her raven-black hair in place. Her gown, a deep velvet blue, was the height of Saemarian fashion, with a high-necked collar and ruffled sleeves. Deep blue and silver embroidery covered the gown, creating the illusion of stars whenever she moved.

Vinet was glad she had dressed well. Her own dress was from Jyria, made of a light yellow cotton-linen blend cut low with an asymmetric hem, too pale to be true gold, but that just made the golden trim stand out even more. She could never wear this dress in the north, as the Jyrian styles were only suitable far to the south.

"And how is your niece doing?" Pellalindra asked as she began to pour the tea.

"Quite well. And your son? Percival, isn't it?" she asked.

Pellalindra's political smile tinged with genuine fondness. "Oh, he's quite a handful. Gives his nursemaid more than enough trouble."

Vinet had to laugh. "They all do at that age." She burned to ask about Pellalindra's elven guard, but such questions didn't meet the criteria for polite conversation. Just from the behavior of Pellalindra's servants, this lady stood on propriety. Asking about a guard would be a social faux pas.

"I assume you've heard of the Council's topics by now?" Pellalindra's voice was casual, but Vinet heard the weight behind it.

Vinet accepted the cup of tea Pellalindra handed her. "Indeed. I am certain we are all aware by now."

"I hardly need to ask what option you will argue for." Pellalindra poured her own cup.

Vinet allowed herself a small smile. "My reputation precedes me."

"Indeed." Pellalindra sighed. "I am not a gambling woman, Lady Vinet. And an expedition like that would certainly be a gamble."

Vinet felt her ears twitch. There hadn't been a condemnation in that statement. "Everything is a gamble, Lady Pellalindra. The question is what has the potential for the most gain."

"And I suppose you are prepared to gamble the safety of the kingdom for a chance at exploration?" Pellalindra's neutral expression gave nothing away.

Vinet looked at Pellalindra sharply. "No," she said. "But I have not heard anything to make me believe that letter is anything more than bandits, which the Regulars stationed there should be taking care of."

"That is a fair point. And your thoughts on the other matter? The dwarven armor and weaponry?" Pellalindra pursed her lips.

"That would require far more resources than funding an expedition." Vinet took one of the biscuits and ducked it in her tea. "Even then, I'm certain we would not be able to outfit the entire Regulars, and so what would be the point?"

Pellalindra nibbled on a slice of apple. "Another fair point. You have a shrewd mind, Lady Vinet."

Vinet bowed her head in acknowledgment of the compliment.

"I am still not convinced of the merits of the expedition, though." Pellalindra took another sip of tea. "You speak of potential gain, but there is nothing that convinces me of that. What if this group are scoundrels, looking to fleece us?"

Vinet took one of the other fruits, a peach, and bit into it. "Perhaps we should investigate that?" she offered. "I could send my guard. It wouldn't be too hard to discover where they're staying."

Pellalindra's expression lightened. "I think that's an excellent idea, Lady Vinet," she said. "If you have no objections, I'll send my personal bodyguard as well."

"Would that be the elf we met in the hall?" Vinet seized the opening.

Pellalindra rolled her eyes. "Was Saihid there? I hope he didn't make a scene."

Vinet laughed. "No, not at all! He seemed very polite."

"He is." Pellalindra's expression smoothed into a smile.

They sat in silence for a few moments, each sipping their tea. Vinet waited, unsure what to expect next.

Pellalindra broke the silence. "What are you prepared to gamble for this expedition?" she stared intensely at Vinet.

Vinet leaned back, thinking hard. What was she willing to gamble?

"A vote," she said finally. She looked up to meet Pellalindra's eyes. "This is an issue quite dear to me. If you come across such an issue, I would be willing to return the vote."

Pellalindra sat up, a considering expression on her face. "I must admit, I was not expecting that."

"Sometimes, when you trade, you have to gamble." Vinet allowed herself a small smile.

Pellalindra didn't appear to be convinced, but she nodded. "I will consider this," she said. "I will depend on our guards' report, after all."

Vinet raised her teacup in acknowledgment. "I could ask no more."

Vinet read the report Gwyn handed her with increasing pleasure. The dwarf in charge of the expedition planning, Yderdochter, had done these kinds of things before. She had a good crew and was reliable and discreet. Gwyn had been impressed, and that was hard to do.

She hadn't told Gwyn she'd sent a message to Ellil. Inspired by a memory that the worship of Mazda was mostly confined to Saemar and the Duchy of Tigri, she'd sent a quick note to the high priest explaining that exploring new territories would be an opportunity to spread the worship of Mazda. She didn't want to bring that argument up in the Council.

She put Gwyn's report in her satchel as the other councilors started arriving. There would be time to bring it forward later.

Pellalindra swept into the chamber behind the rest of the councilors and almost immediately took charge. "Well, I'm sure we all have our various opinions about the options presented."

Dannan sat down, his citron eye looking even more pronounced than usual. "Opinions," he growled.

Remaining silent would be better than engaging Dannan, Vinet thought. He looked ready to bite someone's head off. She admired the solid oak of the table instead, polished so smooth she could see her reflection in the wood.

"Opinions," Pellalindra nodded decisively. "I'm sure we are all aware of some of each other's?" Her eyes flickered to Vinet.

"I think the expedition sounds like a fine idea," Kamian declared with a smile. He surveyed the table. "We need something new! Maybe they'll find another civilization. Give us someone else to trade with."

Vinet exchanged an approving glance with the young lord. Kamian's opinion was hardly a surprise.

Dannan growled. "Of course, you would care more about trade than children." His head jerked to the side, and he started massaging his temples.

Pellalindra nodded. "The note from the south is worthy of our concern," she said. "We should at least discuss it." Her hands folded deliberately on the table in front of her. Vinet avoided meeting her gaze. The two of them had already decided their votes.

Kamian snorted. "What is there to discuss? An illiterate letter that someone got handed to the Council? Such a concern is for the local Regulars, not the Council."

"I think the dwarven weaponry has something to recommend itself," Conn interjected. "It would be a good precaution in case there is something in the south."

"In case!" Dannan's eyes were wild. "In case! There is already something there!"

Vinet couldn't keep silent anymore. "We are all concerned about the letter from the southeast, Lord Dannan, but we need to balance the benefits of all the options."

"Balance?! Balance!! What will balance accomplish? While children might be abducted and precious crops burned and who knows what else, we sit here and simply talk about 'balance'? When has 'balance' ever gotten any of us anywhere?" Dannan stood up abruptly from his chair and started pacing.

Well, she had gotten herself into this. "Balance has gotten me quite far, Lord Dannan. Now, please, listen. If our worst nightmares about this message prove true, and there are abducted children and burned crops, that is one thing. If it is something made up by a frightened farmer, however, then a balanced judgment is certainly called for."

Dannan's pacing changed to prowling. Eerily, his citron eye seemed brighter than normal. "Balance, milady, or caution? A lady such as yourself, almost a spinster, would you consider your life as balanced? You have no husband, no children, no love in your life except what you borrow from an idiot sister's child. You sit alone in your lands as a ruler, you have power, but what of love? Where is the balance in that?"

Vinet felt as if she had been slapped. She whirled toward Dannan, furious, but he had already turned his attention from her, his heterochromatic gaze falling on Ellil. "As for you, nephew of the Lord General, it is obvious where your loyalties lie. With strength and power," he scoffed. "You pretend at balance while wearing a priest's robes. But did such a noble thing as balance get you where you are now? Hardly."

Ellil sat quietly, either unaffected or extremely self-disciplined, under Dannan's accusations. Vinet watched in silent astonishment as he switched his attention to Kamian. "And you. Your life has been a balance of whoring and adventure. You refused to take any responsibility as the heir until you were publicly insulted by your tutor and your favorite wine splashed in your face. Shame is what compelled you, boy. Not balance."

Vinet winced. She had heard those rumors about Kamian before.

Dannan's gaze met Pellalindra's for a long moment, glaring. She refused to back down, and to Vinet's astonishment, he turned away from her and to Conn.

"But let us not forget you, Lord Conn MacTir." As he paused, the torches mounted on the walls started burning brighter. The hairs on the back of Vinet's stood up. "What balance compelled you to kill your uncle and his family? Was it to balance the scales? Was their blood enough to satiate your own bloodlust? Was seeing his children dead enough to bring you balance?!"

Dannan's citron eye practically glowed in the bright light of the torches. Vinet held her breath in horror with the unshakable feeling that something terrible was about to happen.

Suddenly Dannan winced and groaned, bending in half over the council table. His hands reached up to grab his head, and he took several gasping, ragged breaths. The torches darkened, almost going out. Dannan jerked up, panic in his eyes. Without saying another word, he turned and ran out of the council chamber.

Vinet stared after him, trying to process what she'd just seen and heard. For a moment, she couldn't meet the gaze of any of the other councilors.

"The man's not cursed," Conn muttered. "He's insane."

Vinet forced herself to look at Conn. Though she'd never heard it stated in so many words, the rumors about the death of his uncle's family had been following him since he had inherited Dunbarrow. The northern lord's face was pale but otherwise composed.

Slowly, she managed to examine the other nobles. No one wanted to meet anyone else's eyes. Even Pellalindra's face was pale, and she had somehow escaped Dannan's accusations. Vinet winced in pain as her nails dug into her palms, only then realizing they were clenched into fists. Taking a deep breath, she flattened them with an effort and placed them on the table.

"Well, I hardly think he's one to be lecturing us about balance," she said, trying to make her voice light.

Her feeble attempt worked. Conn barked a laugh. "Indeed."

Vinet took another breath. "Perhaps a short break in the session would be in order?"

Her suggestion was accepted with alacrity. Vinet exited the council chamber, still trying to hold back her anger. Gwyn raised an eyebrow when Vinet appeared but said nothing as she fell into step behind her. Vinet hardly cared where she ended up but was unsurprised her footsteps led her to the palace garden. She had a knack for finding the gardens wherever she went. Almost bare this Manyu's Time, the naked limbs of the cherry trees contrasted sharply with the stately rows of still-green hedges.

"Lord Dannan came storming out," Gwyn finally said in a low voice.

Vinet shook her head. "Not now," she said. "Not here."

Gwyn nodded in silent acquiescence.

She rolled her shoulders, trying to shake the tension of the council chamber out. "So, tell me about Saihid."

Gwyn's look was wry, but she answered without hesitation. "Well, he's been in Lady Pellalindra's service for over five years," she began. "Doesn't remember much of his origins. Was sold as a slave, bought and freed by Lady Pellalindra, stayed to become her personal bodyguard. He has a sister too. Apparently, she's Lady Pellalindra's hunts-mistress."

"Two elves?" Vinet was incredulous. "How?"

Gwyn raised an eyebrow. "They do come to Saemar occasionally. After all..." she let her words hang.

Vinet gave her a sharp look. Gwyn knew better than to even reference that.

"It's been twenty-six years since the last one was seen in Saemar that I'm aware of. And now Lady Pellalindra has two serving her." She shook her head as she paced along the gravel garden path. "I wish he remembered more of his heritage."

Gwyn nodded sympathetically, but said nothing more, for which Vinet was grateful.

They walked a little further, the only sound the crunching of gravel beneath their feet. "Will they vote for the expedition?"

Vinet shrugged. "Dannan's outburst made that hard to predict. I think so. I hope so."

"What did he say?"

Vinet rolled her eyes. "Accused us of all the worst rumors he'd ever heard about any of us."

Gwyn's head jerked around. "What did he say?" she repeated.

"Just the fact I'm a spinster and my only family is my bastard niece." Despite attempting to keep her voice casual, she could hear the bitterness in it.

Gwyn relaxed. "Well, at least he didn't accuse you of anything worse. There are plenty of other things he could have said."

Vinet sighed. "I should go back in soon," she said. "I doubt Lord Dannan will be back, but we need to call a vote. And then we have a change of plans."

Gwyn gave her a questioning look.

"We're not staying here for Niara's name-day," Vinet said. "She likes traveling, so she should be delighted when I tell her we're going to Kreutzer." If Dannan had outbursts regularly, she wanted to know more about him. His old home was the best place to do that.

3

THE LABYRINTH

S o, the expedition is on its way, I hear." Pellalindra took a sip of her tea and raised an eyebrow across the table. "I trust you'll remember my contribution?"

Vinet raised her own tea in a small salute. "I wouldn't dream of forgetting it," she assured.

Pellalindra nodded in satisfaction.

They met at Vinet's townhouse this time. In deference to the fact that Manyu's Time was still upon them, they were not, as Vinet would have preferred, in the garden. They sat in a small sitting room on the east side of the house. The curtains hung wide open, letting as much sunlight as possible stream in. A fire crackled in the fireplace, warm and welcoming.

Despite the sun and the fire, Pellalindra shivered. "It is cold today, isn't it?" she asked.

Vinet suppressed a smile. She never had to wait long to be reminded that Pellalindra had no notion what a northern Manyu's Time was like.

"The snow is still thick on the ground in Ilhelm," she said instead of answering. "The children are delighting in it, although it does make for difficult traveling."

Pellalindra huddled her hands around her tea. "Niara must adore it."

"Niara adores almost everything outside." Vinet wrapped her hands around her own teacup, enjoying the warmth herself. "She's been having a wonderful time exploring the capital."

"She will turn into a fine lady." Pellalindra smiled, a real, genuine smile. The mention of Niara was one of the few things that could bring it to her lips.

Vinet nodded her thanks. She couldn't keep a smile from her own face.

Pellalindra took another sip of tea, then sighed and leaned back. "As lovely as talking about children is, there is another matter I wish to discuss with you."

Vinet hadn't doubted it. Pellalindra would not have arranged a meeting the day before a council session if she didn't have something political to discuss. She set her teacup down and looked at Pellalindra attentively.

Pellalindra fiddled with her napkin. "I didn't entirely leave the matter of the south alone," she admitted. "I sent a scouting group there, hoping to find some information. They reported nothing particularly unusual, but one of them disappeared."

Vinet tilted her head, confused. "Were they on the border of Tigri? There's still border conflict there, as much as we try to claim it's settled."

Pellalindra shook her head. "They were, but...well, I never would have brought it up, assuming what you did," she paused, and the fire popped and crackled, "but she's been found. Alive. Though not entirely...whole."

Pellalindra's tone of voice made Vinet's ears twitch forward. "What do you mean?"

"She's not conscious, for starters." Pellalindra wouldn't meet Vinet's eyes, instead examining the falling snow outside. "And she has...marks. Scars on her neck which look like tattoos. And a tattoo on her ankle." The noblewoman tucked her napkin under her empty teacup.

The room took on a deathly quiet, only the crackle of fire audible as Vinet waited for Pellalindra to continue.

"The tattoo was of a skull surrounded by eyes."

Vinet's heart skipped a beat. She'd seen that symbol before. Some-where...and it had foul associations.

Pellalindra selected a biscuit and examined it for a long moment before continuing. "Have you seen such a symbol in any of your scholarly pursuits, Lady Vinet?"

Vinet looked down at her forgotten cup of tea. She picked it up and took a long sip, ignoring the now lukewarm temperature.

"It sounds familiar," she admitted. "I will have to do some research."

Pellalindra nodded. She sighed again as she set her teacup down. "That is the other reason I'm here. The Duskryn and court healers have been

33

unable to revive her. There is a specialist, apparently offering to cure her, but for an outrageous price. Something that would drain the kingdom's treasury, I'm being given to understand. It will be put to the Council at the next meeting."

Vinet raised an eyebrow. "You want me to vote to heal your scout?".

Pellalindra shook her head emphatically. "I cannot ask that of anyone," she said. "It is a great risk. We may drain the treasury and find out all she can say is 'I do not know.' And I have heard the other matters may be more pressing."

"Then you have heard more than I." Vinet took another sip of her tea. "Care to tell me more?"

"Have you not been in the capital the past two months? I would have thought you would have heard the same rumors as I." Pellalindra frowned.

Vinet forced herself to shrug. "We've mostly kept to ourselves," she said. If Pellalindra didn't know about the trip to Kreutzer, then she did not intend to enlighten her.

Pellalindra looked baffled. Still, she continued without commenting. "Well, there was a murder. Surely you've heard about that?"

Vinet's head came up. "A murder? No! Who?"

"The Venian ambassador. Murdered in his own chambers."

Vinet sat back, her mind doing quick calculations. "The Jyrians."

"It must be," Pellalindra sniffed. "They've withdrawn almost everyone, and word is they've started a blockade of Venia's harbor. The coalition has broken down."

Vinet thought hard. The coalition of the western city-states was the only reason Saemar had ever been prevented from expanding to the western sea. "So, Venia is likely to ask for our aid," she said slowly.

"I assume so." Pellalindra shrugged. "If we can prove it was the Jyrians, I am certain they will."

Vinet could only agree as her mind raced through the implications.

"I do not want us involved in a war for no gain, of course," Pellalindra said. "Though if Venia offered to join Saemar in return for protection..."

Would that be a good thing? Vinet forced her attention back to the present. "Rest assured, Lady Pellalindra, I try to avoid war whenever possible."

Pellalindra's satisfied smile was cool. "I can believe that of you, Lady Vinet."

Vinet raised her teacup again. "I will take that as a compliment."

"As you should, Lady Vinet," Pellalindra said. "As you should."

"So, are you going to tell Dannan you visited his home city without telling him?" Gwyn's voice was audible even a half-step behind her, even over the buzz of the city streets.

Vinet laughed at the question. "No," she said. "Although if he's any sort of councilor, I'm sure he already knows. Especially if that book of his is anything to go by. Who would have suspected Dannan to write a book about magic?"

That had been the most miraculous find on the visit to Kreutzer. Discounting their wonderful 'University' which was almost purely a large collection of books and the suspiciously burnt empty plot next to it, the small selection of magic books had been a treasure trove. None of them had any spell work in them, but Dannan's went extensively into the theory of magic.

"Careful around him, Vinet," Gwyn said. "A man with those kinds of talents, and that kind of temper, is not to be trifled with."

"I'm not trifling with him," Vinet held her head high. "I'm investigating. And investigating for my own interest, too. Who's to say I didn't hear of the magic books in Kreutzer and decided to visit it because of that?"

Gwyn shook her head in exasperation, but their approach to the palace made it impossible to continue the conversation.

The two unmoving guards were at the doorway. Vinet wondered if anyone ever mistook them for real statues.

She was early, so she took her time getting to the council chamber. She paused in the hallway to examine one of the paintings on the wall. Faded paint on plaster covered the brown sandstone of the palace, depicting a dragon flying overhead, breathing fire. Below stood a man in shining armor, deflecting the fire with a golden shield which spread out, covering an entire army.

"Admiring our dear founder?"

Vinet turned at the sound of Dannan's voice. "Admiring the artistry, actually. Though there is much about King Enlil to be admired."

Dannan snorted. "We know almost nothing about him besides legend. What can be admired about that?"

She raised an eyebrow. "The fact that he apparently did something which allowed him to be remembered as a hero throughout the generations."

Dannan shrugged.

Curiously, he didn't seem inclined to move past her toward the council chamber. She decided to take a risk.

"Speaking of things we know little about," she said. "I found a copy of your book. May I ask where you learned so much about magical theory?" She smiled guilelessly. "I'm doing an academic study, and I'm having trouble finding material."

Dannan stared at her, his gaze disconcerting. "Magic isn't something to be trifled with. It's dangerous, even for mages."

Vinet smiled tightly. "I am aware of the dangers, which is precisely why I wish to learn more. Ignorance is the most dangerous weapon of all."

"But of what use could the knowledge be to you?" Dannan asked. "You are no mage."

Oh, if only you knew. Though it's good you don't. Not until I know more myself.

She forced a casual shrug. "Mages occasionally travel through Ninaeva. It's a center of learning for everyone, after all. I'd like to know who I'm dealing with."

"There are better ways about learning about mages than learning about magic," Dannan's voice was harsh. "Especially the books you've consulted. 'Poddingstonstan's Guide to Incantation Magic?' Please. That mage was an idiot."

Well, he had given her proof he knew about her visit to Kreutzer, anyway. That had been one of the books in the University Library.

She laughed. She had no reason to conceal her visit. "Then perhaps you'd have better suggestions?"

Dannan narrowed his eyes. "Yes. Stop reading about magic. You'll only get yourself and others hurt. Or worse." He turned and stalked away.

Vinet stared after him. No one had wanted to talk about the burnt-down house next to the University, nor answer any questions about Lord Dannan. But he had lived there, she was certain of it. As had his family.

A family which no longer existed.

She shook her head. Dannan might mean well, but her pursuit of magic was not going to stop because he advised it. If anything, magic was pursuing her.

Sighing, she followed him into the council chambers. Today would be an interesting session.

Sure enough, she had barely opened the door when she heard Kamian, Pellalindra, and Conn already involved in a heated discussion.

"This situation with Venia gives us an opportunity," Kamian was insisting. "If we intervene, they've indicated they are willing to cede their independence and join the kingdom. Do you have any idea the kind of trade goods Venia produces? We'd have a port on the sea, a stepping stone to the trade routes of the wider world! Do you really want to deny the kingdom that kind of revenue?"

"We need to deal with the threat from the southeast first!" Conn's voice rose. "Let the city-states bicker among themselves, we have a problem of our own to deal with!"

"A problem which could very well be minor," Pellalindra sounded like she felt obliged to point that out.

Conn rounded on her. "Mazda's sake, Lady Pellalindra, she's your scout!"

"And it would cost the treasury a great deal to heal her, if she was healed at all," Pellalindra refused to back down. "I am not inclined to take risks with the kingdom's welfare like that."

"You were more than willing to take a risk for Lady Vinet's expedition," Dannan's voice broke through the arguing.

Vinet shot him a sharp look as she sat down. It was hardly her expedition.

The look Pellalindra bestowed upon Dannan was cool. "That, as Lady Vinet pointed out, has the promise of reward," she said.

"And healing your scout doesn't?"

"We know nothing about the marks she bears," Pellalindra said firmly. "For all we know, it could mean nothing."

Vinet sat in silence, listening to the various arguments as the sun shone through the large glass windows, barely blocked by the tall leafless ash tree standing outside. Pellalindra appeared firmly inclined not to ask anyone else to fund the healing of her scout. Perhaps she was scared she would be accused of putting Duskryn interests before the kingdom's.

Kamian was intensely interested in securing Venia. They had offered a tempting deal. Break the trade blockade, and they would join Saemar unconditionally. It would give Saemar a port along the coast, and access to all the trade goods that passed through the city. Of course, it would also anger the Jyrians, who wanted Venia as well.

Conn, on an interesting note, seemed far more concerned about the wounded scout than she would have given him credit for. Maybe part of his reputation was right, and he cared intensely for the lives of his men. Perhaps he felt sympathy for a fellow soldier.

Ellil sat silently, watching the argument. Dannan made cutting remarks about the wisdom of every decision.

Finally, Vinet couldn't take it anymore. "It seems we're hampered by a lack of information," she broke in. "Someone needs to talk to this healer and see if there is actually a chance he would be able to heal her. Someone also needs to find out about the Venian ambassador's murder, maybe speak to a representative to find out exactly how much resources it would cost us to help them. And someone needs to follow up on the scout's tattoos and find out if they mean anything or not."

Pellalindra raised an eyebrow. "Are you volunteering for one of those?"

Unbidden, the image of the old crone hunched over her book stand entered Vinet's mind. Perhaps she would have answers.

"I am," Vinet said. "I may have a lead on investigating the tattoos."

The rest of the councilors looked at each other.

"I will speak to the healer," Ellil spoke for the first time. He flushed a little as all eyes turned toward him. "As a priest, I am aware of some matters of healing."

"I will talk to those in charge of the inquiry into the Venian ambassador's death," Pellalindra said. "Perhaps they will know more about the strength of the Jyrians."

"And I will speak to his secretary," Kamian nodded.

Vinet couldn't help but glance at Dannan, who had sat silent during the allocation of tasks.

"Don't look at me," he said, raising his hands. "You seem to have everything handled."

His smug smile made her anger flare, and Vinet narrowed her eyes. "Are these plans made by a northern idiot satisfactory to you?" she asked pointedly. To her surprise, Dannan paled.

"That," he said quietly. "I am sorry for that, for what I said. I was...not myself."

Vinet frowned at him for a moment, curious. The man was the prince's tutor. The king placed an inordinate amount of trust in him. He couldn't be untrustworthy, and yet...he didn't seem entirely stable.

Finally, she nodded. "Shall we reconvene in say, four candlemarks?" she asked.

The councilors chorused agreement. Vinet sighed in relief. At least something had been agreed on.

The marketplace population was sparse, usual for late Manyu's Time. No Jyrian merchants, however, and only one Venian, who looked rather worse for wear. Vinet's lips tightened. Saemar could not remain insular, ignore its neighbors, and expect to be unaffected.

The book stand was nowhere in sight. Vinet stifled a curse. The spot where it had last stood was empty. However, something, perhaps nothing more than curiosity, drew her to its location. Although the weather was dark and cloudy, or perhaps because of it, a glint of light on the ground caught her attention. A gem. Dark red, it seemed to pulse slightly. Against her better judgment, Vinet crouched down next to the gem and hesitantly reached out to touch it. In the instant her fingers made contact, the faint pulsing ceased. She felt a slight tingle on her backbone, right between her shoulder blades. Hastily, she removed her hand.

The tingle vanished, but the gem started pulsing again. This was unlike anything Vinet had ever read about. She reached out again, slightly more confident this time. Instead of simply touching, she reached out to grab it. As she did, the gem sank into the pavement.

Vinet stared at the gem in astonishment. What on earth had caused that to happen?

She bent forward to examine the ground more closely. There were scratch marks around the gem, as if someone had taken a dagger and attempted to pry it out of the stone.

She sat back on her heels and shifted her satchel to her front. Slowly, she pulled out the black book the bookseller had given her. She had meant to ask about it.

A thought occurred to her. She glanced around. No one was paying attention to her. "Gwyn, would you keep watch, please?"

Gwyn gave her a look full of apprehension, but she nodded and started scanning the marketplace.

Vinet took a deep breath and situated herself cross-legged on the ground next to the gem. She flipped the Book of Truths open on her lap. "AeresThonEsia, may I speak with you?"

A laugh, low and pleasant, emanated from the book. Vinet nearly dropped it in astonishment. Gwyn gasped and turned toward her as the laugh changed to a chortling cacophony. It nearly deafened her as the page changed in front of her eyes. A face, vaguely reminiscent of Niara's, though more elven in nature, appeared on the page, set in the middle of a vast and intricate labyrinth.

Vinet felt a hand on her shoulder. "What's going on?" Gwyn demanded.

Vinet stared at the labyrinth, mesmerized. "It's all right," she said. Carefully, she reached out to touch the page and began tracing the labyrinthine pattern.

She needed answers. And the skull tattoo was the most pressing question. She set the image of the tattoo in her mind. "I have some questions, if you do not mind."

As she reached the center of the labyrinth, her vision went black and blue. The laughter grew louder and louder, filling her ears. She couldn't hear Gwyn, though she could see her friend's panicked face in front of her. She tried to reach out, but a light flashed, and then darkness overwhelmed her.

Laughter filled her senses. It changed, growing from a chuckle to a malicious cackle that sent shivers down her spine. Then it changed again. Screams split her skull, and she opened her mouth, trying to cry out in fear. No sound came out. Nothing. Her eyes flew open.

Silence. There was silence. Vinet stood, gasping, staring straight into a mirror. But instead of her own reflection, a full-grown Niara posed for her. Elven features, however, sending a pang through Vinet's heart.

Then she blinked. It wasn't Niara. It was her. But as a full-blood elf.

She took a deep breath. Somewhere, deep inside her, was buried the remainder of the panic, but it somehow hovered just apart.

Two paths led from the mirror, one to the left, and one to the right. She could distinguish no difference between them. Two tunnels stretched out into infinity.

She couldn't just stand here. Determined, she turned to the right and set off. Something made her peek over her shoulder as she did. Swallowing, she noticed the passage closing behind her.

Well, there's no turning back now.

It took an eternity. Finally, suddenly, another mirror appeared before her. Her reflection again. But this time, she was fully human.

Vinet stared at the mirror for a long moment. It was her mother. Or, almost her mother. The features were still definitely her own, if slightly different. She smiled, feeling the familiar warmth of affection. She had lost her mother too early.

Something else hung in the air, though. An admiration, unfamiliar to her. Centered on a man she had never met.

My father. Vinet resolutely moved away from the mirror. As before, two paths stretched before her, one right and one left.

Well, it had served her well so far. She started down the right passage, not bothering to check behind her this time. If the passageway was going to disappear behind her, it would.

It seemed like no time at all had passed when a third mirror appeared before her. Vinet stared at it blankly. This time it was her.

Her features hadn't changed. The same mix of elven and human present in her own blood reflected before her. Try as she might, Vinet could not muster any emotions.

She looked around again and swallowed as she realized she stood at a dead end. No other passages appeared for her to choose from. The passage behind her, however, was still wide open. She didn't want to go back, vaguely aware of a niggling voice warning against retracing her steps. But what else could she do?

Hesitantly, she turned and started walking back the way she came. Maybe it would lead to the second mirror, and she could take the turning left. She only made it a few steps before the path narrowed. She tilted her body sideways to squeeze through, trying to push down the fear rising inside her.

Suddenly, a cry sounded behind her, and she nearly turned back. It sounded like her own.

She stopped.

All around her, she could feel blood rushing, a low thumping, like the sounds of a heart. Her own heart quickened, keeping pace with the rhythm around her.

Then she saw it.

A skull, floating and grinning, ringed by eyes, eyes that gazed everywhere and nowhere. It moved toward her.

She swallowed and stared at the skull, terror rising. "What are you? Where do you come from?" She tried to sound authoritative but her voice cracked. Her mouth felt dry. Her demand made no impression on it. It kept approaching, floating in the air, its jaw opening and closing. Three tongues simply floated in the darkness of its maw.

She couldn't hear anything. She couldn't think. All she could do was watch in mounting terror.

Then, behind her, a voice, male, soft and melodic. "Vinet Elfsdaughter..." She looked over her shoulder. She could see nothing beyond the black passage.

A scream from the skull made her jerk around again. It moved faster now.

She glanced behind her again. She knew the dark tunnel ended at the mirror, offering no route of escape.

The voice sounded again, saying nothing but her name. Another scream made her jerk back toward the skull. It was almost upon her.

Fear overwhelmed her. She turned and bolted back down the passageway towards the mirror, heedless of the fact that it would end. Screams followed her, and she could hear the licking of the tongues reaching out to her.

The mirror rose up in front of her, a stark barrier. She nearly wept. The only part of her reflection left was her eyes.

"Elfsdaughter. Daughter! Come here."

Vinet stared at the mirror, from where the voice seemed to be coming. She reached out desperately, her hands braced on the mirror. "Father! What do I do?"

The screaming was almost upon her. She closed her eyes.

A sharp pain burned between her shoulder blades. She heard a low rushing, and then silence. The mirror disappeared, and she fell forward onto her knees.

She scrambled to her feet, gasping. She was no longer in the labyrinth. Around her grew a lush garden, apple blossoms, and hyacinths and roses all growing in jumbled joy. Clear paths were laid out in front of her. The garden was still, with no sound of birds, animals, or wind, but nevertheless, a sense of peace settled on her.

Ahead of her, on a low, wooden bench, sat AeresThonEsia. The woman, no longer a crone, regarded Vinet with a tilted head and a smile.

Vinet stared at her. Somewhere, in memory of her panicked run, she was still breathing heavily. "How...where..." she stopped herself. This was no ordinary woman. And considering what she had just been through... politeness was most definitely in order. She took another deep breath and bowed. "Greetings, lady," she said.

As if in answer to her greeting, she began to hear sounds from the garden. The soft lilting of birds flitting about, singing their songs. A cricket. In a tree next to AeresThonEsia's bench, a small, tiny woman with wings was singing gently.

AeresThonEsia gestured and a branch grew out from the tree, a shallow in it filled with water. "Drink, curious child. Drink and breathe. You are in Sanctuary now, though there are," she seemed to chew over the next word, "easier ways to get here."

She managed a small smile and took another deep breath. "I would have taken one of those if I knew how."

"Curious child." AeresThonEsia stood up and moved over to Vinet. She dipped a hand into the water. Vinet couldn't help but note that all her fingers were now present. Cupping her hands together, she filled them with water and took a long drink. The water did not seem diminished in any way.

"Drink, Elfsdaughter."

Vinet watched AeresThonEsia for a long moment. She wasn't a crone, but nor was she that other Vinet had caught a brief glimpse of, that of a maiden. She seemed almost...motherly.

She closed her eyes and forced herself to relax. Mimicking Aeres-ThonEsia, she cupped her hands and took a long sip of the water.

Instantly, she felt refreshed, even elated. Then her emotions settled and she felt as close to at peace as she ever had. The animals were gone, as well as the little woman, but she didn't care.

AeresThonEsia took Vinet's hands in her own and led her to the bench. Vinet followed, unresisting.

"Did you learn anything from your experience, mother's daughter?"

She managed a short, breathless laugh. "To be honest with you, my lady, I don't think I've had time to process it yet. Other than the fact I have no idea what I'm doing." She winced. "I want, no, need, a teacher. Or my curiosity will get me somewhere where there is no escaping from." Despite her own critique of her curiosity, she couldn't help asking, "The voice...back there in the tunnel. Was that my...my father?"

"Yes, Elfsdaughter. I'm as surprised as you are. Well, maybe a little less so." She didn't laugh, but the garden took on an atmosphere of mirth. "Curiosity is the best teacher."

Vinet smiled. "Curiosity killed the cat, but satisfaction brought it back," she quoted. It was one of her favorites, though people always misquoted it.

AeresThonEsia laughed delightedly. "I like that!"

43

Vinet withdrew her hands from AeresThonEsia's clasp and straightened her shoulders. "May I ask you some questions, lady?"

AeresThonEsia placed her hands in her lap and looked Vinet in the eyes. "Ask away, dear."

It seemed to Vinet that out of the corner of her eye she could see a white cat wandering around the garden, clearly curious. She shook her head, banishing the vision. "What is this place? And how did I get here? Can I do it again?" the questions came pouring out of her. She shivered. "And that skull...what is it? I saw it in a vision, before, and then it was a tattoo on a scout, and it...it frightens me." She lowered her gaze, aware the rush of questions could be construed as impoliteness.

"This place. It is any place it needs to be. Now it needs to be the calm. A sanctuary. As it often is when the Labyrinth wanderer survives." She paused, processing the second part of the questions. She then raised Vinet's face with a gentle hand, her touch warm and soothing. "Child, speak clearly now. What skull?"

Survives? Vinet swallowed. "I've seen it three times. In a vision, the first time. Then it appeared tattooed on one of Lady Duskryn's lost scouts. And just now, in the labyrinth." She shivered. "It is a skull, surrounded by rolling eyes, that seem to look everywhere and nowhere. In the labyrinth, it had three tongues, and it screamed..." She took another breath to calm herself.

A certain darkness seemed to briefly flicker through the garden, but then the birds and bugs and fairies started singing again.

"That's a new form for the monster of the Labyrinth. One you took with you into that place. Normally, it is the loss of a loved one. Once it was a rabbit! But this...this is disconcerting." AeresThonEsia rested her left hand on Vinet's back, just between her shoulder blades. "Ah. Yes. Disconcerting." She winced. "You brought it with you."

Vinet winced as well. "Yes," she nodded. "I was thinking about it when I opened the book. I wanted answers. I didn't...I had no idea what would happen."

"I know. I was watching." AeresThonEsia stood up and walked a few steps away, an old woman again. "Mortals playing with immortality." She turned back to Vinet. Her eyes were kind, pitying almost. "You've been marked, child. Marked, mother's daughter. Know you what I mean?"

Vinet shook her head, bewildered. "Marked by who? And for what?" she asked.

"Had she been swifter quicker smarter in the Labyrinth, Lord of mine.

If only. If only." A hand gestured in the air. An index finger was missing from it. The sanctuary began to flicker. "By Manyu himself, mother's daughter. By Manyuanmazda itself!"

Vinet's eyes widened in shock. "By Manyu…" her voice trailed off to a whisper. She got to her feet and walked over to AeresThonEsia. "What can I do?" she asked.

"Better she had stepped through one of the other mirrors than now." AeresThonEsia sighed. "Come, Vinet. Support an old woman?"

Automatically, Vinet offered her arm. AeresThonEsia took it. "I will protect your soul, mother's daughter." She leaned heavily against Vinet. "Walk slowly."

Slowly, they started walking forward. Vinet couldn't tear her eyes away from the old woman.

"We cannot harbor your dreams, though, girl. There he will walk and know. You must practice your focus. Lessss…bro-broad curiosity. Concise," AeresThonEsia coughed, "thinking. The sanctuary will not permit talk of this kind. We have yammered and yimmered long enough, yes yes yesssss." She coughed again. "Nor can I stop Manyu's mortal plaything."

Vinet kept her gaze on AeresThonEsia, trying to take in every aspect of her words. As she did, the sanctuary disappeared around her. For a moment, they seemed to walk in starlight and shadows. Then they were back in the marketplace, behind the book stand. In front of her stood Gwyn and Dannan.

Vinet gasped in relief. All serenity from the garden was gone, and she was shaking. She nearly ran forward, pulling Gwyn into a long embrace. "I'm so sorry," she murmured.

She could feel Gwyn shaking as she returned the hug. "Don't you ever do that to me again," she breathed.

A cough drew her attention and she pulled away, suddenly remembering Dannan's presence. Why on earth was he, of all people, here?

He inclined his head in greeting. "Lady Vinet. How goes your investigation?"

She nodded politely back, even though she was still shaking. She could see AeresThonEsia fade back into the shadows of the book stand.

"All vague, and nothing comforting," she said, taking a deep breath.

His eyes flashed. "Magic rarely is."

Vinet winced.

Dannan looked directly at Gwyn. "Take your lady home. Be sure she has tea or drinking chocolate. It will help." He turned away, heading back towards the palace.

Vinet forced herself to steady. "Wait," she managed. She waited until Dannan faced her again. "I know you and I have not seen eye to eye, Lord Dannan, but you must know. That tattoo is dark magic. Manyu's magic."

Dannan stared at her a long moment, then nodded slowly. Their eyes met in perfect accord.

Vinet nodded shakily. "If you could tell our fellow councilors I'll be resting a while, that would be greatly appreciated, Lord Dannan."

Something could not wait, however. She walked back to the stall where AeresThonEsia watched, eyes observing everything. "Thank you," she said, relief evident in every bone of her body. "If I can ever do anything for you, please, let me know."

AeresThonEsia's voice was low and amused. "I will, my lady." Her voice rose as Gwyn began to lead Vinet away. "Mother's daughter! Remember these words. Stone and hair. Blood on the rose. Gentle paths there, dear."

A vision passed before Vinet's eye, that of the gemstone from earlier. She knew at that moment AeresThonEsia had just given her the key back to the garden.

Vinet barely made it back to the townhouse. Gwyn hovered next to her, trying to help, but Vinet refused. Appearances. Why were appearances so damn important?

Once they entered the doors, however, Vinet collapsed against Gwyn. Gwyn shouted orders and nearly carried Vinet up to her room. There, she began to help Vinet undress.

"Gwyn," Vinet protested. "Get a maid to do that."

"They're drawing a bath." Gwyn retorted. "You are going to be in it as soon as possible."

Vinet subsided. When Gwyn used that tone, there was no arguing with her.

She froze as her gaze passed over her bed. The familiar, black leather-bound book that had gotten her into all this trouble was resting there on top of the blankets.

"Gwyn," she managed, indicating the book. "Did you carry that back here?"

Gwyn looked up, and her hands tightened on Vinet's arms. "No," she managed.

Vinet tore her gaze away. It had to have been AeresThonEsia. Whoever she was. Whatever she was.

The maids bustled in, filling a large tub with hot water, as Gwyn continued to strip Vinet down.

Vinet felt Gwyn freeze as she unlaced her shift. "What?" she asked, turning to peer over her shoulder.

Gwyn stood still, not saying a word. Vinet reached for her in confusion. "What, Gwyn?"

Gwyn shook her head. She waited until the maids had left the room, then stalked over to the bed stand and grabbed a small handheld mirror. Without saying a word, she held it so Vinet could see her back.

Vinet hesitated, then blanched. There, between her shoulder blades, was a familiar scar. A skull, surrounded by eyes. Around that scar, however, was a tattoo, of green thorns and red rose petals intertwining.

"Marked," Vinet whispered. "AeresThonEsia, she..."

"She marked you?" Gwyn's voice was furious.

"No. She...protected me." Vinet stared at the mirror again, then pushed it away. She couldn't bear to see the skull and eyes. The mark of Manyu. Of Manyuanmazda, according to AeresThonEsia.

"Is this going to cause lasting harm, Vinet?" Gwyn demanded.

Vinet turned toward Gwyn, her best friend and confidant. Her eyes were haunted. "I don't know."

4

VENIA

F ire. Blood. Unearthly screams. Vinet tried to run, tried to fight, but she couldn't. The earth was shattering around her. A piercing shriek rent the air, and a dark-winged creature rose up in front of her. She stumbled backward, trying to shield her face from the dust.

"Mama!"

Her eyes widened in horror. Niara was screaming, thrashing, trying to fight as she was carried off into the sky. The black figure carrying her had no face.

She tried to scream her daughter's name, but nothing came out. She couldn't move. Huge roots ensnared her feet, dragging her further and further down into the earth. She struggled, trying desperately to keep her head above the ground. Her hands grasped roots only to have them slip away. She flailed. She couldn't breathe!

Vinet's eyes flew open, and she stared at the sudden, silent darkness. She took several deep, gasping breaths as she came to awareness, shivering in the sweat-drenched blankets. The area between her shoulder blades burned. She was at her townhouse, at the capital. Only a dream.

Somehow, she couldn't convince herself of that. The pain on her back was a reminder of the events of two days ago. The day she'd been marked by Manyu. AeresThonEsia had said something about not being able to protect her dreams.

She took another shuddering breath and pushed off the blanket, swinging her legs off the bed and fumbling for her oil lamp. She couldn't find the flint. Gasping, she reached down, inside, to a trick she'd learned ages ago. She snapped her fingers, and a tiny spark leaped out and caught the wick. She sighed in relief as it started burning.

False dawn didn't even hint outside. Still, she couldn't sleep anymore. Without stopping to think where she was going, she grabbed a shawl and slipped her feet into slippers before picking the lamp up and padding softly down the corridor. Wandering, she ended up in the library. For a long moment, she stared blindly at the rows of bookshelves. Her small lamp barely illuminated enough for her to see the shadows of the books, dancing in the wavering light.

She shook herself. The maids should have left kindling and logs in the fireplace before they went to bed. It would be easy to light it. She made her way to the fireplace mostly by memory. Carefully, she knelt. She had been right, the firewood was ready, needing only a small spark to bring it to a blaze. She didn't feel strong enough to replicate her trick from earlier, so she resorted to her lamp. The kindling caught easily, and she blew gently on it to encourage it to burn. It crackled and sparked as the logs caught, finally dancing high in the fireplace. The fire was a balm to her soul. The warmth sank into her bones, banishing the memory of the nightmare.

Vinet sat there, staring at the flames. What had the dream meant? Was it a warning, threat, or just something delving into her darkest fears?

She couldn't answer these questions. And for some reason she doubted AeresThonEsia would, either. The woman...*the women?* Vinet wondered. They had been unwilling to speak any more about the being who had placed their mark on Vinet's back. The protection during the day seemed as much as she would, or could, do.

She shifted, wincing as pins and needles attacked her calf. The sensible thing would be to go back to sleep. She didn't think she could face that.

Well, she was in the library and she had plenty of research to do now that the Council had voted. She hadn't told any of the councilors about her experience, only that the scout's mark was one of Manyu. What Dannan guessed, she didn't know.

Nevertheless, the knowledge of the mark's origin hadn't been enough to sway anyone except Conn and Ellil toward healing the scout. The rest, including Vinet, had voted to help Venia. She closed her eyes as she remembered. She had presented her arguments in a logical manner. It would benefit Saemar the most to consolidate Venia as part of the kingdom, and to stop Jyria from swallowing up all the city-states under its rule. Jyria couldn't threaten Saemar at the moment, but only if the councilors took steps to keep it that way. By taking Venia, they would also block Jyria's expansion to Hillsdale, adjacent to Vinet's lands. That had been her argument, anyway. That, and the fact they would now have a seaport. But in truth, all she had wanted to do was stay as far away from whatever had marked the scout as possible.

No one would believe that of her. She was the curious one, the one whose curiosity led her blindly and happily into danger. No one would believe she had avoided investigating something out of fear. She'd built that reputation to explain any research which might lead to others suspecting her secrets.

She opened her eyes and stared into the fire again. Well, if no one believed she would back down from fear, that was all to the good. Her reputation had allowed them to help Venia. And she should research their new city now. All they knew of Venia was what came through the merchants. To integrate Venia as part of Saemar they needed to know more about it.

Vinet kept hold of the oil lamp as she stood up. She started pacing the shelves, trying to recall if she had anything on Venia. Had there ever been a merchant agreement, a treatise, or a traveler's journal? She couldn't recall. She would have had more luck if she was using her main library at home. Nonetheless, she continued searching.

Finally, she found a small pamphlet, describing a ball hosted by one of the Venian nobility. She sat down in her chair in front of the fire and sighed. It told her there were nobility in Venia but little else. Perhaps there was more in her main library back home. That didn't help her now, when she wanted, needed a distraction from sleep.

She looked up at a sound from the door. In the firelight, she could see the glint of steel as Gwyn entered the room, her sword held in her hand.

"It's me, Gwyn," she assured.

Gwyn lowered her sword. She was still dressed for bed, her long blonde hair flowing unbound her back, and only a simple shift providing any modesty. But she held her sword with the ease of someone who would use it.

She would, too. Vinet had seen it.

"I heard something. What's up? You're not usually in the library at this hour."

Vinet shrugged, her stomach dropping uneasily. "I couldn't sleep," she said. "Nightmare."

Gwyn gave her a sharp glance and Vinet swallowed. They didn't have secrets from each other. That had been their earliest pact, when they'd sworn blood-sisterhood.

"Nightmare?" Gwyn asked slowly. She sank into the chair next to Vinet's. "Want to talk about it?"

"Not really," Vinet said softly, not making eye contact. She shuddered. "I think... I think it was because of... of what happened the other day." She couldn't bring herself to say the words.

"When you were marked," Gwyn had no such compunctions. She sighed. "Mazda's light, Vinet..."

Vinet shook her head. "We'll deal with it," she said. "Just...not right now."

Gwyn kept silent a moment longer, then nodded. "Alright. But don't take too many more risks like that, please."

Vinet managed a low chuckle. "Believe me, I don't intend to."

"Good," Gwyn sat forward, ready to stand up. "Anything else?"

The pamphlet in Vinet's hands drew her eyes. "What would you say to a detour on the way home?"

The skeptical look Gwyn gave her was enough to make her chuckle again.

"Nowhere too dangerous. Just to Venia. I want to see what they're like, and how easy it will be to integrate them."

"Vinet. There's a naval blockade there right now."

"It's just a trade embargo," she said, frowning. "And our men have already been sent out. The city should be secured by the time we get there."

Gwyn looked on the verge of objecting again, then shrugged. "Alright. But we send the majority of the guard to escort Niara home and do this detour separately. Do not take her to Venia with you."

"Alright," she agreed.

Gwyn stood up. "I'm going to get some sleep," she said. "You probably should too."

Vinet suppressed a shudder. "In a little bit," she temporized. "I want to read this first."

Gwyn narrowed her eyes but didn't say anything. She departed, leaving Vinet alone in silence.

The Lady of Ninaeva stared at the crackling fire. She didn't think she could fall asleep again. Not tonight.

Would she ever?

"Halt!"

Vinet sighed as she reined her horse in for third time this journey, despite the house colors and crest emblazoned prominently on the guards and horses. She was beginning to suspect Gwyn might have been right about this journey.

As if she could read her thoughts, Gwyn met her eyes and gave hers a brief roll. Vinet suppressed a chuckle.

The guard, a man in the red uniform of the Regulars, approached them. As he drew closer, his expression lightened.

"My lady!" he exclaimed. He straightened to attention. "Lady Rochelle," he said, more formally. "What brings you to Venia?"

Vinet blinked. The man did seem vaguely familiar. Was he one of her own subjects who had joined the Regulars?

"Business, soldier," she said formally. She looked at him more closely. She had seen that sandy hair before. "You're Ninaevan, right? You were one of my guards?"

The soldier nodded. "Maarten, my lady. I was a guard at your coronation as Lady of Ninaeva. My Tryza, my wife, works in your kitchens still."

Vinet let a genuine smile cross her face. "Tryza! She makes a delightful custard."

"That she does, my lady." Maarten grinned. He glanced back at Vinet's retinue, and his expression darkened. "I wish you had brought more guards, my lady."

Vinet exchanged a look with Gwyn. "Is it dangerous? I understood from the last patrol the city had been secured."

Maarten shrugged. "Secured... Well, it's not my place to say. By your leave, my lady, I'll take you to the Lord General. He can answer your questions."

That seemed as good a solution as any. Vinet nodded. "Lead on."

The gates of Venia loomed, made of hard, black stone absorbing every ray of light. She didn't get a chance to examine them further, though.

Maarten quickly ushered her party through the gates and down the streets. She caught glimpses of people scurrying here and there, but the presence of so many soldiers made everyone fearful. Hardly surprising. She would have to convince Gwyn to just let the two of them wander around.

Maarten appeared on edge as he led them through the streets. They cut straight through the city to the harbor. To Vinet's surprise, a keep stood on a small jetty, surrounded by a patrol of Regulars.

"Lord General Torainn is inside," Maarten said, stopping at the beginning of the jetty. He saluted. "Good fortune, my lady."

"Safe travels, Maarten. I'm sure Tryza wants to see you home soon."

A smile brightened Maarten's face for an instant. "I'd like to see her too." He was still smiling as he rode away.

Vinet exchanged another glance with Gwyn. Well, a general. This was a first for her. She'd negotiated with numerous types of people, but her own guards comprised the extent of her military interactions.

The inside of the keep was exactly as she'd ever imagined a military fortification to be. Everything, from the men patrolling the halls to the messengers running back and forth with scraps of paper, screamed military bureaucracy.

A page met them as she entered the keep. At her request to see Lord General Torainn, he only took one glance at her clothing before gesturing that she should follow him.

She felt Gwyn's approval as they ascended a flight of spiral stairs. She suppressed a smile. Like Ilhelm, this place was built for defense. Unlike Ilhelm, it seemed they might need it.

The page showed them into a tiny, sparse office. A single desk and chair comprised all the furniture in the room, and the desk was covered in papers. A man rose from the desk as they entered. His uniform marked him as a Regular, and the decorations on his chest a general. Other than that, he did not look particularly militaristic as he looked at her with guileless eyes. "Lady Vinet! So good of one of the Council to take an interest in the proceedings here."

Vinet smiled. "It is in everyone's best interests this is over as quickly as possible, and that the integration of Venia into the kingdom is smooth."

"I believe you mean New Venia, Lady Vinet." Torainn stood straight. "That's what my boys have been calling it, anyway, and the locals seem to be following suit."

"New Venia?" Vinet looked at him, nonplussed. "Why? It's still Venia."

"Oh, it's part of a kingdom now, new beginnings, you know, that sort of thing. It's good for morale." Torainn stepped around his desk and came to stand in front of her, attempting to look down at her even though he only came up to her eyes.

Vinet frowned. She couldn't decide how she felt about that, so she tabled the thought for further contemplation and changed the subject. "So, how are things here? Is everything secure?"

"As secure as they can be, right now," Torainn said. "Blockade's still out there, but they'll leave soon enough now that the city's ours. Jyria doesn't have an army, not a large enough one to challenge us at least."

Vinet nodded in satisfaction.

"Say," Torainn blinked again, seeming to be struck by a thought. "The Venian nobility are hosting a little get-together this afternoon. I'm sure they'd love to have a Saemarian councilor as their guest. Someone to show their gratitude to."

Vinet could almost hear Gwyn's suppressed chuckle. Her eyes widened briefly in alarm. "Actually, I'd rather not," she said hastily. "I just came to assess the situation, talk to the merchants, that sort of thing. With your permission, I'd like to tour around the city a bit."

"As you wish. I'll designate a patrol to keep you company." Torainn shrugged.

Vinet raised a hand. "I was thinking just my guard and me," she said. "I think people would be more willing to talk."

"Absolutely not."

"Excuse me?" she asked, taken aback by his tone.

Torainn flushed but didn't back away from her. "Pardon me, Lady Vinet, but that is out of the question. There are still Jyrian agents in the city and having a Saemarian noble wander around alone would be like placing raw meat in front of a wolf. They aren't as... straightforward as you or I. So, like it or not, you will have a patrol with you."

Vinet stared at him, trying to read how serious he was. His dark eyes met hers unflinchingly. She got the feeling that even if she refused, a patrol would still follow her.

"My lady..." the warning in Gwyn's voice was clear.

She glanced sideways at Gwyn, who shook her head slightly. Vinet sighed. While she would have ignored the general's advice, she could not avoid Gwyn's. "Alright," she said. "But make it as small as possible. I want to talk to people, not frighten them."

"As you say, Lady Vinet. Is there anything else I can do for you?"

Torainn walked back behind his desk, his posture obviously wishing her gone, but too polite to say so.

Her lips tightened. "That will be all, General. I will tell the Council of your accomplishments here."

"I'm sure Lord Conn will visit me as soon as I return. He has quite an interest in military matters, that one." He smiled, but it didn't reach his eyes.

Vinet couldn't read his tone, so she simply took his words at face value. "That he does. Have you met?" She knew Torainn wanted her to leave, but her curiosity kept her asking questions.

"He was interested in how the Regulars were run. As Lord General, I believe I know that as well as anyone else." Torainn remained standing, too polite to sit while Vinet still stood.

"I'm sure you do." Vinet knew it was time to extract herself. "I'll leave you to your duties, Lord General Torainn."

He saluted as she turned to leave. He was already settling back at his desk as she walked out the door.

"I am not going to get any information this way," she hissed at Gwyn as they exited the keep.

Gwyn didn't back down. "If he says there are Jyrian agents here, then I believe him," she whispered back fiercely. "It's my job to keep you safe. I have no experience with anything Jyrian agents will do."

Vinet gazed skyward and tried not to roll her eyes. If she heard the term 'Jyrian agents' one more time, she would scream.

Her desire was not tempered when they exited the keep. Already, somehow summoned by the general, a good dozen Regulars waited to swell her own guardsmen. No one would talk to her with this retinue.

Nevertheless, she was determined to try. She led the retinue along the docks, ignoring everyone except Gwyn. No one else tried to do the same thing, however. People scurried out of her way long before she came within reasonable hailing distance. None of the shops looked open, either. Everything was shut down.

After wandering down the entire harbor and up two streets, she gave up. She shifted her focus, looking instead for an inn. An innkeeper would have to be open. And if they couldn't be persuaded to talk immediately, then perhaps staying the night would loosen their lips. Coin tended to do that.

She spotted an inn just a block ahead. She walked toward it, her steps purposeful, suppressing a smile as she heard Gwyn's intake of breath.

Gwyn knew what she was thinking. The Regulars following her didn't, however. To her relief, most of them waited outside, only their captain following her into the inn.

The place was nearly empty. Only a few fishermen sat in the corner, and they averted their faces from her as she entered. The innkeeper looked as though he would like to do the same, but sighed and asked, "Can I help you, my lady?"

"Lodging for me, my bodyguard, and six guardsmen," she said, naming her personal retinue. The Regulars were not staying with her overnight.

The innkeeper's eyes widened, but he nodded. "Very good, my lady."

"Lady Rochelle," the Regulars captain tried to interject.

Vinet gave him her best noble glare. "Yes?" she demanded.

He shrank back but persisted. "I am sure Lord General Torainn would be more than willing to host you in the keep."

"I am sure he would," she said sharply. "And yet my guards and I will stay here."

She didn't leave any room for further questions. As she turned away, she noticed Gwyn sidling up to the captain and whispering something in his ear. Whatever it was, she hoped it would satisfy him.

She glanced over at the fishermen and frowned before asking the innkeeper, "Is there a library in this town?"

He nodded warily. "There is. Two streets down, a right, then three blocks and a left. Large wood building. You can't miss it."

Wood? Vinet refrained from shaking her head incredulously. *Who would keep books in a wooden building?*

"That's where I'll be the rest of the day," she told the captain. "If you want your men to stand around watching me, you're free to."

He stood stiff. "I have my orders, my lady."

"I'm sure you do," she grumbled. Well, she'd be rid of them tonight.

She and Gwyn retired late for the night. Gwyn shared the room with Vinet, absolutely insisting on it and damn any rumors they were lovers. Similar rumors had surfaced before and likely would again.

Vinet closed her eyes, trying to call up sleep, hoping another nightmare wouldn't claim her. She didn't want to deal with one, not so far from home. The nervous tension in the air was starting to get to her, and she needed her wits about her.

Sleep did not come to her easily. She tossed and turned, trying to get comfortable. The bed was harder than she usually slept in, despite it being an upper-class inn. The air felt stuffy and oppressive as well, as if the city was waiting for the Jyrian blockade to break.

She eventually drifted off, but her dreams were not restful either. A giant skull with dozens of eyes dancing around it floated toward her, laughing an evil laugh as it got closer and closer. She couldn't run, as much as she tried. She opened her mouth to scream.

Her eyes flew open at the sound of a shout. She nearly screamed again at the glint of steel in the air above her. The blankets were tangled about her, no doubt from tossing and turning. She couldn't move!

The sword froze above her, and she heard a choking sound. The dark figure next to her bed doubled over, and she saw the tip of a sword sticking out of its chest. Blood dripped to the floor.

She finally freed herself from the blankets and scrambled to sit up as the body slumped to the floor. Gwyn tore her sword from the body and hissed a little in disgust. Vinet stared at Gwyn, wide-eyed.

"Assassin," Gwyn said succinctly.

Vinet gasped at the body slumped on the floor. She couldn't determine what gender it was, layered as they were by many robes and scarves. The face was entirely concealed.

"Jyrian agents?" she whispered. She hadn't taken the General's concerns about them seriously.

Gwyn shrugged. "Only one way to find out." Without waiting for Vinet's questions, she turned the body over, wincing as she got blood on her hands. She began unwrapping the scarves.

Vinet jumped at the pounding of feet on the stairs and a heavy knock on the door.

"My lady! Are you all right?"

"I'd better deal with that." She shook her head, trying to clear it.

"Wait." Gwyn's voice was sharp, a tone Vinet rarely heard her use to address her. She stiffened, immediately on alert.

"What is it?" she asked, dropping her voice to a whisper.

In answer, Gwyn beckoned. Reluctantly, Vinet moved to where she had a view of the face that Gwyn had just revealed from the scarves.

Bright green eyes stared sightlessly up at her, still clear in the shock of death. It was as if she looked at a mirror of her own. But the face...

Sharp angled cheekbones, slanted eyes, and bright golden hair did not distract from the one feature that made identification certain. The long, swept ears of an elf were prominently visible on the assassin.

"An elf?" she whispered. "How is that... why..." she closed her eyes, then opened them again, trying to process her emotions. This woman had just tried to kill her, and she should be glad she was dead, but still...

"I don't know," Gwyn said. "But look at that." She pointed to the elf's forehead. Right in the center was a tattoo of a single teardrop, ringed by thorns.

"What does that mean?"

Gwyn shook her head but was prevented from answering by a pounding on the door. "My lady? Forgive me, my lady, but are you alright?"

Gwyn rolled her eyes and stood up. She walked over to the door and threw it open, pointing her sword at the entrance.

"Gwyn," Vinet began.

The innkeeper took a step back at the sight of the sword in Gwyn's hand, his eyes wide and terrified. "Forgive me, my lady, but... the shout, the scream..."

"Gwyn, stop threatening the poor man," Vinet said.

Gwyn backed up a step to let the man have a clear view of the room but didn't lower her sword. When the innkeeper saw the body on the floor, his eyes widened even further.

"Go summon the town watch, or the Regulars, or whoever is in charge of this sort of thing," Gwyn snapped at the innkeeper. "And send someone with an urgent message to Lord General Torainn in the keep. Now! Someone just tried to assassinate my lady!"

The man's eyes looked like those of a fish. He babbled something unintelligible, then turned and ran. Vinet could hear his feet pounding down the stairs as he shouted for someone named Mara.

"Was that really necessary?" Vinet protested weakly.

Gwyn glared at her. "Someone just tried to kill you, Vinet. I am not letting that go unnoticed. Someone had better investigate this, or they'll have me to answer to."

Vinet sat back on the bed. She wasn't certain whether she wanted to deal with Lord General Torainn or any of the Regulars or Venian officials.

Gwyn's gaze softened. "I'll answer all the questions. You try to get some rest before the hordes descend."

She tried not to roll her eyes. Gwyn's description was far too apt.

Despite Vinet's protests, they were escorted out of Venia the very next morning. Gwyn was no help, siding firmly with Lord General Torainn's opinion that the sooner Vinet left the city, the better. Vinet supposed they were right, but she disliked the almost condescending way the Lord General had talked to her, just because she didn't have any military experience.

They stopped for the night in a town a hard day's ride out of Venia. Normally, Vinet would have stopped in the market, talked to the innkeeper, and tried to discover everything she could about the surrounding area. Tonight, however, she barricaded herself in her room, telling Gwyn not to let anyone in.

"What are you up to?" Gwyn demanded.

Vinet met Gwyn's eyes. "I'm trying to figure out who that assassin was."

"And how do you plan on doing that?" Gwyn asked, her lips firming.

Vinet didn't answer. Packed in her personal belongings, the Book of Truths rarely left her side. She didn't feel comfortable leaving a magical artifact like that out of her reach.

Gwyn knew her too well. "Vinet…" she began, her tone cautioning.

Vinet shook her head. "I nearly got assassinated, Gwyn." She paused, willing her voice not to shake. "I only survived because you were there to protect me. I…thank you for that."

"Vinet…" Gwyn stepped forward to put a hand on Vinet's shoulder. "You know I'd do anything for you."

"And I for you." Vinet managed a smile. "But I will not sit back and let others take action when I have tools which could help me figure out how to prevent this from happening again."

Gwyn hesitated, clearly still not convinced. "The last time you did something like this…"

"The last time I did something like this I was foolish," Vinet cut in. "This time I know what I'm doing." *I hope*, she mentally added.

Gwyn didn't question her. She just sighed. "Call me if anything goes wrong. Absolutely anything, understand?"

Vinet nodded solemnly. She breathed in relief as Gwyn shut the door behind her. She had been worried Gwyn would insist on staying with her.

She dug in the roll of belongings the maid had brought up to her room and pulled out the book. It looked the same as it always had, an unmarked binding of black leather. Steeling herself, she sat down on the bed and flipped it open. She didn't want to enter the labyrinth or speak to Aeres-ThonEsia again. But this was the Book of Truths. There had to be a way to make it show things she wanted to see!

She closed her eyes and took a deep breath. Mentally, she focused on the assassin. She wanted information about where the elf woman had come from. She visualized the woman's face in her mind, the tattoo appearing prominently on her forehead.

Immediately, memory intervened. She saw the sword piercing the elf woman's chest as Gwyn stabbed her, and Gwyn's fierce scowl as she protected her. The eyes, eyes that could have belonged to her, danced in front of her eyelids.

She shook her head, forcing the image of the tattoo back into her mind, focusing on its central teardrop and surrounding thorns. She reached out and placed her hand on the shifting pages of the book.

About her, she heard the rush of wind. Distantly, so distant that she wasn't certain if it was memory or vision, she heard the choking of the assassin dying. Warmth surrounded her, the comforting knowledge that Gwyn would always be at her side.

She blinked. She no longer saw the room she had rented in the inn. Instead, she stood at the edge of a lake, in the middle of a lush, green woods. Haze lay everywhere, so thick she couldn't quite see through, despite the beautiful calm.

The image of the assassin and her symbol fell from Vinet's mind. Where was she? What was she seeing?

"Vinet Elfsdaughter."

She turned, opening her mouth, whether to answer or inquire as to how the speaker knew her identity, she didn't know. Instead, she froze.

The haze around the forest lifted. The shore of the lake was now clear to view, so bright and vivid, like a painting. The trees loomed tall about the lake so that the water appeared more wood than liquid with the intensity of the reflections. But that was not what made her freeze.

Before her stood an elf, a man this time. He wore a long brown robe, belted with a simple cord of green and gold at his waist. A silver band bound his long hair on one side of his head. His eyes were the same as the assassin's, and as hers, but far older. Although his face was ageless, those eyes spoke of more years than she could ever dream of.

"Elfsdaughter, we do not have much time," the elf's voice faltered as he looked at her. Vinet could not prevent a sense that her every feature was being examined and memorized. Her throat caught at an intense feeling of familiarity.

He swallowed. "Know that the Thorn who came after you is not representative of us all."

He bowed his head, then glanced sharply to one side. He seemed startled, then he waved his hand and the vision faded.

"Wait!" Vinet exclaimed. "Who are you? What are the Thorns?"

No one answered. She stared at the wall of the inn. The Book of Truths lay open before her, its pages suspiciously blank.

5

DARKMANE

Mazda's light, Lady Vinet, are you alright?"

Vinet had to smile at Pellalindra's concern as she stepped into the council chambers. "I'm fine, Lady Pellalindra."

Pellalindra shuddered. "You are taking this far more calmly than I would in your shoes."

"Why? What happened?" Kamian interjected.

Vinet looked up to see all the other council members except Dannan already seated. Kamian and Conn were looking with curiosity at the two women, while Ellil stared into the fire.

"What? You haven't heard?" Pellalindra exclaimed before Vinet could answer. "Lady Vinet was nearly assassinated!"

"What?" Kamian jumped up from his seat, his feet tangling in his long red cloak, and he almost tripped before catching his balance. "Tell me who the blaggard is. I will most certainly challenge him for you, my lady!"

Vinet stifled a laugh. "I am afraid Gwyn already took care of the agent, Lord Kamian, and I am at a loss as to who was behind it. Has anyone seen the symbol of a tear surrounded by a ring of thorns, by chance?"

Kamian shook his head as he sat down again, disappointed, but Conn shifted uncomfortably. She raised an eyebrow at him.

"Some strangers were seen up by Dunbarrow recently," he said slowly. "They haven't done anything, just watched. I wonder if they were connected." His eyes slid away from her to the window, refusing to meet her own.

Vinet's eyes sharpened on Conn. "What kind of strangers?" she asked.

"We haven't managed to talk to any of them yet." He shrugged, still not meeting her eyes. "They are sneaky enough to avoid the guards. But I've set a trap for them, so hopefully they'll take the bait."

Sneaky might fit elves, Vinet thought. More details did not seem to be forthcoming, however, and she didn't feel like pressing the issue. She straightened her shoulders as she took her seat. "Well, are we waiting for Lord Dannan, or shall we look at what options the Council has to spend our kingdom's resources on now?"

"Well, there is one thing I thought you would find very interesting, Lady Vinet," Pellalindra said, smoothing the blue velvet sleeves which clung tightly to her arms. "Or hadn't you heard the expedition has returned?"

Vinet managed a tight smile at Pellalindra's coolness but couldn't contain her excitement. "No, I've been traveling! Did they discover anything?"

"A lost city!" Kamian declared, his eyes bright and enthusiastic. "They found it! An entire civilization that just vanished! It appears to have been elven. They found thousands of book covers too, but for some reason, all the pages are missing." He sounded as disappointed about it as Vinet felt.

"I must admit, Lady Vinet, I am impressed they found anything," Lady Pellalindra put in. "It seems your intuition was well-founded."

Vinet couldn't tell if Pellalindra was being sarcastic or not. She decided to take it as a compliment. "Thank you, Lady Pellalindra," she said.

Pellalindra smiled in return.

"Lady Vinet, someone else has decided to ask us to sponsor an expedition in light of the success of the first one! This is a different group, and they'd be heading north, along the coast. Past your lands, if I'm not mistaken." Kamian's eyes gleamed.

Conn snorted. "In light of the first one's success? They found nothing that can be of use to us!"

Vinet stared at him for a long moment, trying to decide how to explain that knowledge was worth far more than military might, but she couldn't think of a way to explain that to a man whose entire life was built on war and power.

Kamian had no such hesitations, however. "Don't you see the value of the knowledge they could find, fool?" he asked.

Vinet winced.

Conn's eyes darkened. "Who are you calling fool, you arrogant puppy?"

Kamian snorted. "You're calling me arrogant?"

"Gentlemen, please! Leave insults for outside the council chamber, if you please," Pellalindra interjected. She glared at them until they both subsided. "While an expedition may be the most promising idea for you and Lady Vinet, Lord Kamian, there are other options to consider. At the very least, they need to be discussed." She took a sip of her wine before speaking again. "Someone healed my scout."

Vinet blinked. She had seen the price attached to that healing. It had been the primary reason the Council hadn't voted to deplete the treasury. "Who?" she demanded. Who would have the money to spend on something like that?

Pellalindra shook her head. "He left no name. Just said he was an admirer of...of me," she flushed slightly, then sat up straighter. "Regardless of who it was, she did not live long after she recovered. She did, however, tell a strange tale full of dramatic imagery. A red horizon, an ambush by shadows, an orange glow on metal, and someone debating how best to eat her. She seemed certain there is something dark going on in the southeast."

Vinet could tell she was deeply disturbed.

Conn leaned forward. "Did she say anything else? Anything to give us some clue as to who or what might have been behind her attack? Any idea of their strength and numbers?"

"No," Pellalindra said. "She remembered nothing of her attackers. It seems she was..." she swallowed, "tortured."

Conn's face darkened. "That is an insult to all good men of Saemar. We should avenge her! Send a unit to the southeast to deal with this!"

With longing, Vinet thought of the proposed northern expedition, but she pushed it to the side. "Wouldn't it be better to send a scouting party first? We can't send a unit down there blindly. They may be walking into a trap."

Pellalindra looked intrigued, but Conn shook his head. "They already walked into a trap! A unit will have the resources to deal with it!"

Vinet forced herself to remain calm. "A unit will also be seen as a sign of aggression by Tigri," she argued. "And Lady Pellalindra's scout was killed because they did not know of the threat on our side of the border. The next patrol will. Knowledge can save many lives, Lord Conn." She couldn't resist that little jab.

Kamian's chuckle ruined it. Conn glared at both her and Kamian. "I suppose now you'll be making some argument that this northern expedition will give us the knowledge to fight this threat in the south?" he asked.

Vinet shook her head. "No, I..."

"You fools!" The heated discussion came to an abrupt halt as Dannan burst into the chamber. He held a paper in his hand. "How can you discuss anything when this just arrived!"

He threw the paper down on the table, and Vinet blanched. It was a message of some kind, but it contained a gruesome souvenir: a child's finger, preserved in clear wax.

Stunned silence fell in the council chamber. For a moment, all Vinet could think of was Niara, and feel profound relief she was safe. This finger was not hers.

She glanced around the table and could instantly tell that Pellalindra and Conn felt the same way. Even Kamian seemed shocked by it, and Elbl had been jerked from his meditation to stare.

"I told you," Dannan said, breathing heavily. "I told you to look to the east. And you ignored me. Well, let this be on your hands!"

Vinet released a breath. She was not going to get any information from Dannan, she knew this. Steeling herself, she reached forward and carefully took the message, leaving the finger on the table.

To the Royal Council,

   I write to you to report an increase of the Cossack raids to the Northeast. Everything is under control, but I felt you should be informed. The last raid left this behind as a message. My men tell me it is the signature of a Cossack leader known as Darkmane. We will intensify our efforts to capture or kill him.

   Once again, I assure you everything is under control.

   Yours,

   Lord Artosbern, Warden of the Bern Forest

"What does it say?" Pellalindra asked. In the silence, her quiet voice seemed like a shout.

Vinet shook her head and passed the message to Pellalindra. She stared at Dannan. Surely, he had read the message? Did he have no trust in their northern warden? She waited as the message was passed word-lessly around the table.

"We must send a unit to support Lord Artosbern and deal with this Cossack raider," Conn said sharply. "Let him know we are not to be trifled with!"

Pellalindra nodded. "I agree. To think of that poor child," she closed her eyes and didn't continue.

Dannan growled. "The Tigrians have gone too far this time. We will make them pay."

Vinet frowned. "The Cossacks are not the Tigrian army," she pointed out. "They are merely raiders. Lord Artosbern seems to be confident and capable."

She regretted her statement instantly as both Dannan and Conn rounded on her.

"We must defend our borders!" Conn shouted. "This Darkmane is killing children!"

"There is no price too high for this Darkmane to pay for this atrocity," Dannan's eyes flashed.

Vinet chose not to respond. There would be no reasoning with them in this mood.

"He must be brought to justice." Everyone turned to look at Ellil. These were the first words he'd spoken all session. He looked back, eyes calm and sure. "Mazda demands it."

At that, Vinet knew anything else she said would be dismissed. How could anyone say no to a blessing from the high priest to exact the vengeance everyone already wanted?

"But what about the southeast?" Kamian asked. "Weren't you all worried about that just a few minutes ago? Are we ignoring our scout's report now?"

Dannan snorted. "Rumors. Unsubstantiated rumors. This, however..." his eyes flashed again, and Vinet swore the torches all flickered. "This needs to be dealt with."

Vinet met Kamian's eyes and shook her head slightly. They would not win this argument.

As the rest of the councilors started discussing what resources were the best to send, she leaned over to whisper in his ear. "We are outnum-bered, but we should do our duty regardless. We should investigate this Darkmane character to see if he actually is a threat and see if there's anything in the southeast that actually needs our attention. And I intend to visit the sponsor of this northern expedition."

Kamian met her eyes and smiled, the two of them in perfect accord. "I shall join you to talk to him. I've met Jimesseran before. He's an interesting character."

Vinet waited for Kamian outside the palace, Gwyn a silent shadow behind her. The votes had been cast, as everyone had expected, to send a unit north to deal with Darkmane. Vinet couldn't shake a feeling they had missed something terrible by doing that. *We should have investigated Pellalindra's scout's death. If I can acknowledge that instead of trying to convince everyone to vote for an expedition, then they should be able to see beyond their impulses.*

Kamian appeared, his bright silk clothing instantly recognizable. He shook his head as he approached her. "Fools," he said.

"They have their reasons," Vinet temporized. "Most of them have children."

Kamian snorted. "That doesn't excuse them not acting with their heads," he said. "If only…" he looked at her. "You understand. If we sent the expedition north, who knows what allies or resources we might find! Ones that could help us in dealing with these threats!"

Vinet's lips quirked. "It's too great a risk for them," she said. "They see the potential for more enemies, or for the current ones to take advantage of our distraction."

"If anyone will take advantage of our distraction, it's whoever is in the southeast," Kamian said. "Cossack raiders are something that has happened before. This Darkmane character is just a new iteration of it."

Vinet shook her head but couldn't help but agree. They walked in silence for a bit. She restarted the conversation, hopefully on a lighter note. "So, tell me about this expedition leader. You apparently have some knowledge of him?"

Kamian nodded, looking relieved by the change of subject. "Yes, indeed. His name is Jimesseran, as I said, and he's a cartographer from Venia. That's about all I'm aware of, I'm afraid, but he's apparently conducted several mapping expeditions up and down the coast before."

"From Venia?" Vinet couldn't contain her delight. "So, us annexing Venia brought him to us?"

Kamian chuckled. "I am not certain our fellow councilors would approve if they knew this is the part about annexing Venia you enjoy the most."

She laughed. "They would not be surprised."

"Indeed. And I can't say I do not approve," there was a strange gleam in Kamian's eyes, but before she could react to it, he gestured. "This is where Jimesseran lives. After you, Lady Vinet."

Vinet smiled as she stepped forward. It was a modest little house, well-kept, but worn with time. She knocked on the door.

"Come in, please!" a voice called from inside.

Vinet looked at Kamian and shrugged.

"I'll go first, my lady," Gwyn interjected.

Kamian seemed surprised at Gwyn's initiative, but Vinet just chuckled as she stepped to the side.

Gwyn opened the door, then turned back to nod at the two nobles.

Kamian frowned at Vinet. "You let her speak to you like that?" he said in a low voice.

Vinet frowned back at him. "She's my bodyguard and in charge of my safety. Not all of us are as skilled with blades as you, Lord Kamian."

Kamian grinned, but that was all they had time for as they were led down a corridor and into a small office.

An older gentleman sat at the desk, poring over an array of maps. He looked up as they entered and rose to his feet. "My lord! My lady! Forgive me, I was not expecting such company!"

Vinet smiled and raised a hand. "We are simply visitors, Jimesseran," she said. "And I have something for you. Hopefully, you can find it of use." She reached into her belt pouch and dug out a copy of the map fragment she'd discovered.

Jimesseran's face brightened as she handed it over. Eagerly, he bent over his maps, rustling through them and finally discovering where it fit. "There!" he exclaimed, pointing. Vinet saw the piece she'd given him extended the map he'd had of the land north of Hillsdale. He grinned up at her. "This will come in most handy, my lady…?" he tilted his head as his voice trailed off.

"Lady Vinet Rochelle of Ninaeva," she answered. "And this is Lord Kamian Silas of Hinswold."

"Councilors!" Jimesseran obviously recognized their names, if not their appearances. He smiled hopefully. "Dare I hope you've come with an answer for my proposal?"

Kamian shifted angrily, and Vinet made a small, abrupt gesture with her hand, hoping to avert a rant. "A disappointing one, unfortunately," she said. "The Council has…other matters to occupy them. But Lord Kamian and myself are quite intrigued by your expedition, and I believe both of us might fund you privately."

"The others don't understand," Kamian growled. "Exploration for exploration's sake should be enough. Otherwise, we all stagnate and die.'

Jimesseran shrugged philosophically. "It was a long shot, in any case. But if it brought you two to my door, I cannot say that it was in vain. Already you have helped a great deal, Lady Vinet."

Vinet smiled. "I just wish we could have convinced the Council to sponsor you. The kingdom's coffers are much larger than mine or Kamian's, or both of ours combined!"

Jimesseran shrugged again. "As you say, they have things to deal with. And I am already indebted to the Council for accepting Venia into your fold. My people would have starved to death otherwise." He paused. "Might I ask a question of you two, humble commoner that I am?"

Vinet laughed. "Of course!" she said.

"Absolutely." Kamian leaned back against a bookshelf.

"Have you ever heard of Utgard? Or perhaps Utheim?"

Vinet frowned and glanced at Kamian. He shook his head. "No. I haven't. Are they places?"

Jimesseran nodded. "Old sailors' tales, while most certainly exaggerated, though likely based in truth, speak of two cities of giants divided long ago by the angry sea. One city, Utheim sat in glory amidst the plains while the other, Utgard loomed as a fortress with mountains for walls. I've wanted to find these places since I was a young boy on my first voyage. This is my primary motivation for making a map of the northern coastline."

Vinet exchanged a delighted glance with Kamian. "But that sounds fascinating!" she exclaimed. "Oh, I hope you can find the cities, or at least what happened to them. Are these sailor stories written down anywhere? I'd love to read them. Or if you'd like to visit me in Ninaeva, you can have free rein in my library in exchange for telling me stories of your travels and adventures."

Kamian laughed at Vinet's exuberance, but Jimesseran smiled sadly. "I'm afraid I must harbor my energy, Lady Vinet. This will be my last voyage." He looked down at his desk and began ruffling through the maps and papers splayed out on it. "No, they are not written down, I apologize.

Hopefully my survey of the northern coast and, as your map suggests, the other coast where Utheim might be, will provide the foundation for further exploration. I cannot promise hard gold from this expedition, obviously."

Vinet nodded. "I understand completely. My hope is that you will meet other peoples and cultures that we could trade with and learn from. I know you cannot promise that either, but that would be fascinating."

Kamian tilted his head. "Are you retiring after this expedition, then, Jimesseran?"

"I'm dying."

Vinet stared at the cartographer at this blunt statement. He didn't look a day over forty! She boiled over with questions, but she didn't want to press him.

After a moment, Jimesseran sighed. "I would love to meet the occupants of these cities. The legends speak of nephelm, the children of both giant and man through ancient ritual. What a sight they would be."

"I... I hope you get to see them before..." Kamian's voice trailed off.

Vinet's imagination was captured. The children of giant and man? What kind of creature would that be? "I wish I could go with you," she stated.

Jimesseran smiled. "I am certain you would be marvelous company. It will be a long voyage with only the company of Yderdochter and she, well...she doesn't like talking as much as I." He stood up and bowed. "Is there anything else, Lady Rochelle, Lord Silas?"

So Yderdochter is going with him! That's good. She proved herself on the last expedition, Vinet thought. The female dwarf had given the Council a fine report of the ruined city.

He was giving her a hint. No doubt he had to conserve his energy and was politely, if vaguely, asking them to leave. She bowed in return, a mark of respect. Kamian gave her a startled glance but followed her example. Vinet said, "No, thank you. I wish you all the luck in your voyage, Jimesseran. You will be certain to receive a donation from me before you sail."

"From me as well," Kamian said.

They were silent as they left the house. Vinet could not help feeling sad at the thought of Jimesseran. He seemed too full of life to die.

Kamian appeared to be sensing the same solemnness. He bowed. "I will take my leave of you now, Lady Vinet. I hope to see you at the next

Council session. Don't forget to put in your vote for Lord of the Council before you leave the capital."

Vinet stopped in her tracks. She had forgotten completely about that. Had it really been a year since she'd taken her seat on the Council?

"Who did you vote for?" she asked, to cover her confusion.

"Who do you think?" Kamian smiled at her. "You."

"Lady Vinet! I was told I would find you here."

Vinet turned, slightly irritated at being interrupted. She had just been about to enter the palace library and archives, in the hope that someone might have written information down about Cossack raiders. Kamian had refused to accompany her, insisting she was far more suited to such scholarly pursuits than he.

Pellalindra, on the other hand, did not strike her as a researcher, but also not as someone who would avoid responsibility.

She managed a smile. "Good afternoon, Lady Pellalindra. Can I help you with something?"

Pellalindra raised an eyebrow. "I do hope I'm not interrupting," she said.

Vinet shrugged. "I was just on my way to the archives to research the Cossacks."

"Oh!" Pellalindra's expression brightened. "Then you are taking this seriously?"

Vinet frowned. "While I may think that haring off when our Warden states so clearly the matter is under control shows little faith in our own men, I am not about to ignore something we've committed to just because I think it was a bad idea." She suppressed a wince. She shouldn't have snapped like that.

Pellalindra didn't even blink. "I am glad of that, Lady Vinet. Perhaps I could help you?"

"I don't see why not." Vinet glanced at Pellalindra, puzzled. "Although I have never heard you had much inclination for sifting through books and reports."

"I do when the fate of the kingdom is at stake," Pellalindra said.

Vinet shrugged, declining to mention her own suspicion that Dark-mane wasn't really a threat to the kingdom. Instead, she gestured for Pellalindra to precede her into the library.

"What do you want?" a grouchy voice from behind a bookshelf greeted them as soon as they walked through the door.

Vinet smiled. "Good afternoon, Jaysk," she said. "It's Lady Vinet. I was hoping you could point me in the right direction for a little research."

"Lady Vinet! Why didn't you say so at once?"

Vinet refrained from pointing out that she had. She shook her head in amusement as the old man poked his head around the bookshelf. He looked as disheveled as he had when he'd shown her his private collection.

"Well, what is it? Something magical in nature again? Or another map I can help you find? Quickly, I have my own research!"

Vinet winced, wishing he hadn't brought up magic in front of Pellalindra. She tried to keep her voice casual as she answered. "I need information on the Cossack raiders in the northeast, Jaysk. Do we have any reports on their activity?"

Jaysk waved a hand and started rummaging through the shelves. "Of course, of course. Dates? Times?"

"Recently," Vinet asked. "If there's any mention of a leader called Darkmane?"

The effect on Jaysk was remarkable. He stilled, the frown completely fading from his face. "This is what you interrupt me for?" he asked. It should have been an annoyed question, but his tone was curiously flat.

"Yes. Is there a problem?" Vinet asked.

"It's a fairy tale," Jaysk said. "A child's nightmare story."

Before Vinet could say anything, Pellalindra interrupted. "There is nothing imaginary when a child's finger is sent to the Council!" she exclaimed.

Jaysk blinked. "A child's finger?" He ignored Pellalindra entirely and directed his question to Vinet. "Encased in clear wax?"

Vinet nodded.

Jaysk closed his eyes. "Was the letter signed?"

"Lord Artosbern, Warden of the Bern Forest," Vinet said.

"My condolences to his family," Jaysk whispered.

Vinet couldn't stand the suspense. "Jaysk, what is it? What do you know?" she demanded.

His eyes opened. "King Andreas III forbade this tale," he said. "Though it is likely still told in commoner households. I always viewed it as a fairy tale, a story to frighten children."

Pellalindra's nose wrinkled a little at the mention of smallfolk households. Vinet sent her a quelling look. They needed to hear what Jaysk had to say.

"The Cossacks might also be using the legends to boost the fear their men inspire. But I hope you understand most fairy tales and legends have their basis in reality."

Vinet nodded, almost feeling the mark of Manyu burning into her skin between her shoulders. She knew that better than most.

"Whoever receives such a finger, and signs his name bearing such a message, is marked to die by Darkmane's hand," Jaysk said. "But there have only ever been forgeries, wax fingers. Has Lord Artosbern's signature been verified?"

Vinet frowned in confusion. "What are you saying? That if Lord Artosbern sent the message, he is going to die? That doesn't make sense."

Jaysk shook his head. "No, no, no. Lord Artosbern would never send such a mutilation along with his letter. If it is *not* his signature, then he is in grave danger."

Pellalindra cleared her throat. "It hasn't been verified," she said slowly. "Lady Vinet, I had not a chance to tell you, but Lord Conn went to Lord General Torainn about it. His reaction was...distressing."

Vinet blinked. "I thought Lord General Torainn was in Venia."

"He'd just returned yesterday. Lord Conn apparently knows him from the Tigrian War. But...he nearly broke down at the mention of this Cossack and called him a...a revenant." She stared at Jaysk. "Was he right?"

"No, no...fairy tales and legends! That is all it is!" Jaysk looked around frantically.

Vinet bit her lip. "Are there any of these legends you could show me?" Much as she hadn't believed this was serious, she had to investigate it if both Jaysk and Lord General Torainn were reacting so strangely.

"I'll find them and send them to you, Lady Vinet." Without stopping for farewell, Jaysk disappeared back among the bookshelves.

Pellalindra stared after him, clearly shocked. "The nerve!" she exclaimed. "To just leave!"

Vinet had to stifle a laugh, despite the gravity of Jaysk's news. "That's just his way," she explained. "He's old enough to have earned that right."

Pellalindra shook her head in clear disapproval but said nothing.

Vinet sighed. "He'll send the reports to me when he's ready and not before. Are you heading anywhere now, Lady Pellalindra?" Inwardly, she hoped Pellalindra would return home. She didn't want to be polite to fellow councilors anymore.

To her disappointment, however, Pellalindra just tilted her head to one side. "Would you join me in a stroll about the gardens, Lady Vinet? The flowers are beautiful this time of year."

There was no way to gracefully back out of it, so Vinet nodded. They walked in silence through the palace and into the gardens.

The flowers were gorgeous, Vinet had to admit. Mazda's Rise had dawned with full force, and the flowers took full advantage of the sunlight, roses, lilacs, peonies, and lilies all blooming under the boughs of cherry blossoms.

"Have you cast your vote yet for Lord of the Council?" Pellalindra asked casually. Too casually.

Ah. So, this is what this conversation is about.

She shook her head noncommittally. She should have been thinking about this, true, but she'd had other things on her mind.

Pellalindra smiled. "I have spoken to both Conn and Dannan, and they have announced their desire to vote for me."

Vinet blinked. She had not been expecting that. "Congratulations?" she asked.

Pellalindra pursed her lips. "Neither our high priest nor Kamian will vote for me. That leaves the deciding vote in your hands. I want to call in that vote you promised me."

Vinet caught her breath. She stopped and turned to look at Pellalindra, crossing her arms over her chest. "And what did you promise them to get their votes?" she asked. "I owe you, yes, but if I vote for you on this, I give you twice the power for an entire year, while you've given me one vote. Hardly a fair exchange, you must admit."

Pellalindra's lips tightened. "I am the only option that will not cause strife on the Council," she said. "Everyone else is too firm in their own beliefs. I am at least willing to compromise. If you will not support me, I will let it be known you broke your promise and name you oathbreaker."

Vinet stared at Pellalindra, her mouth nearly falling open. "That's a little extreme!" she finally exclaimed. "Especially as I hadn't declared one way or another yet!" She hardened her tone. "I promised you a vote for a vote for a decision, Lady Pellalindra, not for Lord of the Council!"

Pellalindra waved her hand dismissively. "Will the others see it that way, I wonder?" she asked.

Vinet narrowed her eyes. "And will they see it my way or your way, I wonder, when I tell them how manipulative you were in bringing this about? You still haven't told me what you promised them."

Pellalindra hesitated, and Vinet felt a moment of satisfaction. It vanished quickly, however. Pellalindra's threat could not be taken lightly.

"I promised them nothing more than I could offer," she said.

"As you will promise me," Vinet said, pressing her advantage. "I vote for you, and you promise me to avoid potential war, and to seriously consider exploration. I do not think that too much to ask for the disparity of our votes!"

Pellalindra's jaw dropped. "Of course, I would avoid war!" she exclaimed. "I am not like Lord MacTir!"

"You threatened to call me an oathbreaker," Vinet kept her voice low. "That is something Lord Conn would do. I would not have expected it of you."

"I did not threaten you, Lady Vinet," Pellalindra said. "But you did promise me a vote. You do not get to decide how it is called in."

Vinet glared at her. "I did not expect to have to word my agreements with you as if I was dealing with fae creatures." She didn't care how harsh she sounded. She was tired, angry, and had suffered too many disappoint-ments already that day.

Pellalindra straightened her shoulders. "You gave me a tool, Lady Vinet. I am merely using it."

"As I said, manipulative," Vinet said. "I will vote for you, but only if you give me your word on the exploration."

Pellalindra hesitated. "As long as there are not situations that directly endanger the stability of the kingdom," she said.

That was all she would get, Vinet realized. She nodded shortly. "Then done," she said. She turned to start walking away, hoping to disappear between one of the hedgerows.

"Lady Vinet…"

She almost didn't turn back, but the hesitation in Pellalindra's voice made her pause. She looked over her shoulder.

Pellalindra seemed uncertain, but she continued. "I am intending to host a ball in celebration if I am elected. Everyone on the Council will be invited, of course. Perhaps, if this is the case, you would like to arrive a few days early? I would like to meet your niece, and mayhap she would like to meet my son."

Vinet wanted to refuse. She really did. But that was her anger speak-ing, and it would not be wise to make an enemy out of Pellalindra.

Besides, this was a peace offering, at least as Pellalindra knew to give them.

"I will come," she said and forced a smile. "Niara loves seeing new lands, and Duskryn is much farther south than she's ever traveled."

Pellalindra looked relieved. "Then I look forward to welcoming you to Duskryn."

Vinet nodded, more courteously this time, and walked away.

As soon as she was out of sight, she leaned against a wall and clenched her hands into fists. Mazda's light, she hated aristocracy and politics!

6

MASQUERADE

Remember what I told you."

Niara nodded. "Yes, Aunt Vinet."

Vinet bit her lip. She'd tried to teach her daughter how to properly greet nobility, how to talk, how to act, but...she glanced sideways at Gwyn.

"Don't ask me. I certainly don't have any advice in this matter," her faithful guard and friend declared with an amused glimmer in her eye and a shrug.

Vinet sighed. Aside from the MacTir children, Niara hadn't met any of the other nobility, even in an informal setting, and the MacTirs were hardly typical nobility. And meeting Lady Pellalindra and her son...she didn't think Pellalindra was capable of being informal.

She couldn't worry about it now, though, as the carriage drew close to Pellalindra's estate. There Pellalindra would host them for three days, with whatever entertainments she deemed appropriate, and then Vinet would attend the masquerade ball to celebrate Pellalindra's election as Lady of the Council.

"I still can't believe you roped me into this," Gwyn grumbled.

Vinet managed a smile. Since it was a masquerade, she'd convinced Gwyn she should come. After all, what better place to guard Vinet than right at her side, disguised as a member of the nobility?

Glancing at Niara as the carriage pulled to a stop, Vinet wondered, *Is it too early to start introducing her around? She's only six.*

Niara looked out the window of the carriage, oblivious to Vinet's thoughts. She was looking at everything with wide-eyed amazement. It reminded Vinet of her childhood self. The same persistent curiosity had started her interest in traveling, kept her researching, and kept her searching for new stories. She felt a surge of protectiveness. Niara deserved to keep that wonder as long as possible.

You can't shelter her forever, she reminded herself. As much as she might want to. And if she wanted Niara to become her official heir, then she had better get the support of other nobles. Her second cousins would fight the named succession if a bastard niece, at least to their knowledge, became Lady of Ninaeva instead of them.

Gwyn got out of the carriage first, as always. After Vinet stepped out, she turned around and lifted Niara out, straightening the girl's dress before looking around at the entrance to the Duskryn estate. She blinked. She knew Duskryn was wealthy, one of the wealthiest holdings of Saemar, but she hadn't expected it to be this apparent. The blue-stoned manor sat in the middle of a picturesque lake filled with waterlilies and swans, with a drawbridge which didn't look like it had ever been raised in Pellalindra's lifetime anchored to the shore via black-iron spikes formed into intricate flowers. The lack of obvious defense stated blatantly that Duskryn was powerful enough to not need to defend itself.

Vinet's sharp eyes, however, noticed guards stationed at various points along the wall, aside from the two at the edge of the drawbridge. The guard who caught the majority of her attention, however, waited at the end of the drawbridge for them. She'd met the elven guard at Pellalindra's townhouse in the capital. *What was his name? Saihid, that's it.*

He seemed a great deal more confident now than he'd been when he'd just stumbled upon them the first time they'd met. He bowed as Vinet approached. "Lady Vinet of Ninaeva, welcome to Duskryn."

Vinet nodded at him. "Thank you, Saihid," she said. Saihid jumped slightly, and she realized he'd never actually told her his name.

Niara saved everyone from awkwardness. She stared open-mouthed at Saihid. "You're an elf!" she exclaimed.

Saihid looked down at the little girl. "Ah, yes?"

"Are your ears real?" Niara demanded.

"Niara!" Vinet exclaimed. "Yes, his ears are real, and that's a very impertinent question."

Niara flushed. "Sorry," she mumbled.

"No need to apologize." Saihid crouched down. "Would you like a better look?"

Niara glanced at Vinet, and she gave an encouraging nod. Niara hesitantly stepped closer, peering at Saihid's ears.

"Why do they do that?" she asked.

Vinet suppressed a smile. Niara never did shrink from the difficult questions.

Saihid blinked. "Um... I don't know," he said. "Because I'm an elf?"

"That's not an answer!" Niara folded her arms.

"Niara," Vinet cut in.

The warning was all Niara needed. "Sorry," she said again.

"I know it's not an answer," Saihid chuckled. "There are many things I don't know."

Niara frowned. "I don't like not knowing things."

It seemed to Vinet that Saihid's eyes darkened slightly, out of sadness or anger, she couldn't tell. She instinctively placed a hand on Niara's shoulder.

He just shook his head. "Neither do I, my lady."

Niara flushed in pleasure. "I'm not a lady!" she exclaimed.

"Yes, you are," Vinet squeezed her shoulder. "Didn't I explain this?"

Niara brightened at the reminder.

Vinet smiled at Saihid. "Would you be so good as to tell Lady Pellalindra we've arrived?" she asked.

Saihid started and straightened. "Of course! I'll take you to her at once."

Vinet caught Gwyn's eye as they crossed the bridge and raised her eyebrow questioningly. Gwyn and Saihid had struck up a friendship that first encounter, and if there was any chance to learn more about him, Vinet wanted to take advantage of it. Gwyn rolled her eyes, but nodded, a smile on her face.

Saihid led them straight through the manor, turning neither left nor right. The main entrance hallway was magnificent, with portraits and other paintings lining the walls. The stairway upstairs was made of polished birch, with intricately carved banisters. Vinet didn't get a chance to examine any of the decorations, however, as Saihid led them through to the back entrance.

"My lady is waiting for you in the garden with some refreshments," Saihid said.

"Thank you, Saihid." Vinet met Gwyn's eyes and nodded. As she and Niara entered the gardens, Gwyn turned to walk with Saihid.

Pellalindra sat on a little patio with a table and chairs set out for tea. Vinet looked around the garden in appreciation. Although very different from Ninaeva, the flower beds and plants were arranged with impeccable taste, with ordered rows of tulips and hyacinths.

Pellalindra rose as they approached. "Lady Vinet! I hope your journey was pleasant."

Vinet smiled. "I love journeys, Lady Pellalindra. And I had company this time." She gestured at her daughter. "May I present my niece, Niara? Niara, this is Lady Pellalindra."

To Vinet's relief, Niara managed a credible curtsy. The young girl screwed up her face briefly as she remembered the phrase she had memorized. "Thank you for inviting us, Lady Pellalindra." She beamed that she had remembered.

Pellalindra clasped her hands in front of her, and Vinet could see the expression of delight in her eyes. She relaxed. Niara had made another conquest. There was nothing to worry about.

Pellalindra dipped a small curtsy to Niara. "The pleasure is all mine, Lady Niara," she said. "Would you and your aunt be so kind as to join us for some tea?"

"Yes please," Niara said eagerly. Vinet's lips twitched as she tried to ignore the tightness in her chest. Niara had seen the cakes on the table.

They sat down, and Vinet handed Niara one of the cakes without prompting. Niara gasped in delight as she took the first bite. Vinet made sure she had a napkin ready. If she didn't, Niara would get crumbs all over her nice dress.

Pellalindra raised her teacup to her lips. "Do you like cake, Lady Niara?"

Niara nodded so hard her hair tumbled into her face, then paused in the middle of a bite and glanced at Vinet worriedly. Vinet smiled reassuringly. Niara went back to eating with barely restrained delight.

Vinet took a bite of a cake herself. A little sweeter and lighter than she was used to, but then again, down here in the south things didn't need to be as hearty as in the north.

"So, Lady Niara, are you taking any lessons?"

Vinet relaxed. Pellalindra could not have chosen a more perfect topic.

Niara took another pastry. "Lots! I love the library! There're all kinds of books about these strange places and creatures! I don't like figuring much, but the seneschal says it's important, and Aunt Gwyn is teaching me to use a knife!" She reached for another cake, despite still chewing on the first one.

Pellalindra's eyes darted to Vinet, and Vinet concealed a wince. She had forgotten to tell Niara not to call Gwyn her aunt. And as for knife-fighting...

"A knife?" Pellalindra said, feigning at having not heard Niara clearly

Niara continued, oblivious. "She says if I'm going to travel like I want then I ought to be able to defend myself. She says I'm already better than my Aunt Vinet!"

Vinet felt her cheeks flush. She'd never had any aptitude, or interest, in any kind of martial art.

She decided to make light of the conversation. "Gwyn would be training me if she thought she could," she said. "Unfortunately for her peace of mind, I never wanted to learn, so she rectifies the situation by staying close to me."

"Saihid has never offered to teach me," Pellalindra said, trying to match Vinet's lightness.

Vinet hid a laugh at the mental image of Pellalindra dressed in anything other than an elaborate dress for combat training. "Well, Gwyn's first offer was when I was eight," she said. "Things are a bit different that young."

Pellalindra nodded and turned back to Niara. "So, you like reading?" she asked.

"Yes!" Niara exclaimed. "Especially the old tales. Aunt Vinet has a whole collection. I must be quiet when I read them, though, or the scholars get all annoyed at me. It makes it hard to act them out," she finished in a disappointed tone.

Vinet suppressed a smile, then shared an amused glance with Pellalindra when she saw she was doing the same thing.

Pellalindra kept her voice remarkably level. "It is important to have a quiet place to study."

"I know," Niara nodded. "But sometimes I just want to act things out! Like the tale of King Enlil and the Dragonriders!"

That was a Saemarian legend so common every child had heard it. She wasn't surprised Niara had mentioned it. The Dragon's Day parade had been the day before they'd left Ninaeva.

Pellalindra inclined her head. "That is a good legend. Maybe you'd like to tell it to my son? Would you like to meet him?"

Vinet saw Niara visibly brace herself. She had warned her this would happen.

"I would be honored," Niara said in a formal voice.

The formal voice seemed to charm Pellalindra. She waved for a servant, and a few minutes later a woman dressed in servant's clothing came out, leading a toddling boy by the hand.

Niara glanced at Vinet, then stood up. Vinet and Pellalindra followed suit.

Pellalindra smiled warmly at the boy. "Percival, this is Lady Niara. Lady Niara, my son, Lord Percival."

Niara looked very confused about curtsying to a boy half her height, but she managed anyway. Percival gave her a stiff little bow.

Pellalindra gazed at them in approval. "Maddy, why don't you take Percival and Lady Niara down to the fountain, and Lady Niara can tell him the tale of Enlil and the Dragonriders."

The woman nodded. "Yes, my lady."

Niara waited for Vinet's approval before following the two. As they walked out of earshot, Vinet heard her say to Percival, "So, do you like dragons?"

Vinet watched the two of them until they were out of sight. Hopefully, Niara wouldn't scandalize Percival too much.

"Your niece is a treasure," Pellalindra said.

"I adore her," she replied. She looked at Pellalindra, aware her next statement might be shocking. "I want to make her my heir."

Pellalindra raised an eyebrow. "Your sister's daughter?" she said, tactfully leaving out the part where Niara's father was unknown.

"Yes," Vinet said firmly. "She's my closest relative, aside from my sister, who can't inherit now she's in the convent."

Pellalindra absently brushed a strand of black hair behind her ears. "It might be possible. Bastards have inherited before."

Pellalindra had studied her history. One of the more famous Saemarian kings, King Darrien II, had been a bastard. Granted, there had been no other contenders to the throne because his father's wife had been infertile, but still.

Pellalindra frowned but nodded once and slow. "Well, I'll support you if you do decide to make it official. She's a dear."

Vinet suppressed a triumphant smile. "Thank you, Lady Pellalindra."

Pellalindra leaned back in her chair and raised a cup of tea to her lips. "Not at all. Are you looking forward to the masquerade?"

Was she? She didn't tend to like parties. But it had the potential to be fun. "Of course," she said politely. "I had a lot of fun picking out my mask."

Pellalindra took another sip of her tea. "Do let me know what it is. Although it is a masquerade, at least one person needs to know who everyone is, and as hostess that is my duty."

Vinet took a small bite of another cake. "You mentioned we could bring a guest. Gwyn will be there as mine."

Pellalindra's eyebrows rose, but otherwise she didn't react. "That's good. Saihid will have someone to talk to."

So, Gwyn wouldn't be the only guard in a mask. Vinet briefly wondered if Aed, Conn's bodyguard, would also be there.

"Have you heard of the new issues for the Council to discuss?"

Vinet blinked at the shift in topic. "Seems things have settled down a bit since last time."

Pellalindra nodded. "There are still one or two things I want your opinion on."

Vinet leaned back as Pellalindra started to elaborate. Pellalindra was trying to win her good opinion by asking for counsel. She wouldn't forget her manipulation as easily as that, but it would do no harm to listen.

"I can't believe you got me into this thing," Gwyn complained.

Vinet suppressed a smile, then realized she didn't need to with the mask in front of her face. She grinned. "You look absolutely wonderful."

Her friend truly did. Somehow, Vinet had been able to choose the entire costume. Gwyn's long blonde hair was braided into golden tresses instead of tied up neatly in a bun, and it contrasted magnificently with the feathered black gown. The mask, also black, was a stylized raven.

"I can't move." Vinet didn't need to see Gwyn's face behind the raven mask to know she was glaring.

Vinet laughed. "Nonsense. The skirt can be torn loose, and you have your daggers strapped to your thighs. I took these things into consideration."

Gwyn shook her head, but Vinet sensed that part of the argument was over. "And I can't believe you are wearing that mask," Gwyn said.

"What's wrong with my mask?" Vinet asked, her voice saturated in mischief. Her outfit appealed to her own spark of rebellion. She wore a green dress, simply cut, but made of the finest silk, and trimmed with blue and brown reminiscent of a sylvan glade, a Tigrian style, though few were likely to recognize it. Her mask was a simple green, but no one could miss the long elf ears attached to it. Gwyn sighed. "If someone guessed..."

"That's the beauty. It's right in front of their faces, but no one will ever guess. This is a masquerade, remember?"

The truth of that statement confronted Vinet as they entered the main ballroom. From the top of the stairs, she could see people swarming about, all dressed in elaborate costumes with masks. Vinet halted a moment to take it in. She had never realized how accustomed she was to seeing people's faces. She was glad of Gwyn beside her; at least she knew one person here.

As her gaze swept the hall, she noticed a woman in a dark blue gown standing at the bottom of the stairs. Although she wore a mask, it was only a thin strip of blue cloth, and the ornate black hairstyle marked her as Pellalindra. Well, the hostess would want people to be able to recognize her.

Especially Pellalindra, her cynicism said. *She wants congratulations for becoming Lady of the Council.*

She silenced that voice as she and Gwyn descended the stairs. Pellalindra was deep in conversation with four other nobles. From the broad shoulders and the wolf mask, one of them would be Conn, which meant one of the women was Maeve. Whether she was the woman in the starling mask or the plain aqua mask, Vinet couldn't tell. The other man wore a golden peacock mask, and even standing still he still strutted enough for one.

"Lady Pellalindra, this is a wonderful ball," Vinet said as she approached the group. "I have never seen such finery." Purest flattery, of course, but expected.

Pellalindra smiled. "It is only what we should provide." Her gaze switched briefly from Vinet to Gwyn. "You two simply must give me the name of your seamstress."

The four other nobles perked up. They were expecting a location, Vinet realized. Something to give them a hint of her identity.

She shook her head. "I'll let you know once the ball is over," she promised.

The woman in the aqua mask whispered something in Conn's ear, and he laughed.

The woman in the starling mask stared at them, and then grabbed Conn's arm, saying lightly, "Let's dance, dear."

Well, that answered the question about which woman was Maeve.

The man in the golden peacock mask nodded amiably to the ladies before swaggering off.

Vinet glanced at Gwyn. She seemed to be observing everything. Still in bodyguard mode. She rolled her eyes in amusement.

"Are you enjoying the ball?" Vinet asked the woman in the aqua mask.

The woman gestured with her embroidered fan. "Indeed! Oh," she turned to Pellalindra. "You have my sincerest congratulations on your new position, dear."

Vinet blinked. Did she know that voice?

Pellalindra looked taken aback but managed to accept the expression graciously. Before anything else could be said, a man clad all in royal purple approached them. His mask had a crown.

He bowed smoothly. "My greetings, ladies. Lady Duskryn, it is a pleasure to make your acquaintance."

Pellalindra nodded politely but Vinet could see the stiffness in her shoulders. Pellalindra had no idea who this man was.

Politeness dictated Vinet should move on and let the other guests greet Pellalindra, but curiosity bade her stay. She compromised, curtsying to Pellalindra and the man then wandering off, staying just within earshot.

"Greetings, sir," Pellalindra said. "I hope you shall enjoy the festivities of the night."

"We shall see," the man said. He bowed again, reaching for Pellalindra's hand and kissing it.

Pellalindra laughed, and Vinet could see she was flattered. "Well, let me know if there is any assistance I can offer to make it more pleasurable."

"The only assistance renderable to me is the presence of your company, my lady."

Vinet raised her eyebrows. That was flattery bordering on flirtation.

Pellalindra scanned the room. "Well, it seems most of the guests have arrived, so shall we take a stroll around together?"

The man bowed. "Your wish is my command."

Vinet started to follow the two of them, only to be intercepted by the man in the golden peacock mask. She stopped, cursing inwardly. She wanted to find out who was flirting with Pellalindra.

"Might I have this dance, my lady? You look absolutely charming."

Vinet glanced at Gwyn, who gave a shrug. She nodded as the musicians struck up a tune.

The man took her hand and led her to join the line of dancers. She tilted her head slightly as she studied him, waiting for the music to signal the start of the dance. Who was he?

The dance began, and he took her hand as they took the first steps together. He knew how to dance, at least.

"Where did you learn to dance, my lord?" she asked.

"Oh, in the frozen north," came the answer. "We have to do something to keep ourselves warm."

Well, he was connected to Conn, then. She wracked her brain. His seneschal wouldn't have come down. His bard? Aed? His shoulders were broad enough for Aed.

"And you, my lady?" the question was pointed.

Vinet laughed lightly. "Oh, I learned everywhere I went," she said. "One has to know the local dances, otherwise one is likely to commit a faux pas."

The man shook his head. "My wife would agree with you."

His wife! Well, that ruled Aed and Conn's bard out. Who? Conn wore the wolf mask, that had been obvious, so...

She nearly missed a step as the thought occurred to her. They couldn't have switched masks... Pellalindra had been adamant about knowing which mask was worn by which guest.

Should she tell Pellalindra? It would probably cause her concern, but...

No. Conn wasn't harming anyone. It was nonsensical and defeated the point of the masquerade, but perhaps the only things he'd heard about masquerades were from some of the risqué romances she was keeping from Niara. Mask trading and mistaken identities were always a part of those.

The dance came to an end, and Vinet curtsied to the man she now knew was Conn. She looked around, trying to spot where Gwyn, or Pellalindra and the strange man had gone.

To her surprise, Pellalindra and the man were not far off, over by the refreshment tables. She wandered over under the pretense of getting a drink to cool herself.

"I would love to know your name, but alas, this is not the night for such revelations," Pellalindra said playfully as Vinet approached.

Vinet nearly choked as she reached for a glass of wine. *I didn't think Pellalindra flirted with strange noblemen.*

"We must all play the game," the man bowed slightly. "Though some, I daresay, play it better than others."

For a moment, Vinet thought the comment pointed toward her. But it couldn't be. She wasn't near enough to be casually listening. Her elf ears allowed her far sharper hearing than any noble should expect.

"Oh, you refer to the northern wolf?" Pellalindra waved a hand derisively. "His blatancy will be practiced only at his own peril. Because of the status of everyone here, security is at its highest."

Vinet nearly snorted. Conn's identity wasn't as obvious as Pellalindra seemed to think.

"My lady! You wound me!" the man clapped a hand over his heart. "I spoke only by my own humble broad observations. I accuse no one lest I myself be accused."

Pellalindra laughed. "Of course, of course," she said. Their conversation paused for a moment before she continued. "As newly elected Lady of the Council, I must voice we are all intrigued as to what everyone else's thoughts on the Council are. We've been established a year now. Might I pick your brain, taking advantage of anonymity?"

The man bowed. "My wish is your command."

Pellalindra smiled her thanks. "What are the nobility's thoughts on some of our most recent decisions?"

The man didn't answer, just took Pellalindra's hand and joined the next dance without consulting her. Pellalindra followed without resistance.

Vinet moved along the row of dancers, stretching her hearing as far as she could. She wanted to hear this.

"The Council has most certainly made some curious decisions," the man said as they stood, waiting for the dance to start. "The wild goose chase most recent concerns numerous nobles, myself included. If I may impart, my Lady of Council, we have taken to calling it the wild ghost chase!"

"I'm afraid I may agree with you on that. You don't see the debates within the chamber, only the results from it. But it was a decision not easily made." Pellalindra was silent for a moment as the dance swept them up. "How would the lords like us to vote in the future, as I assume investment in other expeditions will continue to be options?"

Vinet nearly broke her cover and stared at Pellalindra. *The expedition was no wild goose chase!*

The man in the purple mask missed a step but recovered so quickly Vinet couldn't be sure if she had seen the mistake. "You mistake my statement, I'm afraid. I would hardly consider the deployment of two Divisions an expedition!"

Darkmane, Vinet thought. *I knew chasing after him would come back to haunt us.*

Pellalindra seemed to realize the same thing. "We wanted to bring a murderer to justice. Anyone would have done the same."

"Deploying the Regulars in force to chase a murderer seems a little extreme, does it not?"

Vinet felt a harsh feeling of vindication as she heard the man's words. It had been extreme.

"As you speak it, I must agree somewhat. We wished for Lady Justice to strike quickly, as idealistic as that seems," Lady Pellalindra said.

Vinet eyed Pellalindra. She was certainly adept at appearing to agree with anyone's statements.

The music faded, and the man led Pellalindra off the dance floor. "Ah yes. Lady Justice. I know her well. Most assuredly the idealist's lover, but not the wife of a ruler."

Vinet stared down at her drink. She had been accused of idealism time and time again. Maybe she wasn't suited to being on the Council.

Pellalindra and the man started walking in her direction, and Vinet got ready to greet them. Before they reached her, however, the man in the golden peacock mask, Conn, as she now knew, walked up to intercept them. "Come now, is this really the place to be discussing politics, with such fine wine and finer company?"

The man in purple gave Conn a short bow. "A ball is the perfect place to discuss politics, good sir."

Conn nodded. "Well, in that case, did I hear you correctly? You disapprove of the southern expedition? I thought they found a whole heap of gold!" he laughed heartily, as if at a joke.

Vinet's hand tightened on her glass. She had known Conn didn't approve of the expedition. And the anonymity of his new mask gave him the freedom to express that opinion.

"Good stranger," the man's voice was calm and level. "You mistake my words. I have spoken no harsh words against the Badlands expedition."

Conn looked taken aback. "Apologies. Then what did you mean?"

"A conversation held with a lovely lady is not one best repeated, good man. I'm sure you, of all those here, would understand this truth." The man took a goblet from a passing servant and sipped it, but Vinet noticed he never stopped looking at Conn.

Conn chuckled easily. "That is fair. Well then let us not repeat what was said but bring new information to the table. What do you think of Saemar right now? Is trade your major concern or are you one of the warlike types?"

Vinet wanted to roll her eyes at so obvious a division of the Council. Pellalindra seemed to have the same thought. "People's ideals are rarely so dualistic." Lady Duskryn interjected.

"One might say I am a trader of sorts." The man in the purple mask paused, fixing Conn with his inquisitive look once more. "And your own concerns?"

Conn shrugged. "Oh, I am concerned for the safety of Saemar, nothing more." He turned. "Might I have this next dance, Lady Duskryn?"

Pellalindra accepted his hand, and he led her to the dance floor, leaving the purple-masked man alone. He stood in contemplative silence for a moment, then walked in Vinet's direction. He bowed. "Greetings, my lady. Are you enjoying the ball?"

She curtsied in response. "As much as you," she responded.

He laughed. "An enigmatic response."

"Perfect for an enigmatic evening." She couldn't take the measure of this man and had no idea what to make of him.

Like an angel, Gwyn appeared at her elbow. "You need to see something," she whispered. She glanced at the man. "Pardon me, my lord, but I must claim my friend."

"Of course," the man waved. "Do not let me stop your enjoyment."

Vinet followed Gwyn through the crowded ballroom and out to the garden. "What is it?"

Gwyn simply shook her head and continued leading her. The gardens were also full of guests, though nowhere near as crowded as the ballroom. Gwyn led her to a small, secluded grove and drew her behind one of the bushes.

She quickly took in the scene. Conn's bard sat with his mask off and a harp in his hands. The mask beside him was the gray wolf mask Conn had originally been wearing. A young elf woman stood next to him, as well as a slender man in a black fox mask. The woman in the aqua mask, from

89

the beginning of the ball, was there also, staring at the bard. "A lie is a lie, sir," she said.

Vinet poked Gwyn. "Who's who?"

"Elf woman, Saihid's sister. Black fox, Saihid. The woman..." Gwyn's voice trailed off as the bard replied to the aqua-masked woman.

"Oh, no harm is done. Let my lord and his lady have some fun at the southern lords' expense. You have no idea how often they mock him, calling him barbarian and savage. This is just a bit of innocent fun," the bard implored.

Vinet knew that was true. But Conn encouraged that by appealing to every stereotype they had. He seemed to enjoy the image.

"I hardly doubt it will be innocent," Saihid said. "Lady Duskryn assigned the masks for a reason. She knows everyone in the room simply by looking at them. Speaking of which, who are you?" The Duskryn guardsman looked at the lady in the aqua mask.

Vinet watched as the lady laughed. "Ah, my darling fox of the platinum. You cannot lecture on the meaning of a masquerade and then immediately ask me my identity. Truly the fox is cunning." She walked near him, circling. "You can call me Maiden."

Saihid's reply was utterly confused. Vinet couldn't suppress a smile. "I...very well, Maiden. What brings you outside on this cold night? Surely the ballroom is more comfortable and suited to your tastes?"

"The cold is what suits a bitch like her," Conn's bard muttered under his breath. Vinet raised an eyebrow, knowing he had not meant anyone to hear.

The woman raised a hand, and there was a loud twang as every one of the harp strings snapped. Vinet stared. What had she done? How had she heard?

"Come with me, my black fox," the woman said, taking Saihid's arm.

Saihid seemed even more startled but didn't resist. As they passed near Vinet and Gwyn, the woman looked in their direction. "Have a good night, mother's daughter."

Vinet stiffened, and she felt Gwyn do the same thing beside her. *What was AeresThonEsia doing here?*

Her thoughts were interrupted by the arrival of Conn, his wife, and several other masked figures, all talking at the top of their lungs. Apparently, the mask switching had been discovered.

Vinet tugged Gwyn's arm. She didn't want to deal with this. "Let's go dance," she said to Gwyn. "I've had enough of politics, intrigue, and deception for the night."

7

THE GREAT HUNT

Lady Vinet? There's a dwarf here to see you. She said something about an expedition?" The page peeked into Vinet's study.

Vinet glanced up from her reading. "Here? In Ninaeva?"

The page nodded.

Vinet closed her book. "Show her in."

"Yes, my lady," the page left the room. Shortly afterward he returned, followed by a female dwarf.

"Lady Vinet?" The short, red-haired dwarf crossed her arms over her chest.

Vinet rose to her feet. "You are welcome here..."

"Yderdochter," the dwarf said. She uncrossed her arms and raised one hand to her smooth cheek, then lowered it again, shifting from foot to foot. "Went north with Jimesseran."

Vinet tried to throttle down her excitement. "Is Jimesseran here? Did he find what he was looking for?"

Yderdochter shook her head. "Jimesseran's dead. This is for you." She took a ragged journal out of her jacket and thrust it toward Vinet.

Vinet took it, still trying to process Yderdochter's words. "Dead?"

"Just read it." Without another word, the dwarf turned on her heel and walked out of the room.

Vinet stared at the journal in her hands. She had known Jimesseran was dying when he set out, but she hadn't thought he'd die on the journey. *Did I expedite his death by funding the expedition?*

No, Jimesseran would have gone anyway. It had been his life's dream, and he would want someone to know what he had discovered. She sank back down in her chair in front of the fire and began to read. Excitement rose in her. He'd been successful! He'd gone further north than anyone, through N'Dar's Dagger and the Channel of Sorrows. And after two weeks of traveling, he'd found nephelm sites! Abandoned, unfortunately

She flicked through the pages impatiently. Surely, he'd found more! He described a marvelous bridge, with dragon statues, and another statue of a curiously-garbed female nephelm warrior poised to slay them. So, the nephelm had been dragon-slayers? Were they the reason there were no more dragons left?

She froze as her eyes moved to the next line.

A dragon! We saw a dragon, albeit far in the sky above and only a glimpse since the road, even traveling north along this strong river, is heavily wooded. I'm sure it was a dragon. Yderdochter...be safe, we are not using the road, sticking to the woods with the road just in sight.

She stared at the sentence, trying to verify she'd read it correctly. Dragons had been extinct for hundreds of years. Yet Jimesseran's writing reported a sighting of one, not more than a month's travel northward?

She wished the journal contained more detail, but the last pages were ragged and nearly illegible. His illness, whatever it was, had been catching up to him, and for some reason he'd sent Yderdochter away. He mentioned another strange creature only briefly, and another bizarre segment at the end which implied he would die fulfilled. Did that mean he'd found the nephelm? Another fragmentary sentence mentioned someone watching, but was that real or delusion? She couldn't tell.

She put the journal down, torn between elation and frustration. Something existed in the north, that was certain. She just wished Jimesseran had been able to make it back himself.

She would send Kamian a copy of the journal. He'd be as interested in this as she. After the conversations of the masquerade, she was less inclined to think anyone else on the Council would want to see an expedition's journal.

"Lady Vinet?"

She looked up to see Kildar, her seneschal, at the door. She smiled. "Yes, Kildar?"

The old man approached her, a thin envelope in his hand. "A messenger arrived and brought this for you."

Her eyebrows rose as she saw the address on the letter. *Lady Pellalindra Duskryn.*

She opened the envelope and pulled out the most expensive piece of parchment she'd ever seen, trimmed with gold illumination.

The wording was suitably formal for such a piece of parchment, but Vinet quickly gathered the gist. An invitation to the 112th Great Hunt of Duskryn. Apparently, now that Pellalindra had been elected Lady of the Council, she was inviting the councilors to all her grand events. She leaned back in her chair as Kildar left the room. Did she have to go? She really didn't want to deal with all that politicking again.

A flash passed in front of her eyes, and she grabbed at her chair. *Not now. Not again!*

On the corner of her desk, the Book of Truths opened on its own. She gasped.

The vision took her so fast she could do nothing to prepare. A forest, with trees taller than she'd ever seen. A lone wolf. A scream of horror. The twang of an arrow. And a feeling of something familiar. Something...

She gasped, and her vision dissipated. She was back in her library, Pellalindra's invitation having fallen to the floor in front of her. The Book of Truths was closed.

She stared at the paper. Normally, she had no idea what her visions meant. This time, however, she felt a certain connection with Pellalindra's invitation. Gwyn would probably tell her to leave well enough alone. But there was something...something in that vision, a deep sense of familiarity that gave her heart a pang of longing for something she'd never known. She picked up the paper, noticing her hands were shaking. She'd missed the postscript.

Please bring Niara. She and Percival got along so well last time. They can entertain each other while the hunt is going on. I've invited Lord Conn's children as well, so they won't be alone.

"Welcome, one and all, to the 112th Great Hunt of Duskryn! The

competition is simple, the hunter who brings back the largest prize wins!"
The announcer bowed with a flourish.

Vinet sat astride her horse, dressed for the occasion in a green leather
split skirt with yellow leggings. Beside her rode Gwyn, dressed in her
usual mail. Gwyn had refused all offers to join the serious hunters and
had insisted she was staying with Vinet.

Vinet could not help being grateful about that. Though she was trying
not to be paranoid, she knew something was going to happen.

The rest of the nobles milled around, all mounted on various steeds.
None of them were serious hunters. They would be riding, following the
main hunt. *Well, unless Lord Conn rides out to join them. He looks very
unhappy being stuck here with the rest of us. His bodyguard has already ridden
ahead.*

Pellalindra brought her horse alongside the Ninaevans. "It's a perfect
day for a hunt, isn't it? Are you enjoying it, Lady Niara?"

Vinet smiled at her daughter seated on the pony beside her. She had
garnered no few raised eyebrows already, and no doubt some muttered
speculations as to why Vinet had brought her along and not left her at
Pellalindra's estate. But Niara had wanted to see the forest and the
animals, and Vinet saw no reason to deny her.

Niara nodded vigorously but didn't answer verbally, staring around
her wide-eyed.

Pellalindra chuckled. "I'm sure you'll have a wonderful time."

Conn chuckled. "Probably best for a child to be back here instead of
with the real hunters. Though my oldest son has done a fair amount of
hunting on his own. He'll be ready for his first solo hunt soon."

Niara sniffed, and Vinet remembered her daughter's outspoken, at
least in Ninaeva and in private, opinion of Niall. *He's like a donkey in silk
trousers, Aunt Vinet. Do I have to be nice to him?*

She was saved from having to prevent Niara from answering by an
exclamation of joy from Pellalindra. "My lord! You made it! I wasn't
certain you would come!"

Vinet glanced up and froze. Even though he wasn't wearing his purple
mask, she recognized the man from the masquerade ball, the enigmatic
one who'd flirted with Pellalindra. She remembered his broad shoulders,
the sandy hair, the confident way of carrying himself. He was exquisitely
handsome, perfect in every way, even his horse a perfect white stallion.
He sent a shiver up Vinet's spine.

The man rode up beside Pellalindra. "It is a pleasure I hoped I would not have to miss. Although my duties are ever present." That settled it. His voice was the same, musical and deep.

Pellalindra nodded sympathetically. She gestured to Vinet. "Lady Vinet, may I present to you Lord Auriel?"

Lord Auriel turned his gaze on Vinet, and she found herself held by his piercing eyes. "A pleasure to meet you," she managed. She forced a smile. "Though I believe we met briefly in more anonymous circumstances."

Lord Auriel inclined his head. "Ah yes, the masquerade. You were the elf woman, correct? A most daring costume, if I do say so myself."

She sensed, more than saw, Gwyn stiffen at her side. *Easy. It's a figure of speech. There's no possible way he could know my heritage*, she thought.

"Flowers!" Niara exclaimed. Without waiting for Vinet's permission, she slid off her pony and darted for the forest.

"Niara!" Vinet exclaimed.

Gwyn hesitated, glancing worriedly at Vinet before dismounting her horse, handing the reins to a servant, and following Niara into the woods.

Pellalindra spoke. "I'm sure she'll be fine, Lady Vinet. Any dangerous game will have been scared away by the passage of the hunters."

Vinet stared into the woods after Niara and Gwyn for a moment, trying to convince herself Pellalindra's words were true. She couldn't very well go dashing after them. Gwyn was more suited to that than she was.

"We are acquainted with Lord Auriel in a way beside the masquerade," Pellalindra continued. "He is the one who paid the fee for my scout."

Vinet forced her attention back to the nobles and blinked at Lord Auriel in surprise. "I…you have the Council's sincerest gratitude."

Lord Auriel smiled pleasantly. "It was the least I could do for the kingdom. Especially considering the post I will soon be assuming."

"Post?" Vinet noticed Ellil and Dannan were riding closer, intrigued by the conversation.

"Ah. Well, I suppose it does no harm to make it public," Lord Auriel smiled, more at Pellalindra than Vinet. "I am to be appointed His Majesty's steward. So, I shall be seeing a great deal more of all of you." Somehow, he managed to make his words seem directed only at Pellalindra.

"A steward? Why does His Majesty need a steward?" Dannan's words were sharp.

Before Lord Auriel could answer, Ellil interjected. "It's a traditional post," he said, his voice smooth. "But it has been vacant for some time now."

"His Majesty has decided it is time for it to be filled," was Lord Auriel's casual response.

Vinet was full of questions. Why him? Why now? She'd never heard of Lord Auriel before and was certain several of the others had not either.

"Well, I do hope your duties will allow your presence at other events such as this." Pellalindra seemed intent on steering the conversation away from the potentially dangerous subject of Lord Auriel's abrupt appointment. "I hope you will enjoy yourself while you are in Duskryn lands."

"Indeed, they are as beautiful as I remember," Lord Auriel seized on the change of subject.

Pellalindra started. "Remember? That must have been some time ago. Before I married my husband, as I am sure I would have recalled meeting you before."

"Ah yes. Nihlas." Lord Auriel's voice was flat.

Vinet kept her expression blank with an effort. Lord Auriel was aware of the rumors surrounding Lord Nihlas's death, then; principally, that it had been far too conveniently timed.

The chatter of her daughter distracted Vinet from the conversation and she turned her head toward the woods.

Three figures appeared. They did not step out of the shadows, they just appeared, as if they willed themselves to be shown. All of them were carrying longbows, and they all had long, pointed ears. One of them held the corpse of a wolf slung over his shoulders. Seconds later, Niara walked out of the woods, holding hands with another, older elf, chattering happily.

The elf looked directly at Vinet, and the blood drained from her face. She knew that man. She had seen him in a vision, heard his voice. He was far more intimately connected to her than any of the nobles all about her, for all she'd never met him.

"There's Aunt Vinet!" Niara exclaimed. She started bounding over. "Aunt Vinet! He says I should have pointed ears too!"

Vinet paled even further as she slid out of the saddle. Niara flung herself into her arms, still chattering happily. Vinet held her but could not tear her eyes away from the elf. She barely noticed the other nobles moving.

Pellalindra's sharp voice interrupted her thoughts. "There was a woman with the child!"

Vinet's eyes widened just as Gwyn burst through the trees. Gwyn assessed the situation before quietly walking to Vinet's side.

Vinet swallowed. "It's alright, Lady Pellalindra." Even to herself, her voice sounded strange and distant.

The older elf smiled at her. "Lady Vinet, I presume? I found this one wandering the woods. She nearly killed this wolf here had we not put it out of its terror."

Vinet felt another spike of fear. Had Niara run into a wolf? She nearly turned an accusing glare at Pellalindra. She had said the dangerous predators would have been scared off! The elf's gaze held her attention though. She nodded slowly. "I am Lady Vinet, yes. And...and you?" Everything was silent, waiting with tense anticipation.

He bowed slightly to her, his green eyes warm. "Kinaevan Sindarilae."

Only the presence of the other nobles, and her keen awareness of their assessing stares, allowed Vinet to keep her composure. She had to know more about him!

"Lady Vinet. Perhaps you should allow your guard to take Niara back to the estate, and we can submit the wolf as this elf's contribution to the hunt." Although phrased as a question, it was clear Pellalindra meant it as a command.

"Heathens," Ellil's normally calm voice was exceptionally sharp.

Vinet tore her gaze away to see several guards had ridden up. Kinaevan and the elves appeared supremely unconcerned.

To her surprise, Lord Auriel rode up next to Pellalindra and took her hand. "Stay your hand, your blades, and call back your guards. I know this elf."

Her gaze switched to Lord Auriel in shock. *He knows Kinaevan? How? Why? When not even I...* She took a deep breath. "I am not letting Niara out of my sight," she said to Pellalindra. She wasn't letting Kinaevan go easily, either, not if she could help it. "Kinaevan and I will go back to the estate together."

Pellalindra appeared surprised. "If that is what you wish...my guards are available for you should you need them."

Vinet met Kinaevan's eyes. He smiled slightly at her. She swallowed, nearly overwhelmed by the sense of familiarity.

"No guards," she said.

Lord Auriel rode closer and dismounted. Mazda's light, he was an intimidating man. So poised, so confident, so sure. He extended a hand to Kinaevan. "You have our hospitality, old friend."

Kinaevan took his hand and clasped it. Vinet stared at them both, bursting both with questions and fear.

"How do you know this elf?" Conn's voice was whip-like with suspicion.

Vinet bit her lip. She needed to get Kinaevan out of there. She wanted him to answer questions, but her questions, not questions of her fellow councilors.

Lord Auriel turned to rest his eyes in Conn's direction. "Do I know you?"

Despite the tension, Vinet had to conceal her amusement. Conn seemed quite taken aback at Lord Auriel's insistence on politeness.

Pellalindra cleared her throat. "Lord Auriel, Lord Conn MacTir, one of the council members."

"I am certain it is a pleasure," Lord Auriel said as if dismissing a syco-phant or servant.

Vinet seized the moment before any other councilors could get involved. "Would you like to ride back to the estate with me?" she asked Kinaevan. "I must...I must thank you for rescuing Niara."

"I have not ridden in a long time. If we might walk, then I would be happy to discuss a great many things." Kinaevan's eyes met hers with understanding.

Vinet nodded, and they set off without saying goodbye to any of the nobles. She would need to apologize to Pellalindra afterward, but right then, she just couldn't care.

The other three elves vanished back into the trees. After a few minutes of walking, there was no one around but Vinet, Niara, Gwyn, and Kinaevan.

The silence was unbearable to her, but Vinet couldn't think of anything to say. The one question she burned to ask lingered on the tip of her tongue, but she couldn't blurt something like that out. *Are you my father?*

Niara was completely unaffected by the awkward silence. Supremely happy, she skipped along between Kinaevan and Vinet.

"You saved her life," Vinet spoke. "Whatever other reason you had for coming here, you have my sincerest thanks for that."

Kinaevan smiled down at Niara. "How could I not? She is queen of the forest. Are you not, little one?"

Niara beamed. "He says I should have pointed ears!" she told Vinet. "He says that means we're the chosen of...of...The Lady of the Leaf and

Lake!" she beamed triumphantly at Kinaevan. "I remembered!" She looked curiously at Vinet. "Why are we part of the chosen?"

Vinet felt her face pale again. She met Kinaevan's eyes as Niara got distracted by a flower. "You know who she is," she whispered. "She doesn't. Not yet."

"And why is that, elfsdaughter?" Kinaevan said. They all drew to a stop. His eyes met hers, his tone one of both sadness and rebuke.

She flinched at the unspoken rebuke and drew back. "It was to protect her. To protect myself. Much as my own parentage was hidden from me until I was old enough to understand." She took a deep breath. "Why are you here? Why now? How have I seen you before?"

Niara seemed to sense Vinet's mood and moved back from looking at her flowers. "Aunt Vinet?" she asked.

Vinet leaned down to embrace her and closed her eyes. The things she had done to keep her daughter as her own. The lies she had told...it was all worth it. She had her daughter. She looked up at Kinaevan.

His eyes flashed. He straightened, his arms at his sides. His plain brown robes flared out, making him appear larger than he was. Slowly, he surveyed the woodlands. "Protection." The single word held a world of disbelief and question.

Vinet tightened her embrace of Niara, swallowing the lump of guilt in her throat. She was not going to let a man who'd disappeared for twenty-seven years tell her what was best for Niara. "Do you know how this land regards bastards?" she demanded. "Or the women who have them? I had been lady of Ninaeva for barely a year. It was the safest course of action."

For a moment, Kinaevan didn't appear to have heard her. Then he knelt to speak to Niara face to face. "Niara, good queen, would you like to run along ahead?"

Niara glanced worriedly up at Vinet who forced a smile. This was not Niara's fault. Nothing was Niara's fault. "Let Aunt Gwyn give you a piggyback ride back to the estate and have her tell the cook to give you some treats. Surely, you'd like that?"

Niara brightened like a ray of sunshine. Gwyn stepped forward and hoisted her up. She stared intently at Vinet. "Are you going to be alright?"

Vinet nodded, trying to act assured. "I'll tell you everything."

Gwyn frowned. "That's not what I meant," she muttered.

Vinet gave her a pleading look, and Gwyn rolled her eyes. Niara started chattering happily to Gwyn as she they walked away.

She and Kinaevan stood together in silence once Gwyn left. For a long while, Kinaevan closed his eyes. Despite that, she had the sense he was still surveying the entire forest around them. Finally, he opened them and met hers. A smile touched his lips, and Vinet could have sworn she saw a flash of pride as he reached out, gently brushing a strand of hair back behind one of her ears.

Her eyes stung. She swallowed. "Will you tell me who I am to you?" Her throat caught, and she looked away. "I know, at least I think I do, but there have been so many half-truths, so many guesses, so many evasions, I...I need to hear you say it." She couldn't meet his eyes. She couldn't let him see her hope and fear.

"You are my sole daughter, my only child."

She met his eyes. He held her gaze. "I see the Lady gave the gift of the eyes to you as well as to Niara." He stepped back. Then he slumped as if the weight of a thousand worlds had suddenly come to rest on his shoulders. "My apologies, Vinet."

Vinet took a deep, shuddering breath and wrapped her arms around herself. She was trembling. She took another breath, trying to calm down. "I don't... I don't think there's anything to apologize for, Father." Her breath nearly caught on the word: *father.*

Kinaevan blinked and seemed about to embrace her, then caught himself. "My exile. Leaving you here. Burdening you with an unguided gift. There is plenty I owe you."

Vinet couldn't deny the probable truth. But none of that mattered at the moment. "You're here now," she said.

Kinaevan smiled. He still appeared sad, though some of his strength was returning. He spread his arms. "Let me embrace you, my child."

Her eyes stung again and she stepped forward into his arms, instantly overwhelmed by a feeling of comfort, support, and a deep, intense familiarity. She tightened her embrace.

"I imagine you have a great many questions. There are many things I can tell you, but there are a great many things the Lady will not permit one so young in the Sight to know," Kinaevan said.

She pulled back from the embrace just enough to look him in the eyes, recalling Niara had mentioned that title. "The Lady?"

"The Lady of the Leaf and Lake, my daughter. She is whom I serve, whom all Elvenkind once served." His voice cracked briefly with the utterance of the last phrase.

A flash of memory. A figure over her bed, blade in hand, slumping to the ground with Gwyn's sword in their chest. She swallowed, remembering her vision. "The Thorn which attacked you is not representative of us all?" Those had been his words, she remembered.

"Fiends." His dark eyes were furious. His grip tightened on her. As he gazed out into the woods, she noticed a long and terrible scar down his neck. She smothered a gasp.

"They are...what is the word in this language? They are Untrue. Unfaithful to the Lady." Kinaevan's voice was harsh as he spoke of them.

"Unfaithful," she whispered. "I see." The nickering of a horse somewhere off reminded her of their location. While they were in private now, that could change.

She stepped back and straightened her shoulders. "What are your plans, Father? Will you...will you come back to Ninaeva with me? I have so many questions, but there are ears here, and I..." *Oh no.* She thought as the implications of her descent came to the forefront of her mind. "Mazda's light, what do I tell the Council?" She stared at her father in wide-eyed admonition.

He chuckled at her alarm. "There is no one at this moment, daughter. I would have seen them. Your secret and position are safe."

Vinet had a suspicion he did not mean 'seen' the way she would have used the word.

"Your wisdom is sound, though," Kinaevan continued. "I am, in fact, the ambassador from the Faithful to Saemar. That is my purpose for being here, but I could not keep myself from coming to this place once I was shown you were here."

He began to walk forward, leading them back to the estate. "Given my position here, at this very moment, I cannot accept your invitation to Ninaeva despite my fond memories of that place."

"Ambassador? Then I will see you on a regular basis, as I am a member of the ruling council." She frowned as a question occurred to her. "But why an embassy now?"

"There is a darkening tide coming. We must be ready. Mount Halon stirs." He met her eyes. "You have seen the signs."

She shivered. Without elaboration, she knew what he must be speaking of: the scout, the mark...her shoulder blades ached.

The estate's outbuildings came into sight, and Vinet slowed her walk. "Before we meet anyone else...you mentioned something you called the Sight. I have had some...interesting experiences. Is there a way..." she paused, trying to figure out how to phrase her question. "I need to learn how to use it, or, at the very least, control it. Is there a way you could teach me?"

"I could be there for you as your Sight develops, but I cannot teach the control. For that, you'll need to see the Lady, though she has been in shadow of late."

Vinet swallowed, remembering her experience with AeresThonEsia. Hopefully, this Lady was kinder than she. "Will you tell me about the Lady, then? This is the first I've heard of her, and I want to know more about your...our...culture and heritage."

Kinaevan smiled. "I am glad to hear it. The Lady is our guide, often called goddess by the ignorant. She does not, however, coerce and demand from her people like divinities. She gave our people numerous gifts, marking us as blessed via ear and eye."

Vinet instinctively reached to touch her own ear. Round to most people, but if one touched it there were angles to it that shouldn't have been there, not on a human, at least. "That's what you meant by the gift of eyes," she said.

"Indeed," Kinaevan said. "I am, and you may yet become, an Eye of the Lady. We are closest to her, blessed by her. She gives us the Sight to see, and the Swaying."

"The Swaying?"

"The ability to use magic," Kinaevan's voice seemed distant. He looked at her. "It is...costly, the Swaying."

Vinet remembered Dannan, his rants against magic, and her suspicions he had once been a mage. She nodded in understanding.

"The Thorns also serve the Lady," Kinaevan continued. "They are our warriors, our hunters, our protectors, and providers."

"Those were the three with you?" Vinet asked.

Kinaevan inclined his head slightly.

"I'm sorry Lady Pellalindra threatened you." Her lips twitched, remembering the situation.

Kinaevan laughed. "They were in more danger than we. The Thorns are highly skilled. If I had been truly threatened, they would not have hesitated."

"Is the Lady the only one you serve?" she asked. "Is there a...an elven government, or kingdom...or..." She stopped as she couldn't think of what else there could be.

Kinaevan smiled. "We are few, but there is a kingdom. There is our

Lord, the Lord of Life and Loss, but he is not..." he paused. "He gave us other gifts. Long memory, long life. But he is not spoken of."

"Why?" Vinet couldn't conceal her curiosity.

"Curious child," Kinaevan shook his head. "Not yet. The Lady..." he winced.

Young in the Sight, Vinet remembered. She wasn't just young. She was a bare beginner, with no knowledge of anything.

"We near the estate." Kinaevan glanced around. "I will rejoin my fellows, rather than intrude on Lady Pellalindra's hospitality. I will see you in the capital, my daughter."

Vinet smiled and blinked. She leaned forward to embrace her father again. "I will see you there," she promised.

Vinet thought she would have a chance to find Gwyn, sit down, and explain, but she got no such opportunity. The hunt seemed to have come to an abrupt conclusion, with many of the main hunters arriving back at the manor disappointed or elated with their prizes. They bustled about, getting in her way as she searched the hall for Gwyn.

Gwyn found her amidst the confusion and bustle. "Niara's playing with Percival and the MacTir children," she said. "Vinet, what in Mazda's name just happened?"

Vinet surveyed the room to ensure no one stood in earshot "He is my father," she said in a bare whisper.

Gwyn's eyes widened. "Your," she cut herself off and stared at Vinet. "You're sure?"

Vinet nodded. "Absolutely," she said. "I saw..."

"Lady Vinet!"

Vinet looked up and suppressed a curse. The nobles had returned.

Pellalindra made her way over, a smile on her face. "Coming to the feast? Where is the mysterious elf?"

"He went to rejoin his fellows," Vinet said, trying to keep her voice calm. "He did not want to intrude on your hospitality."

Pellalindra seemed disappointed. She looked around and drew nearer. "I need to ask. Is everything...alright? Nothing happened? Niara is safe?"

Vinet felt a surge of affection for Pellalindra at her concern for Niara. She shook her head. "Everything is fine. From what I gathered, Kinaevan arrived just in time."

Pellalindra's worried expression didn't fade. "These elves...have they been in Saemar long? We never see them in the kingdom and now this..."

"Kinaevan has not been here long, no. In fact, he was on his way to the capital. He is an ambassador for his people. They call themselves the Faithful."

"So, he came from the southwest?" Pellalindra frowned. "I do not see how else he would have come through Duskryn lands."

She had to deflect Pellalindra's concern about the southwest. She didn't want anyone to associate Kinaevan with the missing scout. "I am afraid he didn't reveal the location of his home," she said, keeping her voice light. "His origin is as mysterious as your Lord Auriel's."

Pellalindra gave a lighthearted groan. Unfortunately, she was not distracted. "He seemed quite interested in you. Do you think he already knew who you were? You and Niara?"

Vinet braced herself. "I don't know how he would," she said. "He only met Niara because she went wandering in the woods. Why do you ask?"

"He appears unannounced and uninvited on my lands, and then pays me no heed." Pellalindra sniffed. "Instead, he only speaks to you and ignores every noble there except for Lord Auriel. What am I to make of that?"

Tension flared in Vinet's shoulders. "Perhaps the manners of the elves are not like our own," she said, fighting to keep her voice level. "You will have your chance to ask him when he is officially introduced as ambassador."

Pellalindra gave her a long, penetrating look, and Vinet forced her expression to stay neutral. Pellalindra's affection for Niara might have softened Vinet's feelings, but she still remembered the manipulation. She was not about to hand Pellalindra anything that could be a key to her secrets.

"Are they connected to the assassins who came after you in any way?" Pellalindra's voice was hard.

Some of the tension eased out of Vinet's shoulders. "No," she said as steadily as she could. "The Faithful are enemies of that group. They name the ones who tried to assassinate me Unfaithful."

Pellalindra raised an eyebrow. "What else did he tell you about his people? Who are they faithful to?"

Vinet paused, choosing her words with care. What Kinaevan told her and what she told the Council would be two different things. "They are faithful to a figure they call the Lady," she said. "She is not a goddess. I am not certain what she is."

To her relief, Pellalindra let that rest. "And would you trust that elf?"

Vinet felt a flare of amusement. *She asks if I would trust my own father. My father, my flesh and blood.* "I would," she said. "That may be surprising, considering my recent encounter with elves, but…Lady Pellalindra, may I be frank?"

Pellalindra blinked. "Of course."

"We are going to need allies soon," Vinet said, keeping her voice low. "Against the Unfaithful, if no one else. We have no idea what their motivations are or why they tried to target me. They could have been working with Jyria and sought to cause chaos by eliminating a Saemarian noble. They may have some other plot entirely. Having one ally who has any idea of their motivations would be invaluable. And…" she hesitated. "If something from the southeast threatens…" The other reason they would need allies tingled in the back of her mind, sending a stabbing pain through her shoulder blades. Whatever Mount Halon was, it would do no good to mention that to Pellalindra until she had more information.

"I see your point." Pellalindra nodded slowly. "Very well, I will welcome him as Lady of the Council at the next council session. And perhaps explain to him proper Saemarian manners."

Vinet let out a laugh and relaxed. "If you do that, I would be prepared to receive a lecture on elven customs in return."

The look Pellalindra gave her was one of incredulous disbelief. Vinet shook her head. "But you're missing your own feast, Lady Pellalindra. Surely you have other guests besides me to attend to?"

"I do." A reluctant smile crossed Pellalindra's face. "We shall speak again, I am sure."

Vinet nodded as Pellalindra left. As soon as she was out of earshot, she gave a sigh of relief. She turned to Gwyn, who had stood silent at her side during the entire conversation.

"Congratulations," Gwyn said. "I almost believed you had no idea what Kinaevan wanted."

Vinet rolled her shoulders, wincing at the tension. "I hope no one else asks me about him. I had to think on my feet there."

"It won't be the last time you have to do that." Gwyn raised an eyebrow. "If your father has arrived, things are about to get very interesting."

8

FAMILY

V inet found no time to explain about her father to Gwyn on their journey back to Ninaeva. She knew Gwyn was concerned, but she couldn't do anything about it surrounded by their escort of guards. And Niara.

Niara, of course, was in high spirits, full of questions about elves, about the Lady, and about pointed ears. Vinet answered as best she could. Her heart tightened every time she saw Niara. Her daughter had come so close to danger without realizing it. And more danger would come, if she believed Kinaevan. Niara would share Vinet's gift.

Upon their arrival at Ninaeva late in the evening Vinet packed Niara off to bed and fled to her study. It only took a few minutes before Gwyn slipped into the intimate room. Vinet gave her a slight smile.

"I was expecting you," she said. "What's bothering you?"

To Vinet's surprise, Gwyn shifted uneasily. Instead of answering, her friend and bodyguard walked over to the small window and looked out. It didn't offer a very good view, being more of a slit for light than anything else.

Vinet stood up and followed her. "What's up?"

"I failed you, back there in Duskryn."

"How can you say that?" Vinet exclaimed. "You have never failed me, Gwyn." She placed her hand on her friend's shoulder. "Ever."

Gwyn shook her head. "I should have been closer to Niara. If I had, then the wolf would never have snuck up on her. If the elves hadn't been there..." she shuddered.

"Oh, Gwyn..." Vinet pulled Gwyn into an embrace. "You couldn't have done anything more," she said. "And Kinaevan was there. Everything worked out."

"But will he be there next time?" Gwyn pulled back to look into Vinet's eyes. "Niara's going to run off like that again. And what if I must stay near you? What if there are no other guards like there were at the hunt? I can't leave you undefended! But it would kill you to lose your daughter."

Vinet stilled. That word had been unspoken between them for years. They'd both deemed it too dangerous to talk about. That Gwyn used it now...

Gwyn pulled out of Vinet's arms. "I'm sorry," she said, her voice now a whisper. "I know we said..."

Vinet shook her head. "It doesn't matter," she said. "There's no one here but us."

"But there could be."

Vinet couldn't stand it, this doubt and fear in her friend. She grabbed Gwyn's hand, the one which bore the scar from years ago. She held her own next to it so that the matching scar was visible.

"Gwyn," she said, her voice sincere and soft. "You're my sister. We swore, remember? You could never fail me. You've saved me more times than I could count."

"You've saved me too," Gwyn was blinking rapidly. "If you hadn't..."

If Vinet hadn't. If she hadn't been an impetuous eight-year-old who wanted a friend, then who knew what would have happened to Gwyn, a ragged girl on the streets, whose mother worked in a brothel.

"You would have done fine for yourself," she said forcefully. "That's not the point."

"No, the point is I can't protect both you and Niara," Gwyn's eyes darkened. "And I have to protect both of you in order to protect the other."

"You can protect both of us." Vinet reached out and grabbed Gwyn's shoulders. "But you are right, you can't be in two places at once."

Gwyn looked up. "What are you getting at?"

"There needs to be two of you," Vinet said. "One for me, one for Niara."

Gwyn frowned. "You mean, get Niara a bodyguard of her own?"

Vinet nodded.

"Who?" Gwyn bit her lower lip.

Vinet released Gwyn and waved her hands. "You know all the guards in the keep. You know who's to be trusted, who has the potential, the patience. I leave that judgment in your hands."

Gwyn's expression was alarmed. "But, Vinet...I..."

"No buts," Vinet kept her voice firm, but softened it by reaching out to squeeze Gwyn's shoulder. "I trust you, sister."

Gwyn shook her head, but a small smile started to form. "Idealistic fool."

"Always," Vinet chuckled. "Now, who do you have in mind?"

Gwyn thought a moment. "Well, there is one guard," she said, measuring her words. "She accompanied us to Venia and on this last trip to Duskryn. She's got six younger siblings of her own, so she knows how to handle younglings."

"She sounds perfect," Vinet said. "Bring her with us the next time we go to the capital. That can be her trial period. If you're satisfied, we'll introduce her to Niara and make it official. What's her name?"

"Evalynna," Gwyn said. "I'll see to it."

Vinet kept a close eye on Evalynna during the next trip to the capital. Quiet, observant, and evidently fond of Niara, Evalynna appeared very different from Gwyn, but that wasn't a bad thing. Gwyn was strong, outspoken, and couldn't hide in a crowd if she wanted to. Everyone knew Vinet had a bodyguard, which helped keep her safe. Evalynna in contrast, was calm, with mousy brown hair and a soft, round face. Most people would think she was Niara's nursemaid rather than bodyguard, and therefore underestimate her. Vinet made a point to watch Gwyn and Evalynna practice, though. A deadly surprise waited for anyone who underestimated Evalynna.

As they rode through the streets of the capital, Vinet noticed with delight that one of the buildings on her street had been refurbished. The front garden now had a lovely array of trees and vines unlike any Vinet had seen, and the entire place looked graceful and pristine.

The usual rush of servants collecting luggage and greeting their lady waited for them as they arrived at Vinet's townhouse. Vinet sent Evalynna to help Niara settle in and went to her study. She needed to see if another message had arrived from the Council. She'd barely been there a quarter of an hour when a loud knock sounded on the front door. She looked up, curious as to who would be visiting so soon after her arrival. She didn't have long to wait.

Gwyn entered the study, trailed by the high priest, Ellil. He was dressed in his formal regalia, with the sun of Mazda emblazoned prominently on the front of his robes.

She rose in respect. "Your Radiance," she said. "What can I do for you?"

He bowed stiffly to her. "You can start with an explanation."

She blinked, entirely taken aback. An explanation of what? That she hadn't officially visited him at the temple? She had her own priest in Ninaeva for the necessary rituals, so it couldn't be that.

"Please, sit down." She gestured at the seat across from her desk. "What can I explain?"

"You can explain why there is now a gathering of heathens not one block away from you, with a man who purports to be an ambassador actually receiving an invitation to the palace, despite his heathen ways. Did you know those elves don't worship Mazda?" Ellil sat down, not relaxing into the soft cushioned chair at all.

So that new building is the Embassy of the Faithful! She suppressed a smile as she sat back down, pleased she could just walk down the street if she ever wanted to see her father.

First, however, she had to deal with Ellil. "I didn't think they would," she said, keeping her voice calm. "The worship of Mazda is not universal, after all. The light still needs to spread throughout so many lands." *There, that was diplomatic.*

Ellil's expression darkened. "The light spreads throughout all four corners of the world. It is only the heathens who do not accept it." He gestured at the light that shone through the large windows.

Well, apparently it wasn't diplomatic enough. "Why do you think I can explain their presence?"

"Because you relate to these elves in some way. I saw the one who claims to be an ambassador at the hunt. He would only talk to you. He failed to acknowledge anyone else's presence, even his host's. Why did he speak to you, above all others?"

"He spoke to Lord Auriel."

Ellil sniffed. "Lord Auriel, whom none of us have ever heard of before. And he's now steward. Very convenient."

Vinet frowned. Lord Auriel was an enigma, intimidating and far too perfect, certainly, but Ellil made it sound like he wasn't to be trusted. *Then again, why is he to be trusted? It's not every day a mysterious noble appears and announces he's to be the kingdom's steward.*

She shoved that doubt aside. "If the king has appointed Lord Auriel to be steward, then I see no reason to doubt his judgment," she stated. "After all, His Majesty appointed us to the Council, didn't he?"

Ellil frowned. Vinet wasn't entirely convinced by her own words, but to question a king always neared treason. And after what had happened to the last council, she wouldn't run that risk.

"Look, Your Radiance," she said instead, fiddling with one of the pens on her desk. "Think of the Faithful's presence here as an opportunity, like the expedition into the southern badlands. Some folk have never seen Mazda's light, despite it being in all four corners of the world. Now is your...our, chance to show them." She hoped he wouldn't notice her slip of the tongue.

Ellil's expression was still dark. He regarded her closely.

"You've heard of the cultists in the southeast, have you not? Or have you arrived too recently for that?"

Vinet's attention focused. "Cultists? No, I haven't heard."

Ellil shook his head. "I thought you'd be first to know, considering they bear the mark of the one who tried to assassinate you."

"The teardrop surrounded by thorns?" Vinet leaned forward, resting her elbows on her desk.

Ellil nodded. "Do you still trust these elves now? These cultists are ravaging the southern border where the elves came from. Something will have to be done."

Vinet swallowed. She could hear the truth of Ellil's words. "The Faithful are not the Unfaithful," she managed. "They are not the same."

"We will see." Ellil eyed her carefully. "You still fear Manyu's darkness, don't you, child? You pray for Mazda to protect you?"

Vinet felt an involuntary shiver down her spine. She'd had another nightmare that very night. She needed no reminders of Manyu, although it wasn't Mazda who protected her.

Something in her expression appeared to satisfy Ellil, at least. He nodded decisively. "Then you, at least, have not been corrupted by those heathens. Stay well away from them, my child." He rose. "Mazda guide you."

Vinet rose automatically as Ellil left the room. That had been an unexpected and unpleasant visit.

"Bloody priests."

She glanced up at Gwyn and smiled. Ellil had, of course, completely ignored Gwyn's presence against one of the bookcases.

Vinet paused, considering. "I think I shall take a walk down to the embassy. Do you want to accompany me?"

Gwyn smiled. "Always, Vinet."

It was only a short walk to the Faithful embassy from her townhouse. Now that she knew what it was, it appeared like the image of an elven dwelling of legend, though that could have been just her imagination.

An older elf woman sat at a desk just inside. When Vinet gave her name, she waved her straight into an office, asking Gwyn to wait outside. Vinet looked at Gwyn for approval before continuing. Gwyn shrugged. If they couldn't trust the Faithful, then they were in far more trouble than she alone could deal with.

In contrast to the elegance of the outside, the office was sparse. No chairs, desks, or tapestries, or any other kinds of decorations, only a few cushions on the floor, set in a circle around a curious flower. Vinet assumed it was a flower, at least. It had alternating red and yellow petals, and the center formed of seeds, shaped like an amber eye.

Kinaevan sat across from the flower. He didn't acknowledge her entrance as he stared at the flower, his eyes slightly glazed.

Vinet hesitated. She had just been waved in. What if the elf woman outside hadn't known Kinaevan was busy? Kinaevan showed no signs of moving. She hesitated a moment longer, then finally whispered, "Father?"

The air rushed quietly, and the light in the room brightened. Kinaevan looked up from the flower. His face was tired, but he greeted her with joy. "Welcome, welcome, my daughter!" He stood up in a fluid motion and moved to embrace her.

Vinet closed her eyes and savored the feeling of comfort and security she had never known.

She pulled back. "It is good to see you, Father," she said. "I hope I'm not interrupting. Were you using the Sight?"

He smiled, though it seemed weak. "Yes, though not of my own desire." A shudder ran through him, as if he were cold. Vinet frowned. Although Manyu's Rise was well on its way, heat still lingered.

"Sometimes the duties of an Eye are demanding. I would not have it any other way, however."

Vinet sobered. "Your visions are not always voluntary, then?" If they weren't, even for him, that would explain so much.

Kinaevan didn't answer. He sat down on a cushion and patted another, gesturing her to sit next to him. The flower seemed to move toward him, attracted to him like a sunflower to the sun. "Are your visions always voluntary, daughter?"

She shook her head slowly as she sat down next to him. "No," she said. "I can call them, sometimes. But they're unpredictable and rarely clear. And I can never predict the dreams." She shuddered.

His eyes sharpened, and he leaned in and snatched her hand. "You have visions in dreams? How many? How often?"

Vinet jerked. She hadn't been expecting his intensity. "I don't always remember them," she said. "They're...they're not very pleasant." *He has to know. Maybe he could help.* "They started recently. After I had a bit of an... accident."

"The Labyrinth?"

Vinet met his eyes and whispered, "So you were there." He had been there. He had saved her.

"That was not pleasant, but the Lady assisted me. Please tell me what happened to you in there. The Sight in that place is very," he paused, "unfamiliar."

She looked down as the words came pouring out of her. She hadn't been able to tell anyone except Gwyn, who could only sympathize.

"I was trying to speak with a lady who'd given me a magical book. I wanted some information. I made a mistake and ended up in the labyrinth. There were mirrors, with different reflections of myself. And..." she swallowed. "There was a skull surrounded by eyes. It chased me." She closed her eyes. Those simple words did nothing to convey the horror she had felt. "That's when I heard your voice. You guided me through the mirror." She opened her eyes again and took a deep breath. Out of the corner of her eye, the flower seemed to draw her gaze. "The lady I spoke to, AeresThonEsia, said it was a mark of Manyu. And that I had been marked."

As her gaze strayed to the flower, the room went dark in a flash. *No! Not now!* She didn't want another vision!

Deep woods. No light anywhere. Dark-barked trees barely indistinguishable from each other. The air was close, oppressing, old.

"Daughter!" The voice was sharp, a command. "Lady, no. She is not..." Vinet struggled, but the voice faded. She looked around, shuddering at the sight. No, it wasn't her. The woods were shuddering! She heard a distant yelling. Elven? It sounded familiar, so familiar...

With a sudden jolt, she found herself in Kinaevan's office again. The flower focused on Kinaevan, as if it eyed him. He stared back. The seeds had changed color. Instead of the warm amber, they were now black with a red center. The petals seemed to be dancing.

Kinaevan was shivering and sweating as he regarded the flower. Vinet reached out hesitantly to touch his hand, almost in a panic. "Father?" she whispered. She didn't dare look at the flower again.

The room darkened, and for a moment Vinet thought she was still in the vision. Dark trees emerged from the walls, choking the light and air. Then Kinaevan's hand shot forward and covered the flower. Light flashed sharply, and a smell, almost like a burn.

The room calmed. As Kinaevan removed his hand from the flower, Vinet saw it was now closed. No eye stared at them anymore.

She watched as her father took a few deep breaths. His eyes, which had been so focused and intent, returned to normal. He still had his hand tightly closed.

She stared, not knowing what to do. "Is everything all right?"

"It is now." Kinaevan stood up in a fluid motion. "Might we leave this place, take a walk in the city?"

Vinet nodded and got to her feet as well. They passed Gwyn on their way out. Kinaevan said nothing as she fell into step behind them.

Vinet remained silent for a time. What had just happened? It had felt like another vision, but her father had been far too worried for it to have just been that. She glanced at him. He was avoiding every tree, every blade of grass, which took them away from the wealthier areas of the city, where gardens and yards adorned every townhouse, to the poorer areas, where smallfolk thronged among the increasingly narrower streets. They drew some odd glances, especially as Kinaevan kept them strictly in the center of the dusty lane.

Changing the subject would be better for now, she decided. "Ambassador? Can I ask you something?"

Kinaevan smiled at her. "Of course, Lady Vinet."

"It's about the Unfaithful." She smiled back, slightly reassured. "Have you heard of the cultists in the southeast?"

Kinaevan's brow furrowed. "I have heard of no cultists, but the Faithful have been busy deterring the threat from Mount Halon. What about these concerns you?"

Vinet took a breath. "The cultists are using the same mark as the Unfaithful. The teardrop surrounded by thorns."

Kinaevan sighed and lowered his eyes to the cobblestones on the path, wincing as he saw a stubborn dandelion and stepping around it. "Then the disease has spread further than we thought. It was from the corruption of Mount Halon that our own people became the Unfaithful. It seems this has now happened to your own. For that I am sorry."

He still seemed distracted, but Vinet wanted to ask him about what had happened. She needed that information. "Where is Mount Halon? How did this corruption start?"

They dodged around two dogs running down the street, followed by a yelling man. "Mount Halon is situated, in your knowledge, to the southeast of the most southern Tigrian border. It is a dark place, a focus point. From there the Corruption started, akin to a burden we Faithful bore before. This time, however, it is less strong, and we are far more prepared than we were," Kinaevan said.

"We've had our warning signs," she said. "It is where we saw the…the symbol I saw in the Labyrinth." She did not want to elaborate anymore on that. She found herself returning to the occurrence within the embassy. "What just happened? Am I…did this mark…"

"The Lady called you." Kinaevan's voice was flat. They turned into an alley, dark and overhung by the neighboring buildings, and he stopped walking and turned to face her. "But it is far too soon."

Vinet stopped as well. "I…" *The Lady called me? What did that even mean?* "How did she call me? And why is it too soon? It seemed," she paused, searching for words. "Dangerous yes, but yet there was something… familiar."

Kinaevan shook his head. "The flower. It is a focus. My focus, but it seems you can use it as well. What do you generally use?"

Vinet blinked. *A focus?* "A focus for the Sight?" she ventured.

Kinaevan nodded. "You must have something to ground yourself. The danger otherwise is far too great."

She shivered. She did not need more danger. "There is a book," she said. "The Lady I met in the center of the Labyrinth gave it to me. She called it The Book of Truths."

Her father's eyes widened. "She gave it to you? Then continue using it. But it is not the only thing which can focus. I use flowers, trees. Perhaps you can one day as well." He sighed. "You cannot control the Sight. Not yet. The Lady is not herself of late, more impatient. The Trial would have taken you entire, and I could not allow that to happen." He hesitated, then dropped his voice to a whisper, leaning forward despite the alley being to all appearances, deserted. "Not when you have just been returned to me, not before Niara knows her true heritage from her true mother."

She winced. "You do not approve that I kept it secret."

"No." Her father took hold of her shoulders. His expression was sincere, but there was no harshness. "I know your reasons, but I do not have to agree with them. The sooner she knows, the better for her."

She met his gaze, then extracted herself from his grasp. She wanted to tell Niara, but how could she justify that? "If I tell her about me, she would learn about you. What happens if, in her childish enthusiasm, she lets slip our relationship?" She felt her voice break, and she looked around, ensuring that they were still alone. "I want to tell her. She is the light of my life. But there is more than my love for my daughter resting on this." Her future, Niara's future, the future of Ninaeva.

"What is greater than love for a daughter?" His eyes met hers, still steady.

Vinet's breath caught in her throat at the implied sentiment. She looked down, eyes catching a glimpse of light on some weeds growing in the corner of the alley. "I will think on it," she promised.

"That is all I ask. I know your burdens are great." He turned away. As he did so, she noticed a harsh eye scar scorched into his right hand.

She grabbed it. "Are you alright?" she demanded.

He removed her hand. "I will survive. I must."

Vinet regarded him for a moment. He seemed so strong, and yet, at the same time, so old and full of cares. She couldn't stand to think of him bearing this alone.

"Tell me if I can do anything to help," she whispered. "I know I have duties, but yours do not seem to be any lighter. I can help."

"Forgive me." Kinaevan turned back to her, opening his hand. The scorch was indeed an eye, but it had been the flower which had burned him. The individual marks were the seeds.

Vinet swallowed, trying to throttle her guilt. If she had not been caught by the flower, he would never have had to interfere and burn himself.

"Make yourself strong. Practice the Sight, but be gentle in your beginning. Find a focus, like your book. Were I the one who had trained you, I would have you concentrate on the young trees, the maple and yew would have been good to you."

The book. She shuddered. While powerful, it was too unpredictable for her. She would try the trees, as her father suggested. "There is nothing to forgive. I will practice. Will you...be careful?" She swallowed, aware of the hypocrisy of her statement. "The path you walk does not seem easy. I do not want to lose you."

He smiled and patted her arm. "I've walked this path since your birth and have prepared for it since my own. The Sight will not take me until the Lady wills it."

Vinet wanted to ask him more questions, but they were interrupted by a group of children barreling down the alley, nearly running them over in their enthusiastic chase. Kinaevan started walking out of the alley, heading back in the direction of the embassy, and Vinet and Gwyn followed in silence. The press of people prevented any further private conversation, especially the closer they got to the wealthier districts, where the crowds thinned and Kinaevan's elven form was more visible.

Kinaevan paused when they came in sight of the embassy. "I hope to speak to you again soon, Lady Vinet." He bowed, hands clasped in front of him.

"Likewise, Ambassador," Vinet said automatically. Kinaevan did not give her the chance to do anything else before he turned and strode into the elegant building.

Vinet stared after him for a time. Gwyn stepped up next to her, looking after Kinaevan as well.

"Well, that was interesting," she said.

Vinet shook herself. "Yes, it was." She looked at Gwyn. "Well, back home, I suppose. We have work to do."

Gwyn laughed. "As always. What's on the agenda for today?"

Vinet forced a smile, her heart tight. "Well, we need to introduce Niara to her new bodyguard." She took a deep breath, making a split-second decision. She had wanted to do this for so long, and with her father pushing... "And she needs to learn the truth about her mother."

"Niara, this is your new bodyguard."

Niara looked at Evalynna. Niara transferred her gaze to Vinet. "Is this because I ran away at the hunt?" she asked, her voice slightly subdued.

"No. Well, a bit," Vinet suppressed a smile. "But you're not in trouble, dearest. Your adventure just made me realize you're old enough to need one now."

"I'm old enough?" Niara's eyes widened.

117

Vinet couldn't suppress a laugh this time as she leaned down to lift Niara into her arms. "Yes, you little minx. If you're going to go running off by yourself, you need someone to watch over you." She winked at her daughter. "After all, that's why I have Gwyn."

"Oh!" Niara seemed to find that a perfectly acceptable comparison. She looked at Evalynna. "So, you're my Gwyn?"

Evalynna gave a slight bow. "If you like, yes, though my name is Evalynna."

"Evalynna," Niara beamed. "I'm Niara. I like you!"

Evalynna chuckled. "Well, I like you too."

Vinet sighed in relief. "Evalynna, Gwyn will show you to your new quarters. She'll give you a detailed description of your duties, as well."

Evalynna straightened and saluted her. "Of course, Lady Vinet. Thank you for trusting me with this."

Vinet waved a dismissal and Evalynna left the room, leaving her alone with Niara.

She walked over to the chair next to the fire and sat Niara down on her lap. "So, you like Evalynna?" she asked.

Niara nodded happily. "Will she play with me?" she asked.

"I should think so." Vinet shook her head. "Evalynna has six younger siblings."

Niara shifted in her lap. "Will I ever have siblings?"

Vinet bit her lip. "Maybe someday," she stroked her hair. *Why was this so difficult? Why couldn't she just come right out and tell Niara she was her mother?* "Would you like to hear a story?" She asked.

"A story! I love stories!" Niara squirmed around in her lap to look eagerly up at Vinet.

She chuckled at Niara's enthusiasm. "Once, not too long ago, there was a young lady who lived at Ilhelm Castle. She was a very free-spirited young woman, who loved to read, to laugh, and to dance. Does that sound familiar?"

Niara nodded. "Those are things I like to do!"

Vinet felt her heart tighten. "Well, one day, this young woman met a very charming minstrel. They danced together, he made her laugh, and he told her stories about lands far away she'd never seen. He told stories of dragons and elves and of magic. They enjoyed each other's company a great deal, but he was a minstrel, and left Ilhelm after only a week."

Niara shifted again. "Why'd he leave?"

Vinet stared into the fire, caught in memory. "Because he loved traveling as much as the lady did, but he didn't have the responsibilities which bound her to Ninaeva. They both knew this would happen and spoke no promises to each other. The lady was content to take up her duties in Ninaeva, and he would continue his wandering."

It had been like that too, at first. Until she had found out the price of that week of pleasure.

Niara smiled, humming before saying. "I'm going to wander too someday."

Oh, my darling. "I'm sure you will." Vinet stroked Niara's hair. "That may have been the end of the story, except for one little thing. The time spent with the minstrel had an unforeseen effect. The lady realized she was carrying a child."

Niara sat up straighter. "This is about Mama!" she exclaimed. "That's me!"

Vinet laughed, though every muscle of her body was tense. "Yes, you little minx, you. Now, the lady did not know what to do about this at first. She wasn't married, you see. The lords of Saemar tend to judge those who have children without a husband rather harshly."

Niara screwed up her face, and Vinet had to laugh again. She'd had to explain long ago to Niara what bastard meant. "Yes, we both know there's no shame in it, but that doesn't change what people think. The young lady was scared, so she talked to her sister and came up with a solution."

"Mama talked to you?"

Vinet forced herself to smile. "Her sister was a religious sort and had always wanted to join the Sisters of Mazda. Many people would consider the Sisters the only place suitable for a woman who transgressed the way she had, so the sisters both went to the convent. The lady's sister stayed to follow her calling, and the lady came back to Ilhelm, pretending to the world she brought her niece home with her. But instead, that child was her daughter, and she loved her with all of her heart."

At Vinet's last words, Niara turned to stare at her. Her mouth dropped open, and her bright green eyes, so exactly like Vinet's own, were wide. Vinet didn't dare move. She didn't dare hope.

"You...you're my mother?" Niara demanded.

Vinet nodded. "Yes, dearest, I am."

"But...you told me you were my aunt! That my mother was your sister who went to the convent!" The confused accusation in Niara's tone was like a dagger through Vinet's heart.

She leaned down to embrace Niara tightly. To her relief, Niara didn't squirm away. "I'm sorry," she said, her voice muffled in Niara's shoulder. "I was scared and foolish, and I should have told you the truth a long time ago. Can you forgive me?"

She pulled back enough to look at Niara. Niara met her eyes for a moment, then tears started welling up.

Oh no, oh no, oh no. She'd ruined it. Her father had been right. She should have told Niara long ago. She should never have kept it a secret. "Niara, I'm so sorry."

Niara shook her head vehemently. "You're my mother!" she exclaimed, throwing her arms around Vinet's neck.

Vinet froze, then tightened her arms around her daughter. "Yes, yes I am."

They sat that way for a long while. Niara's tears stopped, and she relaxed into Vinet's lap again. "Is it still a secret?"

Vinet hesitated. *Oh, my dear daughter. Wise beyond your years.* She couldn't hurt Niara anymore. "No one else knows," she finally said. "Well, except my sister and your Aunt Gwyn. No one else can know yet, dearest. Do you understand?"

Her daughter looked thoughtful. "It's because of the Lady thing, right? Repu-reputation?" Niara stumbled over the difficult word.

Vinet's heart contracted at the ease with which Niara accepted the necessity to lie. *I will find a way to acknowledge her to the world. By Mazda, this I swear.*

"Yes. But no matter what other people believe, you are my daughter, and I will always love and protect you." She felt a fierce wave of protectiveness.

"Of course, Au—Mother." She smiled sheepishly. "Can I call you that?"

Vinet pulled her close again, blinking back tears. "Of course, you can, my daughter," she whispered in Niara's ear. "Of course."

"Mama," Niara snuggled into Vinet's lap and chest, arms wrapped around her mother.

Vinet hesitated. "There's more," she said. "But this part really is a secret."

Niara sat up again. "More?"

Vinet took a deep breath. "You liked Kinaevan, right?"

Niara wrinkled her brow and nodded, confused.

"Well, he's my father. Your grandfather."

Vinet couldn't conceal a smile at Niara's expression of delight.

"An elf?" Her daughter exclaimed. "We're descended from elves? Is that why he said I should have pointed ears?"

Vinet laughed. "Yes, it is. Though, dearest, I think you will have more pointed ears than I do," she ran a hand through Niara's hair, just brushing her ears. "You can't see it, not yet, but you can definitely feel it."

Niara wriggled proudly. "I'm an elf!" she proclaimed.

"Part elf," Vinet corrected. "There's still some human in you, little one."

Niara rolled her eyes. "And my father?" she asked.

Vinet stilled. "I don't know much more than I told you," she said. "His name was Jaim. He was a minstrel who came to Ilhelm for Papsukkal. You remember Papsukkal?"

Niara drew up. "Of course! All the fun! All the dancing, and the world upside down!"

Vinet laughed again. "Yes, indeed. The day outside of time. And he certainly seemed that way to me." She sighed. "I've suspected he may have had elven blood as well. So, you get it from both sides, dearest."

"I like elves," Niara said, pride in her face.

Vinet shook her head but smiled. "I need to tell you one more thing," she said. "You're going to have a gift. It's a gift of our heritage."

"A gift? Like what? A horse? Can I have a horse?"

"Ask Gwyn when she thinks you're ready," Vinet said automatically to the familiar question. "No, not a gift like that. This one is a gift of magic."

Niara's eyes widened again. "Magic?"

"Yes," Vinet said. "I see things, occasionally. Visions of different places You will too."

"Woah!" Niara was absolutely enthralled. Vinet's heart tightened. She couldn't ruin Niara's enthusiasm. Not yet. She couldn't let her know about the pain and terror of some of the visions.

"Promise me you'll let me know as soon as you start having them," Vinet commanded.

Niara stared at Vinet. "I promise, Mama."

Vinet smiled. "And dearest, no one can know about Kinaevan being my father, alright? Can you keep that a secret?"

Niara nodded solemnly.

Vinet took a deep breath. She hoped she'd made the right choice. But only time would tell.

9

———

NEW ACQUAINTANCES

Vinet resisted the urge to hold her head in her hands. The shouting had not ceased since she entered the council chamber.

"You had us call the men back when your precious Lord Auriel called it a wild goose chase!" Conn shouted. "You have only yourself to blame for his disappearance!"

Pellalindra sat firm. "There had been no progress. None. You were the one who told me of Torainn's reaction to that! Panic, absolute panic, from a man entrusted to lead our entire army."

"Torainn disappeared because we showed no trust in him! Because we ignored his warnings about Darkmane!" Conn threw up his hands, his thick cloak catching on some of the papers on the table and sending them to the floor.

"Torainn was a foolish idiot if he went into the north alone," Dannan snapped. "His fears about the revenant finally got the better of him."

Kamian raised a glass of wine to his lips. "Aren't we supposed to be nominating his replacement rather than arguing about his disappearance?"

Conn, Dannan, and Pellalindra paid no attention to Kamian, who merely turned to Vinet and smirked. Vinet shook her head and looked away, examining the intricate wood carvings on the wall instead of engaging in the conversation. There were dragons here too, with eyes of cherry wood that gleamed in the sunlight.

"Lord Artosbern II said Torainn hasn't been seen!" Conn slammed his fists on the polished table surface.

"As if the young lord is paying attention to anything since his father's death," Dannan said scathingly. "Leave it, Conn. Torainn is either an idiot or a deserter."

"He is not!" Conn whirled, fist raised as if to strike Dannan.

"Is this a bad time?"

Vinet glanced up, startled at the new voice. To her relief, Conn stopped mid-shout, giving everyone a moment of blessed quiet.

The voice belonged to an older gentleman, with kind, soft eyes, and silver-white hair. He stood straight as a post and wore the uniform of the Regulars.

"Pardon my tardiness," he said. "General Alexander Priam Lokris-Phythia. I'm to join the Council. Did Lord Auriel not inform you of this?"

Vinet saw the confused glances exchanged around the room. She had not been told of a new member of the Council and felt the others were no better informed.

Conn's eyes widened. "General Alexander?" he asked, his voice tinged with awe. "I've heard of your exploits in the Tigrian war, sir. I am honored to make your acquaintance."

Alexander smiled. "You must be Lord Conn. Likewise," he looked around. "I presume this discussion involves choosing Torainn's replacement?"

Vinet hid a smile as Kamian snorted. "We hadn't gotten to that yet."

"I see. Well, in that case, allow me to nominate my former colleague, General Lairan. A fine old fellow, who was honored for exemplary service in the last war."

As the discussion began again, Vinet regarded Alexander. He had taken command of the volatile situation of the council chamber as easily as commanding troops. She would not have expected such a diplomatic approach from a General.

Ellil, too, regarded Alexander, but with something bordering on dislike. *Curious*, Vinet thought. She'd heard nothing bad of any of their generals.

"General Lairan seems like a fine choice," Pellalindra said. "Anyone have any objections?"

Vinet shook her head. To be truthful, she had no interest in who their next Lord General was. She was more curious why Torainn had disappeared.

"So, what's the next order of business, then?" Alexander asked, smiling.

Pellalindra cleared her throat. "There is the matter of cultists appearing in the southeast. There has been an influx of refugees to the capital because of it."

"Not just refugees," Dannan growled. "Tigrians. Fleeing from something over the border."

Vinet sat very still. Mount Halon. It had to be. Kinaevan had been right.

"We don't want Tigrians infiltrating Saemar," Conn said. "Who knows what kind of spies will slip across with the refugees?"

Vinet frowned. "What kind of information are those spies going to learn?" she asked. "If people are fleeing something, then offering them shelter seems the best thing to do. Maybe we'll impress the Tigrians with our generosity. They worship Mazda's Light as well as we do, don't they, Your Radiance?"

Ellil met her eyes. "They do."

"Then as Mazdians, we owe it to them to provide shelter, and not punish and harass them," Vinet argued. She looked around the chamber, daring anyone to disagree with her.

Dannan blinked. "You'd leave the border unguarded, then?"

Vinet restrained herself from rolling her eyes. "No. We need to find out what they're fleeing from and guard against it; a goal which can be achieved without barring refugees."

"We need to deal with the cultists," Ellil broke in. His eyes were dark. "Let me lead a missionary group to the border. We will bring them back to Mazda's Light."

Vinet caught her breath, trying to find the words to express how inordinately a bad idea that was. Something evil approached from the southeast, something the elves feared enough to seek an alliance with Saemar. Any priests would be in grave danger.

"Absolutely not," Alexander said. "We will not place our high priest in such danger."

Ellil's eyes sharpened. "As high priest of Mazda..."

"Our priority should be finding Torainn!" Conn exclaimed. "He's the one who can deal with this mess of a border situation and bring Darkmane to heel!"

"You have a great deal of trust in our vanished Lord General. Who says General Lairan will not be equally competent?" Pellalindra snapped.

"You drove him away!" Conn started to stand up.

"Enough!" Alexander commanded.

Vinet blinked at the strength. She regarded him with respect. Perhaps having a military man on the Council would not be such a bad thing.

"Blame will get us nowhere," Alexander said in a quieter tone. "That is the first lesson on campaign. Deal with what you must, not whose fault it is you have to do it. Right now, we have to decide what to do with the border in the southeast."

"General Alexander is right," Vinet mimicked the general's calm tone. "Blame is pointless. We need information about the southeast, and to that end I visited the Faithful ambassador earlier."

Every eye turned to her. Ellil glared at her, and Pellalindra raised an eyebrow.

"You went to visit the elven ambassador?" Pellalindra's voice was curious.

Vinet ignored the curiosity and nodded. "The Faithful are fighting a war south of Tigri right now, with something they call Mount Halon. He believes the cultists are part of the corruption which Mount Halon spreads."

If she'd wanted to silence the council chamber, she'd succeeded. She squared her shoulders, waiting for someone to demand why she hadn't shared this information sooner.

"The Faithful ambassador told you this? What is his name?" Alexander asked.

Vinet looked at the general. "Kinaevan Sindarilae," she said, keeping her voice level.

"How are we supposed to trust him?" Dannan demanded. "He could be saying this to fool us, to draw us into a war which has nothing to do with us."

She shrugged, struggling to keep any anger from showing on her face. "I would suggest you talk to him yourself if you have doubts," she said. "For my part, I am convinced. We need to send scouts down there, armed with the knowledge of Mount Halon, and find out more information."

"My scout died down there," Pellalindra put in softly.

Vinet turned to her and nodded. "Because of a lack of information," she said. "We need more."

"I agree," Alexander said. "To the smallfolk, wars are won by heroes. In reality, they are won with information."

"And what about Torainn?" Conn demanded.

Dannan glared at Conn. "Whatever your feelings about us driving him away, Torainn abandoned his post," he said. "He is absent without leave. Your hero may not be such a hero."

Conn's face darkened, and Alexander held up a hand. "I do not believe Torainn is the sort of man to turn traitor," he said. "Nonetheless, Lord Dannan has a point. Torainn was not thinking clearly when he disappeared. Short of following him, there is nothing we can do. And we need our military resources devoted to the southeast."

Conn glared but subsided at Alexander's words. Vinet let out a breath. Having someone on the Council who Conn respected would be a good thing too.

"Well, is that decided then? Good. I shall let the steward and General Lairan know, and they can get to work immediately." Alexander pushed himself up from the table. "Good day, everyone. It will be a pleasure working with you."

Pellalindra stared after Alexander, seemingly shocked by his dismissal. That was her duty, as Lady of the Council.

Vinet hid a smile. If Pellalindra wasn't careful, she would have a rival for her seat next year.

"My lady."

Startled by Gwyn's formal tone, Vinet looked up from her book immediately and set it on the bench beside her. Gwyn only called her that when there was someone around who would object to her bodyguard simply calling her Vinet. She hadn't expected to hear it in her townhouse garden.

"Yes, Gwyn?"

Gwyn met her eyes with a smile. Vinet relaxed. "There's someone here I think you'd like to meet," Gwyn said. "I met him on the street earlier today and suggested he come here. He's a refugee from the south."

Vinet furrowed her brow. "A refugee? Not that I'd object to taking him in, but why would you...?"

Gwyn shook her head, cutting Vinet off. "Talk to him. You'll see why."

Vinet nodded and sat back in her chair. *What would have Gwyn acting so mysterious?*

Gwyn disappeared, and Vinet took a moment to adjust her shawl. Although deep into Manyu's Rise, warmth still lingered outside, and she wanted to savor the sunlight which filtered through the red and orange leaves of the ash tree above her before the snows came.

Gwyn stepped back into the garden, and Vinet's eyebrows rose as she saw the man following her. She didn't need any more elaboration as to why Gwyn thought she should talk to him.

He wore what had once been scholar's robes, simple and brown, and worn and stained from travel. His straggly black hair fell past his ears, implying he hadn't been concerned about appearances for a long time. What stood out more than anything, however, was his jet-black skin. Vinet had never met a man like him before. She'd seen multiple shades of brown on her travels, particularly in Hillsdale and Jyria, where the merchants traveled on the water, but never pure black. It made his white pupils stand out even more, and his brown eyes observed everyone and everything about him.

Vinet stood up as he approached, trying not to let her astonishment show.

He bowed as he approached her. "Nazir et-Alim, at your service, Lady Vinet."

Nazir et-Alim. A name unlike she'd ever heard before! She shot Gwyn a look of gratitude.

Gwyn rolled her eyes from her duty station. Vinet turned her attention back to Nazir.

"I understand you met Gwyn earlier today," she said. "And she told you I might be of assistance to you?"

Nazir nodded. "I am a refugee, I fear. Although I had no home to flee from, so I am better off than some. I seek a place where I can rest a while before setting off on the road again."

Vinet raised an eyebrow. *No home?* "And what is it you do?" she asked.

Nazir shrugged, his expression sheepish. "I am a wanderer. A collector. I listen to people's stories, and I write them down and tell them as I travel."

Vinet's eyes widened. "You're a collector of stories? A researcher?" She caught Gwyn's stifled chuckle. She ignored it.

Nazir's expression lightened at her enthusiasm. "Indeed, Lady Vinet. I have been traveling for over ten years now."

Ten years of stories! "And do you have any of those collections still with you? They were not lost when you were forced to flee?" She would offer him shelter regardless, but if she could see those collections.

The corners of Nazir's lips twitched. "I do. They were the only things I saved, in fact."

"He has an entire donkey packed full of books," Gwyn broke in.

Vinet felt her eyes light up. "Nazir, you will be most welcome in Ninaeva," she offered. "I insist you travel back with us and stay at Ninaeva as long as you like. There will only be one cost." She smiled, trying to make it plain the price was not a hefty one.

Nazir raised a smooth eyebrow. "Indeed?"

Her smile widened. "You have to tell me these stories you've collected," she said. "I won't ask you to allow my scribes to copy them, but if you would, I would be immensely grateful. I am always eager for new stories, histories, and simple descriptions of other lands and places!"

Nazir inclined his head, but seemed slightly sober. "I thank you for your invitation, Lady Vinet." He hesitated. "There is something you should know before I accept it, however."

Vinet saw Gwyn go on alert. There was an intensity to the seriousness in her guest's face.

He took a breath. "There are rumors which follow me. I would hate for your house to fall under scrutiny because you took me in."

She frowned. "What kind of rumors?" she asked.

"That I am a child of demons." Nazir watched her for a moment before continuing. "You have been very kind, not immediately showering me with questions, but a lady of your reputation has to be curious about my strange appearance."

She flushed. *A lady of her reputation? What did that mean?*

"I have never seen a man like you before," she temporized.

"Nor have I," Nazir answered.

She blinked in surprise. "Not even your parents?" she ventured.

He shook his head. "My mother was as pale as you."

Unspoken, Vinet knew the rest. He didn't know his father, which left him unable to answer the accusations of demon heritage. Her spine stiffened. She hadn't known her true father for years. She was not about to turn someone away just because he couldn't name his father.

"You are still welcome in Ninaeva," she said, her voice sincere.

Nazir's eyes widened, and Vinet sensed she had surprised him. "Truly? My...my heritage does not worry you?".

Vinet laughed. "A true demon would not have told me of the rumors," she pointed out. "I think I can trust you."

Her eyes flickered toward Gwyn as she said that. Despite her words, she wouldn't accept a man whom Gwyn disapproved of. Gwyn's eyes rolled, but she was smiling. With more confidence, Vinet turned her smile back to Nazir.

"I'll have a servant bring your things to a guestroom," she said. "And send someone off for any essentials you require. After you refresh yourself, I would love to speak more with you."

He bowed again. "You have my most sincere thanks, Lady Vinet," he said.

She waved her hand to summon the page who waited in the doorway for anything she needed. "Please show Nazir to one of the guestrooms," she said once he arrived. "And let him give you a list of things he requires, including some spare robes."

Nazir glanced down sheepishly.

The servant bowed, his face expressionless. "Of course, my lady."

Vinet smiled as she watched Nazir walk away. His presence would make Manyu's Time in Ninaeva fascinating instead of cold and oppressive.

She turned as Gwyn coughed. "What?" she asked.

Gwyn raised an eyebrow. "Stop looking at him like that."

"Like what?" she demanded.

"Like you want to see if his lips taste differently than Jaim's," Gwyn stated.

Vinet stared at her friend in shock. Neither of them had mentioned Niara's father's name for years. "I do not!"

Gwyn snorted, and Vinet felt her cheeks flush. Nazir was handsome. She couldn't deny that.

"I do not," she said again, aware she couldn't convince Gwyn. "I just want to hear his stories. He's traveled for over ten years, Gwyn! He's got to have stories of all kinds of places. He'll be able to help entertain Niara."

Gwyn looked skeptical but didn't say anything else.

Vinet shook her head. Gwyn was being overly cautious, she decided. There was no danger of her taking Nazir as a lover, not when she had her gift to train, council matters to consider, and Niara to look out for.

10

MANYU'S TIME IN NINAEVA

The snow fell early that Manyu's Time. Blanketed by a thick layer, Ilhelm Castle looked like something out of a fairy tale legend. Vinet loved the sight of Ilhelm in the snow. It reminded her of her childhood.

"Niara? Do you want to go out and play in the snow?" Vinet asked as they rose from breakfast.

Breakfast at Ilhelm was a far more casual affair than at any other noble house. Pellalindra would have shuddered to see the eclectic gathering around the table most days. But Vinet couldn't see any point in excluding those she wanted to talk to simply based on their rank. Scholars of all sorts graced her table throughout the year, as well as the occasional traveler or servant who had a story to share. Today, however, only she, Niara, Gwyn, and Nazir enjoyed the meal. Nazir had been regaling them with a story of a long-lost son fighting to regain his kingdom.

Niara shifted in her chair and shook her head. Vinet glanced at her, startled. Niara never refused an offer to play in the snow.

"Dear? Is everything alright?" she asked.

"I'm fine," Niara's voice was muffled as she looked down at the table. "I'm fine!" With that, she rose and fled from the room.

Vinet stared after her, aghast. What was wrong? Her daughter never did that!

She started to rise and follow her, but Gwyn raised a hand to stop her. "You stay here," she told Vinet. "I'll follow her, make sure she doesn't get into trouble."

"But…" Vinet gazed after Niara.

"She's upset," Gwyn said. "I'll get her to talk. She'll come to you later."

Nazir cleared his throat. "Was it something I said?" he asked.

Vinet glanced at him, startled. "No, I…" she stopped. The story. The long-lost son, fighting to be recognized by his father. She sighed and placed her elbows on the table, holding her head in her hands.

"My…niece has had some troubling news recently," she said. "It will take her some time to get used to it."

Nazir nodded, seeming to understand perfectly. "She is a charming child, and intelligent as well. I am sure she will understand quickly."

A part of Vinet flushed in pride for the praise of Niara, but another part of her worried. Had Kinaevan been right? Had she damaged her relationship with her daughter by keeping their relationship a secret?

"Come, do not let her distress you too much," Nazir urged. "Gwyn has said she will take care of her, and she seems more than capable. Niara trusts her, as well, for she also calls her Aunt Gwyn, if I'm not mistaken?"

A small smile crept over Vinet's lips in spite of herself as she nodded.

"There. If Gwyn says all will be well, then all will be well. Do not distress yourself. You worry too much as it is."

Vinet blinked. What did Nazir mean by that?

"You do not sleep well," Nazir said, voice calm. "Forgive me, but I can tell."

She flushed, embarrassed her thoughts had been so easy to read. Carefully, she lifted her cup of tea, trying to keep her hands from shaking. She'd had another nightmare. She hadn't been able to sleep for hours.

"Well, since Gwyn has said Niara will talk to you later, shall I entertain you with another story until then?"

Vinet smiled as she took a sip of tea. He was trying to distract her. Well, she would let him. He was right. She should trust Gwyn.

"I'd rather know more about you, if you don't mind." She paused. How did she explain her fascination without offending?

He appeared to understand completely, however. He took a sip of his own tea before replying. "I am afraid I doubt I will be able to answer your questions to your satisfaction, but I will do my best. What do you wish to know?"

"Where are you from?" That seemed a safe place to start.

Nazir took another sip of tea. His eyes gazed far away, into the veil of memory. "A small village, not far from the southern border with Tigri. A tiny village, not more than a handful of people. We barely filled up half the temple at service time, and we did not have a large temple."

She nodded, encouraging him to continue.

"My mother...well. She was Saemarian, as far as I ever found out. She was..." he sighed and stared down at his tea. Vinet felt an inexplicable urge to reach across and hold his hand to comfort him.

He sighed again. "She was not...all there. Something had happened. She lived half in a dream world, and on the rare occasions I could get her to look at me," he shrugged.

This time, Vinet didn't resist the urge. He glanced up at her touch, startled.

"What made you start traveling?" she asked, attempting to change the sad subject.

His lips twitched. "Well, as you can imagine, village boys are not kind souls," he said. "Especially not when one looks like," he gestured at himself.

Vinet winced.

"The Temple was the only place I ever felt safe, but I didn't want to be a priest. How could I, with rumors of demon spawn following me even there? I loved the books in the Temple, though. So, I started off in search of more." He shrugged. "A simple enough quest, but it's led me all about Saemar, through Tigri, and some of the free cities. This is the first time I've ever been in the north, however. I must say, I was not expecting so much snow. It is beautiful though."

She took the hint and allowed the subject to change. "It is an early snowfall," she said. "I'm afraid it will make traveling back to the capital for the council session difficult. Perhaps I should have followed Alexander's advice and just stayed in the capital for Manyu's Time."

"No," Nazir shook his head. "You would never have been happy there for months at a time. This is your home."

She looked at him, surprised at how emphatic his words were. Her hand still rested on his, and she started, hastily withdrawing it.

"While I agree with you, I do enjoy traveling," she protested.

Nazir smiled. "But staying in the capital is not traveling. And if you do not mind me saying so, it would be too much a reminder of the stress of politics."

She took another sip of tea, trying to conceal how his observations rattled her. They were too true. How did he know so much about her already?

"Vinet."

She glanced up sharply at Gwyn's re-entry into the hall. Gwyn was carrying a crying Niara. Without care for politeness or decorum, Vinet rushed over, carefully taking Niara from Gwyn.

"I'm sorry," Niara said softly through her tears.

"Shh," Vinet stroked Niara's hair. "It's alright, dearest. I'm here. I will always be here for you."

Niara said nothing else, just buried her face in Vinet's shoulder. "Why?" she wailed. "Why didn't you tell me?"

Vinet froze. "I'm sorry," she said, her voice cracking. "I was scared, dear. I did what I thought I must to keep you. To protect you."

Niara sniffed, and Vinet held her even tighter. "I'm sorry."

Gwyn stood sentinel as Vinet stroked Niara's hair. Niara sniffled some more but seemed to be calming. Finally, she wriggled, and Vinet put her down, kneeling on the floor next to her.

Niara stared into her eyes. They were red from tears but still so bright and shining. Vinet blinked back tears of her own. She never should have hidden Niara's heritage from her.

"I'm sorry, dearest," Vinet whispered again. "Can you forgive me?"

Niara nodded jerkily, but her face still twisted with confusion. Vinet's heart contracted.

She jumped as a shadow stood next to her. But it wasn't a shadow, it was Nazir. She scrambled to her feet. "Nazir, I'm sorry…"

He shook his head and crouched down to look Niara in the eye.

"You have every right to be upset," he said. "It is hard, finding out painful truths. But is this one really so painful?"

Niara frowned at him. "What do you mean?"

"You have a mother who loves you," he said softly. "That is a treasure, little one. A mother who sacrificed much to raise you as her own. A mother who protects and cherishes you. That is not something to be taken lightly, little one." His voice cracked on the last sentence.

"Vinet!" Gwyn hissed.

Vinet stared at Nazir in shock. She hadn't told him she was Niara's mother. She turned to Gwyn and shook her head mutely. Gwyn's eyes were not convinced.

Nazir ignored the two of them and remained focused on Niara. "So what troubles you, little one?"

Niara sniffed. "I...but why did she lie?" her voice was a heartbroken cry. "She's never lied before."

Vinet buried her face in her hands.

"Because sometimes we lie to protect," Nazir answered. "Tell me, Niara. What would have happened if your mother was known to have had a child, unmarried?"

Niara screwed up her face. Vinet had told her about her sister often enough. "She'd be disgraced," she managed.

"And then what would have happened to you?" Nazir asked.

Niara hesitated. "I...don't know?"

"You would have been sent to live with someone who cared far less about you than your mother," Nazir said, his eyes kind but his voice grave.

Niara turned an anguished glance toward Vinet. Vinet nodded slowly. She didn't know what would have happened if she'd openly had a bastard child, but disgrace would have been the least. She had been too new in her position, too lacking in friends and support, to even risk it. Her second cousins could easily have petitioned the king for her removal. She had no one to turn to in case of such an event, and the Sisters of Mazda did not let children live with their mothers. She would have been forced to send Niara away.

"Would you have wanted that?" Nazir pressed quietly.

Niara shook her head vehemently. Without giving Nazir another glance, she threw herself at Vinet. "I'm sorry, Mama."

Vinet shook her head as she returned the embrace. "It's alright, dear," she whispered. "There's nothing to be sorry about."

"You, on the other hand," Gwyn glared at Nazir. "How did you know?"

Nazir stood up from his crouch and shrugged. "I watched."

Vinet eyed him carefully, not releasing Niara from her embrace. Gwyn eyed him with suspicion, but he seemed perfectly calm.

"It's a secret," Gwyn hissed. "And you're an outsider."

Nazir simply inclined his head. "I am," he said. "I understand your concern. I will swear on whatever you want never to reveal it to anyone."

"That's not good enough," Gwyn started.

Vinet raised a hand sharply, and Gwyn subsided. She stared at Nazir, who met her eyes without flinching.

There was no deception in his eyes, only pure sincerity. And after what he had just done, what he had helped Niara understand... "I trust you," she said softly.

"Vinet," Gwyn began.

Vinet shook her head. She couldn't explain how she knew Nazir was to be trusted, but she did. She was sure of it.

Nazir regarded Gwyn. "I will stay here as long as it takes for you to trust me," he said. "But I mean you and your lady no harm. On my life, I swear it."

Gwyn still seemed unconvinced, but Vinet nodded decisively.

"Thank you, Nazir," the childish voice startled everyone.

Niara looked over her shoulder at Nazir. "Thank you for helping me understand," she whispered.

If nothing else, that would have decided Vinet. She couldn't send away someone Niara trusted. Nazir would stay.

The trees in the gardens were bare but beautiful, the small pond frozen over, and everything still and quiet. Snow had fallen again last night, laying untouched and pure, presenting a peaceful, tranquil scene.

Peaceful, at least, until a snowball came out of nowhere and hit Vinet in the shoulder.

"Hey!" she exclaimed.

Gwyn gave her a wicked smile. "Score one for us, Niara!"

Niara giggled and ducked behind a snowbank. Vinet tossed a light handful of snow her way but missed entirely.

"Like this, Lady Vinet!" Evalynna scooped up a handful of snow and flung it straight at Gwyn. Gwyn dodged, avoiding getting it in the face, but still got a handful of snow on her shoulder.

"Oof! I'll get you for that, Evalynna!"

Vinet laughed as the fight started in earnest. Snowballs went flying every which way, some aimed, some not. As Vinet crouched behind a bush, focused intently on Gwyn's assault on Evalynna and awaiting an opportunity for an ambush, she felt a handful of snow slide down her back.

"Ah!" She spun around, tackling Niara to the ground. "You minx!"

Niara collapsed in a pile of giggles. Vinet pushed her into the snow, careful not to hold her too hard. "You ambushed me!"

Niara continued to giggle, so hard she couldn't stand up. Vinet sat up and clutched dramatically at her chest. "Evalynna! I have been ambushed! Avenge me!"

"Sun-bringer!"

Vinet looked up at Evalynna's curse. For a moment, all she could see was a flurry of snowballs, all flying in different directions. She ducked as one flew over her head. Then Evalynna threw herself on top of Gwyn, two snowballs in her hands. "I shall take you with me!"

Taken off guard, Gwyn disappeared into a snowbank, Evalynna on top of her. Vinet sat back on her heels, shaking her head in amusement as the two of them finally emerged, covered in snow.

She reached out and pulled Niara into a hug. "I guess that makes you the victor."

"I win! I win!" Niara squealed. She started dancing through the snow, hugging first Gwyn and then pouncing on Evalynna, who lay on her back in the snow.

Evalynna groaned and pushed Niara off of her. "I'm already dead. Gwyn killed me."

"You killed me," Gwyn pointed out. "In a suicidal attack, nonetheless. You have only yourself to blame."

"It was the only way to take you out!" Evalynna protested.

Gwyn chuckled and reached down to offer her a hand up. Evalynna took it, then pulled Gwyn into the snowbank with her.

Vinet laughed at the two bodyguards wrestling in the snow. She hadn't felt this lighthearted in ages.

She turned at the sound of someone clearing his throat. Her seneschal stood in the doorway, a bit sheepishly. Vinet sighed and got to her feet. Kildar wouldn't be interrupting her if it wasn't important.

"I beg your pardon, Lady Vinet," Kildar said as she approached. "I know you intended to spend the morning with your niece. But you have a visitor."

Vinet blinked. She had not been expecting anyone. "Who?"

Kildar cleared his throat again. "Ah, an elf, Lady Vinet. He said you had met before, that he is an ambassador at the capital?"

Vinet smiled broadly. "Kinaevan! He came to visit? Oh, that's wonderful! This won't disrupt my plans, Niara needs to meet him as well. Show him to the library, will you?"

Kildar bowed. "Very good, Lady Vinet."

She turned back to the garden. "Niara!" she cried. "Come on, leave those two to their squabbling. You and I have a visitor."

"A visitor?" Niara came bounding over. Her eyes were bright with curiosity. "I've never had a visitor before."

"Well, you have one now." Vinet brushed some of the snow off Niara's cloak. "Run and get changed, dear. He's in the library."

Niara scampered off, and Vinet went to her own chambers at a more sedate pace. She peeled off her soaked clothing, changed into a simple wool dress, and slipped her feet into fleece-lined slippers before making her way to the library.

Kinaevan rose from a chair as she entered. Vinet glanced about to ensure no one else stood in the room, then walked forward to hug him. He returned the embrace firmly. Curiously, he seemed to be carrying a book with him, tucked under his robes near his heart. "Greetings and Lady's Guidance to you, Vinet Elfsdaughter," he said, smiling. "It is good to see you."

"You as well," she said. "I'm glad you came. There is someone..."

A little gasp of joy made Vinet turn as Niara entered the room. She stared at Kinaevan, her eyes wide with happiness.

Vinet's smile broadened. "Niara, I know you've met before, but you need a proper introduction this time. This is your grandfather, my father. Father, this is my daughter, Niara."

Kinaevan sank down in a crouch in his usual fluid motion. "Guidance to you, daughter of my daughter."

Niara met his eyes in excitement, but remained silent, clearly not knowing what to say. She glanced around and spotted a book sitting on the table. "Have you read this story?" she asked Kinaevan.

Kinaevan raised an eyebrow. "I have not. What is it?"

"It's a legend about dragons!" Niara exclaimed. "And a princess! And how she outwits the dragon and saves the kingdom!"

"That sounds like a fantastic story, little queen," Kinaevan said.

Niara's face flushed. "It's probably not real," she said. "But it's fun to read." She paused. "Why do you call me a queen? Mother's not a queen, and she'd have to be for me to be one, right?"

"Every lie has an aspect of truth often as many. Do not discard your stories too quickly." He stood up. "As to why I call you queen, it is because it is in your blood."

"A queen?" Niara stared up at him, wide-eyed. "Mama told me about the elf part, but not the queen part."

Vinet shook her head. "You did not tell me about a queen, Father," she said. Her hands clenched, and she hoped her daughter believed her, didn't think she'd kept another secret.

Kinaevan gestured, and they moved to sit next to the fire. After a moment's hesitation, Niara climbed into Kinaevan's lap. He appeared startled at first and then smiled warmly.

"In the Era of Great Fire, in which there came the dragons," he winked at Niara, "The Faithful became four separate realms. Our blood carries the ancient lineage of one line of royalty, descended from Queen Olvae of the Oaken Spear."

Niara's eyes widened. Vinet leaned forward as well.

"Was Queen Olvae a great hero?" Niara asked.

"At one time, yes, but heroes who become rulers rarely remain heroes." Kinaevan's eyes darkened, and Vinet shivered at the shadow which seemed to pass over the room.

Kinaevan blinked, and the sunlight returned. He looked about the room. "Would you like to hear her tale?"

Niara nodded eagerly.

Kinaevan laughed. "Then I will tell it to you in the style in which I first heard it." He took a deep breath. "In the first days of the Age of Great Fire, a great queen, passionate follower, and close friend of the Lady, strode under the boughs of the Greenwood. Her name was Olvae. This is her Memory-in-Voice."

He paused. "There are some words which do not translate exactly. You must forgive me."

Vinet shook her head, gesturing him to continue.

"Olvae, blood-daughter of Aevan Firstborn, blood-daughter of Olathae Duskbrow, kin of Artran Stone-Speaker and Hiliakae Who-Made-The-Trees-Weep, and oath-sister of the Lady. The grandmaster of the Treespeakers-Grove broke his vow of silence to tell Olvae, her apprentice, of the death of Aevan Firstborn, High King of Elvenkind, and father to Olvae. 'Of my mother?' the apprentice asked. 'Dead,' answered the grandmaster. Then the Sight took her in a vision of the coming destruction long forewarned by the Lady."

Vinet frowned as she tried to memorize the list of names. Aevan First-Born. Olathae Duskbrow. Artran Stone-Speaker. Hiliakae Who-Made-The-Trees-Weep. She would have to ask Kinaevan about that one. What had Hiliakae done to make the trees weep?

Kinaevan closed his eyes and continued. "Olvae New-Queen lay down the mantle of Treespeaker and left the Grove behind. She went to her people and ruled them well. There came a day when she was to be tested. The Lady called her to her, to meet and share visions in the Treespeakers-

Grove. On this day, her path grew harsh. For as she entered the Treespeakers-Grove, the Great Burner and her Consorts Three attacked."

Niara gasped. "The Great Burner?" she whispered.

Kinaevan nodded. "The ancient one, the one who caused the Age of Great Fire. The ancient enemy of the Faithful."

Niara's eyes widened.

Kinaevan continued. "Fire and fury, battle bitter. The Thorns of the Lady were broken and cast aside. The grove-sacred screamed as the Great Burner laid waste. Queen Olvae, she-who-abandoned-her mantel reached out to a great Oak-of-the-Beginning. This noble tree surrendered its essence to her and from it she fashioned an oaken spear. This she cast toward the Great Burner; the power behind it was the pain of ancient trees. The throw, though true, was intercepted by the third Consort who cast himself before it. With a great roar, he tumbled, slain. The Great Burner and the final two Consorts fled, aware now of their own vulnerability. On that day, the Lady named her True Queen Olvae Oaken Spear. And so she was named, and so she is remembered."

Kinaevan looked at Vinet. "And Olvae had a son, and from her son's lover I was begotten. The ancient line of a queen."

"But you are not a king," Vinet said quietly. This wasn't the entire story, Vinet knew. Something had happened to Olvae, something to make her no longer a hero. Kinaevan had said it himself. *Those who become rulers rarely remain heroes.*

Kinaevan shook his head sharply. "The Faithful no longer have kings or queens," he said.

"Are there more stories like that?" Niara demanded. "I've never heard one like that before!"

Vinet smiled at her daughter's enthusiasm. "Nor have I." She met her father's eyes. "There is very little on elven history which is written down. I have collected what I can, but I cannot separate truth from fiction."

"Indeed," Kinaevan said. "We rarely write our stories down, though in these dark times, I have begun some of the work myself."

Vinet raised an eyebrow as her father withdrew a small book from inside his robe. "The tales hold their power when told in our own tongue. A tongue which I need to teach you both. Particularly you, Vinet, as you progress down your path."

The look Kinaevan gave her spoke volumes. She nodded in understanding.

"I have written some of the tales in this tongue, as well as our own. Study them carefully, my child."

"Will you teach us Elvish?" Niara looked up.

Kinaevan smiled. Before he answered, he handed the book to Vinet. It was small and light, but Vinet held it as if it was more precious than any other book in her library. And, in a way, it was.

"Indeed. That is why I came during Manyu's Time. There is no business to hold me in the capital, and it is far more important I spend my time guiding you both." He nodded decisively. "Our first lesson shall be now."

Maple is curious and fun. She laughs until the day is done.
The old children's rhyme rang through Vinet's head as she closed her eyes, the image of the maple in the garden firm in her mind. She wondered, now that Kinaevan had started teaching her, if that old children's rhyme had been translated from an elven teaching song. It certainly seemed accurate.

The tree in the garden. Strong, supple. Seemingly dead to outside eyes, but so alive and full of life. Sleepy, but it gave a warm chuckle as it welcomed her.

She saw Gwyn and Evalynna sitting side by side. Someone had cleared the snow off a bench. They sat close together for warmth, deep in intense conversation. She wanted to pay closer attention, but that wasn't the point of this exercise.

Yew is wise and full of life. He guards the watcher from all strife.
The next tree her father had recommended. Further uphill from Ilhelm Castle, on the road into the Gray Mountains. Hardly anyone there this time of year. Strong and hard, watchful. Not playful like the maple, but comforting. Snowy hills, soft in the snow. A cardinal, bright red, chirping on the branches of the tree. The sigh of the wind.

She stretched out again, further this time. Toward Duskryn, and the trees she'd taken note of there. A hawthorn.

Thorn is a prickly one, beware! But clearest vision is his prayer.
Harsh pain. She gasped as she settled in. Everything was sharp. The thorn didn't care. It prickled everything. Her sight was sharp, too, sharper than it had ever been. She could see for miles. No snow here. Saihid paced

the hall. Pellalindra curled up by a fire, draped in furs. Sobbing? Tears streamed down her cheeks.

She tried to hang onto the vision, to figure out what was wrong, but it pricked at her, forcing her away. She flung her mind out, trying to reach a nearby tree.

Pain! She gasped and doubled over. Malevolent and dark, it bent over her, obscuring everything else. She fought back, trying to free herself. Dark eyes. Heavy, oppressive. She couldn't breathe!

She opened her eyes with a gasp. The last verse of the child's song danced in her mind.

Elder, he has deadly teeth. Death comes for those who lie beneath.

She steadied herself with a few deep breaths. *Mazda's light!* she thought. "Lady Vinet?"

She glanced up at Nazir's voice. She'd been in the library, gazing out the window to where she could just make out the maple tree in the garden. Not entirely private, but she hadn't expected to be disturbed.

"Nazir." She looked down at the papers scattered in front of her. Notes, mostly, translations of fragments of Elvish from her father's book. And a copy of the children's poem.

"Interesting research?" Nazir asked. "Anything I can help with?"

She hesitated. She shouldn't. "I...I think I'm fine," she said.

He smiled. "Very well. Let me know if you need assistance." He turned and started walking to where a desk had been set up for him.

"Nazir," she called.

He stopped and looked back at her.

Mazda's light, why had she done that? *I can't tell him anything. He already knows too much,* she argued with herself. *Gwyn would kill me if I told him about Kinaevan as well as Niara.*

He still stood there, waiting for her. She searched through her mind, frantically looking for a topic. Stories! He had to have heard stories. And she'd been unable to draw any further stories about this from her father. "Have you ever heard of the Age of Great Fire?"

He frowned. "The Age of Great Fire...let me think..." he walked over to his desk and started flipping through some of the books and papers stacked on it. She made a mental note to assign him a secretary.

"Aha!" Triumphantly, Nazir pulled out one of the books and brought it to Vinet. He held it out, fingers framing a passage.

"A tale from my childhood, actually. I'm afraid it's just a brief mention in the prologue. 'Many years ago, in the Age of Great Fire, darkness ruled the skies. But then came the Age of Green, and our people rejoiced.'"

Vinet sighed. That told her little more than Kinaevan already had.

"Where did you hear about that?" Nazir asked, interested. "I've only ever heard of it in this prologue. Do you think it was an actual event?"

She nodded without thinking. "I was talking to Kinaevan and he told me..." She shut her mouth abruptly.

Nazir looked at her curiously. He didn't press.

"It was just a mention then too," Vinet lied. "It seems to be an important event everyone in the story's original audience would have been well aware of."

"Those are always the things which are lost," he said with a sigh. "Those things that are believed so obvious they needn't be written down."

"Is that why you make a life of writing stories down?" Vinet asked.

Nazir shrugged. "That, and no one else would ever write down the stories of commoners," he said. "Most nobles are interested in legends which glorify their past. Since they're the ones with money to fund any research..."

Vinet smiled sympathetically. She didn't need him to clarify that most nobles did not include her.

He hesitated before asking. "Any other tidbits from Kinaevan's tales?"

Oh, Mazda take it. Surely telling him the story of Queen Olvae wouldn't hurt, she thought.

"The Faithful used to have kings and queens," she said, gesturing for him to pull up a chair next to hers. "The one in the story, Queen Olvae, fought the Great Burner during the Age of Great Fire. Olvae nearly killed her, but one of her consorts took the blow meant for her and died instead."

Nazir looked fascinated, so she continued. "Queen Olvae was kin to a number of the elven leaders," she said. "Kin to their Lady, who is not a goddess." She smiled wryly. "I've yet to meet this Lady myself. But she's also kin to mortals, kin to Kinaevan, and—" She shut her mouth abruptly again. What was getting into her? What was it about him that just made her want to talk? To her relief, he, once again, didn't press.

"And he's teaching you elvish?" he asked, gesturing at the papers strewn in front of her.

She glanced down sheepishly. Her notes made no sense, not even to her. She needed a secretary as badly as he did.

"May I?" he asked, reaching for one of the papers.

She nodded. If he could make any sense of the little tidbits of which word was which, he was more than welcome to it.

"The fourth born from the Mountain-God's hatred of the dragons, his Brother's chaotic creation. The Mountain-God made them in the form of his domain, colossal and strong. It was they, in friendship with the Goldwood Realm who cast down the Great Burner after her long reign." Nazir stopped reading. "What does any of this mean?"

She hesitated. She had told him so much already.

"It's part of a creation story, as far as I can tell," she said. "Kinaevan didn't translate that one for me, I've been working on it myself. The elves were first, before even the first of the realms splitting, then the humans, whom the Great Burner cursed with short lives, then the rest of the races. I'm not sure which race this passage refers to."

Nazir frowned. "Mountain-God, colossal and strong. And friends with the Goldwood Realm."

"The Goldwood Realm are the elves," she said. "At least, I think so."

Nazir nodded.

An uncomfortable silence fell as the two sat together. Finally, she couldn't take it anymore. "Nazir—"

"Vinet—"

Both of them stopped. Vinet laughed nervously and gestured for Nazir to go first.

He shook his head and returned the gesture. She looked down, flustered.

"Nazir, I...there are some things, I can't..." *Mazda's light! Why can't I talk straight? I'm not a flustered child!* Vinet scolded herself mentally.

"Vinet," he had forgotten to use her title. She didn't correct him as he continued. "There's something I should tell you. It...it might..."

Her eyes widened as he avoided her gaze. Was he flustered too? He'd always seemed so calm, so assured! "What is it?" she asked.

Nazir looked up again. "I saw part of what you were doing, earlier," he said. "I think I know what you were doing too. And why you can."

She swallowed. Did he mean...did he know?

"I didn't mean to," Nazir said. "I just...I've heard about elves before. Their abilities. I met a few, traveling in Tigri. They told me about the Sight."

"They told you?" Vinet couldn't believe it. She'd had to drag the information out of Kinaevan piece by piece, and Kinaevan was willing to tell her!

"One was taken by a vision right in front of me," Nazir said. "They had no choice. I swore never to reveal any of it."

She narrowed her eyes. "Then why are you telling me?" she asked.

"Because you already know," Nazir said. He took a deep breath. "Because you have the Sight. You were practicing it earlier."

She flushed. Had she been that obvious? She paused as a thought struck her. Elves had told him about the Sight. He had made that direct comparison between her and them. Did he...

"You know," she whispered softly.

Nazir met her eyes. "I didn't mean to know," he said. "But when Kinaevan came to visit, and you started spending so much time together...and Niara is hardly subtle in her affection. She's very careful, she never calls him anything but Kinaevan around me, but the resemblance..."

Vinet winced. All that care, and for nothing! She felt a flare of panic. *If Nazir has guessed, then who else knows? Who would sell that information for a pretty price?*

"I don't think anyone else knows," Nazir said hastily. "No one you didn't intend to, anyway. Evalynna might suspect, but that's just because she spends so much time with Niara. I doubt she'd care, though. She loves Niara like one of her younger siblings."

Vinet took a deep breath and stared out the window again. The maple tree danced in the wind. Another storm was coming. Gwyn and Evalynna were hopefully inside by now.

She looked down at her notes. "Queen Olvae is my great-grandmother," she said.

Nazir's eyes widened. "And Kinaevan your father." He shook his head. "I'm sorry," he said. "But you were struggling...and your work is so fascinating..." he gestured at the pile of papers again.

She had to laugh. A scholar's curiosity, like her own. "You just want to study Elvish with me." She was surprised at the teasing in her voice.

Nazir let out a breath.

She glanced up, surprised at the relieved expression on his face. "What?" she asked.

"I was afraid...afraid if I knew too much, you would be angry," he said. "I can't help it. I listen and look at everything. It's what made me a good collector of tales."

She should have been angry, Vinet supposed. She had concealed her heritage from everyone except Gwyn for over twenty years. To have all

that secrecy revealed by a man who saw more than was good for him...
but it was a relief. She didn't want to conceal anything from Nazir.

"Look at this passage," she said. "It's the end of the creation story. It
says that the fall of the Great Burner was what brought the Age of Great
Fire to an End, and that some now call that Age the Age of Birth. What do
you think of that?"

Nazir frowned. "Well, fire can be cleansing..."

He broke off at a laugh from the hallway. Both fell silent as Gwyn and
Evalynna walked by.

"You don't really mean..."

"I do," Gwyn said.

The footsteps stopped. "Gwyn, I...I don't know what to say."

"Are you...are you upset?" Gwyn's voice was full of uncharacteristic
hesitance.

"No!" Evalynna said immediately. "Gwyn, I...I've been wanting to
approach you since you recruited me," her voice became the softest
whisper.

Gwyn's laugh sounded full of relief. "Well, why didn't you?"

"Because you're intimidating, Gwyn! You should know that." Evalynna
sounded flustered.

Gwyn kept silent a moment. "We're still both bodyguards. Whatever is
between us, nothing will change that."

"Of course," Evalynna said.

"We're going to need to discuss this more..." Gwyn started walking
again, and their voices passed out of earshot.

Vinet clapped a hand over her mouth. Had she interpreted that
conversation accurately? Were Gwyn and Evalynna...Gwyn and
Evalynna!

She turned to Nazir, her eyes dancing. His face was full of suppressed
amusement of his own.

"Seems they have much in common," he said lightly.

"As do we," Vinet said, equally lightly. She flushed. "I mean, like our
scholarly interests. Not..." *Mazda's light!*

Nazir nodded quickly. Perhaps too quickly. He hesitated. "You truly
don't mind that I know?" he asked.

Vinet thought for a moment. Gwyn would certainly mind. But as for
herself, it felt right. "No," she said. She smiled. "Now I can draft you
into research projects without worrying about concealing vital
information."

"I am at your disposal, Lady Vinet." He bowed as well as he could from his chair.

She hesitated. "You called me Vinet earlier," she said.

He flushed beneath his dark skin. "I'm sorry. I shouldn't have…"

"I prefer Vinet," she interrupted. "When we're alone, at least. In public I have to be Lady Vinet, even to Gwyn."

Nazir nodded. "And will I see you much in public, Lady…I mean, Vinet?"

She smiled. "Well, you'll come with us to the capital for the next council session, won't you? Someone will need to entertain Niara, and Kinaevan will be going back to his embassy."

Nazir laughed. "Your wish is my command."

Vinet relaxed as they bent down to study Kinaevan's book together. This felt right.

1 1

A WEDDING

I don't care where she is, show me to her immediately!"

Vinet glanced up from her meditation, startled. It was the height of Manyu's Time, almost Niara's name-day. Even in the capital, the air chilled bitterly, but it hadn't stopped Vinet from bundling into her heaviest cloak to take her daily walk in the gardens. She found it comforting to be near the trees, especially the hazel by the bench. *Hazel laughs and dances well. Comfort lies beneath her spell.*

To Vinet's surprise, Pellalindra came through the door, wrapped in the finest wool cloak she had ever seen. She was dressed impeccably, as usual, but she had dark circles under her eyes and an anxious look on her face.

Vinet walked over to her, waving reassuringly at the anxious servant who had followed Pellalindra outside. "Lady Pellalindra? What's wrong?"

Pellalindra stared at her for a moment, as if she tried to gather her thoughts. "I need your help," she whispered. She shivered, wrapping her cloak around her tighter.

Vinet took her arm, guiding her back toward the house. "Let's talk in my study," she said, knowing it was both warmer and more secure.

Pellalindra followed as Vinet handed a servant their cloaks and ordered tea. Pellalindra remained silent until they were both seated in the sitting room, cups in front of them, and the last servant had left.

Pellalindra raised haunted eyes to Vinet. "Promise me you won't breathe a word of what I am about to tell you."

Vinet blinked, taken aback by her words. Before she could answer, Pellalindra elaborated. "It's nothing to do with the security of the kingdom, or dangerous in any way, I swear, but still..."

Vinet shook her head. "Of course. I promise," she leaned forward and took one of Pellalindra's hands. "I will help you."

Pellalindra stared at her hand for a long second, seeming to gather her courage for something. Finally, she looked Vinet in the eye. "I'm with child."

Vinet's eyes widened. Pellalindra was the last noble she would have expected to make the same mistake she had. The Lady of Duskryn was so noble, so aware of propriety!

"I see," she said softly. *Who is the father? Another noble? Is he married?* These questions buzzed through Vinet's mind. "And the father?" she asked. She blinked, realizing Pellalindra might not want to reveal that. "You don't have to tell me."

"Saihid," Pellalindra said miserably. "My elven guard."

Vinet sat back, feeling her mouth open in surprise. She would never have expected that from Pellalindra. Saihid was smallfolk, a foreigner, and an elf! "What do you need from me?" she whispered. "I will help you however I can."

"I don't know!" Pellalindra exclaimed, burying her face in her hands. "I don't think there's much you can do, but from woman to woman, I need some advice." She paused, her shoulders shuddering. "I don't know what to do! If the other nobles find out, then everything I built for Percival's future will crumble! I saved him from the taint of his father's reputation, but if my own reputation falters..." she shook her head. "Saihid...he says it's my judgment, that he will support me. I've considered a political marriage, but when the child is born half-elf, the truth will be obvious," she nearly choked, "and I don't want to lay aside the child."

Vinet stared at Pellalindra for a long moment, caught in the memory of her own fears. She had panicked at the discovery of her pregnancy. But she'd had options, a sister who was willing to go to a convent.

"There are several things you could do," she said, fighting the memories. "You could go to a convent for a religious retreat for a few months and give birth there. Find a discreet one and take only your most trusted maidservant."

"But what of the child?" Pellalindra's hand shook as she raised her cup to her lips.

Vinet shrugged. "Perhaps it could be the maidservant's? Or have the child raised separately for a few months, then allow Saihid to bring his child to raise at Duskryn. You can still raise a child without acknowledging it's yours." The words nearly caught in her throat as she spoke. "You can tell your child later when they're old enough to understand," she managed.

"And raise them smallfolk?" Pellalindra's back stiffened. "I will not deny my child their heritage!"

Vinet barely refrained from pointing out the child would be half-smallfolk anyway. "Then you need a noble mother or father for them," she said. "Do you have any family? Someone you can bring in as a long-lost relative?"

"No, there is only me. The rest of my lord husband's family was executed for being complicit in treason." Pellalindra bit her lip. "I've considered going to Lord Auriel. As steward, he might be able to arrange a political marriage for me."

Vinet caught her breath. "Are you sure a marriage is what you want?" she pressed. "What about Saihid?"

Pellalindra shook her head. "He understands the need for survival among the nobility. He's seen it! He wants a happy family, but he must know it's impossible."

Vinet felt her heart breaking for the poor elf. "If you change your mind, I can recommend my sister's convent," she said. "We can circulate that you needed a religious retreat for a month or so. That is enough time to give birth, providing you have a clever dressmaker."

Pellalindra sighed. "I will talk to the steward," she said finally. "But thank you for the offer, Lady Vinet. At least I now have options."

Vinet reached across to squeeze Pellalindra's hand. "Anytime," she said sincerely.

They exchanged a few more pleasantries, but Pellalindra was eager to be off. Since the quicker she arranged a marriage the better she could pass the child off as her husband's, Vinet could see why she was in a hurry. She stood in the doorway of her study gazing after Pellalindra when the noblewoman left.

"Vinet? You seem thoughtful."

She glanced up at Nazir's approach. He had taken to calling her Vinet with far more ease than she'd expected. She shook herself. The subject of the last meeting was not her secret to reveal. "Just...thoughtful," she said. "Do you want to help me with some Elvish?"

He nodded. "Of course. Anytime."

Anytime. She smiled as they entered the study. It was a nice thought.

She lost track of time as the two of them bent over their studying. He had so many insights she would never have thought of. Not that she wasn't holding her own in the discussion. At some point, they'd gotten distracted from Elvish and were poring over an old Saemarian legend about King Enlil and the dragonriders. The stuff of children's stories, some would say, but after reading Jimesseran's journal Vinet was not as inclined as most to think that dragons were extinct.

Someone pounded on the door, and she looked up, distracted. For a moment, it sounded so loud she'd thought someone wanted into the study, but the pounding came from the front door. She waited, frowning, straining her ears to determine who their visitor was.

She heard Gwyn's sure footsteps and heard her muffled exclamation as the door opened. "Saihid?"

"Gwyn. I need your help. Please."

"Of course, of course. This way."

Vinet's eyes widened. *First Pellalindra, and now Saihid?* She hoped Pellalindra had kept it from the servants, otherwise everyone in the capital would know within two days.

Nazir raised an eyebrow. "Saihid? Pellalindra's elven guard?" he asked.

Vinet shrugged. As she raised her eyes, she saw understanding in his. She smiled. "Gwyn should be able to help him. I hope."

Nazir nodded and turned back to the books laid out in front of them. She couldn't shake the feeling he already knew what was going on. He didn't ask any questions, though, for which she was grateful. She didn't want to figure out the morality of answering a question she'd promised not to talk about to someone who already knew the answer. Just the prospect made her head hurt.

Vinet managed to focus on the research until a gentle knock on the door announced Gwyn's entry. "Vinet, I..." she stopped short as she saw Nazir.

"It's alright," Vinet said.

Gwyn hesitated, and Vinet could swear she wanted to glare at Nazir. "That was Saihid, if you hadn't guessed," she finally said. "I think he told me what Pellalindra came here earlier to tell you. I hope he doesn't tell anyone else. He's very distraught."

"How is he now?" Vinet asked.

Gwyn sighed. "Better. I think I talked some sense into him." She eyed Nazir. "Vinet, there's something else, something I think is new since..."

She broke off at another knock on the study door. Vinet frowned, but called, "Come in."

A servant entered the room, looking very apologetic. "Pardon me, my lady, but this came for you, and I thought you'd want to read it right away."

Vinet took the message handed her with a nod of thanks. Her eyes rose as she saw the black griffons of the Duskryn seal on the envelope.

"It's from Pellalindra," she told Gwyn and Nazir as the servant left She opened the letter and unfolded the paper:

Dearest Lady Vinet,

You have my sincerest thanks for your support earlier. I have spoken to our Lord Steward and I have the best of news. After learning the entire truth, he proposed to me himself. The wedding is to take place within a fortnight.

I will be sending out formal invitations within the next few days, but yours will come from me personally. I do have a request, as a sign of my gratitude. Will you stand for me as witness? I would be honored to have you beside me.

You have my sincerest gratitude once again.

Lady Pellalindra Duskryn

Vinet's eyebrows rose higher and higher as she read the note. Pellalindra was to marry Lord Auriel? And she was to stand as witness? She would, of course. One didn't refuse that kind of offer, not if one wanted to retain friendly relations with one of the most powerful noble families and the steward of the realm!

"Lady Pellalindra is to marry Lord Auriel," she said quietly, despite the storm raging in her head. *Why would Lord Auriel propose to Pellalindra himself? He could have made her eternally grateful and won the loyalty of some other lord by arranging a marriage. And why would Pellalindra accept him? He's so...so cold. Nothing at all like Saihid. Mazda's light, poor Saihid.*

Nazir's eyebrows rose. Gwyn, however, only nodded sadly. "That's what Saihid just told me. Pellalindra must have been writing at the same time he left."

Vinet took a deep breath. "Send a messenger out to a seamstress immediately," she said. "I'll need a dress worthy enough to be presentable as Pellalindra's witness. And help me wrack my head for a good bridal gift for this pair. Gwyn..."

Gwyn shook her head. "Don't ask me to accompany you this time," she said. "I'll join the guards at the wedding, but I won't act the part of a wedding guest. Not at this event."

Vinet took another deep breath. She'd been half expecting that. "Then you'll come with me," she told Nazir.

Nazir blinked. "Me?"

"Vinet, is that wise?" Gwyn said at the same time.

Vinet pressed her lips together. "Someone is accompanying me to this wedding," she said. "I am not going there by myself. And if it's not you, my dear oath-sister, then it's Nazir."

"Vinet..." Nazir broke in. "I've never been to a noble's event. Are you certain I'm suitable?"

Gwyn nodded in agreement with Nazir.

Vinet squared her shoulders. "Just act like you did when you first met me, and you'll be fine," she said. "Others will be the center of attention."

Both Gwyn and Nazir gave her disbelieving looks, and she glared at them both. Gwyn sighed in resignation.

"I'll send out the orders," Gwyn said. She gave Nazir one last hard look before she left the room.

"Vinet..." Nazir protested again.

She shook her head. "Please, Nazir, I don't think I could face Pellalindra on my own. Not after..." she shook her head again. *Not after I'm suddenly a confidant, after months of political dancing after she threatened me. Not after she's decided to marry a stranger to preserve her status.*

Nazir hesitated, then nodded. "Then I will be there for you," he said. "For you and no one else."

She smiled at that. "Good." She pushed back her chair. "If you'll excuse me, then, I must prepare."

Vinet stood next to the stone altar on the dais in the center of the temple, the noon sunlight streaming down through the glass skylight in the ceiling. Nobility packed the holly and ivy decorated aisles, dressed in their absolute finest, a multitude of colors and silks, velvets, and furs, all waiting anxiously for the main event, the wedding of Lady Pellalindra to Lord Auriel. The speculations as to why the Lady of the Council was marrying the steward of the realm in such a hasty fashion buzzed through the temple like thousands of worried bees.

Vinet shifted her weight uneasily, trying to conceal her anxiety. Behind the altar, Ellil gazed sternly at both her and her fellow witness, Kinaevan Sindarilae. Until Lady Pellalindra and Lord Auriel made their appearances, the eyes of the nobility rested entirely on them, and Vinet was not used to being focused on in such a way.

At least her dress brought no shame to Ninaeva, made of a dark forest green velvet, decorated with fine golden trim which glinted in the sunlight. Along the bottom of her dress small cat patterns chased each other, representations of Ninaeva's emblem, the golden mountain lion. The cut came from Hillsdale, the city-state closest to Ninaeva, where they had perfected the use of gores for voluminous skirts. A string of ivy crowned her hair, one of the few plants still green in the depths of Manyu's Time.

The crowd stilled as a door near the altar opened. Three guards, a woman and two men, stepped through, all dressed in embroidered burgundy. *Not Duskryn house colors, they must be Lord Auriel's,* concluded Vinet. In the next moment, Lord Auriel himself stepped through the door, dressed in the same burgundy, his doublet embroidered with hundreds of delicate silver designs. Displayed on his brow rested a circlet of inlaid silver and gold, inset with a single red gemstone.

He glanced around, seeming to gaze at everyone in the room individually. She knew that he looked at her, as he smiled briefly before transferring his gaze to Kinaevan. Then he mounted the steps to the altar and stood next to Kinaevan, waiting.

Vinet blinked as she caught sight of the emblem on his shoulder cape: A sleeping dragon, intricate in silvery detail. A trick of the light made it seem to shift as he moved.

The musicians struck up a quiet chord, and the room fell silent. Vinet turned with everyone else as the front door to the temple opened, and Pellalindra appeared. The bride was radiant, and she knew it. Some of the younger nobles even dared to stand for a better view. Silver beads and gems glinted off her elaborate hairstyle, causing gasps of admiration as she walked to the center of the temple.

Vinet saw the determination in Pellalindra's eyes as she approached the altar, her deep blue dress trailing on the floor behind her, its silver embroidery glinting in the noon sun. The determination faded for a moment as she gave Vinet a wide smile and handed her the bouquet of snowdrops and violets. Vinet returned the smile as best she could, then took her place next to Pellalindra.

High Priest Ellil began the traditional song for a wedding. Vinet barely heard as he finished the melody, then concluded with the blessing. She couldn't believe this was happening.

Pellalindra spoke her words next, then sang her song. Her voice sounded clear and firm and carried through the silent Temple like a bell. Lord Auriel's voice, when it came to his turn, rang full of suppressed and controlled strength and power.

"Mazda's light guide and protect you," Ellil concluded. He presented the writ to them. The king had allegedly prepared it but had not deigned to attend the wedding himself, a fact Vinet had spent much time pondering before the wedding, before giving up trying to determine its meaning.

Vinet watched as Pellalindra signed her name with no sign of nervousness or fear. Lord Auriel did the same, and then she and Kinaevan stepped forward to sign as witnesses.

The Marriage of Lady Pellalindra Duskryn to Lord Usumgal Auriel...

She hadn't known Usumgal was his first name. Had Pellalindra known that? She hadn't ever called him anything but Lord Auriel. Vinet signed her name with a flourish and turned to the crowd.

Lord Auriel took Pellalindra's hand and raised it in his to address the assembled mass. "Away with you! To the ballroom. Let there be dancing! Let there be eating! Let there be drinking! Let there, most of all, be joy for this day a bond was forged!"

A cheer rang out through the hall, and everyone began pouring out. Vinet waited for a moment until she spotted Nazir standing quietly at the side of the Temple and made her way over to him.

He bowed and offered her his arm. "May I escort you, Lady Vinet, since I am your guest?"

She laughed and took his arm. She noticed Conn and Maeve walking through the crowd, as well as General Alexander and Kamian. She thought she caught a glimpse of Dannan, but he vanished before she could be certain.

They made their way across the open courtyard of the palace to the grand ballroom. Vinet caught her breath at the decorations, so numerous as to border on ostentatious. Most were maroon or blue, the major colors of Auriel and Duskryn, interspersed with ivy and holly in an effort to enliven the hall. Nobility swarmed in every direction, some heading to the refreshment tables set up on the side, others milling in groups, waiting for the dancing to begin.

Conn and Maeve were the first ones to approach them. She saw Maeve looking speculatively at Nazir and heard Nazir's quick, bracing breath.

"Lady Vinet!" Conn nodded in greeting. "And who is your guest?"

Vinet nodded politely. "Lord Conn, Lady Maeve, may I introduce Nazir et-Alim. Nazir, Lord Conn MacTir of Dunbarrow, one of my fellow councilors, and his wife, Lady Maeve."

"Where do you hail from, Nazir?" Conn asked.

Nazir bowed slightly. "Originally from the southeast border, Lord Conn. Though I have traveled far and wide."

"The southeast border? Of Saemar?" The incredulity was evident in Conn's voice.

Vinet decided she had best step in. "Yes," she said. "He is now my guest at Ninaeva, at least for Manyu's Time."

She caught the briefest glimpse of gratitude on Nazir's face.

"And how is the frozen north treating you?" Maeve asked as she took a glass of wine from a passing page. Vinet took a glass as well.

Nazir maintained a neutral expression. "Very well, thank you," he said.

"You shall have to bring him to visit Dunbarrow sometime, Lady Vinet," Conn said.

Vinet nodded. "Perhaps he could entertain your children with his tales," she said. "He certainly entertains Niara."

She smiled at Nazir's sideways glance.

They were interrupted by the approach of Pellalindra and Lord Auriel. Vinet did not think she could ever bring herself to think of him as Usumgal.

Pellalindra looked like one of the happiest women alive. "I trust everyone is enjoying the festivities?"

Vinet nodded, and Nazir bowed.

"Oh yes, indeed! My congratulations, Lady Pellalindra, Lord Auriel, on an excellent event." Conn said.

Lord Auriel smiled politely at Conn's flattery. "It is mostly the work of my dearest Pellalindra, here," he said.

Vinet could barely stand the pleasantries. Somewhere inside her, a voice was screaming all of this was wrong. Pellalindra shouldn't be marrying Lord Auriel, not just to conceal the true father of her child. And where was Saihid? Gwyn had said she was looking for him.

"Will you be staying at the Duskryn estate, or your own, Lord Auriel?" she asked, trying to appear normal. She took a sip of her wine, her knuckles white as she clenched the stem of the glass.

Lord Auriel shook his head. "I am afraid my duty binds me to the capital. I shall not be able to leave often, much as I appreciate the Duskryn lands."

Pellalindra laughed lightly. "Regardless! I am in the capital often enough for my own duties."

"Duty is burdensome, but without it there can be no purpose." Another voice broke into the conversation.

Vinet glanced up as Kinaevan joined the group. She smiled a welcome, and he nodded his acknowledgment to her.

Lord Auriel chuckled. "Always the sage words, Kinaevan, my friend."

Pellalindra gave Kinaevan a shallow curtsy, as befitting an ambassador. "Thank you for your role in the ceremony. And you as well, Lady Vinet."

Vinet nodded, her hand tightening on Nazir's arm. Mazda, let her escape these inanities! As she thought that, she saw her father go white. He clutched Lord Auriel's arm briefly, then excused himself and left the ballroom through a small side door.

Vinet blinked. He'd had a vision. She knew it.

"Excuse me," she said to the gathering. Pellalindra glanced at her in concern as she left, but Vinet gave her a reassuring look. Nazir pressed her arm comfortingly as they hurried to catch up with Kinaevan.

The elf ambassador collapsed on his knees in the hall, and an older elf woman with streaks of gray in her hair knelt down to steady him. He shook so hard Vinet feared he would break into pieces.

Vinet dropped to her knees at his side. "What can I do?" she asked, reaching out to help support her father.

As her fingers touched his shoulder, she flinched. *Fire. All the world was covered in smoke. A great form in the sky. Fear, such terrible fear!* She gasped. It was gone. She was in the hall. Kinaevan was sitting up, staring at her, and Nazir was holding her.

The old elf woman nodded. "A burden shared, a pain relieved."

Vinet stared at her father, still shocked by the vision. "Where was that?"

"When." His eyes slid past her to perform a cursory sweep of Nazir. "The Lady is warning me the old enemy is near, supposedly at this very wedding. I am skeptical. The Lady has been..." he paused. "Troubled, since the onslaught of Mount Halon."

"Should we tell anyone?" Vinet whispered.

Kinaevan shook his head. "There are a great many things I have both to teach you and tell you, but this is neither the time nor the place." He frowned, then forced a smile and straightened his garments. "I see you have brought your companion from Ninaeva." His words chided faintly, more teasing than reprimanding.

Vinet nodded. "I have told him much about you." She looked uncertainly at the older elf next to Kinaevan. *How much do the other elves know? Can I speak freely in front of them?*

"Then he knows you are my daughter," Kinaevan stared directly at Nazir. "Tell me, Nazir. Have you collected any stories from the Faithful?"

Nazir answered the question calmly. "Bits and pieces only. No full tales, I am afraid, though that has changed since I made the acquaintance of your daughter."

"Indeed." Kinaevan seemed distracted. "Shall we return to the festivities?"

Vinet nodded but held her father's gaze a moment longer. "Will you be alright?"

"Yes," his voice was hard. "Until the Sight takes me."

Vinet swallowed. This was a side to her father she hadn't yet seen. She didn't protest as Nazir helped her to her feet and led her back into the ballroom.

As they entered together, Kinaevan cast a brief glance at the three guards in burgundy. Vinet gazed at them curiously, wondering what had gained her father's attention. The woman raised an eyebrow at her and winked.

She flushed and started wandering through the ballroom again, sighing in relief as she saw her father leave for the gardens. Maybe he would find some peace there.

"Lady Vinet? I trust everything is well?"

How did I miss Pellalindra and Lord Auriel's approach? She forced a smile. "Yes, of course. Kinaevan just needed a breath of fresh air."

Pellalindra laughed lightly. "It is quite hot in here," she said, fanning herself with her hand.

Vinet twitched as she saw the burgundy trio approach Lord Auriel. They whispered together briefly, then he waved them away.

She watched them as they left. Had that been about Kinaevan's vision? She felt certain it was, but how could it have been? How could they have known?

"Enough of this," the command in Lord Auriel's voice was plain. He bowed to Pellalindra, taking her hand. "Let us dance."

Vinet let out a breath of relief. Something to distract the nobles.

The musicians struck up the first dance for the wedded couple, and they swept across the ballroom, drawing everyone's eyes. They looked perfect together.

As the music concluded, Vinet applauded lightly with the rest of the room. The musicians struck up the chord for the next dance.

To her surprise, Nazir turned to her and bowed. He took her hand, a clear mirror of Lord Auriel's posture earlier. "May I have this dance, my lady?" he asked.

She nodded mutely. He swept her out onto the floor, and they effortlessly joined the dancers.

It was a couple's dance, designed for semi-private conversations. Conn and Maeve danced with each other, as did Kamian and a young noblewoman. Lord Auriel and Pellalindra also danced together again.

"I didn't know you knew how to dance," she managed to Nazir.

Nazir smiled. "It is one of the things that is good to know when you travel," he said. "People like it when you join in their celebrations. Of course, they are often country dances..."

She smiled. "None of those at Pellalindra's wedding."

"Indeed," Nazir chuckled. "But this one is simple enough."

It was a simple dance. It allowed Nazir to twirl her around, appearing full of grace and skill, but in truth just letting her flow to the music. She laughed, relaxing as they moved, only stopping reluctantly as the dance came to an end. His arms were strong and sure, and his smile warm as he looked down at her.

A loud conversation nearby startled her, and she drew away from him breathlessly. He seemed to be having the same difficulty focusing as she.

Nevertheless, he managed to bow and escort her off the dance floor. As they reached the edge, Vinet saw Pellalindra detach herself from her new husband and approach them.

"Now...Nazir, was it? May I be so bold to draw Lady Vinet away for a quick chat?"

Vinet frowned, taken aback by the interruption.

Nazir did not seem surprised. He bowed to Pellalindra, then nodded to Vinet. "I will meet you in the gardens, my lady."

Vinet took Pellalindra's arm as they moved toward the refreshment table.

"Is Kinaevan truly alright?" Pellalindra whispered softly. "And you? You seem pale."

"He is fine," Vinet said. "Or so he assured me. And I...I am fine as well."

Pellalindra stared at her, and Vinet knew she hadn't been convincing. "If you cannot confide in me now, then when can you?" she asked softly.

Oh, Mazda's light. "It's nothing," she insisted. "At least, nothing you should be concerned about on your wedding day."

"Vinet."

She blinked at the lack of title.

Pellalindra took her hands. "What troubles you? It has to do with my marriage, does it not?"

She shook her head. "I...a bit," she admitted. She met Pellalindra's eyes. "You are a stronger woman than I, Pellalindra."

Pellalindra seemed pleased with that statement, although Vinet was not certain she'd intended it as a compliment. How could she explain she didn't think she'd ever have the strength to marry a near stranger? *Much less one as intimidating as Lord Auriel,* she thought.

Another noble approached them, and Pellalindra nodded to him politely. Vinet took that as the signal that their private conference had come to an end, and she excused herself, heading for the gardens.

A flash of conversation caught her attention as she walked. "Skin kissed by the new moon..."

"Demons."

She winced and quickened her step. The rumors had followed Nazir.

Her eyes widened in relief as she saw Nazir waiting for her in the gardens. He led her to one of the benches surrounded by hedges and they sat down, hidden from sight.

He took her hand. "Are you alright? You've been tense the entire day."

She closed her eyes and allowed her hand to tighten on his. "You are far too observant for your own good, Nazir."

She opened her eyes in time to see him raise his eyebrows slightly. "Does it have anything to do with Lady Pellalindra's...condition?"

She gave him a sharp glance, then sighed and relaxed against the bench. Well, she had known that he knew. "You prove my point," she muttered. "Yes. At least, partly."

Nazir nodded. "Your father?"

She attempted to glare at him. "Will you stop it?" she asked, but she couldn't put any heat in her voice. "Yes, I'm worried about him. I probably shouldn't show my concern though, he doesn't seem to like it."

He patted her hand. "He might have simply been on edge. From what I understood, what he saw was not comforting."

"Not in the slightest." She stared across the garden, where the fountain still danced despite the cold. Nazir said nothing, just sat beside her, holding her hand.

Finally, she shook her head. "I don't like this wedding."

He simply nodded. Vinet felt the words drawn out of her. "Saihid's the father of Pellalindra's child. He should be the one at her side. He wants to be at her side. Instead, she's letting the pressures of nobility force her into marrying a man she herself has termed an enigma. She doesn't love him, I know that. And while I know that's not unusual for nobility, I..." her voice trailed off. Her chest knotted into a ball of pain.

"You want something more for yourself," Nazir said softly.

Vinet swallowed. "I suppose I do," she admitted.

Nazir's gaze wandered over the garden, then returned to Vinet. "Vinet, take this from a man who has lived his entire life outside normal society. The opinions of the majority of people don't matter. The ones who matter won't judge you. They will accept who you are and the choices you make."

She managed a smile. "You would know, I suppose." Her expression sobered again. "Nazir, the rumors you warned me about..."

"They've followed me here. I know. I've heard the whispers." Nazir sighed. "It was going to happen eventually."

"It's not your fault!" Vinet hissed. "If they'd just talk to you, they'd realize you could not possibly be demonic in any way."

He smiled. "Thank you for that, Vinet."

They sat in comforting silence for a moment longer. Finally, Vinet reached out and squeezed his arm. "Let's rejoin the others then, shall we?"

Nazir nodded and rose to his feet. As he offered her his arm, she smiled. "Thank you," she whispered. "I needed that."

Her eyes widened as they reentered the ballroom. On the edge of the dance floor, away from most of the nobles, Saihid danced with a young noblewoman. Vinet's breath caught. She could not say how she knew, but instinctive knowledge so deep she couldn't deny it spoke to her. The maiden who'd been at the masquerade, the one who'd spoken to Saihid then. The one who'd called her mother's daughter. AeresThonEsia. And Pellalindra was glaring daggers at her.

The maiden led Saihid to the edge of the room near Vinet as the music ended. "Bear not these burdens, sweet Saihid," she said.

Saihid bowed. "Thank you, Lady Hiliakae," he said softly. "Please enjoy the rest of the evening.

The maiden laughed. "Oh, I shall."

Vinet blinked. For a moment, the maiden had changed, into the face of the motherly figure she'd been in the Labyrinth. What was Aeres-ThonEsia? Maiden, mother, crone? A swirl of fabrics distracted her, and when she glanced back, AeresThonEsia had disappeared. She swallowed.

Pellalindra walked over to her. "Have you seen that woman before?" she asked.

"Only once," she said cautiously. "At your masquerade." *In that form, at least*, she thought.

Pellalindra shook her head. "I shall have to question Saihid about her later."

Humble fabric caught Vinet's attention. The plain linen stood out among the fancy garb of all the guests. The older woman wearing it had brown hair mixed with gray and was obviously pregnant. She made her way hesitantly toward Pellalindra.

"My lord, my lady, my congratulations," she said.

Lord Auriel walked over. "Lady Kianna," he said, bowing as he took her hand. "It is so good of you to come."

Vinet frowned. Lady Kianna was the wife of Lord General Torainn. She had not expected the woman, by all accounts distraught at the disappearance of her husband, to be there.

From across the room, Vinet saw Conn and Maeve see Kianna and quickly walk over. "Lady Kianna!" Conn exclaimed.

Kianna turned stiffly. "Hello again, Lord Conn. Is this your wife?"

Again? Vinet glanced briefly at Conn. Then again, he'd considered Torainn a mentor. Of course, he would have met his wife.

"Lady Kianna, my wife, Lady Maeve," Conn introduced.

"A pleasure." Kianna appeared distracted. "I am sorry Torainn could not be here, but his duties kept him home. He would have loved to have met you again. And you, General Alexander," she said, nodding at the older man's approach.

Vinet frowned. *But Torainn was gone...* Something was wrong with Lady Kianna.

Conn gasped. "But...then Torainn is at home? He has returned?"

Alexander seemed just as excited. "You have seen him?"

Kianna shrank back from the excited men. "Why...why yes. He never left. Is it not he who shares my bed?" She looked around, clearly distraught at the idea Lord General Torainn had been gone.

Conn blinked. "Do you not remember why I visited you in the capital, Lady Kianna?"

"Are you sure you did not come to visit my husband?" Kianna's voice was sharp. "No one ever comes to visit me!"

Pellalindra cleared her throat and gave Conn a sharp look. "I am sure they do, Lady Kianna," she said firmly. "As you came to visit me today. I thank you for coming." She snagged a glass from a passing server. "Let us toast the sweet future, Lady Kianna."

"To the future, to our children and grandchildren!" General Alexander nodded at Kianna. "Do you remember my eldest grandchild, Rian? She's become quite the terror. Determined to wheedle a horse from me, because 'real knights ride horses, Granddad, not ponies!' I am determined not to give into her yet."

Vinet smiled briefly but remained standing back. Something was dreadfully wrong. She could feel it. She squeezed down on Nazir's hand.

"I remember. She was a sweet child." Lady Kianna looked at Lord Auriel. "And how is your own daughter, my lord?"

Vinet froze, as did the entire group of nobles. Pellalindra's glass fell to the floor with a shatter. Instantly, a servant rushed over to clean it.

Pellalindra stepped back. "Oh, I'm sorry, so clumsy of me!" She didn't seem to care that some of the liquid had splashed on her gown. She took Lord Auriel's hand. "Would you care to dance, my dear?"

Lord Auriel's expression was implacable. "That would be most pleasing."

Vinet took a deep breath as Lord Auriel whisked Pellalindra away. Lord Auriel had a daughter?

Lady Kianna turned to her. "And who are you? I have not had the pleasure of meeting you before."

Vinet bobbed a shallow curtsy. "Lady Vinet of Ninaeva." She hesitated. "I had the pleasure of meeting your husband in Venia a few months back. Did you ever join him there?"

Lady Kianna shook her head and stepped closer to Vinet. "No, I do not travel," she said. "Not like yourself, I hear. Your life is full of adventures." She reached out, her hand gently brushing Vinet's own.

Raging fire. Dark corridors. Bright meadows. The wind cutting through the willows around a clear lake.

The streets of Venia.

A dragon's laughter tearing through an ancient sky.
A young woman sitting in a hovel, nursing a babe.
A harsh war, the ground torn, the skies rent, bodies where trees once stood.
A seeping darkness in her mind.
The strength of will to draw herself out, barely.

Vinet tore herself back to reality. Nazir was holding her, whispering soothingly. Conn and Maeve were staring in alarm. Alexander's eyes were wide. Only Lady Kianna seemed utterly unaffected.

Vinet stumbled away from Kianna, trying to process what she'd just seen. "I...excuse me," she said. She glanced around desperately. She didn't know where Kinaevan was. He hadn't been in the gardens. Pellalindra and Lord Auriel were on the dance floor...

"Vinet. You need air." Nazir steadied her as she stumbled. She allowed him to support her as he led them to the gardens. The darkness was a blessed relief after the bright light of the ballroom.

"I need my father," she whispered. "Nazir, there's something terribly wrong!"

"I can't leave you alone," Nazir shook his head. "Vinet, you're not well."

"What's wrong with her?" Gwyn strode through the darkness toward them.

Vinet nearly collapsed. "Gwyn. I need Kinaevan. I had a vision. Something is wrong with Lady Kianna."

Gwyn didn't hesitate. "I'll get him. Nazir, you take her someplace more secure than this. There's a servant's hallway off the ballroom. None of the nobles will think to eavesdrop there."

Before Vinet had a chance to answer, Gwyn had disappeared. Nazir took her arm and guided her back through the ballroom. The servants' hallway was deserted. She gasped as Lord Auriel and Kinaevan entered the room together, followed by Gwyn and Pellalindra. Kinaevan strode straight for her and held her shoulders.

"A vision?"

She nodded.

"Tell us," Lord Auriel's voice was calm, but commanding.

She swallowed. "When Lady Kianna touched me. Fire. Dragons. War. Venia, meadows...and darkness." She shuddered. The image of the woman with the child flashed through her mind. Why hadn't she mentioned that? It could have been important. But even now, she couldn't add the words.

She looked up. Pellalindra stared in shock. Lord Auriel and Kinaevan exchanged grim looks.

"The same." Lord Auriel said.

"But not Venia and the meadows." Kinaevan shook his head. "What have you been doing?" His voice chided, but gently. "You must ground yourself, Vinet." He took her hand. At his touch, the pain of the vision began to fade.

She knew what that meant now, grounding. She hadn't been looking through the trees. She took a deep, shuddering breath. "I didn't mean to. This happened without warning."

"Does this mean…Kianna isn't a danger?" The hope in Pellalindra's voice was painful.

Neither Lord Auriel nor Kinaevan confirmed her hope. "We must get her away from the others immediately. To the gardens."

Pellalindra's reactions were a credit to her. Without any further questions, she left, presumably to carry out Lord Auriel's instructions.

Nazir's silent presence was an eternal comfort. She grasped her father's hand. "Thank you," she gasped. "I didn't expect that to happen."

He chuckled. "I never expect mine."

She looked up. Lord Auriel stared at the wall, as if deep in thought. She cleared her throat. "I am sorry for disturbing your wedding, Lord Auriel," she said.

He shook himself. "No, no. It is better you shared this vision. Now we can do what must be done."

"What must be done?" she asked. She wanted to ask more questions, but she glanced between Lord Auriel and Kinaevan uncertainly. She still didn't know how much Lord Auriel knew about Kinaevan, and definitely not how much he knew about her.

Her father sighed, and Lord Auriel returned to staring. Suddenly he started, and without ceremony left the room.

She turned her gaze to her father.

"The great enemy must die," he said softly.

"Kianna?" Vinet whispered. "Kianna is the great enemy?" She couldn't believe that. "The Great Burner?"

"A host," Kinaevan grasped her hand even tighter.

Host. Her eyes widened. "The child?"

"It seems the Lady was correct."

Vinet stumbled backward into Nazir's arms. "What must be done…are they going to kill her?"

"To save thousands upon thousands of lives, of the existence of life on our world, yes."

She swallowed, bile rising in her throat. Despite the conviction in her father's words, all she could see was the swell of Kianna's belly. "I think I might be sick."

"I am sorry, my daughter. I was hoping I was mistaken, but with your vision..." he shook his head.

She reached out a hesitant hand to his shoulder.

He started. "I am sorry," he whispered again. "There is always a great doubt whenever the Sight prevents the Great Burner's return."

She blinked rapidly. "Is it always an unborn child?"

He nodded slowly. A single tear rolled down his cheek.

Her own eyes stung, and she turned, burying her face in Nazir's shoulder. He pulled her close to him.

They stood there in silence for a moment. Then Kinaevan shifted. "Ground yourself, my child," he said softly. "The world still turns." He paused again. "Take care of my daughter."

"I will," Nazir's voice was firm and steady.

"Good."

Vinet heard the door close as Kinaevan left.

Nazir held her a moment longer. Finally, he pushed her away, holding her shoulder, and looked her in the eyes. "Let's go," he said. "You have faced enough today."

"They're going to kill her," Vinet whispered.

She felt a tear on her cheek as Nazir nodded. "I know," he said. "Come, Vinet. Let's go home."

12

WAR

Vinet hesitated at the door to the council session. Whatever was on today's agenda was sure to be derailed. She could already hear the shouting.

"Nervous?"

She turned and raised an eyebrow at Kamian.

He grinned. "I would be. Everyone's going to be peppering you with questions as soon as you walk in there."

"You assume I have answers," she muttered. She stared at the door. "And that they're not too involved trying to kill each other."

Kamian laughed loudly. "Come now. You flee the wedding in a panic, and in the next half hour, Lady Kianna is shot dead by Lord Auriel's guards? And then you ride back to Ninaeva before anyone can speak to you? You are going to be in for the questioning of a lifetime!"

Vinet glared at him. "Those who needed to know already know, Lord Kamian. I am not here to satisfy everyone's idle curiosity."

He blinked in surprise. She took advantage of his momentary silence to push open the door and walk into the council chamber.

Bedlam reigned. Pellalindra and Conn shouted at each other, both on their feet, leaning across the table. Alexander stood as well, prepared to physically intervene if necessary. Dannan watched in fascination, and Ellil merely gazed into the fire. The shouting did not lessen at all as Vinet entered the room.

"Your precious husband killed my mentor's wife!" Conn shouted. "I don't care about his excuses! There needs to be justice!"

"Justice you will administer?" Pellalindra's voice was scathing. "How can you administer justice when you are blinded by your own rage?"

"That's priceless from you." Conn shook. "Who is it who's so blinded by affection that she defends her husband with every breath? Did he enchant you into this wedding? Is that why you're so under his thumb?"

"You dare?" Pellalindra seemed aghast. "I am Lady of the Council, and he is the Lord Steward of the realm! Are you accusing him of treason?"

For a moment, Vinet thought Conn angry enough to make the accusation right there and then. He glared at Pellalindra for a long moment. "No, but I still think he owes us more than an explanation than we got! And there should have been proper justice involved, not an assassination in the dark!"

A small, cynical voice in the back of Vinet's head chided Conn for hypocrisy. No one knew who had given the order to murder his uncle and cousins in their feasting hall, but since the perpetrators had escaped, all the safe bets were on Conn himself.

"What more justification do you need than that she was a danger to the kingdom?" Pellalindra asked.

"That's not good enough justification," Dannan's voice was low. "I agree with Lord Conn. We are the ruling council until the king decides otherwise. How are we to best protect the kingdom if the truth is hidden from us?"

"I want the truth!" Conn yelled. "Are you so far gone as to trust the word of a near stranger? One who hasn't told you the complete truth?"

Pellalindra paled slightly but held her ground. "He had already told me about his daughter," she said steadily. "That was one of the reasons he knew Lady Kianna was not who she said she was!"

"She what?" Conn jerked back. "You speak nonsense, Pellalindra," he snapped. "I've met the lady before; a kind, gentle soul, who wouldn't harm a fly!"

"It wasn't her!" Pellalindra shouted.

Vinet blinked. It hadn't been Lady Kianna there? She sat down as unobtrusively as she could and thought hard. It either had been Lady Kianna or a very good magical disguise. Or...Kinaevan had called her a host. Had the Great Burner been working through her? Had Lady Kianna already been dead? Or simply possessed? Could they have saved her? She looked down at the polished oak wood. Could she have saved her? She had hidden one small part of her vision, even from her father. She hadn't been certain why at the time, but she knew why she was keeping it. The mother and child, somewhere in a hovel in Venia. If she told her father, it would almost guarantee another assassination.

"Lord Conn, Lady Pellalindra, please," Alexander tried to intervene. "This is getting us nowhere. Please, calm down."

"Calm down?!"

Vinet winced. That had been the wrong thing to say to Conn.

"Calm down?!" Conn continued at the top of his lungs. "A pregnant woman is murdered in front of my eyes, and you expect me to calm down?"

Pellalindra gasped, and Vinet looked up sharply. Pellalindra had bent over and was clutching her stomach. Vinet leapt to her feet in an instant. Unheeding of anyone else in the room, she walked quickly to Pellalindra's side and took her arm. She could feel the desperate strength in those fingers as Pellalindra clutched at Vinet. She was so pale.

"I'm going to faint," she whispered.

"No, you're not," Vinet whispered back. "Come on. Out of here. One step at a time."

By some miracle, no one intercepted them as they walked to the door. Vaguely, she heard Alexander talking to Conn, but she kept her attention focused on Pellalindra. She pushed the door open to reveal Saihid. He stared at them both in concern.

"Saihid," Vinet snapped. She didn't give him any time to think. "Take your lady to her bedchamber and call a healer."

"I'm fine…" Pellalindra protested weakly.

Vinet grasped her hands. "You will be. But someone needs to verify it. And provide an official diagnosis for the announcement."

She met Pellalindra's eyes, trying to communicate her meaning.

Pellalindra's eyes widened slightly, and she nodded in understanding. Vinet sighed in relief as Saihid took her arm and guided her down the hall.

She turned back to the council chamber to find both Dannan and Ellil staring at her. Alexander still tried to calm Conn. Kamian wasn't helping. Now that Pellalindra had left, he was making snide remarks to Conn.

She cleared her throat. To her surprise, the argument stopped.

"I suggest we all take a recess," she said, surprised at how calm her voice sounded. "We'll reconvene here in half an hour."

She didn't wait for anyone to disagree and get wrapped up in an argu-

168

ment, simply turned on her heel and walked out of the council chamber, walking quickly down the corridor to the palace gardens.

The fresh air brought a sigh of relief. It was still Manyu's Time, but Mazda's Rise could be felt. It tingled beneath the cold, the breath of fresh life.

Vinet sat down on the same bench where she and Nazir had sat after the wedding and closed her eyes, breathing in the smell of life around her. Her senses tingled, as if she physically reached into the ground, living growing, nurturing. Her shoulder blades throbbed, but she was so deep she barely noticed.

Someone cleared their throat, and she opened her eyes in irritation. She bit back a sharp question when she saw Conn standing next to the bench, partially hidden by the large hedge.

"Lady Vinet. Might I have a word?"

Well, at least he seemed calmer than he had been a few minutes ago. She took a breath and nodded. "Of course, Lord Conn."

He glanced around the garden suspiciously. Her eyes involuntarily followed his, checking that no one was eavesdropping on their conversation.

"Is Lady Pellalindra well?" he said.

Vinet narrowed her eyes. "She will be, yes," she said shortly.

Conn nodded, seemingly distracted. "Good. Despite our disagreements..."

She waited. This was not what he wanted to talk to her about. Her entire body felt as tense as a harp string.

He cleared his throat. "The wedding," he said. "What happened? When Lady Kianna touched you, you were taken ill, or something. But you were not the only one she touched. I know this is the truth," he said as she opened her mouth. "Do not try to deny it."

Vinet closed her mouth again. She waited until Conn asked his question. "Why were you so affected by it?"

Ignorance. Ignorance was the best defense. "You and I wonder the same thing," she said, putting all the bitterness she could summon into those words. Bitterness about how little she knew. Bitterness that she could not reveal the child in her vision to anyone.

"What exactly happened?"

The best lies have truths. "She touched me, and I saw..." She didn't need to pretend to shudder. She closed her eyes, banishing the memory. "I knew something was wrong," she said. "I told Kinaevan and Lord Auriel.

The rest…well, you know." She waved a hand. Such a simple summary of such a horrible event!

Conn regarded her steadily. "Let me be frank, Lady Vinet. Are you a mage? Or training to be one? Because it is odd that 'a great enemy' would reveal his plans on purpose, and Alexander, myself, and Lady Pellalindra all touched her without being struck down."

Her lungs stopped. Conn suspected her of being a mage? Well, he wasn't far wrong, but still! She supposed she should be grateful he didn't suspect her of collaborating to murder Kianna! She took a deep breath, thinking quickly. Part of the truth. "I have studied some magic, yes," she said. "But mostly theory. I am no mage; not like you mean. But…do you think that just the knowledge could have been enough to trigger the vision?" She let her voice fill with hope.

Conn smiled grimly. "I see. I didn't think you could have concealed being a mage, not since Dannan, as much as he tries, cannot conceal his great power."

Vinet suppressed a flash of anger at the satisfaction in his voice. He didn't think her capable of deception?

He nodded. "It makes sense you are merely a novice. Tell me, what kinds of practice have you done? Perhaps simply being exposed to magical theory is enough to waken a sensitivity."

She closed her eyes, thanking Mazda Conn did not read many books. He did not know magic followed bloodlines. She could lie, and he would never know.

"I've mostly read." She smiled, realizing she could draw on Dannan for an alibi. "Lord Dannan was not pleased when he discovered I had gone through Kreutzer's library. As to practicing, I can light a candle. But that's barely anything."

From what she knew the 'barely anything' part was the most blatant lie. Most mages operated on the theoretical level, a mental plane of energy. To be able to operate on the elemental level was a gift only a few could manage. Dannan was powerful indeed, if her guess about the torches reacting to his emotions were true.

Conn smiled triumphantly. "Then that's probably it. That is more than I, or Alexander, or Pellalindra can do, which is why you were the one affected."

She shrugged. "I suppose that makes as much sense as anything." She held her breath, praying that he left it at that. She didn't want him inter-rogating her further.

"Thank you for telling me, Lady Vinet. You are far more open than some I could name."

She suppressed a wince. If only he knew... "If you could keep it from Lord Dannan," she said softly, "I would be grateful. You and he are friends, I have seen you talking. You must know his feelings about magic."

Conn chuckled. "You have my word. Let us hope the rest of the council session goes smoothly. Shall I escort you back inside?"

She nodded gracefully and let Conn take her arm.

The atmosphere in the council chamber lay as stiff and quiet as the gold-embroidered backed chairs. Pellalindra remained absent, to no one's surprise.

As everyone sat down, a servant knocked on the door. Vinet had only to glance at the blue and black Duskryn livery to know his purpose.

"Pardon me, my lords, my lady, but I bear a message from Lady Pellalindra. She is bearing Lord Auriel's child and has taken to bed for the rest of the day. She sends her apologies."

Vinet smiled. "Please convey my congratulations," she told the servant.

The other councilors joined in politely, even Conn. She was grateful for that. She could understand his feelings about the murder, but he was too prone to violence, too unpredictable, to ever be considered safe. And pregnancy made one vulnerable in unexpected ways.

She regarded the rest of the councilors and met Alexander's eyes. He smiled at her. "Well, shall we address the first order of business, then?" she asked.

Another knock interrupted them before anyone could respond. Vinet turned with the rest to see a servant in the livery of the palace messengers. He looked exhausted.

Her throat tightened. Somehow, she knew the words he was about to speak would be terrible news.

"My lords and ladies of the Council," he said, swaying on his feet. "I bear urgent news. Since the king has taken ill, the Lord Steward directed me to come here immediately."

The king ill? Vinet glanced up, seeing equal shock on every other face, including Dannan's. If even the prince's tutor hadn't known, the illness must have been sudden and recent.

The messenger took a scroll from his belt and unrolled it.

"From Lord General Lairan. My liege, I have urgent news. Our scouts report an invasion from the south. An army sweeps across our lands. Our Regulars have managed a defensive line, but we have lost fertile land.

More urgently, two of our nobles appear to have turned traitor. They have been seen collaborating with the enemy. I await your instructions and beg you and the Council to authorize the redeployment of the troops from Venia here at once. The situation is urgent. Strange beings have been seen with the army, and we will need every warrior we have. I serve you faithfully, now and forever. Signed, Lord General Lairan."

Vinet made her way back to her townhouse in a state of exhaustion. The Council had granted Lord General Lairan's request. How could they not? Jyria had made no aggressive moves toward Venia since they had withdrawn their naval blockade. And all the councilors seemed to understand the gravity of the threat, even if they didn't understand what lay behind it.

Mount Halon. It had to be. Kinaevan had warned her often enough these past months. The corruption had reached Saemar. She had no doubt that was why the two lords had turned traitor. Her shoulder blades ached, and she was acutely aware of the mark on her back. Was Manyu the one behind the corruption? How could they fight against a God?

She missed Gwyn's presence at her side. Gwyn had decided Evalynna should accompany Vinet today, as bodyguard training. In theory, Vinet approved, and she liked Evalynna, but the woman wasn't her oath-sister.

It was a relief to be back home. She dismissed Evalynna and made her way to the library. She just wanted to curl up with a book in front of the fire; a storybook, one unconnected to the darkness rising from the south.

"You think she'd risk a second bastard?" She stopped outside the door of the library. Nazir's voice came from inside.

"Don't play the fool, Nazir. You are exactly the sort of man she'd fall for. Charming, smart, a scholar, obsessed with history and travel, and completely ineligible." Gwyn's voice rang sharp and reprimanding. "So be an honorable one as well. Don't tempt her with what she can't have. She's having enough difficulties right now."

Vinet caught her breath and steadied herself against the wall.

"I see," Nazir spoke quietly, so quiet Vinet had to strain to hear. "And what of her heart, Gwyn? Don't you think she deserves a chance at happiness?"

"She cannot have a lover, Nazir, and that is the only way nobles and commoners can ever love." She'd never heard Gwyn this harsh before. "And if you do anything, anything at all, to upset my lady, or toy with her heart in any way, I will make it my business to deal with you, understand?"

Vinet turned blindly away. She didn't want to hear the rest of the conversation. She'd heard enough already. She didn't pay attention to where she went, but she wasn't surprised her steps led her to the garden. She sat down on the ground underneath the hazel tree, next to a bed of snowdrops and witch hazel, and took a deep breath, trying to process what she'd just heard. Nazir fancied her? Enough that he stood up to Gwyn?

She closed her eyes, feeling her chest tightening. Ever since Pellalindra's wedding, they had been closer than ever. He had supported her without question, without judgment. He had given her the strength she'd needed to face this council session. She wanted...

"There you are."

She glanced up at Gwyn's voice, hoping her emotions didn't show too clearly on her face.

"Evalynna told me you were home," Gwyn said, sinking to the ground next to Vinet. "Bad council session?"

Vinet winced. "We're at war," she said. "Mount Halon. From the south. Two nobles defected."

Gwyn sucked in a breath. "Mazda's light," she breathed. "That's bad."

Vinet nodded. "We redeployed the Regulars," she said. "Lord General Lairan sounds confident enough. But I don't know what they can do against..." she shuddered.

Gwyn placed a hand on her shoulder. "They'll figure it out," she said. "We have the Faithful, who've fought this evil for a long time, remember? They'll help. And Lord Auriel, despite his mysteriousness, seems devoted to the safety of Saemar."

Vinet grimaced. "The king is ill too."

"How does that make a difference? He's been absent since the queen died. That's why there's a council, isn't it?"

She shrugged. "Yes, but he's just been withdrawn, healing from grief. If he's ill..."

Gwyn snorted. "Healing from grief for three years? Uninterested in his duties, if you ask me."

Vinet frowned at Gwyn. As much as she might agree with the sentiment, one did not say that kind of thing about a king.

Gwyn sighed. "We need to talk," she said.

Vinet turned her gaze to the hazel tree. Now it came. "What about?"

"Nazir," Gwyn was never one to mince words. "Vinet, this has to stop."

"What does?" Vinet asked stubbornly. "There's nothing between us."

"Vinet," Gwyn sighed. "Don't try that on me."

She winced and met Gwyn's eyes. No harshness existed in Gwyn's expression, just pity.

"There isn't," she insisted weakly. "He's a friend. A good one."

"One you want to be more than a friend," Gwyn said. "I was there when you fell for Jaim, Vinet. I know you."

Jaim. Vinet closed her eyes and shook her head. "This is different."

"I should hope so. Vinet, you can't afford another bastard."

Vinet opened her eyes, wincing at the bluntness of Gwyn's words.

"You're a member of the Council now," Gwyn continued ruthlessly. "Just look at what Pellalindra did. You can't afford a four-month religious retreat. There will be questions, questions you can't afford. And what of Niara? What would happen to her after such a disgrace?"

Vinet felt her throat closing. She couldn't deny the truth of Gwyn's words. Pellalindra had married a near stranger to save herself and her son. The scandal for Vinet, who would never marry like Pellalindra, would be devastating.

"Don't ask me to send him away," Vinet begged. "Whatever else, I need his support right now. With this war…"

Gwyn sighed. "Be careful, Vinet."

"I will," Vinet reached out to grab Gwyn's hand. "I promise, Gwyn."

Gwyn did not appear convinced, but at the same time, she looked resigned. She squeezed Vinet's hand once before standing up.

A cough from the door made them both look up. Evalynna stood there, looking sheepish. "Pardon me, Lady Vinet, but Lord Dannan of Kreutzer is here to see you."

Vinet exchanged a glance with Gwyn. She stood up, brushing herself off. "Show him in." She nodded to Gwyn, and Gwyn retreated deeper into the garden, out of sight of Dannan.

Dannan was just as grim and intimidating as ever, dressed all in black velvets. His citron eye glared at everything around him.

Vinet put on a pleasant smile as she walked forward to greet him. "Lord Dannan! This is a pleasant surprise."

He snorted. "Hardly, I'd imagine. No need to pretend you're glad to see me. I need to ask you some questions."

His bluntness relieved her. She allowed her smile to fade and crossed her arms over her chest. "What can I help you with?"

"I was at the wedding," Dannan said. "I saw part of what happened, but not all. And for the life of me, I cannot discover what happened when Lady Kianna touched you."

She gritted her teeth. She couldn't lie to Dannan. He knew far more about magic than she did.

"A vision," she said shortly. "One of destruction and darkness."

A single raised eyebrow. "I see. Can you tell me more?"

She took a breath and closed her eyes. "Venia. A meadow. Fire, war and hundreds of corpses. Then absolute darkness."

The baby's wail echoed in her mind. The poor mother in the hovel. She shoved the image out of her mind, not wanting to give Dannan a hint she wasn't telling the whole truth.

"I see," Dannan said again.

She waited as he turned to regard the garden. They stood in silence for a long moment.

"Tell me, Lady Vinet, how long have you had visions?"

She had been half expecting the question. She stared at Dannan, trying to read him. She couldn't see any anger in his expression.

"Since I was thirteen," she said quietly.

He didn't turn toward her, but she saw the slight smile. "Indeed. Thirteen. It always seems to manifest then, doesn't it." It wasn't a question.

Her hands tightened on her arms. "Lord Dannan, I know your feelings on magic. But this...I can't help it!" Frustration leaked into her voice. "I can't not see things! It doesn't work that way."

His gaze snapped to hers, startled. "Oh, I know. You're not enough of an idiot to go looking for visions of the future, I think. Too many mages fall for that trap, constantly obsessed with it, blinding them to the present. That does not sound like you." He paused. "Do you have any idea why you would have this ability? I can sense you have it, but not why."

She paused, still trying to figure out whether the first part of his words had been a hidden compliment. She shrugged as casually as possible. "I don't know. I've always had it. It's the reason I research magic, but there is so little written down." There was no lie in that sentence. To her knowledge, only her father had ever written anything about the Sight.

"These things are usually hereditary," Dannan said. "There's nothing in your heritage? Your mother? Your father?"

"Not that I know of." She didn't know how her voice remained calm.

He stared at her for a long moment. Vinet met his gaze squarely. She didn't dare break away.

Finally, he nodded. "Thank you for your time, Lady Vinet. It seems we both have secrets we'd rather not share. I appreciate your candor about this vision, all the same. I will continue to look into this matter."

He knows I am hiding something, but he won't press. At least, not yet. Vinet hesitated. "You might want to talk to Kinaevan, the Faithful ambassador," she said. "He knows a great deal about magic and this vision. He may be able to tell you more. He told me it was connected to Mount Halon and the south." She would let her father judge how much Dannan should know.

Dannan nodded. "It is clear something in the south wants us destroyed," he said. "This war..." he shook his head. "Thank you for the information. I will speak to him when I can."

She nodded in return. "Anytime, Lord Dannan."

He bowed slightly, then turned and left. Vinet stared after him. Somehow, she had the feeling she'd just made another ally.

A baby's wail. The sound of animals grunting. Mud. Screams. A soothing voice, broken by tears. A skull! It was coming for the child. Hundreds of eyes rolled around and around, over and over each other. They followed her down dark tunnels with no end. She couldn't escape!

Vinet woke in a cold sweat, staring at the ceiling. It was midnight. She was still in her townhouse. There was no danger. There was no danger, she told herself again. She took another deep breath before sitting up and rolling out of bed. She wouldn't be able to sleep now. She never could.

She didn't have the patience to fumble with a light for her oil lamp. She reached inside and twisted, snapping her fingers. A small spark and the wick lit. She grabbed the shawl beside her bed with shaking hands and wrapped it around her shoulders. Taking the lamp, she started for the library, her bare feet padding softly on the floor.

One of Niara's tales, that was what she needed. Or maybe her father's book. Studying: that would distract her.

The fire in the library still lingered, though it had died down from the day's blaze. Only small embers remained, dancing with the occasional pretty flame. It still illuminated the room, though, and with her lamp, enough to read by. She sat her oil lamp down on the small table next to her chair with a sigh of relief.

"Vinet?"

She whirled. Who would be in the library at this hour?

Nazir rose from one of the chairs where he had been ensconced with a book and oil lamp of his own. His face was full of concern. "Vinet, are you alright? What's wrong?"

She stepped back a pace, her heart still pounding. She couldn't face him now. Not like this. Gwyn had been right. This was too dangerous. She fancied him. But she couldn't talk to him now! Not like this!

He took a step toward her, and she flinched. "I'm fine." She cursed inwardly. Her voice had trembled. Nazir was far too observant for his own good. He would surely notice.

Nazir stopped and tilted his head to the side. "Vinet," he said softly. "You don't have to tell me. But you are so pale, I almost thought you were a ghost. Maybe I can help?"

His kindness was too much. She covered her face with her hands and headed for her chair by the fire. Its familiar comfort enveloped her as she sat. She stayed there for a moment, trembling in every limb, letting the heat from the dying fire warm her. She heard, more than saw, Nazir make his way hesitantly to the chair next to her.

He didn't speak. Why didn't he speak? Why didn't he ask? If he had, she could have defended herself. But this...she couldn't withstand this.

"I'm cursed," she whispered.

She heard Nazir move and looked up into his startled eyes. "I'm not being melodramatic. I am. I had an...accident. I got in over my head. And it left me with...these..." she shuddered, "nightmares."

Nazir reached hesitantly toward her shoulder. She grasped his hand with her own, grateful for any human contact. It anchored her, stabilized her. She could remember which world she lived in.

"What kind of curse?" Nazir asked. "If it's a simple one, there are mages who specialize in removing such things."

She swallowed. "If only it were that simple." She met his eyes again. "Nazir, it...this curse..." she couldn't get the words out. He was a devout Mazdian. He had found sanctuary in the Temple of Mazda as a child. How would he react if he knew?

His eyes were kind and understanding. "Vinet, it's alright," he said softly.

She looked down. Then slowly, she stood up, leaving her shawl in her chair. She felt Nazir's eyes on her as she turned her back to him and started unlacing the back of her shift.

"Vinet?" Nazir asked, surprise clear in his voice. Vinet ignored him until the laces were untied past her shoulders.

"Between my shoulder blades."

She heard Nazir stand up and walk closer. She wrapped her arms around herself, bracing herself for any reaction, for shouts, questions, curses, and demands for information. But all she heard was a quick intake of breath.

She waited, trembling, but he said nothing. Finally, she couldn't stand it and looked over her shoulder at him. "I'm no Manyu-worshipper," she said. "But he marked me. I'm protected during the day, but at night…"

Nazir's face was blank, a picture of shock. She waited for him to say something, anything, but he just stood there, unmoving. She turned away to lace up her shift again. She nearly cried as her hands shook so badly she dropped the laces.

Suddenly, she felt other hands on hers, warm, steady hands which took the laces from her and deftly tied them. She stood still, shaking slightly, until Nazir gently tugged her shoulder to get her to turn and face him.

"Is there any way to remove it?" he asked.

She risked a glance at his face. No judgment could be read there, only concern and sympathy. She nearly collapsed in relief. He believed her.

"The most powerful mage I know could only place those protections." She swallowed. She knew nothing of AeresThonEsia's motivations. "Or else, that's all she wanted to do."

He nodded slowly. "Maybe there is knowledge out there we do not have." He smiled, and despite herself, Vinet's spirits lifted. "There'll be a way."

She returned the smile, although even she could tell it was small and shaky. "Thank you," she whispered.

He smiled at her a moment longer. "Will you be able to sleep now? Would you like something? Tea, perhaps? Or something stronger? I can raid the kitchens for you."

She managed a laugh, feeling her tension draining away. She was exhausted. "I think…I actually think I might be able to sleep now." She blinked, surprised. "This helped."

"I'm glad," he said.

They stood there together, a little awkward. Vinet knew she should head back to her room. She should heed Gwyn's warning and not get too close to this strange outcast scholar, but something held her there.

Nazir moved first. "I should let you get to sleep," he said. "Goodnight, Vinet."

Before she could react, he leaned down and kissed her briefly on the lips. She stared at him in shock as he turned and walked out of the room. The sensation lasted, tingling as she brought her fingers to her lips.

Feeling more unsteady than before, she carefully lowered herself into her chair. She couldn't sleep now. She fumbled briefly for the book her father gave her. Study, that would take her mind off things, she would be able to ignore what had just happened, she would...

She sat there for hours, staring at the fire. When Gwyn found her in the morning, her father's book was still unopened on the table next to her.

13

A SECRET TRIP

Vinet, are you certain about this?"

Vinet didn't look up from her packing. "I'm certain," she said firmly. "Pack a small bag. We're going in secret."

She could see Gwyn's trepidation, but she didn't back down. She'd had steady nightmares for the past week, and she could no longer stand the cries of the screaming baby. They were going to Venia.

"I wish you'd take a guard."

"I am. You." Vinet did not want an escort that would draw attention to herself. Some of the other council members surely employed spies. The Faithful, if they weren't all involved in the southern conflict, also. The Unfaithful probably did as well. She didn't want anyone to know where she was going.

Gwyn sighed. "Mazda's light, Vinet, you're worrying me."

Vinet finally looked up to meet Gwyn's eyes. "There's a newborn child somewhere in Venia," she said. "Somehow, it's connected to this darkness from Mount Halon. I do not want anyone else finding out about this until I've had a chance to verify whether it's a threat or not." Her voice cracked. She didn't think she could stand it if a small child truly was a threat.

Gwyn gazed at her sadly. "It wasn't your fault, Vinet."

She squeezed her eyes shut. Although she hadn't seen it, the assassination had been described often enough. Kianna, three arrows in her chest and throat. And the unborn child.

She opened her eyes again as Gwyn walked across the room. She blinked as a packet was thrust toward her.

"Commoner's clothing," Gwyn said. "If we're going secretly, we're going in disguise."

Vinet's eyes stung. "Thank you, Gwyn," she whispered.

Gwyn shook her head. "Don't thank me yet. We've got a long way to go. How do you plan on getting to Venia? The road will be full of soldiers and someone is bound to recognize you, commoner's clothing or not."

She smiled grimly. "We'll go to Hillsdale," she said, "and take a ship from there. The trade blockade is over, ships have been going in and out of Venia for months now. Providing us quite the trade revenue." She added that last sentence with bitter satisfaction. She had fought tooth and nail for trade, and the peace and prosperity it was bringing to the west was welcome validation.

Gwyn sighed again. "You've planned this all out, haven't you? Does your seneschal know?"

"I told him this morning," Vinet said. "He knows to cover for me for two weeks. It shouldn't take us any longer than that."

"Three days ride to Hillsdale, two days sail to Venia...we should be fine," Gwyn muttered. "Very well. I'm ready."

Vinet glanced up, startled. She'd been so absorbed in her own packing she hadn't even seen the small pack Gwyn had slung over her shoulder.

Gwyn shrugged. "I knew I wouldn't be able to convince you not to do this if you'd thought about it."

Vinet smiled. "Then let's go."

They walked side by side through the castle. Vinet had already said goodbye to Niara. Her daughter wasn't happy about her mother disappearing for two weeks, but accepted it.

They had reached the gates when she heard Nazir hail her. She turned to see him walking up to join them. Tall and dark, he was dressed in his old travel garments, repaired but worn, a small pack on his back.

"Nazir," Vinet couldn't deny the relief which filled her chest.

Gwyn glared at him. "What are you doing here?"

Nazir seemed determined. "I'm coming with you."

"Absolutely not," Gwyn hissed.

Vinet held out a hand to Gwyn and met Nazir's eyes. "Do you know where we're going?"

Nazir shook his head. "No. But you're going in secret, and therefore, knowing you, it's dangerous, so I'm coming with you."

Gwyn opened her mouth to argue, and Vinet waved her to silence. She stared into Nazir's eyes for a long moment. Sincerity and concern but also stubborn determination.

She nodded. "Alright."

"Vinet!"

Vinet turned to whisper in Gwyn's ear. "It's either this or he follows us. At least this way, you can keep an eye on him."

Gwyn narrowed her eyes, then transferred her gaze to Nazir. Nazir let out a sigh before falling into step with them.

"So where are we going?" he asked.

"Venia," Vinet said.

He raised his eyebrows. "What for?"

"To find a child I saw in my visions," she answered. "When we get there, I'll use the Sight to…"

"Absolutely not!"

Vinet turned at Gwyn's sudden outburst. "What?"

"The last time you used the Sight, you took two days to recover," Gwyn said fiercely. "I won't have you using it again so far from home."

Vinet opened her mouth to protest.

"I agree," Nazir said quietly.

Vinet transferred her startled gaze to him.

He raised an eyebrow. "You need to practice more. Preferably under the guidance of your father. Do you know what he meant by grounding?"

"Yes, I…"

"And you haven't slept for a week," Gwyn cut in. "No Sight, Vinet. Not unless it is desperately necessary. You said she's in a hovel, yes? We'll search on foot."

She couldn't win an argument with the two of them united. "Alright," she agreed unwillingly.

"Good," Gwyn nodded in satisfaction, and Nazir appeared relieved.

"There's something following us. Something in the sky."

Vinet looked curiously at the ship captain. The two-day voyage to Venia was nearly over. Why would he only mention something following them now?

He shook his head ominously. "My men have seen a dark shape. Been strange reports on these waters. Makes them nervous."

Gwyn laughed. "How many times have you made this voyage, captain?"

He tugged his mustache. "Oh, I don't know. At least twice as many times as you are old, miss."

"Then you have absolutely nothing to worry about," Gwyn said with all appearance of confidence. "Besides, we're almost to Venia, aren't we?"

The captain nodded, not looking reassured in any way. "Aye, that's true. Time to get the lads on the oars, then!"

He strode off, grumbling to himself under his breath. Vinet raised an eyebrow at Gwyn.

"Sailor's superstition," Gwyn muttered. "They can't have an uneventful voyage. There always has to be something wrong."

Instinctively, Vinet turned her eyes to Nazir. He shrugged, but she could see the uncertainty in his eyes.

"These are the trade routes the explorer, Jimesseran, sailed, yes?" Nazir asked.

She hesitated. "He left from Venia and went north," she said finally. "Past Hillsdale, up the coast."

Their eyes met, and she suppressed a shudder. Jimesseran had written about something dark in the sky, convinced he had seen a dragon.

She glanced skyward. They only had a few more hours to Venia. Surely Gwyn was right about it being a sailor's superstition.

Gwyn's opinion seemed to prove itself when they landed without any trouble. As they disembarked, Vinet took the captain aside for a quiet word.

"Would it be possible for you to stay here a day longer and head back to Hillsdale tomorrow rather than this evening?" she asked.

The captain blinked. He knew her identity. She'd paid him well to conceal it.

"Of course, my lady," he said quietly.

She smiled and fished out a few coins from her purse. "Thank you," she said. "And remember…"

"No one knows you're here," the captain laid a finger against his nose and winked. "Aye, my lady. I'll remember."

She gave him a smile and disembarked with Gwyn and Nazir. They were heading to the hovels and slums, a district she'd never been.

She felt awkward in her borrowed clothing. She had worn smallfolks clothing before, especially when she negotiated trade deals. It helped her relations with the merchants. But merchants wore high-quality dresses, and hers emphasized the wealth of Ninaeva. The dress she wore now was common-spun linen, and she kept having to scratch the back of her neck. It helped them blend in, at least. Nazir still got strange looks, but neither she nor Gwyn warranted a second glance. Well, Gwyn did, occasionally. But she couldn't help her striking looks. *Evalynna is a lucky woman,* Vinet thought.

Vinet winced as her foot sank several inches into the mud, grateful she'd worn proper traveling boots. She'd hate to be going barefoot, like most of the people who lived in this quarter. She tried not to see the children running about. They were skin and bones and barely half-dressed, even though Manyu's Time still wasn't over. Papsukkal, the new year, wasn't for a month yet.

She hadn't left herself much time to get back to the capital before the next council session. She'd have to leave almost immediately after getting home, assuming they found the woman in this maze-like slum. It didn't help that the hovels seemed the same, ramshackle places held together by straw and thread. It must have rained last night, as well, for their feet sunk into mud six inches deep in places. Vinet was grateful for the wool cloak wrapped around her shoulders, the one clothing item she hadn't compromised on. Then again, neither had Gwyn nor Nazir. Gwyn's, at least, had the additional benefit of concealing her sword.

"Do you have anything to help us narrow down the search?" Gwyn asked.

"No," she said. "If I used the Sight…"

Both Gwyn and Nazir shook their heads in firm disapproval. Vinet sighed and looked about. She did not like their chances of doing this on foot, not when she had only a vague image of the woman's appearance.

Still, she followed Gwyn, slogging up and down the back streets, meeting the eye of every young woman of childbearing years. Each time was a disappointment. But she couldn't give up.

She slowed her stride. Gwyn and Nazir both walked ahead of her. For the moment, they focused on their surroundings, not on her. She closed her eyes and took a deep breath. The world spun, and everything seemed to crash loudly together.

She stood by a lake, a calm mirror of trees. Rich grass cushioned her bare feet. She wore only a soft green dress made of a fabric she couldn't identify. Ancient trees loomed over her. She could hear their whispers despite the whirlwind; the whirlwind that didn't disturb the water of the lake, or the leaves of the trees, or her dress or hair.

Then, a single ripple in the center of the lake. A hundred lily pads broke the surface, forming a path out to the lake's center from the shore at her feet.

"Approach." The voice was firm, female, and commanding.

She hesitated a fraction of a second, then placed a bare foot on the first lily pad. As she did, it withdrew, and she fell face-first into the water.

It was neither cold nor warm, nor did it feel like any water she'd ever swum in before. She wasn't floating. She couldn't float. A rising panic caused her to open her mouth, and a distinct taste of copper, of blood, consumed her. The color of the lake changed from easy blue to angry green to empty blackness. She was sinking, sinking. A sharp pain stabbed between her shoulder blades, over and over again, settling to a consistent throb.

"Pawn." The voice echoed dully in her mind. More pain. Two voices .. no, three...in her mind, in the darkness all about. Each was filled with fury and surety, a pulsing argument. She couldn't understand anything. The argument threatened to tear her in two!

"Niara."

Niara! Panic-fueled love gave her a burst of strength. This was a vision! She could control it!

She reached out with her mind, reaching for the nearest wood. The woman! The child!

The vision snapped, changing to a hovel, the same as all the others she'd seen, and she felt a moment of despair.

A branch! Above the door. Ash. Mountain ash. *Ash is hard and cold, I fear. She likes it when you shed a tear.*

Vinet jerked out of her vision, tears streaming down her face. She knelt in the mud of the streets of Venia alone. No, Gwyn knelt too, holding her close as she shook her shoulders. Nazir knelt next to her, worry clear on his face.

"Vinet? Vinet!"

"I..." she couldn't speak. Her head hurt. Between her shoulder blades, the mark stabbed her with fury.

"What were you thinking?" Though Gwyn meant to rebuke, the relief in her voice was clear.

"Mountain ash, a branch." Vinet managed. Her throat was dry. Breathing hurt.

"What?" Gwyn demanded. "Vinet, what do you mean?"

She coughed, trying to find the strength to answer.

"There!" Nazir exclaimed. She couldn't see where he pointed. "The hovel!"

He disappeared from her field of vision. A moment later she heard a scream.

"Get back, Nazir!" Gwyn shouted. A moment later, Nazir stood by her side again.

A pause. "Watch over her," Gwyn said.

Vinet didn't have the strength to resist as Nazir took her in his arms. *And why should I*, came a brief flicker of thought. "Can you stand?" he asked.

She could, barely. She blinked as she saw flashing steel in Nazir's hand. Had Gwyn given him her sword?

She clung to Nazir as another wave of pain swept through her, radiating out from between her shoulders. She managed to steady herself just enough to see Gwyn emerge from the hovel, escorting a young woman carrying a bundle made from Gwyn's cloak: the baby.

"We'll find Lord General Torainn," Gwyn promised. "This is Lady Vinet of Ninaeva. She's a member of the Council. Come back with us to Ninaeva, and you'll be safe. I promise."

Lord General Torainn? How is he connected with this? Vinet thought, but she didn't have the strength to think about it further. The young woman looked doubtfully at Vinet, but something in Gwyn's manner convinced her to assent.

Vinet didn't remember getting back to the boat. The captain and Gwyn exchanged some heated words, but Vinet just sank to the deck, shivering. She couldn't see. Her entire body was filled with pain.

"Vinet?" Nazir's eyes flashed in front of her face. "Vinet?!"

She tried to answer, tried to reassure him. But the world faded.

Darkness. Floating. At least there were no screams. Almost peaceful, more peaceful than she'd been in weeks.

A sharp pain. She cried out, or tried to. She didn't have a mouth. She didn't have a body. Where was the pain coming from? It burned all around her, all through her. She shook her head frantically. She had a head!

A scream. Niara! Her head snapped around. Niara stood at the foot of her bed, her eyes wide with fright. "What's wrong with Mama?" she demanded.

"We don't know," Gwyn's voice broke. "We'll find out, Niara, I promise. We've sent for Kinaevan."

Niara turned a tear-stained face toward the bed. Vinet tried to reach for her, but she couldn't move her arms.

"Don't leave me, Mama," she begged. "Please."

"She wrote this for you," Gwyn said. "To be announced the day after Papsukkal."

No! Don't show her that! I'm supposed to be the one to show her that! Vinet thought, helpless.

Niara looked at the scroll Gwyn handed to her and then burst into tears. "No! I don't want to be heir! I want my mother!"

She ran out of the room, sobbing. Vinet tried to follow her, but her legs were like lead.

Her vision shifted. Back on the boat to Venia. No, Venia to Hillsdale. No, back to Venia. The captain stared at the sky. A dark figure dove down, enveloping the world in fire.

Gwyn in Vinet's study, Evalynna bending over the desk next to her.

"Someone has to know Vinet won't be attending the council session," Gwyn said. "She can't just not appear. I've written the Lady of the Council that she's had an accident. That'll have to do."

"If you're sure," Evalynna said hesitantly.

Gwyn threw her hands in the air. "No, I'm not sure!" she exclaimed. "My best friend could be dying and I…" she broke down and covered her face in her hands.

Evalynna said nothing, only leaned down to hug Gwyn. Gwyn returned the embrace, trembling.

"Thank you," she whispered.

"Anytime."

"Pawn. Pawn. Pawn." A whisper, a chant. Vinet's eyes stung. *No!* She tried to cry out. She would not be a pawn.

Fire burst from her hands. No, from Dannan's hands. A demon laughed and cackled. Dannan cried out, trying to stop it. His face was a mask of panic. Fire consumed him, his crackling demise nearly drowning out the screams of a young girl.

"Release the little one to me." Vinet recognized the voice: AeresThonEsia?

"No!" Dannan's eyes widened in panic. "I cannot!"

"Cannot, or will not? You should be more careful with your words, mage."

Fire stabbed through her shoulders, and her body arched, drowning out any other sensations. She floated again.

"Nazir?" Gwyn sounded soft and uncertain.

Nazir looked up from her bedside. His eyes were red. "I'm fine, Gwyn."

"No, you're not." Gwyn's voice was hesitant, but no longer uncertain.

"What do you want me to say? You've already made your opinion about my feelings perfectly known."

"I...I'm sorry. I didn't know..."

"I love her, Gwyn," Nazir's voice choked. "And now I might never be able to tell her."

He loved her! Vinet tried to rise, tried to tell him she loved him too, that she would be there, but she couldn't do anything but watch.

A soft curse. Gwyn's eyes glistened. "I was afraid of that," she said. "I'm sorry."

Nazir shook his head. "No, you were right. We couldn't. I shouldn't." He buried his face in his hands.

"Mazda damn the noble conventions," Gwyn cursed.

Nazir blinked.

"Vinet is bound by them, as much as she wishes she wasn't," Gwyn said. "Look at what she did for Niara."

Nazir buried his face in his hands. "I don't know what to do."

"Neither do I, Nazir," Gwyn whispered. "Neither do I."

I do! Vinet wanted to scream. She didn't care about noble conventions. She wanted Nazir by her side, as her lover, her husband, her partner, her consort. What sensible reason was there why she shouldn't have him?

Sense. Sense. "What sense is there in this?" Lord Auriel's voice. He stared at a map, his three burgundy-clad guards around him.

"It will set us free," the woman spoke.

He shook his head. "Not yet. We still have much to do."

War! Battle. The screams of the dying. Arrows flew, striking men and women all around her. The shield wall held, though the men were rattled.

A dark figure, flying down from the sky. Fear rose up inside her as it came closer and closer. She knew that figure. The white of bone became visible, and the hundreds of circling eyes. She tried to run. The skull kept coming closer and closer, empty eye sockets grinning at her.

"Back!"

Father! Vinet turned, seeing her father move to stand between her and the skull. "You will not have her. Not now, not ever!"

The skull laughed, a horrible shrieking laugh which rent the air. Vinet covered her ears, but she couldn't cease the vibrations that ran up and down her body.

"Back!"

The world exploded. Screams rent the air as she went flying. She had a mouth now, and she screamed. She flailed, trying to reach, trying to ground, trying to do anything.

"Daughter!" Firm and commanding. "Calm. I am here."

Her heart was racing, but she stopped flailing. She still couldn't see. She felt warmth start to sink into her, and only now became aware of the fact she had been freezing. She began to shiver.

"Hush."

She released a breath as her father bent over her. Her shivers calmed.

"Will she be alright?" Gwyn's voice, low and worried.

"She will be." Her father sounded ragged and exhausted.

"What happened?"

"The protections are failing," her father snapped. "He who placed the mark tried to claim her."

Vinet shuddered, and she could see her reaction mirrored by Gwyn.

"What can we do?" Gwyn asked.

"Keep her from using the Sight," her father said. "I will do what I can in that regard."

She felt his warm, comforting presence again. But this time, a demand, a whisper in her mind.

"Daughter. Listen and obey. Do not use the Sight. You have no desire to use the Sight. Not till we stand together in the city of our homeland."

She was floating, so warm and comforting. "Yes, Father," she whispered.

"Very good, my daughter. Rest now."

She drifted off in obedience to his command.

"I cannot stay," her father's voice again. "She will wake within the day. Be gentle with her. You are her Keeper, Gwyn. Her care is on your shoulders."

Gwyn nodded solemnly. Kinaevan turned to Nazir.

"Nazir. Take care of my daughter."

"I will, sir."

Kinaevan bent over, leaning on a wooden cane. He looked so old. He spoke to Nazir. "The blood which flows in your veins is blessed. It will not corrupt her, or your children. Take care how you use your gifts and teach them well."

"Children? Blood?" Nazir's eyes widened.

Kinaevan staggered, and Gwyn went to his side. Angrily, he shrugged her off. "The Lady calls," he said. "I must leave."

"You can't leave like this!" Gwyn protested. "You need rest, as much as she does!"

Her father's eyes were dark. "I will have rest soon." He bent over, coughing again. "I must return to my duties. And the saving of my child. In six months time, we shall meet again."

Six months? Vinet tried to protest. What was going on? Why did he have to leave? Why did he seem so old, so worn?

Kinaevan gazed at her again, and a smile smoothed his worn features. "Sleep now, daughter."

She couldn't resist the hypnotic lull. She took a deep breath, and the world calmed.

Small, quiet sounds. The crackling of fire. The crinkling of paper as someone turned a page. She sniffed. Someone was burning oak wood, a healing plant.

She opened her eyes. She lay in her bed in Ilhelm Castle. Nazir sat in a chair at her side, reading a book.

"Nazir?" she whispered.

He glanced up sharply and dropped the book. It fell to the ground as he scrambled to his feet and sat down on the edge of the bed. "Vinet? You're awake! Thank Mazda!" He grabbed her hand, looking elated.

She smiled. Awake or not, she felt weak as a newborn kitten. "I'm awake." She placed her other hand on top of his.

Nazir beamed, squeezing her hand tightly, then turned toward the door. "Gwyn!" he called. "She's awake!"

Vinet heard running footsteps, and the door burst open as Gwyn came into the room.

"Mazda's light!" Gwyn nearly flew to her side. Vinet laughed as she claimed the hand Nazir hadn't. "In Mazda's name, Vinet, swear you won't ever do that to us again."

Vinet laughed again, but tears stung her eyes. "How long was I asleep?" she asked.

"Two weeks," Nazir said quietly.

Two weeks? Her eyes widened. "I missed the council session."

"Don't worry about that," Gwyn said hastily. "I wrote Pellalindra. Mazda knows what she'll think of receiving a letter from a bodyguard, but I used your seal, so that should help."

She had to smile. "Niara?"

"I'll get her," Nazir volunteered. He rose and left, pausing only for a moment to exchange a look of joy and relief with Gwyn.

Vinet looked at Gwyn, raising her eyebrows. Gwyn simply shrugged.

"He's helped a lot since you've been ill," Gwyn said. "He's not a bad man, Vinet. Just…"

"Smallfolk. I know," Vinet sighed.

Gwyn winced. "It's not…"

Her words remained unspoken as a squeal of delight interrupted her. "Mama!" Niara shrieked, flinging herself across the room and into Vinet's arms.

Vinet let out her breath in a whoosh as Niara slammed into her chest. "Easy there, darling," she said.

"I was so scared." Niara buried her face in her neck.

Vinet stroked her daughter's hair. "It's all right. I'm better now."

Niara pulled away. "Are you really going to name me heir?"

Vinet glanced sideways at Gwyn, who shrugged sheepishly. She turned her eyes back to Niara. "Yes. Does that bother you?"

"No!" Niara shook her head. "I want to be your heir, just not Lady of Ninaeva. Not yet." She wrinkled her nose.

Vinet laughed. "Not yet, dearest. Not for a very long time."

"Good," Niara snuggled back into her mother's arms.

Vinet looked around the room. It was perfect. Nazir sat at her side again, Gwyn smiled down at them, and Niara was in her arms. All felt right.

She straightened. The woman! The child! She remembered finding them, but as to what had happened, she hadn't a clue.

"What happened to her?" she asked Gwyn.

Gwyn blinked in confusion, then her eyes cleared. "To Eithne?"

"Is that her name?"

"Yes." Gwyn sat down in the chair Nazir had vacated. "Eithne and her son are safely in one of the guest apartments. I assigned the most trustworthy of servants and guards to them."

There was something more. "What does she say?"

Gwyn hesitated and exchanged a look with Nazir.

Vinet's ears twitched. "What's wrong?"

Gwyn's eyes were dark. "She was Lord General Torainn's mistress while the Regulars were in Venia," she said. "The child is his. She's named him Kishtar, after Torainn's father."

"And he abandoned her?" Vinet's eyes widened. "To live in that hovel?"

Gwyn shrugged. "She says he didn't, that he always intended to come back, but," she shook her head again. "She also insists they were married."

"Married!" Vinet exclaimed. "But Torainn and Lady Kianna..."

"Were married for many years," Gwyn interrupted. "I know. I checked. If Eithne only met Torainn during the Venian campaign, then even if they did marry, it wasn't valid."

Vinet caught her breath, trying to reconcile the friendly, jovial man she'd met in Venia with this new information. How could he justify abandoning a woman and child, a woman he'd seduced and deceived, to the slums of Venia?

"I'll speak to her," Vinet said. "I'll let her know."

"You'll speak to her when your strength returns," Gwyn's voice was firm. "You've only just woken up. Your father said you need to get your strength back.

Her father. "How is he?" she whispered.

Gwyn exchanged a glance with Nazir, who shook his head slightly.

"How is he?" Vinet demanded. "I know something was wrong."

Gwyn looked at her in surprise. "He seemed troubled," she said. "But he was determined. I couldn't stop him from leaving."

"To find a solution to my curse," Vinet murmured.

Gwyn appeared even more startled. "Yes. How did you know?"

She shook her head. If that part of her dreams had been real, then what else had been?

Gwyn waited. "Never mind. You need to rest." She stood up, gesturing to Niara and Nazir to follow her. She turned back at the door and smiled. "I'm glad you're well again, sister."

Vinet smiled back, despite a lingering fear that this was far from over. "So am I."

14

PAPSUKKAL FESTIVAL

V inet could tell the capital was preparing for Papsukkal. Colorful streamers hung over the city streets, and tense excitement filled the air. Papsukkal was the day which didn't belong. It marked the beginning of the new year, a new planting season, but it didn't fit with the rest of the calendar. It was out of balance, out of place, out of time. Anything could happen on Papsukkal, with no consequences the rest of the year. Servants became masters. Masters became servants. Vinet preferred this holiday above all others back in Ninaeva, but she had to be in the capital this year for some morale-boosting scheme the Council had thought up. She could see their point, what with an ill king and war in the southeast. Her understanding didn't change the fact she would much rather have been back in Ninaeva, participating there, in her home.

She looked across the carriage and smiled at Niara, who bounced up and down in excitement as she stared out the carriage windows. Niara would enjoy the celebration, at least. It would be spectacular, if the rumors Vinet had heard were even half true.

She glanced sideways to glimpse Nazir sitting next to her. He and Gwyn seemed to have come to an agreement that one of them should always be with Vinet. On the one hand, she welcomed the arrangement. On the other, she had been so busy she hadn't had a single moment of privacy with Nazir.

She knew he loved her. And she loved him, she was certain of it. They needed to talk about it, but not with anyone listening, not with Niara, Evalynna, or even Gwyn around. This was between the two of them. Though it appeared unlikely she'd get a chance for that until after the festival.

She sighed in relief as the carriage rolled to a stop before her townhouse. Niara scrambled out, while Vinet and Nazir followed at a more sedate pace. Gwyn immediately dropped into step behind them.

Vinet kept herself from sighing again. She half suspected Gwyn was actively preventing her and Nazir from having privacy to talk. While Gwyn's attitude toward Nazir might have changed, her opinion about their potential relationship and its dangers had not. Vinet shoved that thought away as she made her way to her study. She needed to check if any messages had arrived and whether any pressing business awaited. If nothing else, her attendance at Papsukkal needed to be confirmed, her costume chosen, the constant pressures of positioned nobility. She sank into her chair and closed her eyes briefly, trying to relax. Why couldn't things ever stop?

She wrote a hasty note confirming her attendance at the Papsukkal festival. Briefly, she wondered if Lord Auriel had taken charge of the celebration. He was the king's steward, after all. But maybe he would have delegated it to another noble. There would be plenty of nobles eager to gain favor with the king or his steward for their own social advancement, rather than the good of the kingdom. *Sycophants who won't do anything which doesn't benefit them directly,* she thought.

"Mama?"

A smile spread across Vinet's face as her daughter poked her head into the study. "Yes, dear?"

"Would you play outside with me? It's so much warmer here!" Despite her obvious eagerness, her voice sounded tentative. She knew her mother had work to do.

A surge of warmth made Vinet laugh, and she rose to her feet. Business could wait. "Of course," she said. "Get your cloak on, though. Just because it's warmer doesn't mean it's warm enough to be without it."

"Yes, Mama," Niara dashed off to get her cloak.

Vinet followed at a slightly more sedate pace, a smile still on her face. Niara had taken all the revelations in stride. She was her daughter and her heir, and still the most adorable child Vinet had ever known.

Niara, practically bouncing up and down in excitement, waited at the door to the garden when Vinet arrived. Vinet's smile turned to a grin as she saw the little leather ball held in her hands.

Vinet took a deep breath as they entered the garden, taking in the smell of roses and irises beginning to bud, the sound of birds chirping away as they courted, and the soft feeling from the earth which spoke of new growth, of new life. Mazda's Rise was certainly here, although the planting would not officially begin until after Papsukkal. It would be a good year for planting, though. Assuming the war didn't spread.

She shook off the solemn thought as she faced her daughter. "Ready?" she asked.

Niara laughed in delight and tossed her the ball. Vinet caught it, and the game began.

Niara was good at the game, and Vinet found herself laughing with her daughter as they tossed the ball back and forth. She tossed the ball with a little extra strength, and it sailed over Niara's head. "Mama!" Niara exclaimed.

A cough made Vinet spin around. Gwyn stood at the entrance to the garden, an expression of dismay on her face. Vinet felt her own face echoing that emotion when she saw Lord Dannan standing next to Gwyn.

She saw Niara stand still as well, completely forgetting the ball. A flash of pride battled with her dismay as Niara remembered her manners and curtsied.

She smoothed her own expression and gave Dannan a cool nod. "Lord Dannan," she said. "I was not expecting you."

Dannan seemed stiff and tense, but he gave Niara a small bow in response and nodded back to Vinet. "Indeed. We were all worried about you, Lady Vinet."

Vinet caught Niara's expression and walked over to her daughter. She leaned down to whisper. "It's alright. Fetch the ball and go with Gwyn into the house."

"But..." Niara said.

Vinet ruffled her daughter's hair. "It's alright. I'll take care of it. Find Nazir and ask him to tell you a story."

The little girl could not resist the promise of a story. She collected the ball and took Gwyn's hand, but looked over her shoulder at her mother, a concerned expression still on her face. Vinet smiled reassuringly, and Niara and Gwyn walked away, Gwyn giving her one last lingering look.

There was a moment of silence as she and Dannan stood alone in the garden. *Well, if Dannan isn't going to immediately interrogate me about my daughter, then I'm not going to bring it up,* she thought. "I didn't expect to see you until the festival," she said levelly.

Dannan smirked. "Come now, Lady Vinet. Did you think a tale about an accident would not raise my suspicions, after our conversations?"

Vinet gave a tight smile. "No, indeed."

Dannan waited, but Vinet didn't volunteer information.

"What happened?" he asked.

"I was unconscious," she stated.

"Why?" Dannan's eyes were dark.

"I wish I knew for sure," Vinet said, meeting his eyes without flinching. "I had a vision. It left me like that."

Dannan's only reaction was a raised eyebrow. "Has that ever happened before?"

She shook her head. "Never."

"Did you do anything to cause this vision?"

She had to be careful around Dannan. He knew too much of magic for her to lie to him. "Well, I called it," she said, allowing a wry smile to appear. "But I've done that before." She sighed. "I did not see just what I intended to see, though."

Dannan snorted. "You never do. That is why visions are hardly the best way to gather information."

She tightened her lips. "It was this time."

Dannan's eyes narrowed even more. "What did you see?" he asked.

She shifted her cloak on her shoulders. "Lord General Torainn's bastard son."

Dannan's eyes widened. "He had a mistress?"

She nodded. "They're both in Ninaeva now. Safe."

"And do you plan to keep them there?"

"For as long as they want to stay." She wasn't in the mood to defend her actions.

He frowned. "You said that you didn't just see what you meant to see. What else did you see?"

She should have expected the question. "Barely anything," she said. "I fell into a lake and started drowning. The water tasted like...like blood and decay." She grimaced, feeling the taste in her mouth again. "Someone said 'pawn.' I managed to wrench control of the vision again, and then blackness." She was not going to mention the other thing the voice had said. Niara was not going to come under Dannan's scrutiny if she could help it.

196

"Was that all? No more details?"

Vinet pushed down her flash of fear. He had no reason to suspect she would leave out details. "If I knew more, I might be closer to understanding why I fell unconscious," she snapped.

"A voice that said the word pawn," Dannan began to pace back and forth. "This is why I told you to avoid magic, Lady Vinet. You were tampering with dangerous things."

She felt her hands clench at her sides. "I was not about to have a vision of a child in a hovel and not do anything about it!"

"You had no idea who the child was!" Dannan exclaimed. "He could have been Torainn in the past, or a vision of the future! Visions aren't precise and pursuing them will get you hurt! Magic is dangerous, Vinet. I won't have you ending up like my..." he broke off, panting.

Vinet looked up, startled. Like who? Like his family?

Dannan didn't finish the sentence. He took a few more deep breaths, then said in a more level voice, "If you let your heart lead your efforts and let your passion get the better of you, then magic will betray you. Trust me on this. I did not have this scar when I married my wife." He gestured to his disfigured face and his strange citron eye.

Dannan's talk of passion annoyed Vinet. "If magic will betray me, then how do I stop it?" She was aware she had snapped, but she couldn't stop. "I can't control my visions, Dannan! This one I called, yes. But the one at Pellalindra's wedding happened without any will of mine! I need to learn how to use my visions, Dannan, not ignore them! Otherwise, it will kill me." She cut off, breathing heavily. She had no idea why she had said that. But its truth spoke to the depths of her soul.

"And will you teach your daughter?"

She glared at him.

He appeared entirely unaffected by her stare. "I told you these abilities tend to be inherited. Will your daughter share your talent, I wonder?"

She turned away, she said flatly, "She will." She refused to look at Dannan.

"Has she shown any signs of it?"

Vinet shook her head.

She heard him sigh. "Well, then maybe there is still hope she will not" he said. "You yourself said you didn't have a vision until you were thirteen. Maybe it will pass her by."

Vinet shrugged, although she was certain the magic would do no such

197

thing. Her daughter was too much like her in all other ways. And Kinaevan believed his granddaughter would share his talents as well.

Dannan remained silent for a long time, and eventually Vinet returned her gaze to him. He seemed unaware of the world around him. Finally, he met her eyes again. "The royal librarian may have a few tomes which could help you. Mention my name and you should get access."

"Thank you," Vinet inclined her head, relief suffusing her. He had accepted her tale.

Dannan sighed again. "I must be going. But take care, Lady Vinet. Control your passions and heart in all things. It will affect your magic, you have my word on it."

Control her passion in all things? What of her passion for her family, for learning, for...

Almost on cue, Vinet saw Nazir enter the garden. He stopped a fair distance away, under the hazel tree, when he saw Vinet and Dannan.

Dannan glanced over at Nazir and frowned.

Vinet stiffened. Dannan had no right to give her a lecture on propriety. What happened between her and Nazir was no one's business but their own. "About Niara," she said, forcing him to look at her again. Although she planned to acknowledge her daughter, she wanted it to be on her terms, not Dannan's. "It is not known. I plan on announcing it soon, but until then, if you would be discreet..."

A smile appeared on Dannan's face. "No one shall hear the truth from *my* lips," he said.

She could almost hear the implication that she had only herself to blame if the secret came out. She shook her head, but only said, "Thank you, Lord Dannan. I will not keep you any longer."

He recognized the dismissal. "See you at the festival, Lady Vinet." He walked out.

Vinet turned, but Nazir had already disappeared back inside. She cursed. When was she going to get a chance to talk to him?

"Gwyn, no. I insist."

"But, Vinet..."

Vinet shook her head emphatically. "You have been guarding me night and day for over a month now. You need a break just as much as I do.

Enjoy Papsukkal." She managed a smile. "I *command* you to enjoy the festivities."

She could still see Gwyn's hesitation, so she shook her head again. "No arguments. I'll be at the palace for most of it, along with every other noble in Saemar. If someone harms me there, through all the royal guards, then it's someone not even you would be able to stop." She was being blunt perhaps, but it was the language Gwyn knew best.

Vinet nearly rolled her eyes as Gwyn continued to hesitate. "Fine, but I'll tell Evalynna to…"

"No!" Vinet exclaimed, throwing her hands in the air. "Evalynna's half the reason I want you to enjoy the festival! Now go! Have fun! Be merry! Do the things you can't do any other day!"

Vinet saw the flush rise to Gwyn's cheeks.

"You don't mind?" Gwynn asked softly. "About Evalynna and me?"

Vinet stepped forward and drew her blood-sister into a firm embrace. "I'm so happy for you," she whispered. "And I want you to enjoy your happiness."

Finally, Gwyn seemed convinced. "If you're sure."

"I'm sure!" Vinet pushed Gwyn away and toward the door. "Out, out! Go get Evalynna and enjoy the festival!"

Gwyn laughed as she left the room but threw one more concerned glance over her shoulder. Vinet sighed in relief. Getting Gwyn to think of anything other than her duty could be exhausting at times.

"Are you sure this is the best idea?"

She glanced over her shoulder to where Nazir had been sitting, head bent over a book. She nodded firmly. "Absolutely," she said. "You've seen the way those two have been looking at each other. They need a day to themselves."

"That wasn't what I meant," Nazir said quietly. "Am I still going with you?"

She caught a glimpse of the emotions on Nazir's face. Hope, worry, fear, and excitement all played together, mixed with something else she couldn't define.

"Yes," she said quietly. "I can't be unescorted, after all, can I?"

He didn't seem to know how to answer that. Vinet caught her breath. They were alone together. The first time since she had woken up.

She nearly cursed aloud as a knock on the door below heralded the arrival of Pellalindra. The two of them were heading to the festival together, since Lord Auriel could not be spared from his duties to escort his wife.

She walked over and took Nazir's arm. "Come on," she said. "It's Papsukkal. Things can happen today that would never happen any other time."

She saw his resistance melt away as her hand touched his arm. He stood up without a word and followed.

They made a splendid pair, Vinet thought to herself. As befitting Papsukkal, they wore wild garments, full of colors. Her gown was of various shades of blues and greens, with an asymmetrical hem that swished about her legs when she walked. She wore no jewelry, simply a flower crown braided into her long hair.

Nazir was dressed no less magnificently. Unlike Vinet, his garments were of a single color, the purest, deepest black that anyone at Ninaeva could manufacture. He appeared a man of pure shadow, except for the silver necklace around his neck. She knew a symbol of Mazda lay concealed beneath the high collar of his tunic.

Vinet smiled as she saw Pellalindra waiting for them. Though Pellalindra dressed as magnificently as ever, it could not be more obvious to Vinet that the Lady of Duskryn couldn't care less for a celebration that took place outside of time and order. She still looked every inch the noble. The only difference was that her gown now revealed her pregnancy.

Pellalindra's eyes widened as she saw Nazir, and she gave Vinet a measuring look. Vinet returned her gaze steadily. She would offer no apologies or explanations for his presence.

"Shall we, Lady Vinet?"

Vinet felt her shoulders stiffen at Pellalindra's decision to simply ignore Nazir's presence. *She won't be able to ignore him for long. Not if I have anything to say about it.* "After you, Lady Pellalindra."

A moment of awkward silence fell as the three of them sat in the carriage. Pellalindra took a deep breath and looked directly at Vinet, ignoring Nazir. "You are recovered from your accident, then? I trust there are no lasting injuries?"

Vinet managed a smile. "None, Lady Pellalindra. Thank you for asking."

She could see the curiosity in Pellalindra's eyes. "But what happened? The note was extremely vague."

Vinet took a breath. She did not want to tell Pellalindra about the vision which had struck her down, or the reason her trip to Venia had been conducted in such secrecy. "I fell ill," she said.

"Ill?" Pellalindra frowned. "So there was no accident?"

Vinet carefully avoided looking at Nazir. She didn't want to give any of her thoughts away by remembering the events of her coma. "I do not know what caused the illness," she said. "Gwyn believed it was an accident when she sent the message to the Council."

"I see," Pellalindra said. "Well, I am glad you are recovered."

Vinet inclined her head. "So am I."

An awkward silence fell over them again. Pellalindra did not seem to know what to say with Nazir in the carriage with them. Vinet took advantage of the silence to look out the window of the carriage. The festivities were already in full swing. The morale-raising scheme would be a huge success, Vinet could already tell. She just hoped the Council hadn't beggared the treasury to do it.

"So, tell me, Lady Pellalindra, what has been planned which made it imperative I be here if I could?" Vinet asked, taking pity on Pellalindra at last.

Pellalindra's eyes widened. "Didn't anyone tell you? The Council is bestowing random acts of generosity and kindness to those who petition during the feast. The entire Council must be present, of course, and my husband will preside over the festivities. The randomness will fit with the spirit of Papsukkal, while promoting goodwill toward the King and Council," she nodded decisively.

Vinet suppressed disappointment. A feast during which there were petitions would take hours. "And after the feast?" she asked, keeping her voice light.

Pellalindra laughed. "Why, afterward is when all the fun really happens! Or so I've been told. I intend to retire early." She placed a hand on her stomach.

Vinet's lips twitched. No doubt Pellalindra would be retiring early even if she didn't have such a ready excuse.

She caught a glimpse of Gwyn outside the carriage window, walking arm in arm down the street with Evalynna. She smiled broadly as Evalynna stopped and drew Gwyn into a long, lingering kiss. The smile remained on her face as she turned back to the other occupants of the carriage. She hoped the rest of her night would go as well as Gwyn's.

Nazir gave her a curious look, but she shook her head slightly, not wanting to explain while Pellalindra accompanied them. If Pellalindra hadn't been there, she would have told him with glee what she had just witnessed. She would have leaned across the carriage, taken him into her arms like Evalynna had taken Gwyn, and…she shook herself out of those thoughts as the carriage drew up to the palace. Now was not the time to act on that impulse.

The carriage stopped, and Vinet blinked as an elven figure stepped up the carriage and offered his arm to her. "My lady?"

Vinet took Saihid's offer of assistance and let him help her out of the carriage, then watched him help Pellalindra out. The look shared between them was one of such painful longing on Saihid's part that it made her heart nearly break. Pellalindra's expression carried sadness as well, but she determinedly straightened her shoulders and turned her back on Saihid. "To the great hall, Lady Vinet, or we shall be late for the feast."

Vinet hesitated long enough to place a hand on Nazir's arm. "I'll have to sit with the Council for the feast," she said in a whisper. "Will you…"

Nazir nodded, interrupting with a light touch to Vinet's hand on his arm. "I'll be fine," he answered her unfinished question. He glanced at Saihid. "Maybe I can keep him company."

Vinet's heart warmed. She smiled at him before following Pellalindra into the palace.

The entire great hall had been redecorated for the event. Red, purple, and gold streamers hung all about. Giant candelabras and torches illuminated the entire room. Tables lined the edges of the hall, but the entire center remained free. For petitioners, Vinet assumed, and to accommodate dancing later in the evening. She couldn't wait for that time to come. That would be when she could slip away from the festival and spend a moment alone with Nazir.

"Lady Vinet!"

She was taken completely by surprise as Kamian approached her, swept her into a hug, and spun her around. "We were so worried! Thank Mazda you seem completely recovered. You are completely recovered, right?"

Vinet laughed as she pulled away, though she had to suppress a flash of irritation. If she really had been injured, Kamian's antics would have been thoughtless and careless.

"I am completely recovered," she assured him. "But tell me what I missed! How was the last council session?"

Kamian shrugged as he drew her away from Pellalindra and toward the high table. Vinet frowned a little as she saw the seat in the center, larger than the rest, almost like a throne. It wasn't the throne, though, which still sat on its dais behind the high table. Was the larger chair for the steward?

"Oh, the council session was a council session," Kamian said. "Lots of shouting and yelling. The only thing anyone could agree on was to host this event to distract everyone from the bad news."

"What bad news?" Mazda's light, she thought, Kamian could be frustrating.

He shrugged again. "The war has stalled, and we don't know what happened to two of the lords. Their estates have been completely overrun, and there's no sign of them or their households. And the king still hasn't recovered, which is getting harder to conceal."

Vinet frowned. "How is an ill king different from a reclusive king?" she demanded, an echo of Gwyn's words.

"A reclusive king does not have the threat of death hanging about him." Dannan approached the two. "And the threat of a regency."

Vinet raised an eyebrow at Dannan. "And how likely is that?" She asked in a hushed voice.

Dannan shrugged. "No one knows, which makes the uncertainty worse," he said. "Lord Auriel has been hiring the best healers to come tend him in secret."

Vinet nodded slowly. "Then we will hope for the best."

Kamian tugged her arm again. "Enough of this talk! It's Papsukkal, it's a festival, and we should be enjoying ourselves. Isn't that the point?"

Dannan scowled. "The point is for the people to enjoy themselves. We have responsibilities."

"Which they can't do if we're discussing fears and politics," Kamian said in an unrepentant voice. "Come on, Lady Vinet. Let's claim the best seats."

"Haven't they been assigned?" Vinet protested, but she didn't resist as Kamian drew her along.

"Well, of course," Kamian said. "And we have the best ones. May I have the honor of sitting next to you, my lady?"

She couldn't help but laugh as she sat down in her assigned seat and Kamian sat to her right. She sighed in relief, however, at the realization General Alexander was seated directly to her left.

The General raised his glass to her in welcome. "It is good to see you back in the capital, Lady Vinet. No lasting ill effects from your adventure?"

Her throat tightened. That had yet to be seen. "None," she said lightly. "How has the time treated you?"

"Well enough, with the war still raging in the southeast," Alexander said. "My grandchildren have been a welcome distraction from that, however."

"Grandchildren?" Vinet nodded to the server as she poured her a glass of wine. "I have heard you talk of one. How many do you have?"

"Three." Alexander accepted a glass as well. "My oldest, Rian, and the younger twins Ianna and Arrex. They are about the same age as your niece, I believe."

"Niara is seven," Vinet said, suppressing a flash of pain at not being able to correct Alexander about her daughter. *Soon. I can't bear for people to believe her my niece much longer.*

Alexander continued. "They just turned five a few weeks ago. You should visit Lokrian at some point with Niara and the four can meet."

Vinet smiled in relief as the servers began distributing the food.

Kamian leaned forward to join the conversation. "I assume one of their parents is your heir? So, one of the three will inherit? Rian, presumably?"

A shadow passed across Alexander's face. "My daughter, unfortunately, is no longer with us," he said softly. "So, Rian is my direct heir, yes."

Vinet swallowed. She hadn't meant to bring up a subject that would remind Alexander of his loss.

She never thought she would welcome the distraction of petitioners coming up to present their pleas to the Council. Lord Auriel had indeed claimed the large chair in the center of the high table. He looked very regal, as regal as a king, although he wore no crown. Pellalindra sat directly to his right, practically basking in the attention she was receiving. She pointedly ignored Conn, her other dinner companion.

Vinet let her attention wander as it became clear Lord Auriel intended to handle the majority of the petitioners himself. Most of the tables were filled with other nobles, all watching the proceedings with varying levels of interest, most more interested in their food or dinner companions. A few, however, cast speculative looks at the council members and Lord Auriel. She could almost read their minds. *Who is this steward who acts like our king? Why does the Council support him?* She dearly wished she knew the answer to those questions. *If I did, perhaps I would be less concerned Lord Auriel might know who my father is.*

She surveyed the room some more, trying to determine where Nazir and Saihid had gotten to. If Nazir was keeping an eye on Saihid, he wouldn't be sitting at a table, but surely, they'd be in the same room. Finally, she caught a glimpse of them, all the way at the other end of the hall, beside the great doors. She spotted Saihid first, slumped against the wall beside the door. Nazir blended almost completely in with the shadows. The only thing that set him apart was his utter stillness. He listened intently to whatever Saihid was saying.

Vinet sighed and turned her attention back to the petitioners. Hopefully, Saihid would confide in Nazir. She couldn't imagine the pain Saihid must be facing, knowing that his child would be raised by another. Whatever Pellalindra intended to happen in private, the world would believe Lord Auriel the father.

She glanced down the hall toward the two men again. She could never do that to Nazir. She could never put him in that kind of situation, or through that kind of pain.

The meal seemed interminable. One after another, petitioners stepped forward, asking for judgments, for help, for blessings, and any other thing they could think of. Lord Auriel listened solemnly to all of them, passing judgments easily, occasionally asking one or another of the councilors for input. She jumped the first time he asked her opinion.

"What do you think of the case, Lady Vinet Rochelle?"

Vinet looked at the young family in front of the high table. Her heart clenched. They were dressed in their best clothes, but Vinet saw they were still worn as thin as threads. The little boy's thinness matched that of his clothes.

"Grant them their petition," Vinet said, keeping her voice as level as she could. "As well, extend an offer of employment from my steward in Ninaeva. If they present themselves to me here in the capital, I will arrange transport to Ilhelm for them."

Lord Auriel's eyebrows rose, but he nodded. "Let it be done," he said.

The family left with exclamations of gratitude and joy, and Kamian leaned over to whisper in her ear. "That was thoughtfully done."

She smiled at him. It was good to know at least someone on the Council approved of her actions.

He smiled back, and a warning tingle ran down her spine. That smile was far too intimate, far too knowing for her comfort. Did he think their relationship something more than an alliance?

She shrugged that thought away and returned her attention to the feast. The servers brought out the last course, and the stream of petitioners had trickled down to a handful. It was almost over.

Eventually, the last petitioner was sent away. Lord Auriel stood, and everyone in the room turned to look at him expectantly. "Let the celebrations commence! Let Papsukkal reign supreme!"

"Finally!" Kamian exclaimed. He swung out of his seat and grabbed Vinet's hand. "Dance with me?"

She could hardly resist as he pulled her along. The musicians struck up a lively dancing tune and everyone paired up. Vinet cast a longing glance in Nazir's direction. He stood as still as ever, watching her. Apart from Saihid and the guards, he was the only non-noble in the room.

As Kamian dragged her onto the dance floor, she felt a pang of longing for her own Papsukkal celebration back home in Ninaeva. There, everyone in the castle, servants and all, would be joining in the festivities. One of the servants would be elected King of Fools, and Vinet would disappear into relative obscurity in the crowd to enjoy the wild country dances. Though this dance was no less wild. Kamian twirled her around with impressive skill and finished by pulling her close into a wild dip.

Laughing, she pled a rest. He seemed poised to convince her otherwise, but another noblewoman came up and pulled him away.

Vinet stepped back against the wall and looked for Nazir. She smiled as she realized he hadn't moved. He still stood there, waiting for her.

She walked over and took his hand. "Come with me," she whispered.

A question shone in his eyes, but he didn't resist as she led him out of the great hall and toward the palace gardens. Her heart started beating faster as they entered the rows of hedges in the palace gardens. Finally, completely alone. It was twilight, and the last rays of sun glinted off the new green leaves.

She forced her voice to be casual. "How is Saihid?" she asked, presenting the first conversation subject she found, avoiding all the things she truly wanted to say.

He sighed. "As well as a man in that position can be," he answered. "Perhaps it would be better if he were not head over heels in love with his mistress, and desperately wanted to be a father to his child. But he is a man of honor."

"You are a man of honor," she said softly.

He turned to her. "Vinet..." he breathed, his dark eyes glistening in the moonlight.

"I would never do that to you," she whispered. "Never."

"Vinet…" Nazir swallowed. "Vinet, I love you. But if we were lovers, it would be inevitable. If you weren't a member of the Council…"

"I have no more sisters to pretend to have bastard children for me," Vinet said bluntly. "It would have to happen anyway. If we were lovers." She said that last phrase slowly, annunciating every syllable.

Nazir looked away. "I have tried to keep my distance," he said. "But Vinet, every time I am near you, I feel…" he shook his head. "I can't bear it much longer, Vinet. I have used Gwyn to keep us apart."

She stepped closer so that she was directly in front of him. As he gazed down at her, she reached up and drew his face toward her in a kiss, stopping any further excuses.

He resisted only briefly before drawing her to him, clutching her tight to his chest. She clung to him, feeling all the warmth and passion and love in his embrace. She could not let him go.

He broke away. "Vinet, I'm not…we can't…"

"Marry me," she whispered.

He stared at her. "What?"

"Marry me." She swallowed. "There's nothing stopping us."

She could see the disbelief on his face. "There's plenty stopping us! You're Lady of Ninaeva, and I'm probably the son of a demon! And born of a commoner mother, to boot!"

"I don't care." She grabbed his arm when he would have pulled away. "I love you, Nazir et-Alim."

"I love you, Vinet, but…"

Loud laughter interrupted them, and they sprung instinctively apart as a young couple stumbled into their path. From the sound, they had drunk a bit too much. They caught sight of Vinet, and blushed and giggled before the man pulled the woman off into the bushes.

"Lady Vinet? Are you out here?"

Vinet cursed under her breath. Nazir stepped backward, so the shadows of the hedges almost consumed him.

Vinet blinked as Kamian stepped into the path in front of her. "Lord Kamian?" she asked.

His face split into a grin as he saw her. "I was hoping to catch you alone!" he exclaimed. "How has your Papsukkal been?" He walked forward, feet crunching only the gravel as he swayed slightly.

At that moment, she wanted nothing more than for Kamian to disappear forever. She nodded. "Well enough."

"Then perhaps I can make it better." His smile widened. "I have a proposal for you."

She frowned. "What kind of proposal?"

He laughed and stepped forward. She could smell the faintest whiff of alcohol on his breath.

"Surely, you've thought of it for yourself. We're close allies on the Council, after all," he said. "We both need heirs. Our lands are near. We marry, make our alliance formal, and join our lands and strengthen our positions."

Her jaw dropped. Of all things, she had not expected this.

He seemed taken aback by her surprise. "It's a sensible solution. And I find you quite attractive. We'll have no trouble producing heirs."

Instinctively, she took a step backward. "I have an heir."

Kamian shrugged. "Your niece? But the nobles prefer direct bloodlines. Together we can…"

"Niara's my daughter."

Kamian stared at her. "Your daughter?" he finally said.

She nodded. "It will be officially announced tomorrow. Niara, my firstborn child, is heir of Ninaeva."

"But," Kamian blinked. "You're not…"

"Not married, no," Vinet interrupted. Her hands were shaking. "And never was."

"You can't name a bastard child heir of the only civilized part of the north." Kamian shook his head. "No, together we can…"

"No." Vinet took a step back. She couldn't listen to this right now. "I'm sorry, Kamian, no."

Kamian followed her. "It makes sense," he protested. "Vinet…"

"No." Her voice was stronger now, punctuated by a cut of her hand through the air. "I don't care if it makes sense, Kamian, I will not marry you."

Kamian opened his mouth to object, but a piercing laugh interrupted them, and a group of giggling noblewomen emerged from around the corner of the hedge. "Lord Kamian!" one of them exclaimed. She ran over and threw herself in his arms. He caught her, a bit unsteady. "Tell us again about that famous duel you fought!"

"Will you fight one for me?" one of the others demanded. "My parents want me betrothed to…"

Vinet took advantage of his distraction and moved away. She saw him glance after her, but gave him no chance to call her back as she ran into the shadows of the garden.

The moon was full, so she made her way through the garden paths easily, heading for a small circle of rosebushes. She needed to get away from Kamian. She needed to think. She turned a corner and sat down on a bench. She was trembling. She wished she'd brought a shawl. The night air was still cold, far too cold.

"Vinet?"

She glanced up at the sound of Nazir's voice. He stepped into the circle, his entire posture uncertain.

"Nazir," she breathed in relief.

He moved closer to her, sitting down on the bench next to her. He kept his distance, though, not touching her.

"He was right, you know," he whispered. "It would make sense."

She closed her eyes. "I won't have him."

Silence fell for a time. "Vinet, I can't give you what he can," Nazir finally said. "I am penniless, titleless, and it would be a terrible scandal if you married me. I can't offer you any protection against the fates of the world. I can offer no influence with anyone else at court."

"Do you think I want any of that?" She opened her eyes again and looked at him. "I am lady in my own right. I have land, a title, and wealth. I have a daughter even, one who will be proclaimed my heir. I don't need a lord to provide me with any of that. And I don't want a lord. I want you."

Nazir took a deep, shuddering breath. She reached out and took one of his hands gently in hers.

"Will you marry me, Nazir et-Alim?" she asked. "I can't bear to think of living without you."

Nazir sat completely still for a long moment, and Vinet felt a spike of fear. What if he tried to be all honorable and claim it would be better if he left? What if...

His movement was sudden and caught her completely off guard as he drew her to him in a hard embrace.

"I couldn't bear the thought of you with him," Nazir said, his voice muffled in her shoulder. "I couldn't bear to think of you married to him, having children with him, in a loveless, political marriage. Yes, Vinet Rochelle of Ninaeva, I will marry you."

15

ELOPEMENT

V inet felt her heart pounding as she stepped into the entry hall of the roadside temple, Gwyn right beside her, a steadying, comforting presence. She glanced over at her blood sister. Gwyn was still dressed in armor, in the Ninaevan colors of green and gold. The only concession to the event was her hairstyle. Evalynna had managed to braid Gwyn's hair into a golden crown.

Gwyn caught the look and gave Vinet a wry smile. "Don't tell me you're having second thoughts now."

"No, just wondering if you were going to persuade me otherwise," Vinet smiled.

"I did that two months ago," Gwyn said. "And you took my advice and waited. If you're still set, then there's nothing I can do except protect you from any danger."

Despite Gwyn's lighthearted words, Vinet sensed an uneasiness in her voice. She knew Gwyn still wasn't certain of her choice, despite the two months, another council session, and she and Nazir staring at each other longingly the entire time.

"I love him," she said simply. "And he..."

Gwyn shook her head. "I know. And that's the only reason I'm not calling you a fool. Perhaps this is the best solution. It's better than the others, for sure."

It wasn't much of a blessing, but it brought a smile to Vinet's face anyway. "I love you, sister."

Gwyn's face warmed. "I love you too. Now get in there before Nazir thinks you've changed your mind."

Vinet turned to the double doors leading to the main portion of the temple. Nazir would already be inside, waiting for her with the priest. Evalynna stood with him, ready to be his witness. Niara would be in the very front row, bouncing in her seat with excitement. She took a deep breath and nodded. Gwyn walked up and opened one of the doors, and they both stepped into the temple sanctuary.

The priest stood at the altar, his arms opened in blessing, the sunlight streaming down on him through the skylight. He was an older man, one who had clearly seen many happy couples stand before him throughout the years. The pews were nearly empty, filled only with the handful of Ninaevan guards and Niara, bouncing in her seat. But Vinet only had eyes for Nazir.

He had forgone his usual dark, sober clothing for the ceremony, and instead dressed in a tunic of Ninaevan colors, green and gold. His eyes were radiant as he saw her.

She walked forward confidently, her eyes never leaving his. She stood next to him at the altar and took his hand.

"May the couple who stands before me give their names," the priest said, his voice warm.

"Lady Vinet Rochelle of Ninaeva."

"Nazir et-Alim."

She barely heard the priest start his traditional song of marriage. Nazir's eyes were filled with a love so strong she could hardly breathe.

Then the priest finished, and she found she could, in fact, breathe. As the higher-ranked individual, she went first. She began her song of vows, slightly modified. She saw Nazir's startled expression as she received a silver circlet from Gwyn and placed it on his head.

The words for a noble marrying a commoner were almost never sung, but she had found them in a dusty scroll in the palace library. "Stand beside me beloved, so the sun may shine on us both, and the world see you equal next to me."

Nazir blinked rapidly as she finished, but his voice remained strong as he began his song. His voice was smooth and melodious, and she smiled warmly at his vows and declaration of love.

"Mazda's light protect you and guide you both," the priest said. He presented the writ.

Vinet's heart warmed as she saw the first line: *The Marriage of Lady Vinet Rochelle to Nazir et-Alim.* She had studied it thoroughly before the ceremony, of course. In many ways, it was identical to the writ she'd signed as witness at Pellalindra's wedding, with only one different clause, a provision that whatever children she and Nazir might have, Niara would remain heir of Ninaeva. That had been Nazir's suggestion, a thoughtful gesture which only made her love him more.

She signed her name with a flourish and handed the quill to Nazir. He signed as well, and Gwyn and Evalynna added their signatures as witnesses.

The priest raised his hands. "You are now husband and wife."

Vinet heard Niara's voice raise in a cheer, and she couldn't help grinning as she embraced Nazir. He drew her to him in a long kiss, and she heard the guards join in Niara's cheering. Nazir was beloved among her people already. Ninaeva would welcome their marriage.

She pulled away from Nazir, still grinning broadly. Not releasing his hand, she turned to her people. "Thank you for welcoming the new Lord of Ninaeva," she said, squeezing his hand. "Let us return to Ilhelm and let the rest of the populace know of their new lord."

Niara squealed and threw herself toward Vinet. Vinet laughed as she caught her daughter in an embrace.

"I have a father!" she exclaimed. She squirmed out of Vinet's hold and threw herself at Nazir, who lifted her up into his arms as Niara squealed in delight.

Vinet smiled at the two of them. They were her family. She glanced sideways, to where Gwyn watched with amused tolerance. They were all here, the people she loved most in the world.

Nazir set Niara on the ground and offered his arm to Vinet. "Shall we head home, Lady et-Alim?"

She felt her breath catch in her throat. They hadn't actually discussed whether she would take his name or he take hers. As a noble, she should have been the one keeping her name, but she could not deny how much she liked the sound of Lady et-Alim.

She took his arm. "Let's go home, Lord Nazir et-Alim of Ninaeva."

"A letter for you, my lady."

Vinet took the letter from the servant with a nod of thanks. She raised her eyebrows as she took note of the seal. *Duskryn? What is Pellalindra writing to me about?*

"Anything important?" Nazir asked.

Vinet glanced across the room to where Nazir sat in his chair, a book in his lap. In the two months since their marriage, they had been blissfully happy together. The people of Ninaeva had accepted him as their lord without question. Vinet wished they could have stayed in Ninaeva forever, but a council session had once again called her to the capital. They had stayed through planting, which gave time for the muddy spring roads to dry a little, though they still needed to dig out the carriage twice.

"It's from Pellalindra," she said, answering his question. She broke the seal and began to scan the letter.

Lady Vinet,

I hope this letter reaches you in good health. It is my joy to announce that I am delivered of a girl, Serana Auriel. Mazda has blessed her with good health, and I am delighted as any mother could be.

Vinet looked up. "She's had a daughter!" she exclaimed.

Nazir's eyebrows rose. "Six months after the marriage? That will cause talk."

Vinet nodded. *No child has ever arrived in six months,* she thought. "Perhaps the talk will be Pellalindra and Lord Auriel anticipated the wedding, and that was why it was so hastily organized," she suggested.

Nazir shrugged. "Does she mention Saihid?"

Vinet scanned the rest of the letter. "No," she said. "She says a bit about not being able to be at the council session, and a plea to not let Lord Conn undermine her authority, and then," she swallowed as she read the next words.

I hope what I have heard about you is not true, Lady Vinet. Do not tell me you have married the smallfolk scholar who has been following you around. Do you know people say he is the child of a demon? Rumors, perhaps, but all rumors

*contain a grain of truth. If the rumor about your marriage proves true, however,
I shall not know what to think.*

"Vinet?" Nazir asked.

She shook her head. "She's heard about our marriage."

"Ah," the understanding was clear in Nazir's voice. "And she disapproves."

Vinet shrugged. "I expected it."

"But you're still hurt." Nazir stood up and moved beside her.

She nodded. "You are my husband and my lord," she said. "The rest of the world should acknowledge you as such."

Nazir smiled. "Vinet, I do not mind," he said. "I am your husband, and that is all I ever wanted to be."

But I mind, Vinet thought. *You are worth so much more than they think.* She turned her attention back to the rest of the letter.

*One last thing you should know, do not let Conn MacTir interrogate you about
my marriage or my daughter. He threatened me most foully last time we spoke,
and I sent him away with harsh words. He dislikes and fears my husband, I
believe. Do not let him threaten you as well.*

Lady Pellalindra Duskryn.

Vinet's eyebrows rose. *I shouldn't be surprised. Conn is not the subtlest of
men, and if he is as suspicious of Lord Auriel, then of course he would try to
interrogate his wife.* She sighed. *Fool. Lord Auriel gives Pellalindra an even
higher rank than Lady of Duskryn. She will never betray him.*

She felt Nazir's hands on her shoulders, and she looked up into his eyes. "Vinet," he said softly. "I do not care what the other nobles think of me. I only care about you."

She reached up and pulled him into a kiss, letting the letter fall to the ground. "I know," she whispered. "And I love you."

She broke away from him at the sound of Gwyn's discrete cough. She glared at Gwyn for the interruption, but Gwyn shook her head. "It's time to leave for the council session, Vinet."

Vinet glanced at Nazir apologetically, but he only smiled and kissed her cheek. "When you return," he murmured, sending shivers down her spine.

Vinet ignored Gwyn's amused expression as they left the townhouse.

The journey to the council chamber was over far too quickly, and sooner than she wanted Vinet stood at the door.

They will all have heard already, she thought. *If Pellalindra knew, they will all know.* She took a deep breath. *I have married the love of my life. I have nothing to be ashamed of.* Before she could lose her nerve, she opened the door and stepped inside.

She could feel every eye on her as she entered the council chamber. She stiffened slightly but kept her head high. Let them judge if they wish.

Ellil acknowledged it first. "I understand congratulations are in order, Lady Vinet. My blessing upon you both."

She smiled. The high priest merely gazed at her speculatively, without the judgment she had expected. Then again, Nazir was a devout Mazdian. No doubt the high priest had noted Nazir's presence at the temple services.

"Thank you, Your Radiance," she said. "Your blessing means a great deal to us."

"My congratulations as well," Alexander said, inclining his head. She nodded her thanks in return.

"Congratulations for what?" Conn asked. He alone of the council members seemed to have no idea what Ellil spoke of.

"Her wedding," Kamian raised a glass of wine to his lips. "She's recently married."

Conn's eyes widened. "To who? I hadn't heard."

"There was no official announcement," Vinet said steadily. "It was not a large ceremony."

"She eloped," Kamian said flatly. "With her scholar, Nazir."

Conn's eyes widened even more, and he stared at her in shock. She returned his gaze as steadily as she could.

"Your scholar?" he asked. "But isn't he?"

She tightened her lips. Let him say straight out what he meant.

"He's smallfolk, yes, but what's done is done," Dannan interrupted. "Congratulations and all that. Now can we get down to business?"

For once, Vinet was grateful for Dannan's brusqueness. She didn't want an analysis of her actions from the Council.

"Yes," Alexander said as he pulled out a stack of papers. "I have here reports from the war in the southeast. The lines are holding for now but will need reinforcements soon. If we could redeploy some units, and perhaps talk about conscripting some of the nobles' guards..."

"The nobles need their guards for their own estates," Conn said. "I, at least, still have raiders from the north to deal with, as I'm sure Lady Vinet does as well."

Vinet opened her mouth to reply that Ninaeva was well protected by the mountains to the north, but others spoke before her.

"What good are your guards going to do you if the armies from the southeast conquer Saemar?" Kamian demanded. "Better to suffer a few raids with a skeleton guard than lose everything to these monsters!"

"Monsters?" Dannan looked up.

Alexander cleared his throat. "As to that, there are indeed reports of various natures concerning creatures in the southeast. Most alarming is the news that two of the estates which used to belong to our nobles have been completely overrun with strange creatures," he said, "And that the nobles seem to be perfectly free and alive."

There was only one way that information could have been gathered. Vinet's eyebrows rose in respect. Someone had good spies and scouts.

"Let the nobles commit their troops voluntarily, first," Vinet said. "You should receive enough initial reinforcements that way. If things become desperate then we can talk about conscription."

Alexander gave her an approving nod, and even Kamian seemed to begrudgingly approve.

Ellil sniffed. "Has anyone sent diplomats to the area?" he asked. "Negotiated for peace, begun conversion efforts among the cultists?"

Alexander seemed taken aback. "They have given us no opportunity for—"

"Mazda respects the man who makes his own opportunities," Ellil interrupted. "I will organize the priesthood."

"Your Radiance, I must protest," Alexander said. "To put the priests in danger like that—"

"It is our calling," Ellil cut him off again. "Fear not, only volunteers will go."

"Volunteers who know the danger," Alexander said firmly.

Ellil nodded as if there had never been any doubt of that.

Alexander sighed and looked around the room. "Are we agreed then? Redeploy the reserves, send a message to the nobles asking for volunteers, and allow the priesthood to begin conversion efforts?" His dry tone indicated his opinion of the last.

Vinet nodded slowly, as did the others. For her own part, while she thought Ellil's motives admirable, she couldn't discount the feeling the lives of priests would be lost without any gain.

"Good. Then on to the second order of business," Alexander shuffled through his papers. "There is a demand from Lord Tiber that we disinherit Lord Artosbern II and hand his lands over to him."

"What?" Conn exclaimed. "And just why should we disinherit the son of the Warden of the North?"

Vinet narrowed her eyes. The Bern Forest had been quiet since the 'wild goose chase' against the phantom Darkmane. Was that about to change?

"Because, according to Lord Tiber, Lord Artosbern II is a cultist, in league with the creatures in the southeast," Alexander's tone was carefully neutral. "He claims Lord Artosbern II killed the former Warden, as well as causing the disappearance of the late Lord General Torainn."

Vinet's head jerked up.

"What proof does he have?" Dannan's voice was harsh.

"None," Alexander said.

"Then we can do nothing."

"Nothing!" Conn exclaimed. "If he knows anything about the disappearance of Lord General Torainn—"

"We cannot afford to divert resources during a war," Dannan said sharply. "The disappearance of Torainn is tragic, but hardly crucial to the outcome of the war."

"But what if his claims are true?" Kamian didn't seem to believe it but looked curiously at Dannan instead. "Would you leave a traitor in our midst?"

"We need more information," Vinet cut in. "We need to investigate the truth of Lord Tiber's claims before we can make a decision on it."

Alexander shook his head. "I'm afraid I agree with Lord Dannan. We cannot afford to divert scouts from the southeast border."

She tightened her lips. She trusted Alexander's judgment, but that left them with precious few options.

"I'll go."

All the councilors turned to stare at the high priest. He merely raised an eyebrow.

"Your Radiance, I must protest," Alexander said again.

Ellil straightened his shoulders. "I am the emissary of our Lord Mazda on this soil. I will be listened to and respected. And if the claims of cultists are indeed true, then I am the best person to deal with them in a way which brings them back into the fold. I shall nominate my second to lead the priests in the southeast, and head north myself."

Pious words, but Vinet's heart contracted. Something would go dread-fully wrong if Ellil went on his own.

"Don't go alone," she said swiftly. "Take a small guard with you, at least." As Ellil turned toward her, she said hastily, "There are bandits in the Bern Forest who care nothing for sanctity. Remember the Cossack Darkmane? That is where he roamed, and we have no notion as to his whereabouts. Take a care of your safety, Your Radiance. Mazda is your shield, certainly, but the trust of good men is a capable defense as well."

She felt the eyes of the others on her, but she continued to look at Ellil. She couldn't explain why her skin was crawling at the thought of him setting off into the northeast by himself.

At last, he nodded. "I will take your advice, Lady Vinet. It is well-thought, and quite pious."

She let out a sigh of relief.

"We haven't agreed he should go," Conn objected.

Kamian rolled his eyes. "Do you have any other suggestions? You're the one who wants to find Lord General Torainn or, at this point, his corpse."

Conn narrowed his eyes, but Alexander interjected. "The floor is open for other ideas."

No one spoke. Alexander nodded decisively. "All in favor of sending High Priest Ellil to investigate Lord Tiber's claims?"

Vinet voted in favor. She still had a slight feeling of doom she couldn't shrug, but she saw no other alternatives.

"Very well," Alexander sighed. "Let us adjourn for a time and see to the rest of the business this afternoon. Lady Vinet, might I have a word?"

Vinet glanced up, startled. What could Alexander want from her?

As the rest of the council members left the chamber, Dannan gave her a last piercing look. "I told you to beware of following your passions."

She met his gaze steadily. To her surprise he looked away, and she heard him sigh as he exited the chamber. She turned her attention to Alexander. He appeared far more tired than he had allowed himself to appear during the council session.

"Are you alright?" she asked.

He looked up and smiled slightly. "As well as anyone involved in these war efforts."

She grimaced sympathetically. "I wish we didn't have to deal with war."

He nodded, his eyes dark. Then he straightened obviously. "To business. I assume you've heard I am to be chosen next Lord of the Council?"

She nodded. She had cast her vote for him just before the meeting.

"All of the various council members have told me how they voted, so I may be forgiven for presuming before the votes are tallied. That will not be my only duty, however, and I must ask a favor of you."

Vinet blinked. "What favor?"

"Please foster my grandchildren, for a time. My lands are to be the center of the supply lines, and I fear if the war goes ill, they will not be safe." He held up a hand. "I know everyone will do everything in their power to ensure the war does not go ill, but an old warhorse does not get to be an old warhorse without being cautious."

She blinked again. "I...of course."

He sighed in relief. "Thank you, Lady Vinet," he shook his head. "Others will think me daft for entrusting them to you so shortly after your elopement, but that is their prerogative. Your lands are the furthest from the conflict, and you have shown a great deal of sense and judgment in everything except your marriage, which can be forgiven, I dare say." He smiled wryly.

She raised an eyebrow. "Even regarding my daughter?" she asked.

Alexander smiled. "Even then. What else could you have done?"

Vinet couldn't answer that, so she didn't even try.

He nodded again. "They are in the capital with me. If they could ride back to Ninaeva with you, I would be grateful."

"Of course."

"Then let us go now." Alexander stood up. "Is Niara with you? We can introduce them."

As Vinet rose to her feet, she felt a wave of nausea sweep over her. She gasped and gripped the table, but it disappeared as soon as she did. Her hand instinctively went to her stomach as it twisted.

Alexander's brow furrowed. "Lady Vinet? Are you alright?"

Vinet couldn't answer him for a moment. Hastily, she did the math. Her eyes widened as she realized she was a week overdue, and she couldn't figure out whether to laugh or curse. She had talked about a child with Nazir. She just hadn't figured on it being so soon.

16

ALFHEIM

The air in the garden was fresh and welcoming. The slightest hint of Manyu's Rise was visible in the red tinge on some of the trees, but the warmth from the sun sank into her like a welcoming fire.

Four children had settled into one of the guest rooms of the townhouse. Vinet had almost feared for the safety of the household furniture before Nazir had offered to tell them a story. She had tried to warn him the children were not likely to be satisfied with one story, not this late in the afternoon, but he had simply smiled and shooed her outside.

She was grateful for that. After the council session, she'd barely had the energy to show the children around, much less deal with their rambunctiousness. They were dear children, certainly, but she was so tired.

She would be tired for a while, she knew. The child growing inside her would take most of her energy. She remembered that from Niara. She wished she'd been able to tell Nazir, but there hadn't been time yet. Not with the arrival of Alexander's grandchildren.

She closed her eyes and sighed as she sat down on a bench near the pond, sheltered by an old willow. Gradually, she let her awareness sink down into the earth. To the roots, to the trees, with which she could see.

The world faded, and she saw a bright city. Gorgeous, beautiful, with houses built into the trees, and colorful lanterns hung all around.

"Elfsdaughter," a voice whispered. "Elfsdaughter, we're waiting."

A piercing cry, a scream. Vinet's eyes flew open, shattering the vision. Her hands clutched the bench.

A vision. She hadn't had a vision for nearly half a year, not since her trip to Venia. She hadn't even thought about her visions, about the Sight. *Not since Father brought me out of my coma! What did he say? Six months?* She brought her hand to her stomach. *Mazda, please. Not now. For the sake of my child, not now.*

"Vinet?"

She looked up at Gwyn's voice.

Gwyn's eyes widened. "Are you alright? You're pale."

"I'm fine," she said. "Just tired," she added, when Gwyn looked unconvinced.

Gwyn still didn't seem satisfied but continued. "You have a visitor," she said. "I think you'll really want to see him."

In an instant, Vinet knew exactly who stood at the door. The very person who had made sure she was untroubled by visions and dreams for the last six months. *Father. He's here.*

"Show my father in, of course," she smiled.

Gwyn stared at Vinet. "How did you know it was him?" she demanded.

Vinet paused. How did she know? She had a feeling in her very bones, the knowledge her kin stood at the door.

Gwyn shook her head. "Never mind. I'll show him in. But I warn you, Vinet, he's not well."

Vinet frowned, but Gwyn disappeared before she could ask any further questions. Two seconds later, her father entered the garden. She gasped. Kinaevan slouched over, leaning heavily on a gnarled wooden cane. His hair, once the same red-brown as her own, was now streaked with white the color of bone.

His smile, at least, was the same, though he showed more than a hint of relief in it. "Daughter."

She concealed her shock at his appearance as she rose and stepped forward, arms open to greet him. "Father. Come in, please."

She suppressed another uneasy jolt as he cast a glare at a tree. They sat down on the bench together.

"Forgive my long absence, my daughter," Kinaevan said. "How have you been?"

She paused, thinking of all the things that had happened since she'd last seen him. "I've been very well." She hesitated briefly. "I'm married, Father. To Nazir."

"We know."

Vinet froze. A strange tone rang in her father's voice, a foreign element, sharp and clear.

"We?" she asked.

"Do you not know me?" Her father no longer spoke. The clear voice seemed to emanate from every tree in the garden. "Are you that far fallen, Elfsdaughter? That far into the darkness for which you are marked!"

The leaves and branches of all the trees rattled, as if a great gust of wind swept through the garden. Yet not a hair on Vinet's head stirred. The hair on the back of her neck, however, stood straight up. Every nerve in her body sang an alarm.

She knew that voice. She couldn't have said from where, but she knew it. She had heard it before: three voices in one, combined to form the clearest voice one could ever hear. *The Lady of Leaf and Lake*, she realized. She sprang to her feet, backing away from the tree behind the bench. "I did not choose to be marked, Lady!" she exclaimed.

As if on cue, a sharp pain between her shoulder blades, one that had been gone for half a year, slammed into her and nearly drove her to her knees. She grabbed at the bench to steady herself, bracing herself until the pain faded. She took a shuddering breath and looked around again. "If I knew how to remove this mark, I would."

Silence. No trees moved, no voice spoke. She took another deep breath. Had she imagined the voice? No, it had been real. She had felt it.

Kinaevan sighed. He leaned forward on his cane. The willow behind him seemed to droop, almost embracing him. "Yet there is no denying its presence." He sighed again. "For one reason or another, you have become the plaything of numerous vying powers."

She stared at her father, still breathing heavily. Was it her father or the Lady speaking? She almost didn't care. The mark bored into her back. Whatever protection her father had put over her was now gone.

"Do you know how to remove it?" she begged.

He looked away, a lifetime of sadness lurking in his eyes. "Yes, there is one way."

She dreaded her question, but she had to ask. "There's a price, isn't there?"

"There is always a price to pay with her," Kinaevan stated. He started to stand, seeking a scrap of strength inside him. Instead, he fell forward, the cane clattering to the cobblestone path. Instinctively, Vinet reached out, catching her father as he fell. His body felt limp and heavy in her arms. She could feel the raggedness of his breath.

"You must take me to the Shaded Lake, to Alfheim. There…a ritual."

"Father," she swallowed. "Father, you're not well. You couldn't make such a journey."

He clutched her arm with surprising strength. "I can. I will."

She hesitated. The pain still lingered in her shoulders. "What is the price?" she whispered.

He shook his head. "That doesn't matter. It is a price I will gladly pay." He coughed, and a seizure wracked his body. As Vinet watched, another long streak of white appeared in his hair. She tightened her grip on him, for she knew it was all she could do.

"For you, daughter. For the little one you bear."

She instinctively brought a hand to her stomach. Nothing showed yet, but it would soon. "Father," she whispered, desperation and despair leaking out with her voice.

His hand clutched her arm even harder. "Child of mine. Heir of the Oaken Spear. Promise me you will take me there. Swear to me you will not stop the ritual once begun."

She stared into his eyes, taken aback by the intensity of his gaze. She hesitated a moment longer, then lowered her eyes. Her hand tightened on her stomach, a reminder she was responsible for a life other than her own. "I…I promise."

Kinaevan closed his eyes and relaxed. He slumped back, allowing Vinet to settle him on the bench again.

"Go then to the Embassy and summon my Keeper. She'll know the way to Alfheim and how to begin the ritual. For now, my daughter, I need to rest." He curled up on the bench in a fetal position. The trees rustled quietly around him.

Willow weeps, and is so sad, but to sleep with her is not so bad. The children's poem ran through Vinet's mind as she looked at her father.

What price could there possibly be? She wondered. Her father knew, of that she was certain. And he didn't want her to know, for fear she wouldn't agree.

A flash of nausea overcame her, and she steadied herself against a thorn tree. The bark scratched her hand, and she hastily drew back.

Her hand went to her stomach again. It wasn't just her life on the line now. The little one inside her, the one she already loved more than life itself, was at risk.

She swallowed. She looked one last time at her father, then turned resolutely toward the house. She had work to do.

———

The journey to Alfheim was the hardest journey Vinet had ever had to make.

Kinaevan's "Keeper," as he'd termed her, had proven to be a taciturn older elf woman who'd barely spoken two words to Vinet the entire month of the journey. She'd shown no surprise when Vinet and Gwyn had arrived at the embassy, she had merely ordered the Thorns to move out. The Thorns traveled around them now, guarding the travelers.

Vinet, Nazir, and Gwyn were the only ones who rode. They kept their horses at a walk, but even so, Vinet had the feeling the Thorns could easily keep up with a trotting horse. The only thing which slowed them down was the cart which bore Kinaevan.

She felt her gaze turn to her father again, as it had already a thousand times this journey. He lay perfectly still, his expression shifting between peace and pain.

Nazir, as always, saw where her gaze lay. "How old is your father?" he asked in a low voice.

Vinet shrugged. She had no idea. Very old, was the only thing she knew.

Nazir looked around at the other elves. "They're not surprised. Perhaps..."

Vinet shook her head. She knew what Nazir was trying to suggest, what he was trying to prepare her for. But she couldn't accept it.

*Until the Sight calls me...*she flinched as she remembered that conversation with her father. He hadn't been well even then, so early in their relationship. Was this the price of using the Sight?

"Vinet."

She tore her gaze away from her father at the wonder in Nazir's voice. As she gazed forward again, she felt her own eyes widening with amazement.

A lake stretched out before them, perfectly situated in the middle of the forest. Alfheim was built around it. Longhouses stretched along the near shore, doors facing the water. They appeared more like the long roots of an ancient tree than any house Vinet had ever seen. Up in the boughs of the trees, rope bridges and small houses lit by multi-colored lanterns blended in with the colorful leaves of Manyu's Rise. Out on the lake, houseboats moved in a lazy fashion, seemingly going nowhere and everywhere at the same time.

Vinet blinked, feeling tears stinging her eyes. It was beautiful. Why did she have to come here like this?

She was given no further opportunity to observe the town. Kinaevan's Keeper led them directly through Alfheim without stopping, though Vinet could see that Gwyn, Nazir, and herself garnered curious looks from the elves living there.

They followed the Keeper to the far side of the lake, away from the houses. Slowly, the lake receded behind them as they entered the forest again. A harsh smell assailed her nose as the forest path began to turn down, winding through clefts in stone and soil, jagged tree roots all about. It wasn't a bad smell, but it made Vinet wrinkle her nose all the same. The path narrowed, and the Thorns abandoned the cart which bore Kinaevan and carried him instead. They left their horses tethered above the path.

Down and down they followed the path until a cave opened before them. The Keeper stopped.

"Are you certain of this?" the Keeper asked in a harsh voice.

Vinet looked around. The Thorns, so unreadable during the entire journey, shifted uneasily in the presence of the cave.

A shiver ran down her own spine. "He told me nothing," she whispered. "Beyond a promise not to interfere. I..." She swallowed. "I am not certain of this at all."

"You may not get another chance. In my experience, she is never pleased with this request we are about to make." The Keeper's face was impassive.

Vinet flinched as a stab between her shoulders reminded her of the stakes. Nazir placed a hand on her shoulder, warm and comforting, a steadying presence. "What is the price?"

The Keeper smiled briefly, a sad smile. She reached forward and took Vinet's hand. "You will feel nothing, child, but your father will die. It is often the price she demands."

There. It was said. It was known. Vinet closed her eyes and shuddered. She had understood this, somehow, deep inside her. Nazir's hands on her shoulders were the only thing keeping her upright.

She opened her eyes and looked at her father, still lying motionless in the arms of the Thorns. "Why would you do this, Father?"

The Keeper released her hand. "We do not have much time. Did you not swear to him? Let this be done then." Despite her brusque words, the Keeper's voice cracked.

Vinet trembled. Was this to be her decision, then? The decision of whether to free her unborn child of the taint of Manyu's mark or let her father die?

"Vinet," Nazir said in a low voice. Slowly, he turned her toward him and made her look him in the eyes. "Vinet. Your father knew this. Your father wanted this. Let him do this for you."

She blinked rapidly. "Nazir, I..." She shook her head. How could she do this?

He squeezed her shoulders again. "Vinet. Your father is already dying," he said softly. "It is his time. Let him do something worthwhile with his last hours." One of his hands moved to her stomach. "For our little one."

She looked at her father again. He lay still motionless. His hair shone almost completely white.

"Your husband is right," the Keeper said shortly. "Make your decision."

Vinet closed her eyes again and took a deep, shuddering breath. Something moved inside her stomach, a small kick. Her heart contracted. That was the first time she'd felt her child move inside her. She couldn't let her child bear the same mark she did. She opened her eyes to meet the Keeper's. She couldn't bring herself to speak, but she nodded shakily.

The Keeper showed no reaction of satisfaction or relief, just gestured to the Thorns and stepped into the cave. The Thorns followed her, bearing Kinaevan, and Vinet and Nazir descended after them, followed by Gwyn.

Small crystals hanging from the belts of the Thorns emitted light as they entered the cave. Vinet followed them down a rough-hewn staircase carved into the black rock which thrust first one way through the cave, then switched back to cut into another side. Soon they reached a chasm, and the smooth path followed the edge of the cave wall. Vinet swallowed, fearing to look down. Something dripped in the distance, echoing curiously louder and louder until it became a harsh demand in her ears.

Finally, they left the edge of the chasm and entered a chamber in the heart of the cave. Vinet could tell at one glance it was no natural cavern, not with the floor so smooth, and the walls so polished they gleamed silver and blue, providing an eerie illumination.

At one end of the chamber stood three chairs. One was of bone, bleached and marked red. The second was of smooth ash wood, tall and ornate in its simplicity. The third was a twisted abomination of stone, iron, bronze, and sap-bleeding maple. Three sources of light in the cavern ceiling illuminated the chairs. In the center of the chamber stood an altar of black iron and copper. It shimmered in the light as if a flickering flame.

The Keeper gestured, and the Thorns placed Kinaevan's body on the altar. One by one they left the cavern.

The Keeper turned to Vinet and gestured to Nazir and Gwyn. "Do you wish to do this alone or will these remain?"

Nazir answered before Vinet could fathom the idea of being by herself for this ritual. "We will stay," he said, moving to stand next to Vinet. He laid a hand on her shoulder.

Vinet looked gratefully at him, and he met her gaze with an understanding smile. Whatever happened, she would not be alone.

The Keeper nodded and moved to the altar. "Vinet, please stand at your father's head. Place your hands on either side and do not move from this place until the ritual is done."

Another shiver ran up Vinet's spine at those words. This was like the trials in the ancient stories, with consequences if she didn't manage to keep her hands where she had been told. Nevertheless, she moved over to stand at her father's head. Dreamlike, but her hands trembled as she placed them on either side of her father's head. She felt Nazir's presence, warm and comforting, right behind her, and Gwyn's presence further off, ready to protect her from any danger.

The Keeper produced a knife from her sleeve and slashed open Kinaevan's robe, once, twice, thrice, so that his chest was bare. Then, obviously steadying herself, she pricked his flesh with the dagger, balancing the blood on the blade and carrying it to the central throne of bone.

Vinet swallowed, staring at the wound on her father's chest. "I'm sorry, Father," she whispered.

The Keeper came back and repeated the process, carrying blood to the second throne, then the third. A sticky fog rose from the floor, obscuring vision of everyone's feet.

The Keeper stood at the foot of the altar, holding the knife outstretched in her hands. She remained perfectly still, staring only at Kinaevan. A single tear began to roll down her cheek.

Vinet trembled as she watched. At the sight of the tear, she closed her eyes briefly against the sting of her own tears. *I'm sorry, Father.*

The fog continued to rise, until it obscured everything but the altar, the Keeper, and Vinet. Vinet felt a tear of her own fall just before a slender, gentle finger of fog rose up, scooping up the tear of the Keeper, then racing over to catch her own.

A slight laugh, trickling warm rain. Then the fog rushed away, whipping like a wind across Vinet's face. It drew into the thrones and revealed three seated women. The Mother sat, concerned, on the throne of ash. The Maiden reclined on the twisted throne. The Crone sat, hunched forward, on the bone throne.

Vinet stared at the three women. She'd met them before, all of them, in the body of the same person. The woman who'd given her the initial protection from Manyu's mark. AeresThonEsia. The Lady of Leaf and Lake.

"Ah. The Elfsdaughter," said the Crone.

"Little shining one," sighed the Maiden.

"Dear child," said the Mother.

Vinet tore her gaze away from the three as the Keeper started to speak. The Keeper was not looking at the three women. "We come to offer the one whose blood has fed your thrones."

The Maiden laughed, and the Mother simply shook her head. "In exchange for?" asked the Crone.

"The purification of she who stands at his head."

Vinet bit her lip and looked down at her father's face.

"What good is purity?" the Maiden asked, shifting in her seat.

"What good is standing?" the Crone cackled.

"What is good?" the Mother was weeping.

Vinet glanced at the Keeper, expecting her to answer. She nearly froze at the confusion on the Keeper's face.

She closed her eyes, remembering all the tales she had read. This was a riddle, a test, and it needed to be answered properly before the ritual could proceed.

Her hands tightened their grip on Kinaevan's head. She had to answer. She had to fulfill her father's request.

"Purity is being clean." Her voice shook. She swallowed, willing her voice to strengthen as she continued. "It is being who you are, without influence from any malicious outside forces." The next was an easy one. Standing: so much symbolism associated with standing. "Standing... standing is the only way you can walk and keep moving forward. It is what gives one strength when facing the world. As to good." A trick question. No one, not even the priests of Mazda, had a clear definition as to what good and evil were. "If I could answer that, I would be a much wiser person than I am. I only know that this is my father's wish, for the sake of the child I bear."

She looked down at her father again, feeling the movement of the child inside her again. This was his wish. Nazir had been right.

She glanced up to see satisfaction in the three women's faces, and a wave of relief rushed through her. She had answered correctly.

"Who are these you bring with you, Vinet? These who stand inside our throne room? What concern have they here? The child of the sun, and the shield-protector?"

The three voices wove together as one and echoed through the cavern. "And you would allow this, Keeper of the one called Kinaevan, our Eye?"

Vinet's breath caught, and she looked behind her at Nazir. He opened his mouth to speak, and she shook her head. This was her ritual, for all that the Keeper was nominally in charge. She had to be the one to answer.

"They are Nazir et-Alim, my husband, and Gwyn, my truest friend. They are here to help me, to give me the strength to do what I need to do." She prevented herself from glaring in defiance only by a supreme effort of will.

Apparently, only an answer was required, for the Ladies ignored the presence of the two 'outsiders' and continued.

"What do you desire of us, child-bearer, Sight-knower, Elfsdaughter?" the Crone asked.

This was the trick. Vinet took a deep breath. She had to be clear and concise. "I wish to have the mark of Manyuanmazda removed, so that he may not follow me, and know my actions, and interfere with my Sight. So that he may not have influence over my child."

"As is known and as is spoken, so we do remove his token." The three voices rang out together. "Do the deed, Keeper."

The Keeper gave a single cry of anguish and plunged the knife forward into Kinaevan's flesh. Vinet flinched but managed to keep from crying out. No blood swelled from the wound, though a large gash was rendered in his flesh. The Keeper gave two more cries, and two more stabs with the knife.

Kinaevan stirred under Vinet's hands, and Vinet clutched his head tightly. His mouth opened, but no sound came forth.

No! She thought. *He isn't supposed to wake! He wasn't supposed to feel any pain!*

Her eyes stung as she looked down at her father. His eyes fluttered open and met hers.

An eternal moment seemed to pass between them. Vinet tried to convey all her apologies, all her feelings, all of her regrets in that moment.

Kinaevan smiled at her. She felt his outpouring of love, and an expression of peace came over him. He closed his eyes and sighed, relaxing under her hands.

Blood now flowed from his wounds, as if numerous hands scooped it out. She had never seen so much blood at once. The Crone cackled, the Mother wept, and the Maiden giggled.

A sharp pain stabbed Vinet's back, making her arch backward. There was a crawling sensation, as if ten thousand worms were eating through her. She screamed, clutching her father's head tighter. Then blessed blackness.

The sun shone when Vinet awoke. The quiet melody of the birds soothed her soul, as did the gentle sound of lake water lapping at the shore. Someone held her close, in a warm, gentle, loving embrace. Nazir.

She opened her eyes. They were back in Alfheim, on the shore of the lake. The Keeper was nowhere in sight. They sat on the shore, Nazir holding her, while Gwyn knelt next to them. She saw the relief on their faces as she awoke.

She blinked, recalling the events: her father, lying on the altar; the three women. AeresThonEsia, also known as the Lady of Leaf and Lake.

She sat up slowly, trying to process everything. The mark of Manyuanmazda was gone. She was free to practice the Sight again. Her child was safe. Her father was dead.

Her father was dead.

She burst into tears. Nazir pulled her close again, and she buried her face in his shoulder. After a moment, Gwyn's hand rested on hers, and she clutched it. Neither of them said anything, they were just there. They would always be there.

Finally, her tears dried. She still felt empty, but her grief was spent, for now, at least. She pulled away.

"It worked, by the way," Gwyn said. "I checked."

Vinet managed a small smile. Trust Gwyn to be practical about the entire situation. "Thank you," she whispered.

Gwyn shrugged, seemingly uncomfortable. Vinet turned to regard Nazir. He gazed back at her, nothing but concern and love on his face.

"Vinet Sindarilae?"

Vinet looked up, startled. That was her father's name. She had never used it before, not even in her thoughts.

Her father's Keeper stood on the lake shore, looking at the three of them. She showed no sign of her grief from the ritual chamber.

Nazir's arms tightened around her.

"I...yes."

The Keeper gave a brief smile. "We must speak."

Somehow, Vinet had been expecting this.

The Keeper glanced at Gwyn and Nazir, and Vinet rolled her eyes. "If you did not object to their presence in the ritual chamber, you cannot object to it now."

The Keeper didn't flinch, just met Vinet's eyes. "Some things are not for the uninitiated to hear."

Nazir squeezed her shoulders. "I will stay if you want," he whispered.

Vinet reached up and grasped his hand but didn't let her gaze stray from the Keeper's. The Keeper held the gaze.

Finally, Vinet nodded. "Just move out of earshot along the beach," she said quietly. "This won't take long."

Nazir squeezed her hand, then rose. Gwyn followed him, staying well within sight but out of hearing range.

The Keeper sighed and sat cross-legged on the sand in front of Vinet. "You know so little," she said. "And yet you must learn, and learn quickly."

Vinet bit her lip. "I have been trying."

The Keeper waved a hand. "I know. He told me. It is not your fault, nor his, only simple circumstance keeping you ignorant."

The Keeper fell silent. "She accepted you fully today, as one who will become an Eye. I don't think you realized that or what that entails."

Vinet shook her head. She knew what the Eyes were, of course, but...

The Keeper sighed again. "This would have been simpler had Kinaevan chosen to have a child with an elf woman," she said. "Then you would have been raised here, with the knowledge of what you would become. But perhaps then you would not have the strength that you show."

Vinet blinked. She had hardly felt strong the last few years.

The Keeper seemed to sense her doubt and smiled briefly again. "Do you think it by chance he chose to mark you? Your strength sets you apart. I do not know whether it is because your mother was human, or the lineage of Queen Olvae showing true. Nevertheless, you have all the strength of one of our strongest Eyes. Your father told me you have the Swaying?"

The Swaying. The use of magic. Vinet nodded without speaking.

"You must take your father's place," the Keeper said.

Vinet's eyes widened. "What?" she asked.

"As an Eye," the Keeper elaborated. "It will take years, and will not happen fully until your exile, but you must begin that path. By accepting your father's sacrifice, the Lady demands it."

Vinet hesitated. She had known from the beginning that her father intended her to train in the Sight, and even be an Eye one day. But she had duties, commitments she could not relinquish.

"What does being an Eye entail?" she asked.

"It means you serve the People of the Lady of Leaf and Lake," the Keeper said. "And you serve the Lady. Whatever that entails. Even if it ends in a sacrifice like your father's."

Vinet felt cold.

"If you do not," the Keeper continued, "Then you will be open to another being striking out at you again. The Lady is not gentle, not in all her forms, but she is a protector and guardian. When she chooses to be."

Vinet grimaced. "And how do I become one?" she asked.

"You practice the Sight," the Keeper said. "You use it as much as you can, as safely as you can. You communicate with the Lady. There are ways to reach her."

"I know," Vinet interrupted. "She's shown me."

The Keeper's eyes widened. "Then you are further along than I thought."

Still, Vinet hesitated. "I cannot move to Alfheim," she said. "I have duties and responsibilities. I have a daughter, and this child. I must return to Saemar."

"Saemar is our ally against Mount Halon," the Keeper said. "I will return to the fight there as well."

Vinet took a deep, shuddering breath. Could she do this? Could she dedicate herself to becoming an Eye? Did she have a choice?

She closed her eyes, remembering her father. His peaceful expression as he lay on the altar. His loving laugh as he gently taught her the elvish language, as he taught her grounding techniques so she wouldn't lose herself in her visions, as he told her the stories of her ancestors, of her people.

She had to do this. For her father's sake.

"I will," she declared.

The Keeper nodded. "Good."

There seemed to be nothing more to say. Vinet looked at her father's Keeper for a long moment before reaching out to touch her shoulder.

"I'm sorry," she whispered.

The Keeper didn't pretend to misunderstand her. "It was his time," she said. "The Sight claims them all, in the end. But it is hard. I had been his Keeper for over three thousand years."

Vinet flinched backward. She had known her father was old, but that old?

The Keeper smiled wryly at her. "The line of Olvae Oakenspear does not die easily. You would do well to remember that."

Vinet shook her head. She had had no idea.

The Keeper sighed again. "I must prepare. We will travel with you back to Saemar, then separate. I go to the southeast. Lady's blessing with you, Vinet Sindarilae."

17

TREACHERY

I lhelm Castle was a welcome sight. A flurry of activity occurred as soon as they arrived, of course. Alexander's grandchildren had to be settled in, having spent the last few months in the capital at Vinet's townhouse. And of course, the mountain of business her seneschal had presented her with as soon as she'd walked through the door waited. She'd been gone far longer than originally planned, after all. As soon as she'd returned from Alfheim she'd needed to be in the capital for a council session. Manyu's Time swept its cold across the land, and it would soon be Papsukkal again.

It was good to be back, though. Good to be in a place where she could relax and prepare for her child's birth. Good to be away from the plotting and scheming on the Council, away from the concern that they'd heard nothing from High Priest Ellil since he left for the Bern Forest, and even away from the worry of the southeast war. At least that would settle down for Manyu's Time. Even the strange creatures seemed disinclined to attack in the snow.

She smiled at Nazir, sitting at his desk in the library. He bent over his books again, back to doing what he enjoyed most. Her own book lay open on her lap in front of her. The fire crackled merrily, a warning the chill of the first month of Manyu's Time only heralded harsher weather to come.

She looked up as Gwyn entered the library. The expression on her friend's face made her frown.

234

"What's wrong?"

Gwyn shook her head. "There's a group of riders approaching. Dunbarrow colors. It seems Lord Conn is coming to visit."

Vinet exchanged a look with Nazir. What could Conn possibly want that he couldn't have talked to her about at the last council session? Not that she'd been in much of a mood to talk then, but he hadn't even approached her.

"How large a party?" she asked.

"Small. A few warriors."

Vinet frowned. Was it merely a social call? Somehow, she couldn't imagine it, not in this weather.

"We'll meet him in the great hall," she said. "Sorry, Nazir."

He smiled at her. "I knew this would be part of the bargain when I married you, my dear. No apology necessary."

His words imparted a warm feeling as she left the library to change into something more suitable. As casual and rough as Conn was, she wanted to be dressed in at least some finery to receive him. They were not friends, after all. Their relationship was still a formal one.

She and Nazir took their places in the Great Hall, Gwyn directly behind them. A servant came to announce Lord Conn of Dunbarrow. Vinet eyed her fellow councilor closely as he entered. He looked the same as he had last she had seen him, still full of poorly suppressed anger and righteousness. He wore a fur cloak to ward off the chill of the season. His burly bodyguard, Aed, accompanied them. The rest of their guard must have been left outside.

She stepped forward, smiling a greeting. "Lord Conn. This is a pleasant surprise."

Conn smiled broadly. "I do hope so."

Vinet raised an eyebrow at Conn. He seemed to be struggling to find his next words.

"Lady Vinet, I..." his eyes widened as he actually saw her. "I...my apologies, Lady Vinet. I believe congratulations must be in order. Did I miss the official announcement?"

Involuntarily, she glanced down. On the journey back from the council session, her pregnancy had become more and more visible. The tight-laced formal dress she had donned made it even more apparent. She exchanged a wry look with Nazir. "No, there has been no announcement," she said. "Thank you for the congratulations, all the same."

Conn nodded, absent-minded again. Finally, he met her gaze squarely.

"Lady Vinet, I have become aware you are sheltering a person I must speak with."

Vinet frowned. "And who would that be?"

"The woman who claims to have birthed the son of Lord General Torainn."

Vinet sucked in a breath. So, someone had told Conn about Eithne's presence at Ninaeva. Not that she had ever kept it a secret.

"Eithne, you mean?" she asked, keeping her voice casual. "Why do you want to speak to her?"

Conn blinked. Vinet tightened her lips. Had he been expecting her to deny Eithne's presence?

"I'm searching for Lord General Torainn," he said. "She may know something."

She felt some sympathy for him, which surprised her. He had looked up to Torainn as one of his mentors. "She won't be able to tell you anything," she said. "I've already asked her."

Conn's expression tightened. "I likely know things you don't," he said. "And she may know more than she realizes."

Vinet exchanged another look with Nazir. He shrugged slightly.

She thought for a moment. She could see no harm in granting Conn's request, provided he did not threaten Eithne in any way.

"Nazir will ask her if she'll talk to you," she said. "Let's go to my study. She'll be more comfortable there, *if* she decides to talk. She's not used to talking to nobility." She stopped herself from biting her lip. She did not know how to warn Conn he needed to be gentle in order to gain any information from Eithne.

Conn nodded impatiently, and she had the sense if Eithne refused to talk, he would attempt other methods. He was worried, far more worried than she had ever seen him before.

Gwyn and Aed were two steps behind them as they made their way to the study. Gwyn followed them inside, but Aed stayed outside. Vinet couldn't help but feel a moment of relief for that. No man should be as large and burly as Aed, and of all people, he would be the one most likely to intimidate Eithne.

Vinet gestured for Conn to take a seat while she remained standing, using all her will to keep from pacing.

"Where did you find her, Lady Vinet?" Conn asked.

Vinet's shoulders tensed, and she braced herself for a line of questions.

Nazir interrupted by opening the door. Behind him, dressed in plain servants' clothing, followed Eithne. Vinet would have supported her unconditionally, but the poor woman was aghast at the idea of living on charity. Finally, Vinet had offered her a place in the household, and Eithne had gratefully accepted.

Vinet smiled at the woman. Poor Eithne's eyes were wide as she regarded the room. Since her arrival, Vinet could count on one hand the number of times she'd interacted with any of the nobility.

"It's alright, Eithne," she said. "This is Lord Conn MacTir, a friend of Lord General Torainn's. He hoped you might answer some questions." She turned to Conn. "Lord Conn, this is Eithne."

Eithne managed a shaky curtsy. Conn nodded. "I'm told you knew Torainn intimately? And that you bore his child?"

Eithne's gaze flickered to Vinet with the same shock Vinet knew could be read on her own face. Conn had never been much of one for tact, certainly, but this was extreme, even by his standards!

Eithne cast her eyes down again. "Yes," she said.

Conn gave her a toothy smile, reminding Vinet of a wolf. "I don't bite," he said. "I just wish to find out what you know."

Vinet couldn't help herself, the young mother looked so frightened and confused. She walked over and gently placed a hand on her shoulder.

"When did you last see Torainn, Eithne?" Conn asked.

Eithne kept her eyes cast down. "In Venia, my lord. Over a year ago, now."

"What was he like then?"

What was Conn trying to ask? Despite her reservations, Vinet didn't bother to interrupt, for the question had clearly put fire into Eithne.

"He is the strongest man I've ever known," Eithne said, slightly breathless. "He is firm, fair, kind, the best of all men."

"Is?" Conn frowned. "How do you know he's still alive? Have you had contact from him?"

Eithne blinked, obviously taken aback. "No one could kill my Torainn," she said. "He is the strongest man alive."

The deep faith in the woman's voice was enough to make Vinet's heart contract. *She loves him so much. I could only wish he were worthy of such faith, for her sake.*

Conn continued his questions as if the woman had never spoken up. "How did you come to be with him?"

Eithne's eyes darted to Vinet again, then to Conn. "I was a slave before Torainn found me." She straightened proudly. "He made me his servant instead, his housekeeper. He visited me often, and we grew to love each other. When I told him I carried his child, I had never seen him so pleased. Then he vanished. Shortly afterward thugs took over the house, and I was forced into the streets where Lady Vinet found me."

Conn glanced at Vinet, who kept her face impassive. He narrowed his eyes before turning his attention back to Eithne.

"How was he in those final days?"

Eithne blinked again. "He was himself. Same as ever. I was not allowed to perform my duties as housekeeper because of my pregnancy, but that was the only difference." She smiled, a sad little smile.

"And he gave no indication why he left?"

Eithne leaned forward, and Vinet could see the intensity in her eyes. "He vanished," she said emphatically.

Conn frowned. "Vanished in what way? As in disappeared in front of you?"

Eithne shrugged. "He has not come back. But he will return. He always does."

"So, he vanished before?"

She shrugged again. "He has responsibilities. But he always returns. And he will again." She turned to look at Vinet, and the pleading expression in her face broke Vinet's heart again. "Won't he?"

Vinet couldn't lie to her. "We don't know where he is, but I am sure he would be glad of your faith in him." Empty words, words she couldn't even know for certain were true, but they seemed to reassure Eithne.

Conn regarded them both steadily. Finally, he said, his voice very deliberate, "I know where Torainn is."

Eithne jerked away from Vinet, staring at Conn. "Where? Where is he?"

Vinet glared at Conn. She would have expected him to volunteer this information first. Instead, he'd come to question Eithne on the pretense of finding out Torainn's location. His deception infuriated her.

Conn's expression didn't change. "Did he ever mention his wife to you, Eithne?"

Vinet caught her breath. Conn didn't know, didn't know Eithne believed herself to be more than mistress.

"He had no wife but me." Eithne leaned forward. "Where is he? Where is my Torainn?"

Conn glanced sharply at Vinet. "He had no wife?"

Vinet didn't know what to do. She placed a hand on Eithne's shoulder again, trying to will comfort to the poor woman. She shook her head at Conn, trying to tell him not to press the subject.

Conn glared at her. "I spoke to him. He told me that he would never betray Kianna, his wife."

"No. No," Eithne whispered. She looked up and nearly screamed, "I am his wife!"

Vinet caught Eithne, who had broken down in tears. Wordlessly, she pulled the woman to her, stroking her hair as she sobbed. Eithne was so much younger than she, it felt almost like holding a child. Except this child was a mother as well.

Vinet glared at Conn. "I think she's had enough of your questions."

Conn's eyes flashed. "No. One of them is lying, Torainn or Eithne, and the safety and security of the kingdom depends on it."

Vinet stiffened, but she kept her voice dry. "Safety and security of the kingdom? Torainn was an important man, I grant you, but that's going a bit far, don't you think?"

Conn met her eyes. "An important man who might either save or destroy the kingdom."

Vinet blinked at the intensity in his voice. What was he talking about?

A soft knock at the door startled her. Nazir opened it, and a young servant woman carrying a baby peeked inside. "My lady? I'm sorry to interrupt, but this little one wants his mother."

Vinet had never been so grateful for an interruption. Eithne eagerly received her son.

"Wait," Conn said sharply. "You said you were his wife. When did that happen? What aren't you telling me?"

Anger flared in Vinet on Eithne's behalf, and she was ready to leap to her defense, but it proved unnecessary. The presence of her son, or Conn's refusal to tell her Torainn's whereabouts, had stiffened Eithne's spine.

"I am his wife, Lord," she said firmly. She looked down at her son, who wiggled and grabbed her hair. She hugged him close. "The details of when we were married should be of no more concern to you than the details of our wedding night!" She stalked out the door. Gwyn closed it behind her without waiting for a signal from Vinet.

Vinet turned to glare at Conn. "What in Mazda's name is going on?" she demanded.

Conn met her gaze, and she could see him breathing heavily. His hands clenched tightly, and she felt a moment's gratitude that he didn't appear to be armed.

Then everything seemed to relax. He collapsed back into his chair, his shoulders slumped. "I don't know."

She exchanged glances with Nazir and Gwyn. Nazir moved to stand in the shadows, while Gwyn stood by the door. Conn ignored them both.

"I traveled to Tigri some time ago. I had to apologize to a lord who I'd...well, I had business there. And while I was there, Torainn met me."

Vinet sat down carefully. She had the feeling this was about to get very interesting.

"Torainn talked about the king's illness, that politicians surrounding him were keeping him feeble, keeping him from making his own decisions. He said none of His Majesty's feebleness had started until the arrival of a certain noble who's been put into far more power than he should have."

Vinet already knew who Conn hinted at. "Lord Auriel," she said flatly.

Conn nodded and sighed.

"Torainn suggested Lord Auriel is poisoning the king?" Vinet asked to clarify Conn's suggestion. The idea sounded so outlandish to her ears. Lord Auriel didn't stand to gain anything from that. He had already become the steward. He couldn't climb any further. He couldn't become king, after all. None of the nobles would accept him, not even now. And especially not while the prince still lived, a true-blood heir to the Saemarian throne. And yet something about Lord Auriel unsettled Vinet. *If the king died...the prince is only a boy.*

"No." Conn shook his head. "Not poison, more that he controlled the king, influenced him. Perhaps the illness is a symptom of that. After all, the king is rarely seen unaccompanied, and the person who accompanies him is almost always Auriel."

Vinet could think of plenty of more innocent reasons Lord Auriel would need to be at the king's side. He was the steward, and there were affairs of the kingdom to handle, for one. There were less innocent reasons as well, however, and the position as steward would make Lord Auriel unlikely to be questioned.

Conn shook his head again, more fervent this time. "You doubt me. I knew you would. I am starting to doubt myself!" He threw his arms wide before letting them fall limply to the armrests of his chair. "That is why I came here. Torainn denied the existence of Eithne and the child, so I needed to verify the truth myself."

"And what did you verify?" Vinet asked, her tone sharper than she'd meant it to be.

Conn glanced sideways at her. "She has benefited a great deal from telling you she was Torainn's mistress."

Vinet didn't bother to remind him that Eithne believed she was Torainn's wife. "That is through my own action, not hers," she said. "Eithne did not find me, I found her. She was not even aware I was in Venia. No one was."

Conn snorted. "No one? Not even Lord Auriel? The man knows far more than he should, even you have to admit that."

Vinet tightened her lips. "No one knew," she emphasized. "No one besides Gwyn and Nazir."

Conn waved his hand as if her statement was of no importance. "I've been trying to find out the truth of the matter," he said. "If Torainn's claims are true, then we are facing civil war. Half the nobility already back Auriel, a man who assassinated Torainn's wife without judgment or regret. The other half..." he let his voice trail off.

Vinet felt her eyes widen. Regardless of her feelings about Lord Auriel or Torainn, this was far more alarming.

"Civil war?" she demanded. She thought back to the council session, the reports of the war in the south. "Lord Conn, are you out of your mind? We are already at war! A civil war would be disastrous, and benefit none except Mount Halon!" *How could Conn even be considering this?*

Conn's eyes were dark. "The king's safety is paramount. And if Auriel is controlling him—"

"Forgive me if I put the kingdom's safety before the king's," Vinet said sharply. "He won't have a kingdom to rule if Mount Halon sweeps over us all. His protection is what he has his knights for."

Conn smiled thinly at her. "But we are sworn to the king."

Vinet felt her fists clench. Of all the times for Conn's sense of honor to appear! "My oath as a noble is to the king," she retorted. "Our oaths as councilors are to the kingdom, and they supersede the noble oath."

Conn's face was impassive, and a fire shone in his eyes. Vinet cursed his inconvenient honor. She had to get through to him. "Lord Conn, you're a military man. You've seen the reports from the southern border just as I have. General Alexander is getting ready to conscript more troops. Do you really think Saemar could withstand a civil war and not be overrun by Mount Halon? If Torainn urges you to consider such a course, you might ask him where his actual allegiances lie."

That, at least, caught Conn off guard. He blinked at her. "Are you suggesting he may be in league with the darkness?" he demanded.

Vinet threw up her hands. "I don't know!" she exclaimed. "I haven't met him since he disappeared. But I know one of the theories about Lady Kianna is she wasn't actually Lady Kianna, and that is why Auriel had to kill her. Where did you meet him, Conn, at the north Tigrian border?" she demanded abruptly.

Conn nodded, taken aback.

With Conn's lands in the north, Vinet had suspected as much. "There have been rumors of dark magic there since we became councilors. Mazda's light, Conn, that's what Ellil is investigating! Who knows what could be going on up there?"

She didn't know if anything she said was true, only that she had to get Conn to stop and think, to not act immediately based entirely on Torainn's word alone.

Conn continued to hesitate. "I had not thought of that."

She breathed a sigh of relief. "Well, think of it, please," she said. "You are an honorable man, Lord Conn. Please do not let your honor get in the way of your reason."

Conn blinked as if he was waking up. "You have given me much to think about." He stood, rising to his feet a little shakily. "Do you mind us intruding on your hospitality for a night?"

Vinet shook her head. "Not at all. Quarters have already been set up for you and yours."

He nodded. "My thanks." Without another word, he left the study.

Vinet turned to Nazir and Gwyn. Both stood silent, waiting for her assessment.

She took a deep breath. "I don't know who's in the right on this," she said, "But I know Conn shouldn't be handling it on his own. There are two people who need to know. I'm writing a report to General Alexander, and I'll tell Lady Pellalindra myself when we're back in the capital."

Gwyn raised an eyebrow. "Do you think Pellalindra won't just tell her husband?"

Vinet hesitated. Gwyn had a point, but still, Vinet felt it was the right course of action. "Pellalindra has contacts all over the nobility. If anyone has heard rumors of civil war, it's her," she said. "Besides, her closeness to Lord Auriel might be exactly what is needed to determine the truth."

Gwyn nodded her understanding.

Vinet turned to Nazir. He looked at her, uncertainty plain on his face. She stepped forward and pulled him into an embrace.

"What's wrong, Vinet?" he asked.

She buried her head in his shoulder. "I'm scared, my love," she whispered. "If Conn is correct, and talking about civil war…"

"Shhh," Nazir stroked her hair, much as she had stroked Eithne's earlier. "It will not come to that. I promise."

He had no authority to promise that, but it made her feel easier. She straightened. She had work to do.

The sounds of celebration echoed through Ilhelm Castle. Vinet smiled in relief and delight. Papsukkal again. A new year, new decisions, a new beginning.

Despite her fears, no civil war had broken out. She'd written to Alexander about Conn's visit to her, as planned, but she hadn't found an opportunity to tell Pellalindra yet. Part of her was worried Pellalindra might tell Lord Auriel. The other half of her hoped she would. *If only I knew more about Lord Auriel! If only I knew if I could trust him.*

She felt her child kick inside of her, and she dropped her hand to her round stomach. "Not yet, little one. Not yet." It was Papsukkal, after all. The day outside of time. Some considered it an ill omen for a child to be born on this day.

Nazir appeared beside her. "A new year, my love. A year together."

She smiled at him. He was right. She'd proposed to him exactly one year ago.

"Mama!"

She turned to see Niara and all three of Alexander's grandchildren running toward her. "Mama, can we play by the lake? Evalynna has said all Manyu's Time that it's too cold, but it's Mazda's Rise now!"

Vinet laughed and looked out the door to the great hall. It stood wide open, letting in the chill of early Mazda's Rise. "Does it feel warm to you, dearest?"

Niara had the grace to look abashed. "No." She dragged the word out.

Vinet shook her head. "I am not going to contradict Evalynna's orders, my dear. You ask her."

Niara smiled. "But she's not looking after us tonight."

Vinet sighed and rolled her eyes. No, she wasn't. Vinet had made sure both Gwyn and Evalynna had the night off. They deserved time together.

Rian, the oldest grandchild, grinned, and Vinet knew with a flash where the idea to play in the lake during Manyu's Rise had come from. Alexander's oldest granddaughter enjoyed seeing just how far she could press the rules.

"Not until it's warm," she said firmly. "You don't want to catch a cold and miss the rest of Papsukkal, do you?"

Niara and the twins blinked. Even Rian seemed startled.

"There'll be minstrels and bards from all over," Nazir put in, picking up her cue. "You wouldn't want to miss that."

Niara's eyes widened. "Bards! I love bards!"

"And Gwyn won't even be around to complain about them," Vinet said. "And until the actual celebration, you can play in the garden."

Niara squealed in delight. "Thank you!" She managed to remember her manners before she dashed off, followed by three giggling children.

Vinet sighed. "Where do they get all the energy?"

Nazir just shook his head. He stepped closer to her and placed a hand on her stomach. "There'll be another one soon."

She had to smile at that.

They might have stood there, smiling at each other, except they were interrupted by Gwyn's voice. "Hello, lovebirds."

Vinet looked up. "Gwyn! Aren't you and Evalynna supposed to be...oh, there you are, Evalynna." She raised an eyebrow as she saw Evalynna enter the great hall behind Gwyn. "Aren't you supposed to be keeping her distracted today?"

"I'm trying," Evalynna said, attempting to grumble but failing.

Gwyn rolled her eyes. "We'll get back to it, but Vinet, there're elves here."

"Elves? Faithful or Unfaithful?" Vinet asked sharply.

Gwyn shook her head. "They arrived openly, so I doubt the Unfaithful. I've arranged a guard for you to meet them nonetheless."

Vinet exchanged a glance with Nazir. She hadn't been to the embassy since her father's death, so why were there elves visiting her?

"This is hardly the best day," she said. "I can't make any official arrangements with them until tomorrow."

"The leader wants to see you anyway. Should I show him in?" Gwyn asked.

Vinet nodded. She and Nazir moved to the dais at the end of the hall.

Nazir offered Vinet his arm to help her up the few steps, and she smiled gratefully at him.

She knew they were Thorns the minute they entered the hall. They moved like the elves who had carried her father. They were a mixed group. About half were women, armed and dressed the same as the men. All were armed with bows, a single long sword, and were clad in leather armor, but there the similarities ended. Some were tall, others not. There had a range of hair colors, from red-brown, like Vinet's own, to black and blonde.

The tallest of them stepped forward to address Vinet. "Vinet Sindar-lae, we are here to serve you."

Vinet blinked. She had not expected this. "Pardon?" she asked.

The elf smiled. "You are to be an Eye. We are your Thorns."

Vinet shook her head. "How...but..."

Nazir placed a hand on her arm. "Your father's Keeper."

She blinked again and looked at the elf. He gave her a small nod.

She sighed. "What does 'serve me' mean?" she asked, curious despite her wariness and surprise.

He shrugged. "Your protection. Your messengers. Whatever else is required. You are not an Eye yet, so you have no Keeper, but I am the person the rest answer to in the meantime."

Vinet glanced at Gwyn, standing as unobtrusively as she could near the wall. "I have a Keeper," she said steadily. "My Father named her such. You will answer to Gwyn." *And Mazda help him if he thinks he can underestimate her because she's human,* she thought.

Gwyn's face remained expressionless as the elf turned toward her. His eyes widened, but he bowed his head in acceptance.

Vinet opened her mouth to ask his name, but a powerful contraction hit her, and she grabbed Nazir's arm to steady herself.

"Vinet?" his voice was worried.

She gasped against the pain. Her child did not want to wait. "Send for the midwife," she gasped.

Gwyn set off at a run.

With an effort, she raised her head to look at the elf. "Enjoy the festival for today," she managed. "We'll talk details tomorrow. I..." she gasped again as another wave of pain came.

The elf nodded, and the Thorns left the hall as silently as they had come. Slowly, Nazir helped her make her way up the stairs to her bedchamber. Every once in a while, she had to stop as another contraction began.

Mazda's light, she thought, *this is going to be a long day.*

She was so tired, but also happy. 'Radiant,' Nazir had said.

She glanced down at the child in her arms. Her son had waited until mid-afternoon to be born, and then he'd arrived kicking and screaming. His skin made it blatantly obvious he was Nazir's son, though it wasn't the pure black of his father, but rather a golden brown. He had inherited his father's eyes, as well, dark brown instead of bright green. Nonetheless, he bore his elven heritage in his name. Thalion Kinaevan et-Alim.

"He's so small," Niara said with wonder.

Vinet smiled at her. "You were that tiny too," she said.

Gwyn laughed and interjected, "And look at you now! Eight years old! Almost grown!"

Niara giggled. "I like having a brother," she announced.

Vinet wrinkled her nose at her daughter. "That's good, because you're stuck with him now," she said.

Niara giggled again. "Can I hold him?"

Carefully, Vinet handed her the sleeping Thalion. Niara's eyes widened in fascination as she stared at the little face.

Vinet exchanged a glance with Nazir, and they both smiled. He was theirs. Together, they had created this gorgeous son.

Thalion opened his eyes, and Niara gasped. Vinet watched carefully, but Thalion showed no signs of crying. Instead, he reached up, grabbing a lock of Niara's hair.

"Hey!" Niara exclaimed.

Vinet laughed and reached down. "Now, boy, let go," she said gently.

Thalion cooed and reached for Vinet's unbound hair instead. She sighed and took him back from Niara.

"You did the exact same thing," she informed her daughter.

Niara giggled.

Thalion stirred in her arms and let out a wail. Vinet immediately shifted him, bouncing him up and down.

"I think he's hungry," Nazir said wryly. "I know I am."

Vinet started unlacing her shift. "Well, you can feed yourself. I'll take care of our son."

Our son. She met Nazir's eyes as she said it and smiled. Our son.

They stayed there for a while longer, until Gwyn ordered Vinet to rest and ushered everyone out of the room. The room seemed unnaturally quiet after they left. Thalion slept soundly in his cradle. Her son. She felt a bond so powerful, only matched by the one she had with Niara. Conn had children of his own. His children would be threatened in a civil war. How could he even consider putting his children in danger to side with a potentially unstable man?

She sat down in her chair. Absently, she reached for the cane which rested against the wall. Her father's cane, the one he'd used in his last days. Smooth, polished, oak. She missed him dreadfully.

She needed more information. She needed to see Torainn with her own eyes. If he was anything like Lady Kianna had been, possessed or a danger, she should be able to sense it. *Gwyn will kill me if she finds out I'm not resting*, she thought, a brief, fleeting thought. Closing her eyes reaching into herself, she began. The trees in the castle welcomed her She'd been practicing regularly, as she'd promised her father's Keeper Now she went further, bouncing from tree to tree, across the breadth of Saemar, to the Bern Forest, a forest of elm and elder. Unfriendly trees.

She searched and found a thorn. Sharp and clear, she settled in watching.

A castle, a fortress. A garden. A young lord clad in armor stood nearby but he didn't look comfortable in it. He was conferring with several older men, all grizzled veterans. Lord Artosbern II. Only one castle stood in the Bern Forest. Why was he in armor? Vinet knew him as a bookish sort.

"Battle...reinforcements...orders..."

The words came sporadically, but Vinet caught enough to get a sense. She frowned. Who was attacking Lord Artosbern II's castle? What was going on? Where was Ellil? He was supposed to be there.

A harsh horn split the air. Lord Artosbern II looked around uncertainly. One of his officers grabbed him and hauled him up a nearby flight of stairs.

She searched around for another tree. Nothing on the walls. Outside the castle grew only elder. Finally, she found an oak, further away than she'd like. But she hadn't meant to see this, anyway. She wanted to find Torainn. *Oak, the king, goes strong and tall. He is the father of them all.*

The oak grew too close to an elder tree. It reached for her, sighing its quiet sigh. She struggled to maintain her focus.

The horn split the air again, an uncanny, eerie sound, the sound of death. The elder reached for her, its sigh echoing the horn.

A host of men came into view, riding horses like wild raiders. The man in front caught her attention. He was a dark shadow, a dark blur on his horse. She gasped, trying to hold onto the oak. The Cossack. Darkmane.

Her vision flickered as the elder reached for her again. The battle cry of the men sounded like death. She caught another glimpse of the dark figure. As her vision flickered, he changed to Torainn.

She gasped and tore herself out of the vision, flying back to her body, her room. Her hands were clenched around her father's cane and sweat dripped down her forehead. A wail split the air, and she lurched to her feet, making her way over to the cradle. She picked up Thalion and held him to her breast as he cried. "It's alright," she whispered to her son. "It's alright."

But it wasn't all right. Vinet took another deep, shuddering breath, and tried to analyze what she had seen. Lord Artosbern II was doomed. Darkmane seemed to be attacking his castle. Darkmane, who might also be Lord General Torainn.

18

DEATH

The midwives had advised against it, but when Vinet assured them she intended to ride in the carriage, they had assented. She had to get to the capital for the council session. Her vision was too important to ignore.

She still didn't know who she should tell. Only one person knew about her visions, and she was not certain whether Dannan would listen to her or dismiss her out of hand. After scolding her for using the Sight again, of course.

The carriage bounced, and she held Thalion closer to her chest to protect him from the jostling. He had been remarkably well behaved the entire trip.

Across from her, Eithne looked up, baby Kishtar bouncing in her own lap. Her eyes were wide with wonder at the sights of the capital, but she regarded Vinet with concern. "Is he alright?"

Vinet managed a smile and nodded. The midwives had insisted she bring a wet-nurse along on the trip. Little Kishtar still nursed, but Eithne had a plentiful supply of milk. And since Vinet was not about to leave Thalion behind, Eithne came with them.

She took a steadying breath as they pulled up to her townhouse. *I have to get this over with now.* Nazir helped her out of the carriage, and she handed Thalion to him.

"Can you and Evalynna oversee things?" she asked. "I need to go talk to Lord Dannan."

Nazir gave her a piercing look. "Are you certain?"

She smiled grimly. "I might as well get it over with."

"We will manage. You're taking Gwyn?" Nazir asked.

She nodded, and his face lightened with relief.

"I'll see you later, then, my love," he said.

She kissed him before setting out on the short walk to Dannan's townhouse. It felt good to stretch her legs. Nazir had been coddling her before and after Thalion's birth, and Manyu's Time in Ninaeva left her mostly unwilling to go anywhere outside of Ilhelm Castle. Despite the threat of a renewing war, she could not help but feel glad for Mazda's Rise.

She hesitated outside the door to Dannan's townhouse. She had never visited him before. And before this, would never have dreamed of visiting him about matters of magic. The house looked no different from any of the ones surrounding it, made of the same sand-colored stones as the palace. A wrought-iron gate set in the sandstone wall out front, however, made an imposing sight.

She squared her shoulders and walked up to the gate. Almost immediately, a servant appeared, bowing low and asking her business.

"Tell Lord Dannan that Lady Vinet et-Alim wishes to speak to him, please," she asked.

The servant nodded. "If my lady will follow me, I will take her to the reception room."

The servant gave Gwyn a long look, then dismissed her as irrelevant. Vinet suppressed a smile. Gwyn was never irrelevant.

The servant led them into a bright, sunny room, far more cheerful than anything Vinet had ever associated with Dannan. Several comfortable chairs were strategically placed around a table, and a few others by the fireplace. After a moment's consideration, Vinet sat in one by the table. Gwyn took her place near the door.

She didn't have to wait long before Dannan entered the room. A frown left furrows on his forehead. "Lady Vinet? What can I do for you?"

She rose as he entered. "Lord Dannan, I..." She hesitated. "I have information the Council needs to know about."

"And you cannot tell them yourself?"

She shook her head.

Dannan grasped her meaning immediately. His eyebrows rose. "And you are certain of the accuracy of this information?"

She withheld a curse. *Now comes the lecture as to the uncertainty of visions. As if I didn't already know!* "As certain as I can be."

He looked skeptical, then gestured for her to sit down again. He sat across from her. "Tell me."

"Darkmane is active again," she said bluntly.

"I had heard," he said.

It was her turn to raise her eyebrows. He smiled thinly.

"I have been placed in a unique position by the King's steward," he said. "I have informants in every corner of the kingdom."

She blinked. "You're the spymaster."

His smile widened. "I would not have put it so bluntly."

She couldn't help but laugh. Oddly enough, his admission made her relax. If he had heard about Darkmane being active, then perhaps the rest of her story would not be so outlandish.

She sobered again at the thought. "That is not all," she said. "He attacked Lord Artosbern II's castle. I do not know what happened there. But it surely cannot be anything good."

"My informant there has been silent for a time," Dannan admitted.

Vinet took a deep breath. *He took that well enough. But what will he think of Torainn?*

Dannan gave her a piercing look. "What else?"

"Do not think I'm mad." She hesitated once more.

He simply raised an eyebrow again, his strange citron eye flashing.

She spat the words from her lips, the distaste of the reality on her tongue. "Darkmane is the former Lord General Torainn."

That caught Dannan by surprise. He stared at her, blinking in shock. "Are you certain?" he demanded.

She nodded.

He looked away, shaking his head. "How is that possible?"

Vinet shrugged. She hadn't the faintest idea herself. "I don't know. But he reacted oddly when Darkmane first appeared, and his disappearance into the northeast fits."

"If it were anyone but you who told me this," Dannan shook his head again.

She felt oddly flattered he trusted her judgment that much, despite his adamant belief she should stop using magic.

He fixed his gaze on her again. "And you want me to tell the Council this in place of yourself?"

She smiled grimly. "Since I would rather my abilities not be published broadly, yes."

He nodded, and relief rushed through her. She had been worried she would need to argue her case.

"Thank you. If I happen upon any more information, I shall be sure to let you know," she managed a smile. "You can simply say it came from one of your informants."

He chuckled. "Indeed. Your information may prove invaluable."

She nodded, then frowned at a sudden thought. "How are you tutoring the prince with your extra duties? I thought he took up most of your time."

Dannan cleared his throat, looking slightly uncomfortable. "Since the boy just turned seven, it has been deemed more appropriate that he has several tutors now. I am no longer one of them."

She raised an eyebrow but didn't press any further. Whose decree had that been? The King's, before he fell ill, or Lord Auriel's? And had Dannan done something to warrant being removed, or did he have too many new extra duties? She restrained herself from asking any of those questions. Dannan was already doing her a favor. She would not press his rare good nature. Instead, she rose to her feet. "Thank you very much, Lord Dannan. I'll see you in the council session."

Vinet blinked as she got out of the carriage to see Pellalindra moving swiftly toward her. Why wasn't Pellalindra already in the council chamber? Had she been waiting for her?

She smiled at her, still confused. "Lady Pellalindra?"

Pellalindra drew her into the castle and ushered her into a small, private parlor. "Lady Vinet, we must speak, urgently."

Vinet frowned. "What is the matter?"

"Have you had a visit from Lord Conn?" Pellalindra demanded. Her eyes were dark.

Vinet's eyes widened. "Yes." She waited for Pellalindra to continue before volunteering any more information.

Pellalindra bit her lip. Darkness flashed in her eyes again, and Vinet realized Pellalindra was afraid. "What did he want from you?"

Vinet carefully weighed her words. "He wanted to talk to a woman I have in my employ; the former mistress of Lord General Torainn." She grimaced. "He *said* he wanted to ascertain Torainn's location, but he lied."

Pellalindra gestured for Vinet to continue.

"He already knew where Torainn was," Vinet said, her lips tightening at the memory. "He wanted to verify the truth of the story Torainn told him. The existence of a mistress was not part of Torainn's tale."

Pellalindra started pacing. "That's all? Nothing else?"

Vinet hesitated, remembering Conn's suspicions about Lord Auriel, remembering the threat of civil war. "He said Torainn was plotting against your husband," she finally said.

Grief flashed across Pellalindra's face. "Not just my husband. Me, and my daughter," she said, her voice strained.

Vinet gasped. "Whatever for?" she demanded.

Pellalindra's voice shook. "Because...because Torainn wants Lord Auriel's wife and child to suffer the same fate as his own."

Lady Kianna. Vinet closed her eyes, remembering the events of Pellalindra's wedding. Her guilt for her own responsibility in those events threatened to close her throat.

She swallowed and forced her emotions away. Pellalindra and her daughter were the ones at threat. "Tell your husband," she said, throwing caution to the wind. Whatever her own suspicions of Lord Auriel, they were nothing compared to an active threat against an infant child. "He has resources and the ear of the king. He'll protect you."

Pellalindra looked down. "But the king is so ill."

What does that matter? He was never involved in ruling anyway. Vinet did not allow that thought to show on her face.

A quiet knock on the door heralded the entry of a servant. He bowed low to the two noble ladies. "Pardon me, my ladies, but the king has summoned the Council to an audience."

Vinet exchanged a startled look with Pellalindra. "He's recovered?"

The servant nodded. "Yes, my lady. He demands your presence most urgently."

Vinet blinked. In the nearly three years, she'd been on the Council she hadn't once seen King Andreas, a recluse since his beloved queen's death. And then his illness on top of that. What could possibly make him want to participate in politics now, so soon after recovery?

"The king is recovered!" Pellalindra exclaimed. "We must go at once." She took Vinet's arm and led her through the palace. "We will speak more of this later, Lady Vinet," she said. "After we ascertain how well the king truly is. It's been so long since any of us have seen him. I wonder if he's changed. My husband spends a great deal of time with him, naturally, but he hasn't told me much."

Vinet ignored the chatter as she tried to remember all the protocols for talking to royalty. She hadn't had to use any of them for some time. In fact, the only time she'd seen the king had been upon her officially swearing fealty as Lady of Ninaeva.

Maybe that was why she had felt no concern for the king's illness, and the only reason she cared about Torainn's plot was the threat of civil war, a war which would wreak havoc across the land and cause great suffering for smallfolk and noble alike. The king certainly hadn't done anything to ensure her loyalty.

In part due to these thoughts, she kept her face impassive as they entered the audience chamber. Dannan, Conn, and Kamian were already there. Ellil and Alexander were still missing.

Vinet straightened as she saw the King sitting on the throne, looking as regal as she remembered when she'd sworn fealty. Lord Auriel stood at his right hand and slightly behind, exactly as a steward should. Around the hall, placed inconspicuously, were figures armored in black, members of the king's private guard.

She and Pellalindra approached the throne side by side. When they were fifteen paces from it, they both dropped into a curtsy, but did not bow their heads. Vinet kept her eyes fixed on the king.

"Lady Pellalindra! I am delighted to see you, my dear. And my greetings to you as well, Lady Vinet. I hear you've gone and married. Congratulations," the king said.

Vinet inclined her head in thanks as she rose, not trusting herself to speak.

Pellalindra had no such reservations. "You are most kind, Your Majesty."

"Nonsense," the king said affably. "You are an old friend, and your services deserve recognition. Now, who else are we waiting for?" He leaned agreeably toward Lord Auriel.

Vinet was the only one close enough to notice Pellalindra stiffen in response to the king's words. What services had she provided the king in the past that she didn't want mentioned in front of the Council?

Lord Auriel shook his head. "No one, Your Majesty."

The king narrowed his head. "But surely there were seven members on the Council?"

"High Priest Ellil has gone north to investigate matters there," Lord Auriel said smoothly. "And General Alexander has been delayed in Lokrian."

That explained why Lord Auriel had been more active in Council matters of late. Since the Lord of the Council was busy, he had stepped in. Vinet recognized his willingness to serve as a good thing, but old suspicions gnawed at her.

"Very well." The king surveyed each of them. "I hear things are a mess in my kingdom, councilors."

Vinet sensed everyone in the room stiffen. She knew everyone was remembering the fate of the first council. Their heads had been nailed to the city gate for months, a stark reminder of the fate of traitors.

The king stared at each of them in turn, staring in everyone's eyes. Kamian dropped his immediately, Pellalindra nodded coolly, and Dannan bowed his head after a long moment. Conn flushed, but held his gaze.

He looked at Vinet last. Oddly enough, she sensed no judgment in his gaze as he gazed at her, only curiosity. She met his gaze without flinching, and she swore she saw a slight smile of approval before he turned away.

"A mess," he repeated, addressing them all again. "A war which threatens to engulf the entire southeast and spread north, and a phantom in the north who kills with impunity, so that the entire northeast falls into disarray. What steps have you taken to combat them?"

Vinet felt a sharp surge of relief that she had ordered what Ninaevan guard she could spare to join the fight against Mount Halon. Pellalindra and Kamian had done the same. Dannan didn't have troops or holdings to speak of, but Conn...Conn had contributed nothing.

None of the others seemed inclined to answer the king. Vinet cursed her own impatience as she spoke up.

"The Lord of the Council, General Alexander, is helping the war effort personally by managing the supply lines," she said. "All of the nobility who volunteered have supplied their own private guards to augment the Regulars. We have kept the coffers full and the army fed and supplied. We have made an alliance with the Faithful, who have proven their worth many times over in this war. Currently, we are waiting for our Generals to tell us their needs."

The king's face remained impassive as she continued. "As to the north, High Priest Ellil volunteered to investigate rumors of cultists, but we have not yet heard from him. The phantom you speak of has only just been identified as the former Lord General Torainn."

She ignored the muffled exclamation from Conn and the smothered gasp from Pellalindra. She continued to address the king. "We are only waiting on the high priest's word or return to give orders for action there."

The king met her gaze for a long moment. She felt as if she were being measured. She didn't dare drop her eyes.

Finally, he inclined his head. "Satisfactory," he said.

She allowed herself to relax just a tiny bit.

"Your answer makes up for your marriage, it seems. I am not pleased I have not met this man you've taken as your husband," the king said.

She dropped a slight curtsy. "I will present him to you whenever Your Majesty is agreeable."

"And you've changed your name to his. What is your title now?"

Where was this going? Still, she dared not refuse to answer. "Lady Vinet et-Alim of Ninaeva."

The king considered that. "Lady et-Alim. An interesting name, at least." He fell silent. Vinet could almost feel the other councilors' thankfulness that they hadn't been the ones to speak up.

The king nodded decisively. "Then, Lady et-Alim, I appoint you acting Lady of the Council in General Alexander's absence. Guide the kingdom to success in these things which trouble us."

Vinet blinked in shock. She glanced at the other councilors. They seemed as surprised as she.

She curtsied again. "I will do my best to serve Saemar, Your Majesty."

"Saemar and your king," he said sternly.

She bowed her head, her memory flashing back to when Conn had reminded her of her duty to her king. Surely, he was remembering her answer as well.

She was saved from answering by the arrival of a page. The boy went straight to Lord Auriel, who received the scroll with a nod of thanks. After reading it, he leaned sideways and whispered in the king's ear.

The king turned to stare at Lord Auriel, then fixed his gaze on Vinet. She froze, holding her breath.

"It seems you will be called upon to exercise your duties immediately, Lady et-Alim. There is a messenger who desires to speak to the Lord of the Council. You will go in his place."

She curtsied without replying, feeling a profound relief she would be able to escape the king's presence. She had not remembered him being so intense.

She followed the page out of the hall before demanding an explanation. "Who is the messenger?"

The page looked up at her. "They carried him in. All hurt and moaning. He asked for the Lord of the Council. That's all he'll say."

"Who?" she demanded of the poor child.

His eyes widened at her sharp tone. "The high priest, my lady."

She stopped as she entered the small room, mostly bare of furniture, just a few chairs and a bed. An attendant stood at the bedside, bending over the man lying there. He certainly wore the robes of the high priest, but if Vinet hadn't known it was him, she wouldn't have recognized him.

She stepped forward quietly, so as not to startle him. The attendant glanced up at her and frowned. "Who are you?"

She opened her mouth to answer, but Ellil groaned and stirred. Vinet smothered a gasp of horror. Cuts and bruises covered his face, and bandages covered his neck. He had more injuries, as well, with splints on his right arm and leg. He blinked up at her. "Vinet?" he rasped.

She moved to his side, heedless of the attendant. "It's me," she acknowledged. "Alexander isn't here. I'm to listen in his place."

He didn't bother to argue. His left hand reached out to grab hers. "Warn...the others," he rasped. "Lord...Artosbern...dead. Lord Tiber .. attacked. Slaughtered..." he coughed.

"Lord Tiber?" Vinet asked. "The one who asked us to disinherit Lord Artosbern?"

"The...same," Ellil coughed again. "He...not the worst, though..."

She braced herself, though she already had a fair idea of what the worst was.

"The...the phantom..."

"Darkmane," she said.

Ellil nodded. "Only...Mazda kept me alive..."

Somehow, she didn't doubt Ellil spoke the truth. She squeezed his hand. "I'll warn the others," she said. "Darkmane has gone too far this time. He must be stopped."

Ellil leaned back in his chair. "He leads...cultists," he murmured. "From the south. And elves. Your...tear and thorns..."

"The Unfaithful," she whispered.

Ellil relaxed, his eyes starting to close. "Stop him..."

"We will," she promised.

Ellil sighed and relaxed, his eyes fluttering. She watched, worried, as the attendant shoved his way forward, checking his pulse.

"Will he live?" she asked in a soft voice.

The attendant didn't even glance at her. "He will. Provided he's given enough rest and time to recover. And that this phantom he keeps babbling about didn't do anything uncanny to him. Mazda knows I don't have any experience with dark magics."

Her lips tightened. The only person she knew with experience with dark magics was AeresThonEsia. "Did anyone else from his party survive?"

The attendant shrugged. "Two guards dragged him in here, half-dead themselves. Others have the charge of them."

Vinet knew the surly attendant wouldn't give her any more details. "Thank you," she said, before retreating to the corridor.

She fell into deep thought the entire way to the Council chamber. She had promised they'd take steps to resolve the Darkmane problem, but how? Lord Auriel had called it a wild goose chase before, and all that had happened was the loss of good men.

She looked around as she entered the council chamber. Everyone had gathered, the king having ended the audience. Something had gone dreadfully wrong though, if she was any judge. Pellalindra appeared horrified, Kamian shocked, Dannan and Conn grim. All gazes turned to her as she entered.

"What did the messenger say?" Dannan demanded as soon as she entered.

Carefully, she made her way to her usual seat. No use claiming the power of Lady of the Council yet. "High Priest Ellil returned," she said. "He's badly wounded. Lord Tiber attacked Lord Artosbern II and slaughtered the garrison. Then the castle was overrun by Darkmane's forces." She took a breath. "Darkmane leads a force of cultists from the south, combined with Unfaithful."

If anything, Dannan seemed even more grim.

"What's this about Darkmane being Torainn?" Conn demanded.

She glanced at him, then back to Dannan. Dannan took the hint.

"It's true," he said harshly. "My informants confirm it. I was going to tell everyone today."

"A bit late for Lord Artosbern," Kamian said, his voice dry. He still appeared shocked about something, but he was recovering.

Vinet looked around. "What happened?" she asked warily.

Pellalindra answered. "Another messenger arrived after you left," she said. "The southeast line broke and the enemy got through to Lokrian. General Alexander's been killed."

Alexander… Vinet caught her breath. The kind old man, the one who'd asked her to look after his grandchildren, dead? She grabbed the table, her hands shaking slightly. "Mazda guide him on his next journey," she whispered. *Did he have a premonition? How else could he have known to ask me to take care of his grandchildren?*

She hardened her heart to the grief. The battle lines. Pellalindra said they'd broken. "How far did they get?" she demanded. "How much of the south has been overrun?"

Pellalindra shook her head helplessly. "The troops are holding them again just beyond Lokrian. But no one knows for how long."

"Well, then someone needs to find out who and what and where, and the best person for that is Lord General Lairan. Does anyone know how to contact him?" Vinet asked.

Conn nodded dumbly. "We've already sent a messenger."

"Well, good," Vinet sighed. She looked around. Something else had happened.

"What else?" she asked, dreading the answer.

"The king was not pleased to hear the news," Pellalindra said quietly. "He went into a bit of a rage, in fact. Yelled at all of us, then stormed out. Shortly after that all the knights were assembled, and the king and his troops rode off."

Vinet's heart missed a beat. "South?" she demanded.

Pellalindra nodded.

Vinet stared at the other council members, seeing her dismay mirrored on their faces. Their king had gone south. South, to where evil creatures threatened to destroy their land. South, to danger and war.

"Mazda protect him," she whispered.

19

THE KING

She tried to guide the Council through the discussions, but no one could focus their mind on anything. She found herself just as distracted as them. The minor points of government, all the Council had left to discuss, seemed petty in comparison to the troubles of the kingdom. Alexander lay dead. How was she going to tell his grandchildren that? They'd already lost both of their parents. What would happen to them now? Rian would inherit Lokrian, of course, but she was barely older than Niara. The king would have to appoint a regent for her.

The Council couldn't do anything that somebody else wasn't already doing. The king had ridden south with all his Knights and any of the remaining Regulars. Any actions there were best left to their king and the generals. They could talk about the war, but they couldn't actually do anything.

Vinet leaned forward and put her head in her hands. She alone remained in the council chamber. The rest had drifted off, to one business or another.

She heard someone clear their throat, and she looked up. She stiffened as she saw Lord Auriel standing at the door, as perfect and impeccable as ever. Despite that, or perhaps because of that, an inhuman aura hovered about him. A shiver ran down her spine. *What does he want with me?* He had never sought her out before, not even after the events of his wedding. Surely, he didn't want to discuss her visions now. Dannan had promised to keep them a secret. She didn't believe she could keep the secret of her heritage from Lord Auriel if he pressed.

"Lady et-Alim, might I have a moment of your time?"

She nodded and began to rise. He gestured for her to remain seated.

She ordered her heart to remain at a normal tempo. As intimidating as the king had been, somehow Lord Auriel was more so. *No one can be that perfect, that cool, that impassive,* she thought.

"My wife told me an intriguing tale," Lord Auriel said. "I hope you might shed some more light on it."

She relaxed slightly. *Not my visions. Thank you, Mazda, not my visions.* Not that this topic was not hazardous in its own way. "You are speaking of Lord MacTir and his visit to me," she said.

Although it was a statement and not a question, Lord Auriel nodded in confirmation. "Tell me what happened."

She suppressed a shiver at the thin edge in Lord Auriel's normally flawless tone. She would not want to be in Conn's place right now.

She cleared her throat. "Lord MacTir paid me an unexpected visit. He heard I had found Lord General Torainn's mistress and bastard son, and claimed he wanted to question her about his whereabouts."

Lord Auriel raised an eyebrow.

"Indeed," Vinet said. "As the conversation progressed, it became apparent he had lied. He had already met Lord General Torainn and instead searched for proof, one way or another, of the veracity of his story. As I heard it from Lord MacTir, Torainn had vehemently denied the existence of a mistress and bastard, so he wanted to listen to Eithne's story himself and judge the truth of the matter."

"And what did he judge?" Lord Auriel asked.

Vinet felt as if she balanced on a razor's edge. But it was not her fate at stake, instead that of a fellow councilor and noble. She chose her words carefully.

"I am not certain what he thought of Eithne's story," she said. "But I think in the end he was convinced that Torainn's plans, whatever they were, had no place occurring during our current situation."

"And those plans?" Lord Auriel's voice had cooled now, having lost the single hot edge Vinet had noticed earlier. She suppressed a shiver. *He almost seemed human before. He was angry. But now he's controlled again. Why? And why does that not comfort me?*

She had to remain truthful. "Lord General Torainn believed the king under the influence of his advisors, specifically you, Lord Auriel," she said. "He told Lord MacTir you were responsible for the king's illness." She closed her eyes. "He did not tell me this part; your lady wife did. Lord General Torainn was distraught to hear of Lady Kianna's death, and swore to do to your wife and child what had been done to his."

She suppressed another shiver at the thought of murdering an infant and opened her eyes. She forced herself to meet Lord Auriel's eyes.

His expression remained unchanged. He simply nodded. "Thank you for confirming the series of events," he said. "Lord MacTir will be dealt with."

She felt her breath catch. "Dealt with?" she asked. "In what way?"

Lord Auriel raised an eyebrow, and she squared her shoulders.

"As temporary Lady of the Council, I need to know what will happen to the councilors," she said. "Especially in times like these."

He made a gesture of concession with his hand. "Since Lord MacTir admitted his actions to me when I questioned him just now, he shall be given a chance to redeem himself," he said. "He did not send his men to the southeast, therefore his garrison is still at full strength. He shall take his garrison and what remains of Lord Tiber and Lord Artosbern II's men. He is to hunt and slay the beast Darkmane, also known as Torainn."

Vinet felt her heart stop. The image rose up before her of the dark figure on horseback, charging the castle of Lord Artosbern II. How did Conn stand a chance against such shadow and fury?

Lord Auriel seemed to know what she was thinking. "He has his entire garrison and the support of the local troops. He is a military man. If anything can redeem him, this can."

Vinet admitted Lord Auriel's words made sense. Although Conn had not committed any act of treason, he had certainly contemplated it. She suspected his confession to Lord Auriel had as much to do with the king's recovery as anything else. Whatever else he had done, Conn was an honorable man. The king's newfound health provided proof enough for him that Lord Auriel had not caused his illness. *Unless Lord Auriel heard the rumors and changed his plans.* She shook the thought away as basest speculation.

Besides, if Lord Auriel had given Conn his orders, she couldn't really do anything. Her own garrison had only the strength to patrol the roads around Ninaeva. She couldn't send him any support. She spoke slowly. "I believe it will."

Lord Auriel smiled. "And this will solve one of the primary issues facing the Council currently," he said. "With Darkmane defeated, the northeast can be rebuilt and secured. Perhaps in a style inspired by Ninaeva, a shining beacon of civilization in the north."

She braced herself for possible irony. But she heard none. "Thank you, Lord Auriel."

She expected him to leave. After all, he'd gotten confirmation of Conn's story. Was that not what he had approached her about?

"There is another matter, Lady et-Alim, that I hoped you might indulge me on."

Her shoulders tensed. "And what is that, Lord Auriel?" she managed to keep her voice level.

"I have heard you know of sightings of dragons?"

She blinked. Of all the things he could have asked her, she had not expected that.

"I..." she hesitated. "Possibly," she admitted. She frowned and tilted her head. "Why do you ask?"

"Simple curiosity."

Somehow, she doubted that. While much of him was an enigma, she did know one fact: Lord Auriel never did anything for simple curiosity. After a moment's thought, though, she didn't see the harm in answering him.

"Some time ago, a Venian explorer came to the Council asking us to fund an expedition up the coast," she said. "Lord Kamian and I invested some of our private resources into it. In the journal the explorer sent home, he mentioned sighting a dragon."

"Could you send me a copy of this journal?" Lord Auriel asked.

"Of course," she said. "I will be happy to order a copy made for you."

She kept quiet about the dark shape she had seen in the sky on her boat ride to Venia. For one, she wasn't certain if it had been a dragon. For another, she didn't really want Lord Auriel to know how she'd gotten there, if he knew she'd even been there at all.

Luckily, Lord Auriel seemed satisfied with her tale. He nodded and rose to leave. "Thank you for your time, Lady et-Alim."

Something compelled her to speak up. "Lord Auriel?" she asked.

Lord Auriel glanced at her. "Yes?"

"Does the king have a plan?" She couldn't say what compelled her to ask that question.

Lord Auriel's eyebrows merely rose a trifle. "He is the king. He always has a plan. And currently, that plan is to rid Saemar of the scourge from Mount Halon."

Lord Auriel turned and walked out of the room.

Vinet stared after him, unsatisfied. Why had the king just packed up and left? He had just recovered. Had he truly regained all his strength?

And what was she supposed to do about it? What could she do?

———

What can I do? That thought haunted her for the next two weeks. Aside from Conn, none of the council members left the capital. No word had been heard from him, or from the front lines.

"Vinet. Stop pacing."

She looked up from the garden path.

Gwyn stared at her, her arms folded over her chest. "Pacing doesn't help. Do something."

"Like what?" Vinet asked. She paced a few more steps before stopping. "I can't do anything about the situations in the south or north, we've heard nothing, our scouts seem to have been lost, and I can't do anything! I'm so distracted I can't even read!"

Gwyn walked over and put an arm around Vinet's shoulders. "It's hard," she said. "But the waiting is always the hardest. That's the first thing a warrior learns when they go to battle."

Vinet suppressed a curse. "Well, I'm not a warrior," she said. She sighed. "I'm sorry. I shouldn't have snapped."

Gwyn smiled. "You're tense," she said. "You need a distraction."

She shook her head. "I can't think of anything."

Gwyn gave her a small shove. "Go talk to Nazir," she said. "The two of you need to spend some time to yourselves."

Vinet flushed at what Gwyn's words implied. "You're incorrigible."

Gwyn grinned. "Hey, you're the one who defied all expectations and actually married the man. The least I can do is keep you two together."

Despite herself, she felt a smile spreading over her face. "Do you know where he is?"

"Your chambers," Gwyn said, smiling impudently.

Vinet flushed deeper. Nonetheless, she walked inside, ignoring Gwyn's satisfied chuckle.

Nazir was indeed in their bedchamber, bent over a desk copying something out. Vinet watched him for nearly a full minute, smiling a little at how oblivious her observant Nazir could be when buried in his work.

He blinked as he glanced up. "Vinet!" He set the materials aside and rose to his feet, avoiding scattering quills and ink by a near miracle. He moved to stand next to her, a question in his eyes. "I thought you were in the garden?"

She shrugged, her frustration bubbling up inside her again. "I couldn't think," she said.

Nazir frowned and pulled her into an embrace. She buried her face in his shoulder, reveling in the warm comfort.

"How are you doing?" he asked softly.

She sighed. "It's the waiting," she said, echoing Gwyn's words. "It's the not knowing. It's going to drive me mad."

Nazir stroked her hair. "I'm told that's common in situations like these."

"It doesn't make it any easier." Vinet grimaced.

She sensed his hesitation, and she pulled away a few inches to look him in the eyes. "What is it?"

Nazir regarded her. "You have to judge how much this is a good idea," he said. "But you are not without the resources to remedy the lack of knowledge."

She stilled. He was right. She could look, could search for Conn and the king. She could find out what was happening to them. She could use the Sight. She wouldn't be able to change anything, but she would at least be able to see.

"Vinet," Nazir held her shoulders. "Do not do this if it will cause you harm."

She gave it serious consideration. She'd used the Sight in the Bern Forest before to witness Darkmane's attack on the castle. And although she'd never used the Sight to see anything in the southeast, it couldn't be that bad now that she no longer bore Manyu's mark. She could end the vision if she needed to. Her father had taught her that.

"I can do it," she said.

Nazir smiled and leaned forward. He kissed her. "Just be careful."

She nodded and moved to sit on the side of the bed. Nazir sat next to her and gently clasped one of her hands. She gave him a brief smile, then reached down. Down to the roots of the trees surrounding the townhouse, to the branches, and then skipping northward, toward the Bern Forest. She found the thorn tree by the castle easily enough. Somehow it had been left standing. Yet destruction reigned around it. The castle had been destroyed. The walls were crumbling as if decades had passed. Bodies lay strewn around, and blood soaked into every stalk of grass.

She sent a plea to the thorn to sharpen her gaze. It obliged, and she winced. The thorns always took their price in pain.

The livery. It belonged to Artosbern's men, as well as Lord Tiber's. This was the aftermath of their battle, then. No sign of Conn.

She reached out, searching. There had to be more than elm and elder in the entire forest. There, an ash. She shivered as she touched it. Cold and hard, but not deadly like the elder.

A hunting horn sounded, and she sank deeper into the tree. She gritted her teeth as the cold sank into her bones. A flash of steel. The pounding of hooves. Blood flowing down to the ground. A dark shape, his horse rearing, shouting in triumph. The screams of the dying. Grimly, she held on. Darkmane himself. And he had found Conn's forces.

As if her thought summoned him, Conn himself came riding forward, his sword held high. He let out a wild war cry and crashed into Darkmane's side. His sword cut deep, and blood flowed down the horse's side.

Darkmane appeared unaffected. He swung his sword, almost lazily, and stabbed it deep into Conn's chest.

Vinet flinched at the heart-wrenching roar that sounded through the forest. Conn's burly bodyguard rose from the ground, charging forward. He had no horse and was covered in blood. He raised an axe and chopped, felling Darkmane's horse with one blow. His second blow took Darkmane. The dark figure shrieked in agony, and all the trees seemed to echo his pain.

Conn's bodyguard yelled his grief to the sky and stumbled over to where Conn's body lay sprawled beside his horse. He fell onto his lord as an arrow lodged in his throat.

Vinet forced herself to move around the tree, to see everything. Conn's men were decimated, but so were the Cossack riders. A few unseemly creatures still milled around, as well as several Unfaithful archers, but no leadership remained. Not on either side.

A hail of arrows flew toward her, and she instinctively flinched. The elder reached for her with its eager branch-fingers.

She flung herself out of the ash tree, racing southward. She knew sweat was pouring down her body, but she couldn't stop now. If that was what had happened to Conn, what about the king?

There were no forests in the southeast. Behind the lines, Vinet could only sense barren wasteland and dead wood. She flinched.

Alexander's Lokrian estate. An old apple tree, still standing. Cautiously, Vinet melded into it. Apples were tricky.

It welcomed her with a sigh and tried to pull her in even deeper. She kept her distance. She had no wish to be trapped in the apples. *Apple is fun, but watch out, oh no! Into the otherworld you may go.*

The battle raged. Lokrian lay ravaged, even worse than Artosberg's castle. The buildings of the estate were nothing but rubble, the orchards were nothing but ash. Vinet felt her heart breaking at the destruction.

Numerous figures made up the massive horde of Mount Halon. They were mostly human, dressed in robes and armor emblazoned with Manyu's symbol, some elves, and other dark figures, but all with the eyes of fanatics. One dark figure rose above the rest, a skull mask in place of a face.

The Saemarian line held firm, though. The Regulars stood shoulder to shoulder, their uniforms splattered in blood. A group of black-clad knights surrounded the king who sat tall and proud on his horse, his golden crown gleaming in the sun. As Vinet watched, he raised his sword high and yelled a command to charge.

The thundering of horse's hooves. The flashing of steel. The screams of pain. The crash as the forces collided.

The apple tree shook, and Vinet fought to maintain control of her vision.

The Regulars fought hard. Despite the screams and the dying, the cultists weren't wearing as much armor, and that made the difference. The Regulars pushed forward, inspired by their king who was ahead of his knights, making a beeline for the figure with the skull mask. The knights were fighting to him, trying their best to keep up.

The ground shook, and the figure raised a huge sword to smite the king. Andreas held his own sword high and let out a triumphant yell.

A flash of light, too blinding for her to see anything. The screams of everyone around her. The light faded, and the battle raged. A black cloud rose in the air, circling darkly. It loomed menacingly at the Saemarian troops.

A cry distracted everyone, Saemarian and cultist alike. The king held his sword aloft and cast it toward the tall figure.

A scream rent the air, and the cloud trembled violently. Then it exploded and dazzling light showered over the sky. A single line of lightning arched down, striking the king.

The king cried out, and Vinet could see the pain on his face. She watched in horror as the tall figure leaned down, the sword still stuck in its shoulder. It picked the king up like a doll.

The king cried out again, and every soldier in the army, as well as Vinet, shook in terror. The lightning arced again. A dark laugh rose from the ground.

A hand. The king grabbed his sword. With all of his remaining strength, he twisted, driving it deeper into the skull-masked figure. It shrieked, stumbling backward. The king disappeared into a pile of bodies.

A roar sounded from the Regulars and the knights, and they charged forward again, re-energized. Vinet gasped as they ran through the lines, slaughtering everyone in their path.

She reached out through the maelstrom of bodies, trying to find the king. He had won the battle, that was clear. The cultists of Mount Halon were routed. But where was he?

She let out a cry of her own at the sight. He lay face-up on the ground, surrounded by the dead. His eyes stared blankly at the sky, and his throat had been slit.

She fled back to her body, away from the roar of battle, away from the death and destruction. She flung herself at Nazir with a sob.

"What happened?" he demanded as he held her close. "Vinet, what's wrong?"

She shook her head, getting herself under control. She couldn't break down now.

"The king is dead," she whispered.

EPILOGUE

LADY OF THE COUNCIL

Hot sun beat down as the Council and the rest of the nobles stood at the entrance to the palace. Crowds lined the streets, all cheering and celebrating. The steps to the palace were reserved for the nobility, of course. Vinet and Nazir, by virtue of her position as Lady of the Council, stood near the very top steps. The only people higher were Ellil, still heavily bandaged, and his attendant.

The cheering grew louder, and Vinet gazed down the street. Finally, the procession was coming into view. At the head of the procession rode young Prince Andreas. Much too small for a horse, he instead rode a well-mannered pony. The boy stared straight ahead, barely acknowledging the cheers and shouts with a wave of his hand. Vinet felt a moment of sorrow for him. The poor lad. His father had just died, and now his responsibilities forced this procession on him.

Behind the prince rode Lord Auriel, sitting straight and tall on his own white mare. He looked kinglier than the child in front of him. He nodded at the people and waving in response to their cheers. Behind him rode his three burgundy-clad guards, followed by six of the king's knights. The prince's knights, now, Vinet realized.

The procession came to a halt at the base of the steps, and the prince and Lord Auriel dismounted and slowly started to climb the stairs to the top. The prince kept his eyes straight ahead, staring at Ellil as he climbed. Lord Auriel watched the boy with a kind, amused smile. Prince Andreas knelt in front of Ellil as he reached the top stair. The high priest raised the golden crown of Saemar high so everybody could see it. Vinet could see the priest wince with the pain from his wounds, but the crowd would be too far away to notice such an expression. Vinet's throat tightened as the high priest began to sing, his voice carrying clear across the now-silent crowd. He finished the list of oaths the prince had to swear.

The prince looked up, and for a moment Vinet thought he would falter. Then his voice rang out, singing his oaths, not as loud as Ellil's, but still loud enough to carry over the crowd. He had a beautiful boy soprano.

Ellil placed the crown of Saemar on the prince's head. It wasn't the old crown, Vinet noticed. For one, that would have been far too large for the boy's head. For another, it had been lost on the battlefield. They had managed to bring back the king's body and give him a state burial, but the crown had disappeared without a trace.

A cheer rang out across the crowd as soon as the crown settled on the prince's head. Vinet joined the applause, but only briefly, as did most of the other nobles. The ceremony was not yet done.

Ellil turned his gaze on Lord Auriel, who bowed low. In the same clear voice, he began the song of the vows of the regent.

Vinet had not been surprised the king had made Lord Auriel the prospective regent. Some of the other nobles had been shocked. She hadn't even been surprised it had been done up properly, with the seals of seven witnesses, including Pellalindra. She supposed she should be grateful. Having such a clear document avoided any jockeying for power among the nobility that would inevitably have followed the king's death. Still, something about the timing of the creation of the document, just before the king's departure, made her suspicious; suspicions she kept to herself behind a tight smile.

Lord Auriel sang his vows as regent in the same clear voice he'd used at his wedding. Vinet noticed without surprise Pellalindra smiling, a hint of satisfaction on her face. After all, Pellalindra was now married to the regent, the most powerful man in the realm.

Ellil nodded once more when Lord Auriel finished. He handed Lord Auriel the scepter, bowing low as he did so. Vinet knew the symbolism. The prince would be king when he turned twenty-five, but until then, the scepter, the power behind the crown, would be in Lord Auriel's hands. *The hands of a mysterious stranger*, Vinet thought.

The prince finally rose to his feet and faced the crowd. Lord Auriel held out the scepter to him, and together they raised it high. The deafening cheer nearly drove Vinet to her knees, but she stayed standing as she applauded with the rest. Her part in the ceremony wasn't done yet, after all.

The prince walked through the doors of the palace, followed closely by Lord Auriel, Ellil, and several knights. Vinet straightened her shoulders and followed, along with the rest of the nobility. The time had come for them to swear fealty.

Uncomfortable, she worked her way to the front of the crowd. In most circumstances, she wouldn't have minded waiting to swear her oath. But circumstances had made this unavoidable. She was Lady of the Council, therefore she had to be first.

The prince sat on the throne, looking slightly uncomfortable in the too-large chair. Lord Auriel sat on a chair placed just beside it. A herald stood at the side of the throne and pounded a staff on the ground, though the throne had all attention already in such a formal ceremony.

"The prince summons Lady Vinet et-Alim of Ninaeva, Lady of the Regency Council, and her husband, Lord Nazir et-Alim of Ninaeva!"

Vinet felt Nazir take her arm, and she squeezed his arm in reassurance. The two of them walked side by side to the throne, where she gave the prince a deep curtsy. Nazir bowed low.

The prince looked nervously at Lord Auriel, who gave him an encouraging smile. The prince began to sing the vows of the nobility.

Vinet answered, her own song steady. She remembered singing these words for Andreas IV. She hadn't expected to be singing them to that king's son, Andreas V, so soon. When she finished, she touched Nazir's arm gently. He braced himself and sang his own vow, one as Lord to her Lady.

The prince seemed relieved when the song finished and gestured for her to rise. Lord Auriel held out a hand to stop her from slipping back into the crowd.

"A moment, Lady et-Alim. You still have in your care the grandchildren of the late General Alexander?"

"Yes, Lord Regent," she answered, startled.

Lord Auriel spoke. "The crown has appointed a steward for the lands of Lokrian, as well as tutors for the next heir. In the next month, they will need to move back to their lands to help oversee the rebuilding."

Vinet blinked. She hadn't been expecting this. "I am more than willing to continue to support them."

"You are gracious," Lord Auriel said. "But as General Alexander died serving the crown, it is only right the crown makes provisions for his heirs. The same provisions will be made for the children of Lord Conn MacTir."

She managed a smile and another curtsy of acknowledgment. Lord Auriel nodded his dismissal, and Nazir led her away.

"Lady Pellalindra Auriel of Duskryn, member of the Regency Council!" The herald proclaimed again. The pounding of the staff did nothing for Vinet's headache born from mounting discomfort at the new regime. *Not that I have any facts to support that discomfort,* she thought. *And until then, I cannot speak of my suspicions to anyone.* She did not want Conn's fate to be her own.

Vinet observed as the prince continued to receive the oaths of fealty from the nobility. First, the council members would be called, and then the rest. Not everyone had arrived for this ceremony, of course. Some were wounded, or ill, or couldn't travel for some other reason. But one by one, they would come and give their oaths. They had to.

She felt a flutter of uneasiness as she watched Lord Auriel guide the prince. He had taken command of things so smoothly. When everyone would have panicked, he had calmly picked up the reins. He excelled at it, certainly. And he gave every indication he would continue to be good at his job, and serve the prince as he grew into manhood and kingship.

"Lord Kamian Silas of Hinswold, member of the Regency Council!"

She groaned at whisper-volume, and Nazir gave her an amused smile. She smiled back at him, wishing she could kiss him. But that would have to wait until after the fealty ceremony finished, and then after the first meeting of the Regency Council. There was business to be conducted, after all. A schedule had to be agreed upon, first off, and if Vinet had her way, they would each have duties agreed upon so that the business of government went smoother, without the bickering of who would handle what part.

She sighed. She had a great deal of work to do. *Not the least a quiet investigation into who, or what, Lord Auriel actually is.* She tucked that thought into the back of her mind.

Nazir squeezed her hand, and she smiled wider. She could handle it. With Nazir at her side and Gwyn at her back, she could handle anything.

ACKNOWLEDGMENTS

I can only take credit for part of the idea for this book. Most of it was a collaborative effort during an online RPG game. Rose, Neil, Nathan, Megan, and Jonathan all had equal roles in creating the characters and the world, and Josh was the one who orchestrated it all. I apologize to them for any liberties I took in writing this book, changing the events of our game and personalities of characters to make it a cohesive novel. I also apologize that since it's from Vinet's perspective, some of the councilers are portrayed as less-than-flattering. Everyone is the hero of their own story, after all. Thank you all for your understanding and support.

My wonderful husband, Josh, was a huge inspiration and help in the writing of this novel. When I announced I wanted to write a book based on our game, he said, without hesitation, "Go for it." He was there for me every step of the way, from the first draft through the editing. Thank you so much, love.

A huge thank you to Sally, as well. She was the first person from outside the game to read it, and her perspective and suggestions were invaluable. And thank you to Melissa, who helped my vision of the cover come alive.

Lastly, thank you to everyone at Falstaff Books. I would not have pursued publishing if not for them.

ABOUT THE AUTHOR

Tuppence Van de Vaarst has long been obsessed with history, writing, fantasy, the ocean, and magic. She taught herself to read at the age of three and read every single book she could get her hands on. At the age of eleven, she started creating her own stories. As she grew, her passion for stories never faded.

When she was eighteen, she decided to pursue her love of the ocean by enlisting in the United States Coast Guard. Although she decided military life did not suit her, she views it as a useful experience that she can now insert into her own writing. She has an MA in Medieval Studies and an MA in Library Science from University College Dublin. When she's not writing she's still surrounded by books as her full-time job is that of librarian.

ALSO BY TUPPENCE VAN DE VAARST

Caribbean Magic

Caribbean Fortune

FRIENDS OF FALSTAFF

Thank You to All our Falstaff Books Patrons, who get extra digital content each month! To be featured here and see what other great rewards we offer, go to www.patreon.com/falstaffbooks.

PATRONS

Dino Hicks
John Hooks
John Kilgallon
Larissa Lichty
Travis & Casey Schilling
Staci-Leigh Santore
Sheryl R. Hayes
Scott Norris
Samuel Montgomery-Blinn
Junkle

www.ingramcontent.com/pod-product-compliance
Lightning Source LLC
Chambersburg PA
CBHW020718130726
47899CB00011B/389